A SIGNAL FOR REDEMPTION

Cover and book design by Damonza

Map by Elena Murphy

ISBN 979-8-9852128-0-8 (paperback)

ISBN 979-8-9852128-1-5 (eBook)

www.acmeehan.com

A SIGNAL FOR REDEMPTION

A.C. MEEHAN

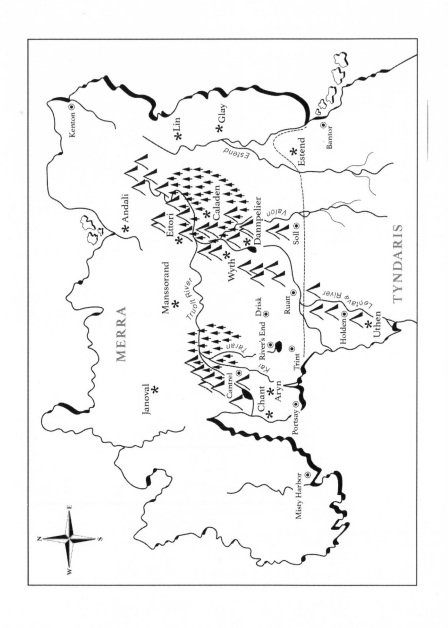

PROLOGUE

I T WASN'T UNTIL Tomas raised his hand to knock on the door of Lord Ettori's council room that the second thought came: this news might not be welcome. He let his hand drop, and tugged at the hem of his tunic, then smoothed back his grey hair and took a bracing breath. He rapped three times, waited for the murmured invitation, and tried to walk into the room with confidence.

Kor, the lord of House Ettori, was at the table with Sergei Benino, his health advisor, papers and ledgers spread between them. A pair of blank-faced House Ettori guards stood just inside the door, out of earshot of their lord but with watchful eyes. As Tomas entered, there was no greeting, but his master beckoned him closer. He heard Lord Ettori tell Benino, in the tone of dismissal, "Start it in Ruatt this time, then. We'll see who it takes."

With gathered papers shoved under his arm, Benino scurried past Tomas with his eyes downcast. Tomas looked toward the table, wondering what had frightened the man, and found Lord Ettori's gaze locked on his face. Lord Ettori had a way of staring that could shatter anyone's nerves.

His eyes were black, so dark that the pupils were indistinguishable from the irises, and he didn't blink as often as lesser men. As usual, Tomas had to resist the impulse to look away as he approached.

"Dan Kor, my lord," he said, "forgive the interruption."

"You hurried here," Lord Ettori commented, lifting one black eyebrow. "I didn't know you still could."

It was a relief to hear the gibe. Tomas was one of a very small circle of people who knew Kor was a lifetime older than he looked; the humor acknowledged that trust. "I'm not quite sixty, my lord," he said. "Not in my dotage yet." Out of context, the smile Kor gave him would have chilled him, but Tomas noted that Kor's relaxed posture hadn't changed. A good mood, then.

"Well?"

"Lady Caladen gave birth to a son, and Lord Caladen says he believes the ark ship is arriving." Something had happened at the birth—he hadn't heard what—that had apparently been convincing to Lord Caladen. Lady Caladen had mentioned it to her lady's maid.

It had been almost a millennium since anyone had expected to hear those words, and Tomas was ready for Lord Ettori to dismiss the simple statement. The lords of the Great Houses of Merra did seem to have access to information—or at least intuition—that eluded others, though, so if Lord Caladen had reasons for believing, Tomas was inclined to accept it. He just hoped Kor wouldn't ask why he'd been hearing secrets from that particular young maid.

He expected questions, but Kor said nothing. A tingle started at the back of Tomas's neck and began to crawl across his skin as Kor's eyes bored into him.

"Who else knows?"

Tomas shuddered. The low, flat delivery of the question

seemed to slide between his ribs like a sharp blade. Kor didn't seem to consider the possibility that it might not be true—but there was nothing in his unblinking acceptance to suggest any excitement at the thought of a myth turned real. "I don't know, my lord. His family, I imagine."

"I've been having dreams," Kor said, mercifully breaking off his gaze and apparently addressing the air. "I wondered."

"Should we Gather the Great Houses?" If it were true, and the settlers were real and here after all this time, the House lords should consider how to manage their arrival.

"It won't be necessary. The ship won't land." Kor's tone wasn't one of prophecy or prediction. It was fact.

Kor's hand brushed the air, and the House guards moved forward in answer. "Take him," Kor said.

To Tomas, he said, "I wish someone other than you had heard this, my friend."

PART ONE

ARRIVAL

1

SCOUTS

Taran River, West Branch
Early Spring, Year 1057

IT WAS HARD to guess how deep the water was, but it didn't look promising for wading across. A tumble of large rocks lay like thrown dice in the river, and the water shattered and frothed silver where it struck. Piers stood on a boulder at the edge, a foot or two above the tumult, and watched a large branch hurtle past and snap against a jutting rock. Beside him, Arthur stooped for a stick, and sent it arcing through the rain to splash into the current halfway across.

The rain was coming down harder, and here at the edge of the water there was no shelter from the canopy of leaves behind them. Piers was soaked, so wet that he no longer distinguished the drips from the sky and the drips from his hair as the water trickled over his face and under the collar of his jacket. Their first two days here had been clear and dry, and then they'd had day after day of intermittent but gentle rain; this shiver-inducing sogginess wasn't nearly as pleasant, but he told himself to enjoy the novelty of it. He wondered where all this water came from.

"Just once," Arthur said, voice raised over the sound of the water. "Just once, I'd like to report back to the ship that we made good progress."

Piers laughed. "We're learning how to cope down here. Exactly what scouts are supposed to do."

He knew what Arthur was thinking—and he didn't need his psi-enhanced Empathy to know how his fellow scout was feeling. Arthur hadn't intended to be a landing scout; he'd trained as a planner. Walking miles in the rain, traipsing through fields and forests, sorting out who to trust and what was safe: landing scouts like Piers were supposed to do all that. Arthur had intended to be comfortable and surrounded by the familiar while he incorporated what Piers and the others learned into *Redemption*'s integration plan. In the two weeks since their shuttle had dropped them here, Piers had coaxed and coached Arthur through more novel situations than either of them had imagined.

It would have been so different if Kathleen were with him. He tried not to think about her, since neither the regret nor the longing would help him focus, but Arthur's cautious reluctance was a nearly constant reminder. If Kath were with him, they would be sharing observations, puzzling things out, and laughing at their surprises. She had trained for this, too—more than he had, really, since she joined the landing scout team before him—and had been nearly out of her mind with excitement as they got closer to their departure. Her accident by itself wasn't the tragedy, since her body would heal. Being unable to be part of the scouting, though, that came close to killing her. Even so, even when she was in the worst of her pain, she'd been sympathetic about the fact that her other ex-boyfriend would take her place as Piers's scout partner.

Knowing them both as well as she did, she'd predicted both their vacillating friendship and the difficulty Piers would have with Arthur's unpoetic, rule-bound determination. For Arthur, nothing mattered more than the assignment. Three thousand people were up there in orbit, crammed in an ark ship that wasn't meant to support even eight hundred, and they were counting on the scouts to arrange a welcome among a population that should have been expecting them but wasn't. As Arthur saw it, there'd be time enough later to marvel at the wonders of planetary life when all of them were on the ground.

"I'm getting sick of surprises," Arthur said, his voice rasping. He squared his shoulders. "Anyway, we have to get across, if we're going to get to the city."

Piers pictured the low-orbit images they'd studied before landing. They'd had limited options for bringing the shuttle down somewhere remote enough to avoid notice but not impossibly far from civilization, and it had been a rough start for them. It had been a relief when they'd finally come to the road that would lead them through the long tract of dense forest between the shuttle's landing spot and the nearest settlement. If nothing else, it was much easier walking for people who'd only ever known the smooth, level corridors of the ship.

Before it vanished under the trees, the road crossed a river that had looked like a small, silvery blue thread from the ship. When they'd come to the bridge, the punishing force of the water had been a lesson in false perceptions. They had watched the rushing, rippling band of water seem to bend against the structure and sentiently flow around obstacles, with a hiss that sounded distressingly like a punctured air-seal. A dropped twig on the upstream side shot out from under the bridge before they could even cross to watch it reappear. It made Piers feel like the ground was sliding under his feet, and he'd enjoyed the peculiar sensation, but it had made Arthur's ground-sickness flare up again.

They knew the road would emerge from the forest just north of the city, with a mile or so of open approach to a clearly visible wall. At the south-eastern edge of the city, there was no wall except the forest itself. They'd left the road to cut through the forest to that more discreet entry—and to try to get some respite from the pelting rain. From the ship's only remaining camera, this second branch of the river had looked trivial, something to step over.

Up close, it turned out to be more turbulent than the branch spanned by the bridge. "The road's north of us now," Piers said. "Backtrack?"

Arthur was fiddling with the dangling end of his pack's strap, and his eyes were fixed on the swirling brown water at their feet. "No," he said. "I don't want to waste time. We need to keep going—and I really want to get into the city without the long hello."

Near where they stood, there was a flat rock almost level with the water, and beyond that, the scattered rocks and boulders made a broken path across the river. Piers put a hand on Arthur's thin shoulder and channeled a bit of his own enthusiasm for the challenge. Arthur wasn't an Empath, and wasn't the most psi-sensitive individual, but Piers could usually bolster him with a Push of confidence or optimism. "Looks like we could step across here." He pointed at a few rocks in sequence. "Just another new experience. Come on. See you on the other side."

Piers stepped out to the rock and discovered that seeing

the motion of the water around him made him a little queasy. Better to focus on the next step rather than his feet, so he plotted his next move—another one-man island. Next was a large rock with several ledge-like angles. Other steps beckoned beyond that. The rocks gleamed, wet, and he wondered if the water would be colder than the rain. Soaked as he was already, he still didn't want to have to wade. He tried not to notice the ferocity of the river, and tried not to be distracted by Arthur's timid progress to his right.

He stretched over to the ledge rock and planted his right foot on one of the ledges, straddling a fury of water until he pulled himself forward. It was narrower than he'd thought, and he had to balance on his toes. Water sprayed his legs and rain stung his face. Now what?

"Careful, Haldon," Arthur called. "Don't want to get wet!"

With a grin at Arthur's wisecrack, Piers looked for a way forward. Nothing convenient. There was a small rock just under the water, a mid-point to a better option, so he stepped there intending to keep moving. It was coated with algae and he started to slip. Ice-cold water poured over his foot—*much* colder than the rain—and his already bruised hip took the impact when he caught himself against a wall of rock, but he stayed on his feet. Adrenaline shot through him, and he made himself slow down. It was maybe forty feet to the other side—probably not even that—but it felt like a good portion of forever passed before he found himself standing on the broad, flat boulder on the western bank.

Arthur seemed to be at an impasse halfway across, stalled and contemplating his choices. He hesitated, apparently debating whether to follow Piers's route or try something else. He looked around for options, and then stepped on a submerged rock. It looked like he was trying to walk on the water.

He started to paddle the air and then fell sideways with a shout. The water started to drag him away, but Arthur grabbed a prominent boulder and fought to hold on against the force of the current. One arm slipped, and he struggled to reattach to the slick rock. The river swept over his shoulders and pack.

Piers shrugged off his own rain-sodden pack and started back toward Arthur, shouting encouragement as he tried to hurry on the rocks he'd just carefully navigated.

He saw Arthur try to stand, but the water jerked him down. Arthur yawped as he fell again, his body twisting. His legs were swept out from under him. His pack dislodged, somehow, and he lunged to grab it. Water smacked into his face and snatched the pack out of his reach.

"Arthur!" A rock Piers had crawled over earlier now blocked his view—Arthur was on the other side. "Hang on, Arthur!" He slipped again, and his legs plunged into the frigid water, over his knees. At the shock, his psi screens fell, and inadvertently he Reached for Arthur, Empathically, as if that would help Arthur find his feet.

Arthur had no capacity to accept the extra psychic energy, and since Piers had left himself Open, the force of Arthur's terror blasted him instead. It tore away his own control. All he could feel, all he could be at that moment was an extension of Arthur. He felt his own legs being dragged by the current, his own face battered by the angry river, not the sensations but the confusion and panic. He fought to find the psychic boundary between himself and Arthur, and to center his thoughts again.

He pulled himself around the upstream side of a

boulder, scrabbling under the water to keep in contact with the rock. He heard Arthur shout again, and saw Arthur's pack ricochet against a boulder before the river tossed it a yard downstream. Then he saw Arthur tumble after it, feet first, arms flailing, knocking against the same sequence of boulders.

"Hang on!" Piers yelled again. He splashed and spidered back to his pack, which was half in the water at the edge of the river. He fumbled with the straps and yanked stuff out until he found the coil of rope and then scrambled along the bank to keep Arthur in sight. The merciless current ripped his partner into the swift center of the river. Only yards away, the water crashed into another span of rocks. Piers shouted for Arthur, who was thrashing sideways. Neither of them could swim, but Arthur kicked and paddled and kept his head above water, and he managed to reorient himself in the smoother water. Piers thought Arthur saw him, and cast one end of the rope out over the water.

Arthur reached for it, but missed. He thrashed harder as he was swept past it, trying to get within reach. The water spun him as it poured into the funnel between rocks. His back slammed into a rock; his body folded over and he dropped into the rapids backwards, his legs pointed upstream. Piers saw Arthur's face just before he was dumped into the violent whitewater. He seemed to be staring right at Piers.

Piers flung the rope aside and forced his way through the woods and brush at the edge of the bank, stumbling and skidding down the incline beside the rapids. Branches lashed at him, roots tried to trip him, but he ran on, shouting Arthur's name with decreasing hope. He Scanned; nothing. He had to climb back up to stay beside the river, but he could still see the racing water. He sprinted as long as he could, high on the bank, then walked while his lungs burned. He thought he was perhaps a half-mile from where he crossed.

The river curved to the southeast, suddenly gentler and shallower. Branches and vegetative detritus were piled in the bend, caught against a tree that overhung the water. Pinned against the pile, a piece of fabric waved in the water. With his heart in his throat, Piers worked his way along the bank to get as close as he could. He knew it was one of Arthur's ship-made shirts.

Piers paced beside the water, oblivious to the rain as he stared at Arthur's shirt. His mind was stuttering over questions, useless ones like: why only one shirt? The more important question, the obvious one, his mind refused to formulate. The river deposited another small branch at the pile and swirled on.

He Reached as far as he could. Nothing. Arthur could be unconscious. Piers strained his psychic senses further, even risked a prolonged Scan. His heartbeat was too loud. His temples started to pound and the nausea began to rise, but he made himself Reach still farther. There was nothing, no one, and the feeling he dreaded—the sense of utter, desolate isolation—started to cling to him. He stopped Scanning before it overwhelmed him.

He shivered. Best to at least keep moving, even if he didn't know what to do. At the farthest edge of his sight, downstream, the river narrowed again and he saw white. Upstream, he could see nothing but the smooth current. Something drifted into his attention—a sock. He watched as the swifter water snagged it and it sped toward the pile of debris.

If there were still things from Arthur's pack being pulled loose, the pack might be caught among the rocks. So might Arthur.

Running back, on ice-water legs that had started to stiffen, was harder. Piers felt like he had to concentrate on every muscle's effort as he retraced his path. Easy to see where he'd been, from the trail of broken twigs and disturbed leaves.

When he got to the woods beside the rapids, he grabbed hold of a tree and leaned out for an unobstructed view. Arthur's pack was barely a quarter of the way from the end of the rapids. One strap had snagged on something, and the flap was open, inviting the water to reach in and take whatever it could carry. Hope flared. Piers moved, and raked his eyes over the next section of the rapids, then the next.

He saw the boot first, when he looked downstream, because the pale sole stood out against the dark rock. Then he realized it was there because Arthur's ankle was wedged between two sharp rocks, twisting his leg at an impossible angle. Piers tasted copper as he saw Arthur's body bucking and slamming against the rocks, face-down, arms reaching downstream as if diving. Blood streamed into the water.

Piers dropped to his knees and retched.

He hadn't noticed that the rain had stopped. He didn't remember making his way back to his own pack. As his senses reawakened, those were his first realizations. Awareness of aching ribs and a burning throat followed, and then he learned he was cold, bruised, and hungry.

Piers discovered he had pointlessly wrapped himself in his blanket, which was now as wringing wet as everything else, and settled on the ground with his back against a tree. He remembered none of that. The sky was still light, and he didn't think he'd been asleep, but he'd shut down so completely it amounted to the same thing—except he didn't feel rested.

The ship chimed in his ear: in range. That must be what pulled him out of the daze. He initiated contact through the implant, and Jon replied.

"Hey, scout! What news?" Jon's encoding was familiar, and that alone almost broke Piers's control. It wasn't Jon's voice, exactly, but he knew how it *should* sound. The words took shape in Piers's inner ear with Jon's resonance and cheery inflection.

His own words were tangled, but Jon teased out the story, weaving the details together until he understood what had happened. There was silence, then.

Eventually, Jon said, "No way you can get to him?"

"No." Cables, harnesses, pulleys...it could be done, if he had help and equipment.

Another long space, and then it wasn't Jon but the captain who said, "Piers, you don't have to play out the tether on this one, if you don't want to."

His eyes brimmed at the sound of his father's voice. It surprised him that Jon had called in the captain for a real-time update, interrupting bridge duties when the scout program was the commander's responsibility, not the captain's. Plus, Jon knew that Piers had struggled to relate to his father after his parents' divorce, despite their best efforts. But the calm concern was Dad at his best, ready to help but leaving enough space for Piers to decide what he needed.

Piers's father said things like *play out the tether* when he wanted to keep a little bit of emotional distance, almost like promising in a code language not to resort to any psi shortcuts. It was just a figure of speech, but Piers *did* feel like he was on a spacewalk—not that he'd ever experienced that. He'd seen the maintenance team do it. Drifting through a vacuum, isolated, with just one tenuous link to safety. Dad meant: do you want to keep going and see this through, or do you want to be reeled in?

Piers closed his eyes. He wanted to shut everything out and think this through. No one would rush him.

He couldn't go back to the ship. He and Arthur had stood at the edge of the clearing with their backs to the trees, and watched the departing shuttle become a toy, then a dot, then a speck, and finally a glint that faded into the sky. They'd known it wasn't coming back.

It was just one more unconsidered consequence of the compromises the people on *Redemption* had made over the years. When the crew on the original manifest of the ship had woken from their suspension and realized they had missed their timemark, they'd had to make hard decisions. To live for three or four generations on a ship that was only meant to hold seven hundred and twenty newly re-awakened humans for a week or so, they knew they would have to make strategic use of everything they had, from the stock of Earth seeds and genes they had in store to the ship itself. Living from the cargo meant when they did finally arrive at the planet that had been prepared for them, they wouldn't be delivering settlers and supplies so much as sending down a fully fledged community of people whose only experience with Earth was generational memory. And that had been the way of it.

Through the decades of realspace travel, three of *Redemption's* four maintenance pods had been cannibalized for various good reasons, their systems and parts sacrificed to repair and extend the ship's own. They hadn't been intended for in-atmosphere excursions anyway. The eight-seat shuttle meant for an advance team's landing had been, unbelievably, half-wrecked by a Manifester in the mad days of despair and disappointment when they first realized what had happened. So the engineers had managed to cobble together two tiny autopilot shuttles for the scouts from the skeletons of the pods and the remnants of the eight-seater, but they were little more than wind-up toys held together with plas-tape.

After the first two scout teams were down, the ship recalled the shuttles. The engineers re-clad them with the last of the heat-shielding from the sabotaged vehicle, and it was just enough to protect the second teams through the fiery entry. There were no resources left to gin up a shuttle to fetch him home.

So. He was on his own.

After Kath's accident, when they had finally been forced to admit that they couldn't wait long enough for her to heal, there had been a lot of discussion about whether a scout could manage alone. There were good reasons why they'd decided it was worth finding a substitute on short notice. Commander Barston had been strong on the argument that a pair of scouts could watch out for each other. Arthur had shown the other truth: the buddy system didn't guarantee protection.

Kath had also raised some thoughtful points about Piers being on his own, considering his potent psi abilities. At the time she was the only other scout who knew that he was being asked to use that ability on the planet. On the crowded ship, there were always other Empaths around. There was no way to avoid it, when there was no way to be more than a few feet away from at least one other person. They were pretty sure the Empathic link wouldn't reach from ground to orbit, so Kath insisted that Piers needed to have someone with him, because they didn't know how he'd react to being cut off from the familiar minds on the ship.

He'd bristled at her caution, thinking he heard subtext that he wasn't self-sufficient. He knew his abilities to Screen and Block were well beyond average, too, and thought she underestimated his experience with being Separated. Despite their history, and the way his abilities had both enhanced and interfered with their relationship, she still didn't recognize how much his psi talent could cost him. It dragged him into vulnerability, and it laid him open to a soul-deep kind of suffering when things went wrong.

When his parents' marriage had disintegrated, he'd felt every poisonous drop of their antagonism—because they were both psi and he was Connected to them both. When his sister had wrestled with depression, Connection brought all the pain into Piers's own mind and heart. And when his grandfather died, that part of his psyche was torn out of him, leaving ragged edges that were still raw even now. Even his connection to Kath, which wasn't truly even a Link because she wasn't psi, had meant that he felt every moment of her intensifying unhappiness before they broke up. That was just the fallout from having made himself Open to her feelings.

All that was nothing rare for an Empath, really; probably the others could match him horror for horror, if they ever compared their experiences. And the same gift amplified love, joy, and happiness, too, so most of them wouldn't trade it. The difference for Piers was one of degree, and from the moment his psi ability had activated, his personal challenge was to learn to calibrate his sensitivity. On the rare occasions when he'd dropped his psi screens completely, he'd been assaulted with psychic cacophony—not just the gentle hum from fellow Empaths but blasts of emotion from Separates as well, all competing for his attention. If he worked at it, he could sometimes corral their contradictory emotions for a while to give himself time to process, but it took so much out of him that it could leave him in tatters.

By now, he had an acquired physical aversion to intense psi efforts. The nausea and headaches were incentive to try to break the habit of his Empathic impulses, to stop him from reflexively Scanning to see how someone was feeling, or Pushing to nudge along a friendship. There had been times in the past few years when using his ability had come pretty close to putting him in medibay; the physical consequences were getting serious. Living like a Separate—a non-Empath—hurt less and seemed safer, even though it meant forsaking the possibility of that deep, connected comprehension, that mutual understanding so complete it was like a saturation of self. He hadn't been Connected to another Empath for years, and hadn't left himself fully Open to anyone else's emotions more than once or twice since Kath.

So it hadn't been the easiest decision of his life when they asked him to join the program, even though he wanted to, and even though there really wasn't a choice. Just like the ship's navigation system was fueled by active Empaths working in concert, the landing sequence depended on an equal amount of planet-side psionic energy to hold the ship in equilibrium through the transition, descent, and landing. Piers was the only strong psi *Redemption* could spare; no one else, beyond a few of the bridge crew, came anywhere close to his level. If there were Empaths here, *Redemption* needed to find them. With his formidable psi talent, Piers was the ship's best hope for this surreptitious scouting assignment—and the only backup plan they had.

He'd been open with Jon and the Commander about his doubts. The ship's nav required eight Empaths at all times, so the crew were all needed just to maintain operations across the shifts. No creative permutation of the schedule made it possible for the ship to do without the three or four crew members whose psi ability was strong enough to be useful for this mission. The other Empaths on the ship didn't have the capacity or the control to do this, and trying to draw out and channel their psi energy would burn through his. All the same, Piers didn't think their chances were too good if they had to rely on any lone Empath, no matter how exceptional. Still, Jon and Barston argued, the long shot was better than no shot, and in any case Piers's talent would be needed in the search for other Empaths.

So his doubts were overruled. His fears, well, those he'd shared only with the Captain. *That* had been a terrifying discussion, but unavoidable. His father knew how bad the pain could be, and knew, too, that Piers had been quite deliberately not using his psi abilities. "As your father, I want to keep you safe and happy, and I wouldn't send you," he had said. "As the captain, I have to deploy the resources I have in the best way I can." They had talked through the stakes, and gone over the realities, and what it came down to was the simple truth that Piers was the only one who could take the assignment.

No one—himself included—really knew what it would take to guide *Redemption* to a safe landing. The plans just said that the Empaths should Connect as equals to create a path for the ship. Based on previous headaches and fever-like exhaustion, it was a fair bet that trying to direct his psi energy as kinetic power, and concentrating it against an eight-strong force, would leave him catatonic, insane, or dead. It had taken some soul-searching, but he'd finally accepted that if giving all he had was enough to give everyone on the ship at least a chance at surviving the landing, he was willing.

The exploration, the adventure, the *purpose* this mission offered was what he had craved all his life, and it was worth the price.

"What else can I do?" he asked. "I knew it was a one-way trip." There was a momentary, unanchored, and nauseating giddiness. Without Arthur, he'd be alone in a way that made Separation seem like companionable silence. Being on his own on the planet with no one to talk to, no one who would understand the impressions and experiences he was facing—*that* felt like exile. "I'll manage." He imagined a tether unspooling.

2

VISITORS

THE CONSTANT FUSS and flurry about her sister's upcoming wedding was wearisome. Arissa felt like it had been weeks since anyone had talked about anything other than dresses and Lyndi's bridal chest. The groom was arranging the wedding for early summer, after the spring rains passed, and with months of waiting ahead, Arissa wasn't sure how she could stand it.

Their mother had been upset that her eldest daughter wasn't going to marry into one of the other Great Houses of Merra, and she didn't like the idea of Lyndi living in Portsay—even though she herself had been raised there. She said it had taken a year after leaving to get the smell of the fisheries out of her clothes. Even so, she hadn't been able to resist getting involved in planning a wedding, and she was more swept up in the romance of it than the bride.

Caleb was nice enough, Arissa thought, but bland. He was in his mid-twenties and already had a receding hairline and an expanding waistline, which he tried to hide by wearing a jacket that was too big for him. They had met him in Portsay two years ago on a shopping trip. He'd been flush with pride from repaying a substantial loan from a backer ahead of schedule, and he'd been enamored of Lyndi from the start. Arissa wasn't sure how he earned his fortune, but he was rich enough that Lyndi would be upgrading her lifestyle, even though she'd be in some townhouse on a crowded street instead of here, in the ancient, noble House on Aryn's sweeping moor.

Arissa wouldn't make that trade for herself. The moor was home, and had its own appeal, and she loved that for centuries House Aryn had stood bold to the wind in the middle of that desolation. Its presence proclaimed its self-sufficiency—a boast it couldn't quite fulfill. Aryn's people made their living from the river that formed the eastern border for the House, or they raised scraggly sheep and thin goats on the wind-scoured land. There was never quite enough, but she loved the wild moor anyway. It didn't matter that House Aryn's attractions had never included wealth.

She hated the idea of Lyndi leaving, but really, it wasn't anything like a surprise. Lyndi was twenty-two, and if their father were still alive she would certainly be betrothed to someone. She was just following the path that every House daughter confronted, though she had been free to decide for herself. Their mother hadn't thought about arranging a marriage, because she didn't think about practical things like that, and Nevin hadn't, because even though he was twenty and Head of House, he didn't think about his sisters much at all.

Lately Nevin had taken refuge in fishing, and spent his days away from the House. For her part, Arissa escaped for walks with the dogs, and sometimes on good days her arthritic pony, Wisdom, hobbled along with her.

Today, Arissa had already endured a long discussion about the relative merits of blue versus rose for Lyndi's dress, and a detailed consideration of whether Nevin alone would be a sufficient escort for the bride or if they should ask their neighbor at House Chant to go along. If Lyndi married into another House, the husband would provide an escort for the bride. This wasn't a House marriage, though, and Caleb didn't have House Guard to send, obviously, and given House Aryn's finances, Lyndi would be going alone. Their mother was concerned about how it would look for a daughter of Aryn to be poorly attended, even making the case that the wedding guests—at least the bride's mother and sister—should go along with the bride. Arissa was glad that Lyndi was resisting the idea; the last thing she wanted was to be stuck in Portsay during her sister's bride-month while the happy couple socialized with all of the groom's family and friends before the wedding.

Arissa knew if she stayed inside with her mother and sister, she would say something unforgivable, so right after lunch she announced that she was taking a walk. Rain was probably on the way, because any day now it would start in earnest, and if she didn't get some air now she'd miss the chance. She pulled on a jacket, because the wind was up today and it was always cutting on the moor. She whistled for Dapper and Belle, and both dogs trotted into the hall with their ears perked. When Dapper saw her take her walking stick and loop her father's old fieldglasses around her neck, he moved to the door and whined, eager to race into the open air.

As she picked her way across the moor, the dogs criss-crossed all around her on secret trails only they could follow. Like her, they knew there were areas where the peat bog was deep and strong enough to pull an animal down. The muck had swallowed one of her shoes years ago, because it wouldn't let go when Lyndi had yanked her out. Arissa often wondered what else was rotting in the mud along with her shoe and the ancient vegetation.

She skirted the west edge of the tarn, which was frosted with tiny whitecaps from the wind, and climbed up the ridge that formed Aryn's northwest border. From the top, she could look out over House Chant's narrow plateau and the sea-carved valley far below. A steep cliff, unsuspected from above Chant, plunged straight into a long lake—the lake where Nevin liked to fish. Toward the east, the moor flowed over a less brutal incline, and it was an easy ride to the village at the head of the lake. The shining river that pierced the lake coursed west through the valley and spread into a broad estuary. This view, which seemed to lay at her feet like a vast map, put humanity's presence in the valley into scale. Sky and river, the land and the sea beyond, all hinted at infinity, while the buildings and boats were mere points. It wasn't a friendly landscape, but it was beautiful to her, even on a day with heavy clouds and rough wind.

Movement among the houses caught her eye. Through the scratched lenses of the fieldglasses, she saw a half-circle of uniformed men on horseback facing the door of one of the houses near the jetties. A man and a woman came onto the stoop and pulled the door shut behind them. Arissa wished the glasses were stronger, so that she could see the details. She saw the man gesticulate, and the half-circle tightened as the horses stepped forward. A rider dismounted and climbed the steps.

The woman went inside, and came back with something small that she handed to the rider, though her man tried to stop her. With some parting comment, the riders remounted, and the horses turned and then trotted away.

Arissa watched for another few moments, while the couple argued and then clung to each other, and then called for her dogs and started down the steep track toward home.

"I know what I saw," Arissa said again. "They were Ettori men and they were collecting." She had been impatient for Nevin to get home this afternoon, and had pushed him to hear her as soon as he'd settled in his study.

Nevin just steepled his fingers and looked at her over the tips, his lips screwed into that pucker he always made when he was trying to seem thoughtful. The silence was an itch she longed to scratch, but Arissa knew that saying more wouldn't help. He tapped his forefingers together a few times, then spread his fingers. "I don't know what you expect me to do about it, 'Riss. If it's in the village, it's Chant's issue, and sounds like it's over, anyway."

She sat across his desk from him, her hands folded on her lap to keep herself from clenching her fists. Dapper lay at her feet, his muzzle resting on his front paws as if he, too, was working at self-restraint. Her brother had listened to her whole account with his feigned consideration, and it amazed her that she'd been able to stop herself from venting her frustration at high volume. Keeping herself on a tight leash, she said, "If they were collectors, what were they doing going after the villagers themselves? And off-cycle?"

"Maybe Chant was short on the Tithe." The people who made their livings from House lands or resources contributed a share to the House. Each House then paid a share to the Council of Houses—and the Council distributed it to communities throughout Merra according to need. The semi-annual Tithe was supposed to be a percentage, a due share of whatever there was to divide. Two years ago, Prime

House had set a minimum for the winter Tithe. For most of the Houses it was a manageable burden, just a little above their traditional percentage in an average year, but neither Chant nor Aryn had ever been reliably prosperous.

"Then they should talk to the House! They have no right to harass Chant's village."

"House Ettori is Prime, Arissa. When it comes to the Tithe, Lord Ettori most certainly does have the right."

Her fingers were flushed and her knuckles were white from squeezing her hands together, but she didn't flare. "What if they went after our shepherds? Our people don't have any extra to give."

"Don't I know it! I'm thankful Lyndi's marrying rich— next time we need a loan, I won't have to shake it out of Petros Gibbon."

"Oh, Nevin...What did you do?" Her hands came unfolded and she dug her fingers into the armrests of her chair. Dapper struggled up to his haunches and rolled doleful eyes back at her.

"Relax, 'Riss. I asked Aryn's head shepherd to help us meet the Tithe, that's all. It's his duty, and he knows it."

Petros Gibbon barely had two chippers to clink together. The old man earned very little, and gave all he could to help his grown daughter raise her family in health.

"He had some saved up," Nevin said, "and I told him we'll pay him back."

That seemed unlikely; their income came from the shepherds in the first place. "With what?" she asked. "Lyndi's bride gift?"

Nevin got out of his chair and came around to her. He put his hands on her shoulders, holding her in her chair. His brown eyes, like their father's except they lacked humor, bore into hers. "That's already spoken for. He gave it to us early and that was most of our Tithe. We'll use yours to pay back Gibbon."

"Mine?" she echoed, feeling dread slither over her.

Nevin patted Dapper's head, then, and gave her a conspiratorial smile. For an instant, it was like they were children again, and he had some plan to tease Lyndi or had found where the cook had hidden the sweets. Behind that smile, though, his adult eyes still held no warmth or sympathy.

His voice was equally barren as he told her that he'd contracted her for marriage. This summer.

Stunned into stillness, Arissa looked up at him and noticed a light wine stain on his collar. The words were just sounds and his lips seemed to move at random.

"Lord Wyth?" She repeated the only bit she'd really heard.

"House Wyth, 'Riss! I never thought you'd get a match *that* good."

He was still talking as she rose from her chair and escaped from the room in a wobbly daze, with Dapper trotting after her and nosing into her hand with concern.

Too soon, the tedious spring rain was lifting, weeks earlier than usual. It took a while for Arissa to notice that the sound of the rain dripping from the eaves to the puddles was easing. The maddening splats of springtime, her father had called that sound. Farther north, especially up in the hills, people had to contend with ice and snow well into the spring, and then the meltwaters would pour into the valleys in early summer. Here on the Aryn moor, the rain just seeped into the already soggy ground, making a lake of mud around the old house that wouldn't fully dry out until midsummer. There were years when she couldn't tolerate the rain that went on for days at a time, but this year she had cheered every watery morning. The rain meant floods, and floods meant delay, and more delay would have meant more time to devise a plan to avoid this marriage. It had been almost six weeks since Nevin told her about Wyth. She could hope for another week or two of rain, maybe, but the fact that there were breaks in the clouds now was the wrong omen.

Arissa looked up from Nevin's desk in the parlor that he used as his study, off the hall just inside the main door. The ledger was open to a page near the middle, and she was trying to make sense of the columns. A column at the far right showed the House's account, diminishing for a few entries, then jumping back up in response to an entry such as, "Sold sapphire ring." There were alternating charges and payments listed, some in a clerk's neat handwriting and some in Nevin's impatient scratch. She flipped at random to a more recent page.

She was nursing a cup of telik; they had already cut back on even that. Her mother had retreated upstairs today, claiming a headache that possibly was real. Nevin had taken Lyndi to Portsay, to meet with Caleb one last time before the bride-month. The rest of the household— just the two servants, now—moved quietly about their tasks, avoiding her mood. She was aware of their caution whenever they had to bring something to her attention. It was a miracle she had her temper in check at all. At least Dapper and Belle never held her moods against her. Both dogs were lolling in front of the hearth, where there was room for them to extend their long legs without contending with the loveseat and the crowd of chairs.

The new page was harder to decipher. No clerk's writing now, just Nevin's sloppy figures, row after row. The charges continued, but there were fewer payments. Every few lines, a deposit was recorded, sometimes with a useful explanation of the source and sometimes with a cryptic note like "50G (E) & 10G (C)." Then there were three or four lines of payments before the unanswered charges resumed.

So this was why her brother hadn't even asked her before accepting an offer from some rich, arrogant lord from the hills who wanted to marry Arissa. She didn't trust his motive—Nevin had said the bride price was the highest he'd ever heard of. There was only one reason why a wealthy House like Wyth would pay so much for a union with a House as poor as Aryn: Arissa was currently the only unmarried House daughter of age in all of Merra. Their children, inheriting from two ancient lines, would be able to claim all sorts of advantages.

There was one particular claim that House Wyth was probably keenly interested in. The Caladen Forest, which lay between Wyth and Ettori, had once made House Caladen the richest of the Great Houses, but when House Caladen fell, its riches vanished. The whole family and many of the House's people had been extinguished three years before Arissa was born, in a terrible fire fueled by the surrounding trees. One way Caladen could be re-established was by the first child of a House union, who would then be considered the founder of a new family line. Lord Wyth would be glad to see Caladen restored as a friendly House, buffering Wyth from Ettori. And marrying Arissa of Aryn was the only way he could ensure that.

Horribly, it was Nevin's right—even his duty, considering House Aryn's debt—to sell her off like this. Aryn had always had a male head of House and their father hadn't renounced that tradition before he died. It fell to Nevin, even though he had no real interest in managing Aryn, and no talent for it. He had too much pride to admit it. So Arissa was here, staring at Aryn's unpaid accounts and trying to think of some answer to their debt that didn't involve the whole rest of her life.

She knew almost nothing about Lord Wyth, just that he was her senior by at least a full decade, had taken over from his father as Head of House—illness, she thought— and people considered him handsome. It was already more than she wanted to know. He would send an escort for her as soon as the floods eased. With the rain tapering, she probably had another three or four weeks at most before they could trust the roads. It would be longer before they could ford the Kai River—her river—if they came by the southern road. But House Wyth was upland, at the head of Wyth Valley, so even while snowmelt inundated the low ground, Wyth's men could take the highroad to cross to the west, and the bridges over the Truolt were high and strong, and hadn't washed out for hundreds of years. They were to come for her, and take her to Ruatt, House Wyth's sponsored city, to prepare for a summer wedding.

Feeling heartsick, she slid a hand under the pages at the back of the book, and pushed them over to clear the way for the thick leather binding. A folded paper clung to the sueded inside of the cover.

House Ettori's emblem scarred the top of the page. The short letter was signed "Kor of Ettori," in spiky writing with spidery downstrokes and razor-sharp points. Written by the man himself? Arissa felt her temper spark.

"To Nevin of House Aryn. Lord Nevin: You will under-stand that it grieves me to write this letter, but House Ettori is not at this point able to loan any further funds to you. As you rightly noted, the amount already owed between us strains charity, and as you wrote to request further

assistance, I infer that no repayment is forthcoming. To show that I am not insensitive to your struggles, I will defer the agreed interest charges until the next winter Tithe, to give you time to find your footing. However, if you cannot repay the full amount due at the Tithe, all interest will immediately accrue. At that point, it must be clear to us both that House Aryn would be proven unable to pay. As Prime House, Ettori would then need to take charge of Aryn's affairs and manage the estate until it is restored to sustainable finances. In friendship, Kor of Ettori."

The paper trembled between Arissa's fingers. In debt to *Ettori*. With House Aryn itself transformed into collateral by Kor's self-serving, expansive interpretation of Prime House's responsibilities. Stupid, *stupid* Nevin. She wondered how much Lord Wyth had agreed to pay for the marriage contract—was it enough?

There was a loud knock on the door, and the dogs started barking in full voice. Arissa jolted in her chair and in her startle, she knocked over her cup of telik. As the dark liquid started spreading across the desk, she snatched the ledger away. The dogs were scrambling in the hall, barking at the door as the knock came again. She shoved the letter into the ledger and hastily stuffed a blotting rag around the base of the cup, then jostled past the dogs into the hall. Anicho, the sprightlier of the House servants, opened the door and stepped back at her gesture.

The air that rushed in was cool and humid, but the clouds were retreating, leaving behind the grey, winter-barren moor. Standing at her door, humbly looking down, was a tall lad she didn't know. He wore a battered cap pulled low and his boots were coated with mud, so he probably worked with the shepherds on the southern fields. His unruly, sandy hair almost hid his eyes when he raised his head, but he greeted her with a polite nod. He had a handsome face. There were probably village girls pining for him.

He smiled, but seemed to think better of saying whatever had crossed his mind. He reached into the bag at his side, and pulled out a large loaf of bread, plainly wrapped in a bit of cloth. He held it out to her across the threshold and said softly, "This is my reason to knock at your door. May I come in?" In a louder voice, and a rougher accent, he added, "It's Mum's baking day an' she said to bring ya this to say thank ya."

Taken aback, she accepted the bread, and looked at him more carefully. His clothes were plain but neat, with no signs of mending. In fact, the fabric of his shirt was remarkably fine, and his vest was well-fitted—and although his cloak was woolen, it was lined. This wasn't a shepherd lad after all. Her pulse quickened. "Thank you," she said clearly, though as she looked past his shoulder she couldn't see anyone else, only a patient, very unremarkable moor pony. "Please come in. I have something for you to take to your mother."

He ducked his head and made a show of wiping his feet, but he winked at her as he walked past her into the front hall. The dogs rushed at him, but he was unbothered. He patted Dapper on the head and let Belle sniff his hand. Anicho shut the door, and the boy straightened, his bearing completely altered. He was older than she'd thought. He glanced around the hall. "Thank you, my lady. I have a message not fit for writing—and there's a good chance someone watched me come here. Are you Lady Arissa?"

She led him into the front room, embarrassed by the mess and the spilled telik on the desk as she set the breadloaf down. He moved toward the fireless hearth—she stayed near the desk and the doorway, glad when the dogs moved between them, although they clearly did not see him as a threat. He seemed at ease, and took a moment to look at the small portrait of her father on the mantel, and the painted glass vase her mother used to keep filled with flowers and grasses from the moor all summer.

"Well?" she asked. She braced her hands on the desk behind her, now aware of her pounding heart. Why had she let a stranger in, just because of a whisper that made her curious? The rules of hospitality were different now, with Ettori's men roaming over the country.

"I bring a message for House Aryn."

"My brother is Head of House," she said. "He's away."

"Lord Chant told me to seek *you*, that you would speak for the House in this. The message is this: House Dannpelier is calling a Gathering of the Houses."

There was an old, old tradition, older even than the Council, of the Houses taking common action in defense of Merra. Gatherings had always been rare, and the Council was supposed to handle most matters. But the Council was paralyzed by Lord Ettori's authority now, and the Houses had no resources beyond what he permitted. Since he himself would be the representative from House Ettori, it was hard to imagine that a Gathering would accomplish anything, either.

"The current Prime House won't be there," the messenger said, as if reading her thoughts.

"Not really a Gathering, then. More of a conspiracy." She glanced at him to see how he had interpreted her impulsive words or her tone. Her quip, the kind of automatic, acerbic judgment that infuriated her mother, could be construed to put her on either side of Ettori's favor. What if the messenger's real errand was to test political allegiances?

For an instant, his face seemed to harden, and she

realized he was closer to thirty than twenty. His eyes locked to hers, and seemed to pin her in place while he considered her comment. Then a tiny half-shrug, and a barely perceptible relaxing of his expression, and he said, "Not yet. Lord Dannpelier just wants a discussion, to see if the Houses have a shared perspective."

She felt a tightness in her throat and a strange, suspended breath, and willed herself to think before she replied. As prosaically as she could, she said, "That could be a dangerous discussion, if Ettori feels excluded."

She watched him carefully, trying to keep her own expression neutral. For a long moment, he gave nothing away, and she felt her color rising. Then, apparently satisfied and with a trace of a smile, he offered, "I was told you weren't one for caution." Seeing her cringe, he smiled again, more broadly. "Please, be calm. I'm a friend."

"And just how do I know that?" She meant to sound sure of herself and skeptical of him. Instead, she heard an edge of hostility in her voice that made her want to apologize for her rudeness—an impulse rooted in her upbringing. Appallingly, he just laughed.

"It was your neighbor at Chant who said to expect you to be candid," he explained. "But he also said I could be sure of you." He drew a deep breath, letting his smile fade. "We could keep testing the air but it's the stronger wind that sets the course, so I'll launch: Dannpelier is calling the Gathering because he feels—as do others—that Lord Ettori is harming Merra, and the Houses have a responsibility to the people to intervene."

Arissa saw him waiting for her reaction, and saw, too, that he was shifting his weight from one leg to the other— not as utterly at ease as he wanted her to believe.

Before she could respond, a light footstep came from

the hall, and her mother appeared in the open doorway. Arissa steeled herself, until she saw that her mother's eyes were clear. Like Arissa, she was dressed simply in faded clothes, but Arissa could see that she had taken the trouble to brush out her long hair and wrap herself in the best shawl they had—a deep color that brought out the startling blue of her eyes. She was still beautiful.

"Arissa, dear, you should have called me to receive our visitor." She swept into the room and moved to the young man, stopping at a carefully calibrated distance. She was giving him a thorough and embarrassing appraisal, but Arissa noted that he was also taking the measure of her mother—much more subtly and, she thought, with discerning caution. Her mother held a hand out toward him, palm down. "I am Issanda, Lady Aryn."

He stepped forward and with perfect style slipped his hand under hers, palm up, and gently lifted her hand. "Gadrin, of Ruatt."

"Ruatt!" Issanda rushed on, "Wyth's city. Arissa is betrothed to Lord Wyth! Have you ever seen him?"

Gadrin glanced at Arissa, saw her dismay, and his eyes danced. But his voice was courteous and smooth: "Indeed, my lady. I have had that privilege."

"Oh, you *must* stay, and tell us everything! Arissa, ask Anicho to bring some telik while our guest gets comfortable. Please, take a seat here and rest."

"I'm sorry, Lady Issanda. That's exactly what any traveler would want today, but I can't linger, much as I'd like to."

Arissa's mother made an effort to ignore this attempt to disengage, and chattered on, though Gadrin still had his cloak on and had taken a step toward the door. He glanced at Arissa, and she saw that his eyes were hazel green, and kind. She watched the play of his expressions as he listened to her mother with expertly masked impatience.

After several minutes of talk about the weather, and his travels, and Ruatt, her mother asked, "Is Lord Wyth as handsome as they say?" There was a coquettishness in Issanda's tone that made Arissa shrink.

Gadrin seemed to suppress a surprised laugh. She could just imagine at what. "I can only suppose that they say he is as excellent in appearance as he is in all things," he said smoothly. He smiled openly at Arissa. "Many women will envy you, Arissa of Aryn, though I'm sure it's difficult to leave your home. I hope you will find happiness at House Wyth."

He seemed sincere, and she hoped she kept her feelings hidden. It wasn't his fault her mother had forced the topic. There were so many other things she would have asked, if she had wanted to ask anything at all about Lord Wyth. She covered her embarrassment by saying, "Mother, I'm sure our visitor didn't plan to spend the afternoon talking about House Wyth."

The look he gave her seemed to contain friendly gratitude. Before her mother could start a new topic, he said, "I wish that I could." He managed to put the perfect amount of reluctance in his tone. "I'm afraid I still have a long trip ahead of me and can't linger. Please forgive me."

Issanda launched a rush of platitudes and courtesies. The messenger had all the right responses, and Arissa could see that her mother had no impulse at all to wonder why a city man from Ruatt would be "passing by" House Aryn. It made no sense—but her mother needed nothing more than some flattery and charming manners to disarm her.

Then Gadrin stepped up to Arissa, just barely leaving enough space between them to avoid a suggestion of intimacy. "A pleasure to meet you, too, Lady Arissa." He turned both his palms up in front of him, and she couldn't ignore the gesture—the most natural courtesy in the world when taking leave of a social acquaintance. But when she rested her hands lightly on his, he leaned forward as if to kiss her cheek, which would have further charmed her mother. He said, very softly, "I need another word."

Before her mother could object or call for Anicho, Arissa led Gadrin back to the door, telling him he should water his horse before going. As he stepped out, he fell back into the posture he had started with, and as he led his pony to the trough he studied the tips of his shoes.

The pony lowered its shaggy head and started to drink. Gadrin rested a hand on its neck and stood as if he were a shy shepherd lad, uncomfortable in her presence. His voice remained steady and low, "The Gathering will be at House Dannpelier on the next Full Dark. You can come discreetly if you pass through Ruatt—it's just a day's ride from there. Will you come?"

Putting it straight to her like that gave her little chance to think it through, but she knew it wouldn't change her decision. Deliberating would only be a matter of trying to articulate her rationale, and it didn't matter. "We need to stop Ettori," she said. "Yes."

Abruptly he pulled the pony's head up, and said, more roughly, "I thank ya, lady." He patted his side, and a few coins clinked together in the pocket of his vest. "Mum thanks ya, too."

3

MENDER

Three Rivers Woodland

PIERS CAME TO the edge of the woods suddenly. He stopped, drew back so he was screened by the trees, and looked at what lay ahead. Closest to him was the windowless back of a large wooden building, blocking most of his view. Past it, he could see a hut, also built of wood, that stood guard over a fenced area where chickens were diligently pecking at the ground. Piers felt like he had stepped into a storybook or an ancient painting. The implications hit him in waves: trees were so common that wood was a basic commodity here; animals were part of daily life—and probably part of daily nutrition.

He'd been on his own down here for almost a week now. For the first two days after Arthur, he'd been unable to bear the thought of interacting with anyone. He would have traded almost anything if he could revise the decisions that had led him to this point, alone and stranded. At first his thoughts crashed and swirled around the ship and all the people he loved and had left. That meant Kath, of course, but also Jon, the other scouts, and his family. He was even regretting that he'd left when there was a young Empath who'd just been on the brink of activation. He'd wanted to help.

The sense of adventure that had buoyed him through the first two weeks, when he'd been the one encouraging Arthur to focus on the excitement, had nearly deserted him. In the beginning, he had blithely dismissed worries that the planet itself could present threats and obstacles. His concern was navigating through society here. It had been funny to him, if painful, that he and Arthur had both fallen so many times, misjudging the uneven terrain. Bruises all over his legs were testament to the very physical learning they needed to do. He was nervous now, and too cautious as he moved. He tested every new surface with one foot before taking a step, wary of slipping.

He had wanted to get as far away from the water as he could, too, but once he was away from it there'd been no orientation for his progress. The ship guided him west, but when he reached the road at the edge of the woods he'd seen people walking, and had instantly turned back into the sheltering solitude of the trees. It had taken him a day or two, then, to admit to himself or Jon that he was deliberately not covering much ground. And then he'd decided that he needed to stop wallowing, and to try not to think too much about what had happened or what was going on up there. This, the very real here-and-now of it, needed all his focus.

Voices, uttering indistinct words, approached the building from the other side. It was time to stop avoiding the work he'd come here to do. He needed to find help. There was a sort of syncopated, soft thudding. He heard the sound of something heavy rattling and scraping, then the voices and the thuds were muffled and he could hear movement inside the building. Taking a deep breath, he slipped around to the side, and crouched under a small, open window so he could hear.

"That door is going to fall off any day now," a male voice said.

"No need to keep saying it, Patterson," a younger-sounding man answered, piqued. "I haven't forgotten. I just haven't had time to get to it."

"Maybe if you just did your work instead of sittin' around complainin' about it, you'd have more time than you think."

Gritting his teeth, Piers forced himself to drop his psi screens completely, leaving himself utterly Open. Gingerly, he Reached, sending out a general pulse of undirected psi Empathy, and he was dizzy but decidedly relieved when there was no response, and no presence for his Empathy to latch onto.

The men stopped talking, leaving Piers trying to confirm his entire linguistics training program by analyzing a tiny fragment of speech while they got on with their work. Without access to the ship, he couldn't get too far, but it sounded like at least some of the experts' theories and conjectures about the rate of vowel drift and weakening consonants had been right. He'd been practicing based on those assumptions, and he and Kath were both proficient now with their best-guess language.

He would need to hear more, with a chance to absorb and adjust, but it was encouraging that he'd understood them. Piers knew he'd be able to pick up the accent without too much trouble. Vocabulary would be a bigger trick, given a thousand years of new ideas and separately evolving semantics, but blending in seemed possible. He had always fallen into other people's speech patterns without even meaning to, and there'd been several incidents as a kid when he was baffled that someone suspected him of mockery. It was part of his talent with language, and it worked best when he didn't overthink it.

A few minutes later, the older man said, "Come on, Foller. Feed the damn horse and let's get out of here."

Piers choked on excitement. A horse! He had to see it, literally in the flesh. His energy surged. He had seen real dogs and cats and rabbits, and there were live fish stocked in the tanks that lined the long walls of the cargo bay. Horses, though, were part of Piers's personal mythology. A few of the original passengers, the ones on the manifest, had actually seen one—a cherished memory that they'd told the children. They all said that the images and recordings were accurate but disappointing. He had always wondered.

As the original captain, Piers's great-grandfather had been part of making the decision to wake up the passengers. Just before he died, he told six-year-old Piers that when they discovered that they were nine hundred and fifty years late and eighty-two years off course, the crew had been unanimous in deciding that the original rules didn't apply. A human body could only survive in a life-suspension bed for a few years. The choice was either to wake people to live out their lives on *Redemption* and leave the journey to their descendants, or let them all die in their sleep and leave *Redemption* to drift.

As they had made their way toward the planet, dragging through real time because of the ship's broken timedrive, they'd gotten used to all of it. The Manifesters never stopped wanting to be back on a planet, but they'd all been selected for the program because they were highly adaptive, intelligent people. The concessions they'd made to their disappointment included creating hydroponic gardens in the empty suspension beds and vivifying a few animals as communal pets. No one ever seriously proposed bringing a horse—or any large animal—back into existence on the ship, though.

Piers moved back into the cover of the woods and sat on his heels to wait until he heard the rattling door again. The men's voices became clearer and then fainter as they left the building and walked away. He could almost hear Arthur cautioning him, and he waited as long as he could stand it. When he stepped out, he stood straight and walked toward the front of the building with casual confidence.

He'd learned that as a kid, too. It probably had something to do with being the captain's child, but it hadn't taken him long to realize that people greatly preferred to assume he wasn't up to anything than to confront the situation—as long as he helped them maintain the illusion. It was just a habit by now; he knew his clothes weren't the local fashion, and a stranger here would probably raise concerns in any case, no matter how at ease he looked. Not quite the same thing as enabling people to decide that the captain's teenage son must have a perfectly good reason for loitering in the corridor outside a door that led to, for instance, adult recreation.

An oversized sliding door hung crooked from a rail that was pulling loose from the barn. The leading edge of the door had slipped out of the guides at the bottom, so the whole fixture was skewed and leaning precariously away from the building. Although an effort had been made to pull it closed, the angle left a gap that a smaller person could probably slip through. A thick piece of rope, anchored on the door, was looped through a bracket on the wall—and fraying from the torsion of the misaligned door. A good push from the inside would easily break the rope, and the door itself would likely topple.

Piers peered through the gap, but it was dim inside and he couldn't see much. There was an animal smell, mixed with a musty odor, and he thought he could hear movement. The horse...

He was starting to untie the rope when he heard a woman shout, "You! Whoever you are, stop right there!"

Piers paused for just an instant, reminding himself that this was what he was here for. He let go of the rope, and turned to face her with every ounce of confidence and bravado he could summon. She was coming toward him, apparently from a two-story house that he could now see. The woman was old, but clearly not frail. She carried a rather significant-looking stick, and there was no sign of fear as she approached.

With his empty hands in full view, he took a slow step toward her and gestured toward the barn. He kept his tone conversational, though he raised his voice a bit to cover what was left of the distance between them. "I heard the men say the door needed to be fixed, so I wanted to take a look. I could help."

She stopped, and stood with the stick ready to swing. The look she gave him would have rivaled that of anyone suspicious of a teenager's claimed innocence. "You're a mender?" The skepticism transferred from her eyes to her voice.

It wasn't hard to imagine how he looked to her eyes. He forced a cheerful little laugh, and said, "Well, I'm pretty good at fixing things."

"This afternoon?"

He nodded, hoping that gesture worked here, and replied, "If you have the tools and a new piece of rope, I'd be glad to do it, if you would let me stay in your barn for shelter tonight."

She considered him with frank eyes and her head at the

slightest angle. Piers couldn't remember the last time he'd been so openly assessed. He Pushed reassurance to her, and dropped his screens for just a second, Open to a response. There was nothing at the surface, and he took that as the answer. He could *still* feel Arthur's terror, and wasn't about to Scan, to go prying into someone else's emotions—not for something like this.

"You sound like you're far from home," she said.

Well, no surprise that he sounded a little foreign—but he thought he heard sympathy in her voice.

"I am. I've been traveling for a long time, and I'd be grateful for a safe place to sleep." In fact he was getting desperate to put physical walls between him and the strange world for a while. The temperature was comfortable, and he still had some supplies in his pack, but he didn't relish the idea of being outside overnight again.

After giving him one more long look, she surprised him by not only agreeing to let him stay, but also asking if he were hungry. She unlooped the rope and shoved the barn door open far enough to let them step inside. There was more light inside than he had expected, and when the woman pointed to some shelves on a wall, he could see the neatly arranged collection of tools.

"Everything you need should be there, mender. Fix the door and I'll bring you some supper before it gets dark." She told him to call her Peggy, and that he could wash at the cistern in the yard, and that there was a water closet at the back of the barn. Piers managed to accept this information just as matter-of-factly as she gave it, but even before she turned back to the house he was wondering which curiosity to satisfy first.

Once her back was turned, he stopped looking at the tools and moved deeper into the barn. Beams and rafters crisscrossed above the large, open space, and light came through open windows on the walls and high overhead, making the dust sparkle. Bales of what he supposed was hay were stacked against the side wall in geometric piles like staircases, as high as the loft. A worktable and chair faced a dividing wall halfway across the barn. Behind that, a row of stalls stretched to the back wall.

The first three were empty, but Piers could see a dark shape swaying in the final stall. He approached slowly, relishing the suspense.

The horse was bigger than he'd expected, despite the records. The Manifesters had been right—nothing about the images or recordings had captured this. The massive head turned so the horse could inspect him with an enormous eye, and he could see his own reflection in it, silhouetted against a light-filled rectangle from the open barn door. The horse seemed benign and curious, but Piers was glad for the barrier between them.

He wished again for Kath. In those awful days after the accident, when they'd been trying to figure out if they could wait for her, he'd told her he would feel guilty if he went without her. As usual, she had been the realistic one from the start. She'd known she wouldn't be healed in time, and she had pretended to be stoic about it. Of course he knew better, and now he knew she would be jealous and probably a little heartsick when she eventually got his message about the whole experience. There was no way to record the sensations or emotions; he did the best he could to describe the feelings, but it turned into a jumble of adjectives. With effort, he forced himself to also record a more scientific scout's report for Jon, with details that would matter for planning and decisions. He wondered if the integration team missed Arthur's artless notes.

The water closet led to another of those minor realizations of the obvious that he somehow hadn't been prepared for: like wood, water could be used profligately here. No treatment and recycling infrastructure, no distillers. Just a pump-filled tank of raw water and a mechanical flush. Ingenuity looked different here.

By the time he had the door hanging level again, the daylight had taken on a sort of amber glow as the sun sank. On the ship, there was a twice-a-day dimming they called twilight—the Manifesters had wanted that planetary reference—but it was a uniform, dull change. Here, the light became more vivid and cast long shadows that seemed alive. Everything here was in motion, changing, shifting constantly, and Piers wondered if anyone had ever considered the effect that had on the human psyche.

On *Redemption*, the unnoticed constant was the fragile and artificial stasis of their environment. Every so often, he had a moment or two of hyper-awareness, just at the edge of terror, of how the ship held the entire universe of everyone's experiences and expectations suspended in the nothingness of space. The tiny, self-contained reality bound their souls to each other and to itself. The walls were what counted.

Given that none of the Manifesters had ever specifically mentioned the way shadows moved, orbiting around the objects that cast them, Piers supposed it was in the same category: an unremarkable, inalienable aspect of living on a planet. It seemed to him that here, the unsettled environment and the absence of walls put the individual into an entirely different relationship with possibilities. The certainty of his experience, the reality of his existence, was no longer sealed in a predictable and controlled domain. Instead, it seemed discretely contained only in his own being. It made him feel more singular, fragile and irreplaceable, which felt like a daunting responsibility.

Piers shook off the feeling and admired the result of his handiwork. It was satisfying to work on something so tangible, and to use some practical reasoning to figure out what was needed. He pulled the door to shut it, and found that it could roll only so far before it glitched on the rail.

He was on his hands and knees on the ground, stabilizing the last guide, when Peggy came back. "Looks like you've done it," she said, and Piers was sure he heard the inflection of surprise.

Piers got up, brushed the dirt off his knees, and added, "I straightened the top rail and reset the guides." The door glided shut when he pushed it.

"Right enough," the woman said. She offered him a bowl of something steaming. Something vegetable-based, Piers thought, and hoped it was something his digestive system could handle.

She cut off his thanks with a curt wave, and said, "Those clothes won't keep you warm enough tonight, even in the barn." From her tone, there were a few other things she might have said about his clothes—but at least his basic shirt and trousers, in muted colors, hadn't shocked her. With narrowed eyes, she directed a judging look at his rucksack. "Never seen a mender who wasn't carrying everything he owned. You're traveling light." An unvoiced question lingered.

"I had to leave a lot behind." He hoped that sounded enough like an explanation to keep her from asking. Under no circumstances did he want to tell her just how much of an understatement that was, even just at the logistical level. Beyond the fact that each scout had brought so little—some protein, a canteen, a change of clothes—in the first place, he'd been dismayed to discover that he'd lost one of his boots at the river.

"Well, you're lucky you didn't have a run-in with Ettori's patrols looking like that. Don't want to look like a foreigner if they're around."

That wasn't happy news. Xenophobia absolutely would be a complication, and *patrols* didn't sound too promising, either. That would all be worth some follow-up, but it was clear Peggy was not in an explaining kind of mood.

She looked him over again. "I think you'll fit. You can have some of my husband's old clothes, may the stars guide him, if you'll see about the gate before you leave tomorrow."

May the stars guide him. Piers took note. Maybe it was a trace of their ancestors, preserved in language, even if something seemed to have wiped out all physical evidence of the foundation ship and the technology it had brought.

Of all the mysteries that had ruined the plans for civilization on this planet, that was the one that tantalized Piers's imagination the most. Yes, there was the great question of why *Redemption*'s timedrive had failed—wrecking the plan for the settlers' arrival. But what had so completely erased the technology and knowledge of the foundation ship? That ship had been the pinnacle of human science and engineering. The men and women who'd been chosen to found the new colony here were experts in their fields, from agriculture and construction to medicine and government. Everything humanity had ever recorded was in *Valiant Star*'s data stores, and the ship carried tools and fabricators to make anything the new colony needed.

That *Valiant Star* had safely arrived was obvious. There seemed to be at least a couple million people here, descendants of those two hundred founders, clustered on the island. The consensus of the experts on *Redemption* was that *Valiant* had landed in the northern half of the island that was now more densely populated. Early on, probably within the first two or three generations, the colony had been wiped out. Enough people had survived to start over—but they had to do it without *Valiant*'s advantages. People had remembered or learned enough over the thousand years since that first landing to harness the planet's resources to create what they needed, all at the domestic scale. Beyond that, the experts had nothing but questions, and so far Piers wasn't finding answers.

Settling into the barn's hayloft that night took some effort. It was better than being outside, but the hay poked through his thin blanket, and unfamiliar smells and sounds pricked his senses. The incomplete darkness was unsettling, his stomach was grumbling, and the adrenalin was still flowing.

Piers got up again and swept his feet along the floor as he made his way to the enormous open window. It was taller than he was, and wider than a doorway. The shutters had been pinned back against the wall, so there was no barrier between him and the fresh air. Some sweet fragrance breezed in with the cool air, and he could see the star-lit sky. It dazzled. "May the stars guide you, Arthur," Piers whispered.

4

RIDER

Briar Inn, Ruatt

RYING TO STAVE off a pang of conscientious guilt, Davyn took another sip of the Briar Inn's excellent morning ale. It felt like a holiday to be having a lingering breakfast with a friend, at a sunlit table in a pleasant tavern far away from his workaday responsibilities. It was mid-morning, but there was no need to hurry. After all, the point of staying overnight in Ruatt when he did the courier run was to make the round trip easier for him, and his horse. It was thirty miles from Trint to Ruatt, and though it was well within Paladin's long-legged limits to make the round trip in one day, it was a few hours' more saddle time than Davyn truly enjoyed. Better to have a leisurely six- or seven-hour ride, a good meal and a good night's sleep at the Briar, and then an equally relaxed ride home.

The Briar made luxuriating easy. It was an elegant inn, and the Briar's public house was very different in character than the Crossroads Inn back in Trint. It wasn't just that the Crossroads was home. Here, instead of ale-stained tables and dart-marred walls, there were polished surfaces and whitewashed plaster. Large windows filled the room with cleansing sunlight during the day and reflected lamplight after dark. At this time of year, the fire in the hearth was usually more for ambiance than need. Add the warm hospitality of the innkeeper, Shea, and the sociable company of her grandson, and it was a hard place for Davyn to quit.

Still. He'd meant to leave right after breakfast. This was the first time he'd left Elanna alone in charge of the livery stable at the Crossroads Inn overnight, and while Elanna was more than capable and certainly willing, it wasn't fair to leave all the work for a twelve-year-old girl to do. They'd expected a quiet night, but there was no guarantee of that.

He must have sighed, because Atto laughed. "You almost did it. I really thought you'd make it through the second cup this morning." Atto reached for another thick slice of bread, though he'd eaten most of the loaf by himself, and slathered it with butter. At fourteen, he'd eat anything he could get his hands on. "Gran says you worry more than you're supposed to. 'Course, she also thinks I don't worry enough." He grinned. "Maybe you got my share."

At that moment, Atto's grandmother approached their table with an empty tray. She was in her sixties, and had probably never been a beauty, but the kindness in her wide-set eyes and her changeable, lively expressions made up for it. When she smiled, which was often, every line of her face made sense. Just now, her look of mild impatience softened when she made eye contact with Davyn.

"I'm sorry to say it, but this imp needs to get on with his day," Shea said, nodding at Atto. "Davyn, my sweeting, I'd gladly have you stay for days, you know, but you've a long ride ahead and you did say you meant to leave early."

Atto slumped. "He's leaving soon anyway, Gran. I'll do my chores after."

She tousled his unruly hair. "Fair enough, boyo. Just remember you've got a long enough to-do list for a day that won't get any more hours in it."

Davyn tossed back the last swallow of ale and pushed back from the table. "Come on, Atto. Help me saddle Paladin."

The stable at the Briar Inn was less well appointed; it wasn't a livery inn and equine guests were almost an afterthought. A row of open stalls for the horses of tavern guests lined the back wall of the building. The barn for overnighters, such as it was, had been erected across the yard without much attention to detail. Paladin had balked the first time Davyn had led him into the close, dark stable, but had relented when Davyn offered freshly baked carrot bread. Now the baked treats were an expected part of an overnight stay at the Briar Inn—Paladin's own taste of luxury, despite the accommodations that weren't up to his standards.

Now the big stallion was standing in the open yard, glossy in the bright morning. Davyn tossed the saddle blanket over Paladin's gleaming black back and settled the saddle over it. Paladin looked back over his shoulder, aiming a benign gaze at his rider, and puffed softly.

"He does that a lot," Atto said. "What's it mean when he huffs at you?"

"Anything he wants it to mean," Davyn said. "Right at the moment, I think he's just letting me know he's ready to go home. Get his bridle, would you?"

Atto handed it to him, and then perched on top of a fence-rail to watch. "I wish I could ride off somewhere." The wistfulness in his face was as familiar as his grin.

"You will, someday." Davyn started to slip the bridle over the horse's ears, but Paladin flung his head up to avoid it. Davyn pushed at the stallion's shoulder, continuing the game. As usual, it wasn't until the third offer that Paladin accepted the bridle, but then he took the bit without hesitation. The metal clanked against his teeth, and he shook his head gently, as if to settle the straps, bit, and reins into place.

"How old were you when you left home the first time?"

Davyn was surprised by the question. Hadn't he told Atto all that? "I was thirteen the first time I went to the market with the farmers," he said. "But I didn't go out on my own until three years ago. I was eighteen."

That hadn't been a leaving he'd chosen, but after Van died, he'd known it was inevitable. He'd been seventeen when the accident happened; by the following spring, Lord Holden had made it clear that the estate was no longer going to support Davyn. He could make a living on the farm, alongside his foster father, or he could find some other occupation, but there would be no more sponsored education. All his life, Holden had provided for him—from the moment that they found him as a nameless infant on the doorstep—but it had been Van's friendship that had tied him to Holden. Without Van, he'd been unmoored, and cast adrift.

Besides his sword and his grief, Davyn had taken three mementos from his years at Holden: his boot-knife, his wanderer's charm, and Paladin. The first two were his only birthright, left with him in the basket at Holden's door. The horse had belonged to Van, but after the accident no one else could even approach the stallion. Lord Holden eventually sent him down to the farm where Davyn lived with his foster parents. Whether the gift signified good will or guilt,

Davyn had never been able to determine. When Davyn had left the estate and ridden away from the Cressidan Hills for good, Paladin had been the only friend he counted.

"And now you travel all the time," Atto said.

"Mostly just along the courier routes, you know. Nothing glamorous."

"But you grew up in Tyndaris, and now you've been all over the place in Merra. I bet you're the only southerner who's ever stayed at Gran's."

Davyn checked the buckles, and tightened the girth just a bit, and hid his smile by bowing his head against Paladin. Atto's enthusiasm was edging into exaggeration. "I live in Trint, Atto. I was raised in the south but I'm a citizen of Merra now."

He interrupted Atto's rebuttal and gave him a hug. Paladin puffed, sending a pulse of hay-scented, warm breath to ruffle Atto's hair. "I'll be back soon," Davyn said, and set his instep on the stirrup.

Before he could swing into the saddle, he heard a man say, "Is that Lord Wyth?"

He glanced back, and saw a tall, white-haired man with old-fashioned clothes and an aristocratic tilt of his head standing just inside the stableyard, holding a canvas bag that pulled him off-kilter. He had a thin, severe face, and deep eyes that seemed to crowd against the bridge of his sharp nose. Those eyes, bright as sun on ice, darted from Atto to Davyn, and rested there. "Lord Wyth?" he asked, in a voice that tumbled in his throat.

Davyn set his foot back on the ground and turned to greet the stranger. "No, sir, far from it. How can we help?"

The man stared at him, his brows low as if trying to decide how to react to a possible prank, then he swayed back slightly and rumbled pensively, "No, no, I see now. Interesting."

"I can take your bag," Atto said, holding out a hand.

"A moment, young sir," the man said. "I believe I am expected. Lord Wyth's men are here?"

After learning that no one from House Wyth had arrived at the Briar Inn, the man wilted. He had travelled from Estend, he said, enduring a long night on a riverboat, because House Wyth had summoned him with promises of a considerable reward. "I'm Oterin, a healer of some renown, though I say it myself. I understand the family is desperate for any hope of a cure. Which I can offer—though hope is a poor substitute for health, of course. There was no one to meet me at the dock, but several good people directed me here. They said it's the likeliest place for House folk."

Excitement fairly radiated from Atto. His thoughts were almost audible to Davyn: he was always excited to meet someone from one of the Great Houses. If House Wyth's men stayed at the Briar, it would amount to an endorsement, which would please Shea. Beyond that, at least for Atto, the Houses represented a fantasy of luxury, power, and tradition—a lifelong fascination.

It didn't sound like the Wyth men were necessarily planning to stop here, and Davyn couldn't quite justify lingering just in case. Truth, though, it was tempting, just for the chance to see them, engage them in some tavern-talk and maybe get some news or insights. House Wyth guarded the heights at the tip of the Wyth Valley, and *The Definitive Guide to the Great Houses* listed Wyth as one of the wealthiest. The Hill Houses were well off, according to the book, and they kept to themselves more than the other Houses; Davyn knew far less about them.

Despite Atto's admiring conviction, Davyn had not been all over Merra. Serving as a courier from time to time did give him a chance to listen at the taverns, and to hear about the machinations of the Houses. His old tutor, Gerald McLennon, had recorded the history of the Houses in his *Guide*, and the book had served Tyndaris well during the war. Davyn had been in Merra only a few weeks before he realized that Ger's book, almost thirty years after publication, was no longer an accurate reflection of the Houses. For one thing, the fall of House Caladen had happened after Ger wrote the book, and the ramifications of that tragedy still roiled Merra. In the three years that Davyn had been living and working at the Crossroads Inn, he'd kept notes on everything he heard about the Houses. Someday, he'd update Ger's work.

"Lady Wyth died over a year ago," Atto informed the old man. Davyn was certain that all three of them knew Atto wasn't offering information so much as hoping for Oterin to volunteer who he'd been called to see.

The healer chuckled, and it sounded like gravel rattling. "So as you might guess, Lady Wyth is not my patient. Lad, you know the Houses keep their business private."

"Well, I hope you can help them," Atto said, blithely accepting his unsuccessful bid for gossip. "Let's go inside, and you can have a drink while you wait. I can go back down to the wharf and see if maybe Wyth showed up down there and you missed them."

Davyn hung back as Atto started to lead the man to the back door of the tavern. When Atto realized Davyn wasn't following, he seemed astonished that Davyn could leave despite the interesting stranger. Davyn said, "I wish I could stay, Atto, but I need to get on the road so I can get back before supper. Sir, I hope you find your way safely to House Wyth."

With a quick step on the stirrup, Davyn dropped into the saddle. He waved to Atto, pulled Paladin around, and

rode through the narrow alleyway that separated the stableyard from the main street.

After a few days of rain, yesterday's spring sun had started
its work and the road was soft under the horse's hooves,
but no longer treacherously muddy. Once they were clear of
town, Davyn leaned forward in the saddle to pat Paladin's
sleek neck, and let out the reins. Speed and wind would
be welcome—especially in the long, flat stretch midway
between Ruatt and Trint—now that they'd left behind the
carts, riders, and pedestrians that meant dodging instead
of flying.

It was freedom. One small part of his attention was
given to the landmarks he was racing past; the rest was concentrated on the sheer pleasure of the wind on his face and
the sight of the road vanishing between the stallion's ears.
Paladin loved to run without the distraction of a rider's
opinion, and he held nothing back. On a day like this, it
suited them both.

Despite his late start, they reached the turn-off to Taran
Lake just on the cusp of late afternoon. They'd be back in
Trint in no time at all, and Davyn was reluctant to end their
liberty. He needed to be home before the evening meal,
or Elanna would get anxious, which would in turn worry
the others and upset the horses. A quick glance at the sun
confirmed there was time for a quick detour, just for a few
minutes' idleness beside the sparkling lake.

The Taran River, a branch of the mighty Truolt, was
fast and narrow and spilled into the terminal lake in a
series of cascades. In spring, the snowmelt and rain made
the cascades thunder and deepened the quiet pools that lay
in between like the landings of a giant's staircase. The road
followed the contours of the lake, and just on the other side

of the venerable hamlet of River's End there was a path to the water's edge. On his first exploration, Davyn had found a tree with low, spreading branches beside the middle cascade. The lowest branch made a comfortable seat against the trunk, and he could rest for a while and lose himself in the sound and motion of the falls.

River's End itself was no one's destination. Only a dozen families lived in the hamlet, and the lake provided what they needed, so there was no tavern or shop. They did have public water, and Paladin knew just as well as Davyn that there was a cool drink not far ahead. Before Davyn could see the hamlet around the bend, he heard raised voices. He reined in, hesitant to ride into the middle of an argument. Paladin flicked his ears, stamped a hind leg, and heaved a sputtering sigh.

"I'm tellin' you, you'll get nothing from me!" The unseen man sounded enraged.

A cold voice replied, "Not your choice to make."

The angry man said, "No tax and no Tithe here. We don't take, so we don't give."

"Oh, you'll give, my man." There was a sneer in the new speaker's voice. "Or we'll take."

With a subtle touch of the reins, Davyn asked Paladin to walk on, and the horse seemed to understand that he wanted a quiet approach. As they passed the bend, there was a sharp cry, in a woman's voice, chased by a man's bellow. The full scene came into view and Davyn saw the woman on the ground, behind a pair of men who were grappling with each other and battling for their footing. They were only steps away from the cracked-open door of a cottage with new thatch.

The man whose back was to Davyn was in a dark grey shirt and dark trousers that had a stripe of crimson down the outside seam. A riderless horse was cropping at some grass beside the road, trying to chew around the bit. Three men on horseback, also in uniform, were watching their comrade scuffle with a man in plain clothes. The woman was trying to get to her feet and get clear of the fight at the same time, all the while pleading for them to stop.

The mounted men saw Davyn as the black stallion closed the distance, and turned their horses to intercept him. The woman noticed, and she called to him for help.

"No concern of yours," the middle rider told him, and the three of them stopped in an imposing row. "Prime House's business." The man who spoke was gaunt, with an angular face that tapered to a sharp chin. One side of his face was deep-lined and pitted; the smooth plaster of a burn scar covered the other side. At the collar of his dark shirt, a fern leaf was embroidered in crimson thread.

These were Lord Ettori's men, then, farther west than they usually came. River's End was in free land, not associated with any Great House, so they wouldn't be part of the Tithe. Such a small hamlet had probably also managed to avoid getting labeled as an independent village, so they would be outside the tax, too. It made sense: they earned nothing, sold nothing, and bought nothing. The hamlet had nothing to offer, unless the treasury wanted lake trout.

"They're free-landers," Davyn said. "And too small to tax."

"Is that so?" The man's interest was too intense to be genuine.

The other two riders moved forward, flanking him and exuding clear menace. They stayed just far enough back to avoid crowding Paladin, which gave Davyn a degree of confidence. Paladin's glare gave him a buffer and if they moved aggressively, Paladin would counter them. Other horses usually had the sense to be wary of the stallion.

The woman called to him again, and he looked between the riders to see. She was on her feet now, with her back against the cottage door. The River's End man seemed to be losing ground and seldom managed to land a blow. He was outmatched by the other's training and control, though he had the power of rage and desperation on his side. The Ettori man was baiting him.

Davyn considered trying to get past the three riders who blocked him. He thought about dismounting and dodging past them to intervene, but they would be able to cut him off—or down—before he'd taken more than a few steps. All three were armed and looked like they'd fight as easily as they rode. Two of them seemed old enough to have fought in the Estend War, and both bore scars that made it seem likely they had.

He had his own blade; he could make them let him through. Paladin would leap forward if he asked, and he could barge between them. If the other horses were intimidated by Paladin, they'd move to avoid him, and he could break through their line. He let his hand drop to the hilt of his sword, not sure if he would—if he could—draw. Despite all the years of training with Carthen the weapons master, and all the skirmishes with Van, he'd never drawn in combat. Paladin was shifting, pressing back on his hind legs as if gathering his strength to launch at Davyn's signal.

"Oh ho! Looks like the pup wants to challenge you, Urvas!"

With a leer, the man facing Davyn drew his sword, and let it rest against his thigh, held lightly in a casual grip. "Is that so?" he said again, drawling. He peered at Davyn's face, as if trying to read his intent. The eye above his undamaged cheek narrowed, but the scar kept his other eye from following suit. It looked like an incomplete, sinister wink. Urvas turned to the man on his right. "He look familiar to you?"

The other shook his head. "Don't think so."

Urvas turned the blade so it flashed in the sunlight, then said, "Well, come on, then, let's see what you're made of."

The other men drew and held their weapons ready. They edged their horses together, blocking the gaps between them. If Davyn tried to rush at them, and the horses had been trained for fighting, he'd be relying on his luck. He'd be risking Paladin as much as himself if those bright-edged swords swung.

"Leave them alone," he said, as reasonably as he could. "They have nothing to give you that would make any difference to Ettori."

"You apparently don't understand the principle here."

There was a different cry from the woman, and Davyn saw that the door was open, and she was trying to push a small girl back inside. The child shrieked for her father and darted out. The man heard her, and tried to break away from the Ettori man to shield her. His opponent was faster, and blocked him, barring the father from the child, and lunged toward her.

The child screamed, and the River's End man hurled himself at the Ettori man, who dropped him with a well-placed blow. He moaned, and the Ettori man stood over him, considering, and then kicked his face. The River's End man was still and silent.

Davyn felt as if he'd been gutted. He saw the victor bend over the River's End man. He ripped a coin purse from the cord around the man's neck, pushed the sobbing child aside, then jumped onto the fourth horse with a strident shout. The other three Ettori riders were unmoved, and the one in the middle laughed at Davyn's shock and raised his sword. Davyn stared at the gleaming metal but couldn't react.

"A lesson in principles, boy." The man pointed the blade toward Davyn and kicked his horse forward.

Davyn recoiled and Paladin reared; Davyn held on with his legs. As he brought his horse under control again, the Ettori men turned their horses almost in formation and galloped away.

A chill spread along Davyn's spine and he felt as if he were alone in a silent, airless space. His senses were dull. Paladin was quiet, though his ears were stiffly back. A neighbor appeared, and then another, and soon a group gathered around the scene. He saw a man at the edge of the group looking at him, judging, and knew he wasn't welcome.

With pressure from his knees, he guided Paladin to turn and carry him back the way they'd come.

Davyn reached the intersection of the road to Trint before the shock released him. As the sequence repeated in his memory, the woman's pleas for help changed into an accusation. Her husband was fighting with all his heart to protect what little he had, and no one had helped.

Her neighbors had hidden behind their own doors, waiting until the danger passed. They weren't prepared to stand up to men like House Ettori's collectors, so they'd chosen safety. Davyn couldn't blame them for self-preservation.

But he—armed, and trained, and riding a stallion who wouldn't falter—should have done something. Instead, he'd balked. Worse, he had considered a few courses of action, and had *decided* to do nothing.

It was proof, if he still needed it, that his training hadn't been entirely successful. He'd been told more than once that he was too slow to act, that he wouldn't be accepted into the Queen's Guard if he didn't learn to assess and remove threats in a blink. "You can't stand there and contemplate the situation, Davyn," Van had said. "Heroes don't wait for someone else to step in."

Hoping that he wouldn't have to talk to anyone yet, Davyn pushed through the wide half door into the welcoming kitchen of the Crossroads Inn. Cooking fires crackled in the two large hearths, and savory smells steamed from the large iron pots that hung there. Lamps lined the walls and hung from the ceiling, filling the large room with a warm, bright light. The red clay tiles on the floor were cracked but shining, and a long, scarred plank table took up the open space closest to the door. Mira's worktable was loaded with serving plates and cooking utensils, but Davyn was alone in the room. Since his dog hadn't greeted him, he must be elsewhere, but Davyn checked the nook beside the stove anyway. Captain's bed of torn blankets was empty.

He crossed toward the worn service staircase leading up to the sleeping rooms. The mingled voices, all male, were muffled through the door to the tavern, but it sounded no different than any night. He knew he should seek out Mira, to let her know that he was back, but he didn't want to face her. As soon as he'd ridden into the stableyard, Elanna had asked him what was wrong. If Mira noticed Davyn's mood, she would be more persistent than her daughter in trying to get him to talk about it. He had his hand on the stair-rail when the door burst inward on smooth hinges and banged against the wall.

Mira spun through the doorway with a tray laden with empty dishes and mugs. "Oh, Davyn! You startled me!"

She set the tray on the end of the worktable and presented her cheek for him to kiss. "Good ride?"

She barely looked at him, but bustled toward the vegetables waiting to be chopped. "It's busy tonight. At least it's a patient lot. Just as well—Elanna's hardly come in all day, just watching your horses with all her might. Her brother's at the smithy with Essen, so I'm on my own. They even took Captain with them." She paused, and noted that he still had his travel jacket on. "You've just come in, then. Go rinse off the dust and when you come back down you can have some stew, and then maybe you'd be willing to pour tonight, at least till Essen gets back?"

Two hours later, Davyn felt like he was sleepwalking as he stood behind the counter in the tavern, pouring drinks, filling pitchers, rinsing glasses, and listening to the bantering customers. Essen, Mira's husband, had come back from his smithy with soot so deeply ingrained in his hands and clothes that Mira had banished him from the kitchen entirely, pending a full bath. Her youngest, ten-year-old Tunny, had worse luck, as she whisked him away herself to deal with the grime. At one point, Davyn thought he heard Elanna in the kitchen, talking to Captain, but he'd just started tallying the bill for a group of rowdies and couldn't walk away just then.

As a general matter, Davyn didn't mind helping in the tavern—or at the forge, or with the guests—even though his official work as the hostler usually kept him busy in the stable. Today had been, by any reckoning, a long day, and he was finding it harder and harder to be cheerful and polite to the men in the tavern. The more they drank, the more they enjoyed teasing him: his accent, his manners, his height, his education, all were points of amusement for the Crossroads regulars.

"Davyn, poor lad," one of the frequent visitors said, with overplayed sympathy. He was leaning on the counter, almost sprawling, and his breath reeked. "How can you stand us Merran louts? You thought you was meant for Court, yeh, and all those Tyndar pretties…"

Another man guffawed, a forced bellow. "He's a Tyndaran pretty, isn't he?" Laughter all around, and Davyn hoped that in the dim light they couldn't see the blush he felt heating his ears. He managed to force something like a smile to acknowledge the joke.

The first man flattened himself on the counter and stretched an arm toward Davyn's face. Blunt fingertips brushed Davyn's cheek. "Yeh, bet the Queen'd like a little—"

"Enough," Davyn said, and pushed the reaching hand away.

The man flinched, and a stunned silence rippled out from the counter. Then someone said, "All right, now, lad, just a joke. Old Trummer meant no harm."

Davyn bowed his head, and picked up his drying towel from the counter. The men scattered to separate conversations, leaving him in peace. He folded the towel, said, "Excuse me, please, for a moment," to no one in particular, and escaped to the kitchen.

Mira was just coming down from the sleeping rooms, and she shot him a curious look as he passed. She told him she'd take over in the tavern, and started to ask something, but stopped and let him go.

They thought he was angry, and he wouldn't correct them. That would make more sense to them than the truth, which was a complex weave of embarrassment and sorrow.

It was strange to think his accent was the only bit of Tyndaris left in him, when he'd spent his boyhood preparing to swear his life to defending the Tyndaran Queen. He might be in the Tyndaris capital now, if only Van had lived.

He picked up an apple for Paladin, and made his way through the kitchen and into the yard. The stallion, too, had trained for a future that had been buried with Van. Lord Holden had encouraged Van—and by extension, Davyn—to spend endless hours with the weapons master, learning to excel in combat.

As boys, their favorite adventure scheme, fully devised before Van was ten and nurtured through their games and studies, was that Davyn would join the Queen's Guard with Van. It was tradition for the eldest sons of the estates to serve until they inherited. Sons who wouldn't inherit sometimes made lifelong careers of it. Van's plan was simple. Van would use his rank to gain a place for Davyn beside him, despite Davyn's lack of pedigree. "Anyone can see you aren't meant to be a farmer," Van said. They'd sworn earnestly that the great deeds they did would be told to their grandsons' grandsons. Davyn had known all along that even with Van's backing the Queen's Guard might not accept him, since he didn't come from a Court family, but he had tried to suspend his doubt, trusting that the rules would bend for Van. They usually did.

"Of course they'll take you," Van had said, on the last of the thousand occasions when Davyn had doubted aloud. "You'll never be the best fighter, but you're better than most." When Van saw that Davyn's pride was stung—though Davyn knew it was a fair assessment—he'd laughed, and patted Davyn's cheek. "Besides, they'll want this face. The southern ladies will *beg* for you to be at Court."

The barn door was closed, though it was early to have settled all the horses for the night. Inside, Davyn took a lantern from the hook beside the door and felt for the matches on the narrow shelf. He heard a soft greeting whicker from Paladin, and his heart eased. The sweet smell of hay and the comforting pungency of the horses pushed away the tactile memory of Trummer's fingers.

He slipped into Paladin's stall and offered the apple. When the horse nudged his shoulder, he felt his eyes sting. What he hadn't been able to explain to Elanna, and hadn't wanted to tell Mira, Paladin understood. As a result of his caution, his cowardice, the River's End man had fought alone to the inevitable conclusion. And Davyn, like Ettori's men, had ridden away from the results. Never again.

The kitchen door was open, letting in cool air and the clear morning light. Mira twisted away from the worktable and sneezed three times in a row, with violence that jolted her and startled Davyn. The chopping knife in her right hand flashed too close to his face—he dodged, aborting his plan to sneak a piece of fresh melon from her cutting board. She froze, then, a look of uncertain anticipation on her face until she was sure no fourth sneeze was coming. Her hair wisped loose from the hardworking pins at the crown of her head, and she pushed the strands out of her face with the back of her knife-wielding hand.

"No question you gave that your all," he said, and reached for the melon again.

She swatted his hand, then relented and pushed a piece toward him with the flat of the knife. "I'll send you to market tomorrow to get more of these," she said. "Nothing better than—"

The fourth sneeze came. Mira clapped the knife down and braced her arms on the table, like a runner catching a desperate breath. She shivered.

"Are you all right?" Davyn asked. He put a hand on

her back, and the fabric of her blouse was warm and damp, though the kitchen was cool. "You should sit."

"No, no, lad," she said. "Too much to do for me to be resting my sorry self. It'll pass."

He tried to insist, but she just promised to rest after she got breakfast to the guests, then gave him a push toward the door to the yard. "Go see to your beasties," she said.

The barn had room to stable ten horses, but it wasn't often full. It was home to four livery horses—though one was out at the moment—plus Essen's own mare and Paladin, who was as out of place as the proverbial prince in a poorhouse and knew it. Just now there were no overnight guests, and no boarding horses, which was not Mira's best news but at least meant Davyn could spend some extra time pampering the residents.

After he'd done his barn chores, Davyn opened Paladin's stall, and the horse followed him as he toted a low stool and his bucket of grooming tools outside. Captain the dog trotted out after him. The stallion bowed his head as Davyn slipped the halter on him, and took up an expectant position at the hitching rail. Davyn tied a lead rope to the halter, and wrapped it on the rail, just as a precaution. Paladin would stand calmly for as long as Davyn was willing to brush him—as long as nothing startled him. Captain sat beside the stool, supervising.

Davyn took his time, singing under his breath as he curried Paladin. "*On a summer day, bright and free, I sat beneath a cherry tree, and thought of chance and love... It happens to be so, my love, and though we don't know why, it happens to be so, because—chance means you have to try...*" He hummed in and out of the lyrics, unbothered by forgotten words.

Paladin puffed and craned his neck around to blink one great eye at him.

With a laugh, Davyn patted his palm against Paladin's shoulder. "Well, I finally slept, that's all," he said. "Does wonders." The previous two nights, since River's End, he had lain awake with dark thoughts. Yesterday, he'd worked at the smithy with Essen and the heavy work had sent him to bed with physical exhaustion that at last overcame his mind.

"Davyn?" Elanna had slipped up behind him without alerting even Captain, and at her soft query the dog gave a startled bark. Paladin tossed his head, but—small mercy—seemed annoyed rather than alarmed. "Can you come in? Mama's sick."

Mira lay crumpled on the floor beside her own bed, her head in Tunny's lap. The coverlet on her bed was pulled back, the pillow still dimpled, and her shoes were neatly set aside. At some point while he was in the stable, Davyn conjectured, Mira had been true to her word and laid down to rest a bit. When she tried to stand up, her legs had given way.

"We heard her fall," Elanna said. Mira's eyes opened to slits and she gave a stifled moan. She tried to move, but her limbs simply slid feebly to the side.

Tunny looked up, his round face stricken. "She's really hot. And sweaty."

The room had a peculiar odor, a sort of kitchen-sweet, burnt sugar smell. Davyn felt a choking coldness as he realized how the pieces fit. "Tunny," he said, his voice tight, "tuck that pillow under her head now and come away."

That scared both children, though he'd tried to sound calm. With a whimper, Tunny reached for the pillow and managed to get it under his mother's head then drew away. Elanna was beside him in the doorway, and looked up at him with knit brows. Davyn held his arm out, beckoning Tunny to him.

When he had both of them in the corridor with him, he saw Mira looking at him and moving her hand in a hint of a shooing wave.

"What's wrong with her?" Tunny asked.

He hesitated. He might be wrong. There hadn't been any reports lately of the Sweep, but Trint had suffered from a bad outbreak of the virus four years ago, just before he came. Nearly everyone knew a family who had lost someone. The disease came in waves that swept through towns periodically. Some years it came and went in a matter of days, knocking out the young, the weak, and the old. Sometimes it led to a lingering lassitude and deterioration that sapped people in their prime. The symptoms varied, but the fast onset and the distinctive odor were always part of it.

"I'm not sure," he said, leaving it at that for the moment. He sent Elanna to the smithy to tell Essen, and told Tunny to go change clothes and wash his hands and face thoroughly. When they were gone, Davyn tied a kerchief over his mouth and wrapped his hands in rags he could burn later, then lifted Mira onto the bed. The Sweep had passed him by three times in his life, even when everyone around him was ill, but precaution never hurt. Direct contact was the usual route to contagion. He settled the coverlet over her and retrieved her winter blanket from the cupboard.

She tried to speak. He hushed her. "I'll bring you some water," he said, "but I want to you to sleep if you can. It's been a few hours, so you could be on your way back out of it already." There was a wish in his words, but it was possible. Sometimes, the Sweep was that fast; it could go as quickly as it came if it didn't claim its victim. It rarely killed quite that abruptly—even in fast years a day or a week of intensifying symptoms was typical. That gave friends and family time to be desperate, and gave the virus time to spread. It was another reason to be glad there were no overnighters, Davyn thought. The family's rooms were all tucked up under the eaves, in a converted attic space at the end of the hall.

By late afternoon, Mira had woken, fever-free, but with racking coughs and seizing pain. He sat in her room, his chair beside the open window, and watched over her.

"Davyn," she said, after catching her breath after a bout, "it won't help if you get sick, too."

"That's why the window is open. Are you warm enough?"

She closed her eyes and murmured, then drowsed until a spasm shook her awake. "Did you tell my cubs?"

"Not specifically. I told them you might be contagious and I wanted them both outside."

She approved of that, and fought through another coughing jag. "Good. You and Essen will have to run the place tonight."

"Take that worry away, Mira. We'll be fine."

The evening's customers, if they noticed Mira's absence, were satisfied nonetheless with the service and the food. Essen cooked, though the only thing he knew how to prepare was bachelor's stew. In the tavern, Davyn served the food and drink, and kept tabs on tables.

When they closed up, Essen checked on his wife and came back down to help Davyn clean the dishes. "Asleep," he said, "but I think the fever is back."

Davyn thought of the healer from Estend that House Wyth had sent for, and wished they could afford that sort of help. There were a few herbalists in Trint, and even a physician, but from what he'd heard, they'd all been powerless in the last Sweep. The only relief any of the sufferers had was at the hands of a wizened Starborn woman who had arrived as the Sweep ended. Some said she had stopped it in its tracks.

There had been a Starborn camp at Taran Lake last summer, on the west shore. They had probably have moved on, because the Starborn rarely stayed anywhere for long, but maybe there was a chance.

"I'll go up to the lake tomorrow," Davyn said. "I'll try to find a Starborn healer." He wouldn't have to go past River's End, but his mouth went dry at the thought of going back to the lake at all.

"That's a good thought, lad. I had a mild case, once, and the only thing the healer here did was get me to swallow telk syrup straight. Helped, but just for an hour or two, and that stuff tastes like deadrot." Essen pretended to shudder, remembering the sensation. "That Starborn woman, last time, she had some secret medicine that helped. Some people were burning mad that she wouldn't share it."

Whatever it was about the Starborn's beliefs that kept them from settling down, they kept to themselves in their small and scattered camps. They were peaceful—people said they wouldn't even keep weapons—and for the most part, no one bothered them. A lot of people didn't trust the Starborn, for no good reason that Davyn had ever heard. They were odd, certainly, edging toward mysticism, but he had never heard of a Starborn man or woman trying to convince someone else to take up their eccentric and nomadic ways. To his way of thinking, if it made sense to them to worship the stars and wander, that was their concern.

"Hope they're still around here these days," Essen said. "Aren't they mostly in the Wyth Valley and the Hills?"

"I'll try the lake first. I'll call for the physician on my

way, and he can help Mira while I'm finding the Starborn. If I have to, I can go to Ruatt and put word around."

"Well, here's hoping you don't have to." Essen put a hand on Davyn's shoulder. "While you're gone, you know, I have to manage all this by myself."

Davyn suggested closing the inn. The tavern would be all right, if Mira stayed upstairs, but it might be a risk for overnight guests. Essen decided otherwise, arguing that if one or two guests came, they could be in the rooms at one end of the hall and never know Mira was in a sickroom at the other.

That night, Davyn lay awake in his room across the hall from where Mira drowsed through fever dreams. He could hear Essen snoring from the extra room downstairs, and knew that Elanna and Tunny were deep asleep down the hall. Dark thoughts returned.

5

ESCORT

East to Trint

EVEN THOUGH ARISSA knew she would probably have ended up in the carriage anyway, because she wasn't a good rider, she longed to be out there on one of the horses. Instead, she was being towed along in the two-wheeled carriage with her luggage at her feet and her wrap tucked around her against the gusts of wind. It wasn't comfortable and it limited her view. At least when Glenn rode beside her, she could exchange amiable, trivial observations with him. When she was left alone with her thoughts, they mostly centered on the unwelcome feeling of living in a metaphor as she was dragged away from her home. Poetically, Wisdom, her pony, was trailing behind them.

The countryside around her was unfamiliar, with bare, undulating fields spreading out in all directions and small, scrubby trees lining the road. Weeks of steady rain had eased into days of intermittent showers, but the sun hadn't dried out the soil enough yet for the crops to sprout. She couldn't remember ever being this far from Aryn, and if she had, it wouldn't have been on this eastward road, winding down through the hills toward Trint. As soon as they had crossed the river—the ford had been no problem at all—and left Aryn's lands, she had felt keenly that there was no turning back. She wouldn't be able to go home for some time, even if she successfully avoided going the whole way to House Wyth.

She had considered leaving House Aryn before her escort arrived, just making her way to Ruatt or even Dannpelier ahead of the Gathering, but they'd come too soon, just a week after Gadrin's visit. Making it work in her favor was her only recourse. She'd have an armed escort to Ruatt, and then could slip away from the guardsmen there. She would make better time, since she wouldn't have to try to travel unseen. A House woman traveling alone would certainly be noticed and noted, and given the nature of the Gathering, she wanted to avoid any risks she could. This way, she'd make half the journey the easy way. Maybe she could even find Gadrin in Ruatt. As long as she didn't raise too many questions by asking too many, she might find someone who could contact him.

"Are you still comfortable enough, Dane Arissa?" Glenn looked down from his horse and smiled at her. "We're just a few hours from Trint, now, so we'll get there in good time to get you fixed up for a good night's sleep at the inn."

She hoped there'd be a decent meal at the inn at Trint, too, and a chance to wash off the grit of travel. "I'm all right, Glenn. Just wishing I could ride."

"I know, but it's colder than you think in this wind. And we've got strict orders—he had this gig done up just for you. It's supposed to be how ladies prefer to travel, and our Lord Wyth would want you to be in style."

"Well, he'd be surprised at how little I care about that. Does it really matter so much to him?"

Glenn looked away for a moment, and seemed to consider his answer before saying, "He likes to have everything done the right way—he's careful with details."

She stared past him at the rolling land, and said, "I don't think we have much in common, he and I."

The guard meant to be kind. "You could still have a good marriage. He will be good to you."

Arissa didn't respond. She could imagine her future as Lady Wyth. She pictured herself in a beautiful dress, sitting in an opulent, stifling room with nothing to do. If her husband walked in, he would acknowledge her with an empty greeting as if he were surprised to find her there. He might tell her that he had ordered some special gift for her—some clothes or trinket that she hadn't asked for—because all the ladies had them. After a year or so, he'd finally insist that they needed to have a child or people would wonder.

Even as she thought about it, she felt herself getting annoyed by his superficial kindnesses and his compliments, which no doubt would really be self-directed. A man who would contract for marriage to her without meeting her or even sending a personal greeting wasn't likely to be very concerned about her perspective on anything. Even among the Houses, a little bit of courtship was a reasonable expectation these days. His transactional approach told her everything she needed to know. All he really wanted was the children.

It was growing dark when they came into the town of Trint, but even so there were people everywhere in the streets. Glenn and one of the other men rode close on either side of the gig. Arissa was protected, but she also couldn't see past them very well, so her first glimpses of Trint were angled past horses' necks. The gig bumped along on the cobblestones; she pushed against the seat to keep herself as stable as she could.

They came to a wide plaza where five roads intersected. A few groups of men stood talking around a small fountain in the middle, ignoring and ignored by the band of children who were chasing each other through the dusk. A woman stood in the doorway of one of the smaller buildings lining the crossroads, calling out to someone to come in.

They stopped the gig near one corner, in front of a large building that was separated from its row of neighbors by a narrow alleyway. Its door stood open, beneath the sign declaring it to be the Crossroads Inn, and she could smell food and hear the tavern's boisterous guests. Her heart sank when one of the guards dismounted and walked in.

"We're staying here?"

Glenn chuckled at her dismay. "Aye, Dane Arissa, we are. Don't worry—the guest house is upstairs and quiet enough when the tavern closes. It will quiet down just about the time we're finished with our supper."

He helped her out of the gig and lifted her case down as the guard and a man from the tavern approached. The man was tall, and walked with his shoulders back and his chin slightly lifted, ready to meet the world on his terms. The clothes he wore were simple, but he looked like he'd dressed down for some reason, like he'd be more comfortable in a House lord's formal coat and sash. Even the fact that his dark hair was a little longer than it should be didn't fully counteract the House dignity. It just made him look young, and tempered the impression that he had everything, always, under perfect control.

The Inn couldn't be as rough as it seemed, if someone

like him was staying here. Arissa waited for him to greet her with upturned palms, but as he strode toward her, he was looking not at her but at the horses. He ran a hand down the carriage horse's neck as he passed, and stopped beside the carriage. Instead of a social greeting, he gave her a deferential half-bow. She recovered enough to acknowledge the bow just before her confused hesitation made it awkward. The horse had turned its head and was watching him. It whinnied, and he held up a hand toward it, a gesture of forbearance. He said to Glenn, "With your permission, I'll see to the horses." She was astonished. A stable hand.

Glenn shook his head. "No, but thank you. We do that ourselves. Back around there, is it?"

The young man looked startled. Arissa supposed most guests were all too happy to let the stable hands tend to tired horses, so she said, "It's kind of you, but it's better for Glenn to do it. His horse is rather unpredictable." She wasn't sure if that were true, but it sounded plausible and she didn't want him to feel unappreciated.

For a moment, it seemed as though he wanted to insist. Then his posture shifted; he glanced toward the horses, then reached for her case. "The livery is behind the inn," he said. "Tunny is back there—he'll help you get them stabled and get you whatever you need. My lady, if you would follow me, I'll take your case up to the inn while your men are managing the horses." She couldn't place his accent.

"No need for that," one of the guards said dismissively. "I'll see to it."

The man set down her case and looked at her, as if for confirmation that she wasn't caught in a bad situation. She smiled at him, and found a coin in her purse to offer him as thanks at least for his courtesy. He accepted it without comment, but there was a stiffness about the way he took it from her.

Somehow she had managed to offend the stable hand when she meant to be kind, and she felt graceless. Her face tingled.

Very formally, he bowed more properly and said, "Safe harbor and safe journey, my lady. I hope you will be comfortable here."

As soon as he was out of earshot, she muttered to Glenn, "You'd think we insulted his mother."

Glenn chuckled. "Takes himself a little too seriously, I'd say. Nothing wrong with that, but we don't need the help so there's no need to pay him for it. Now come on. These two can take the gig around to the stables and get all that settled while you and I let the taverner know we're hungry."

There wasn't much light in the tavern, besides what was given by the fire in the enormous hearth and a few inadequate lamps along the walls. The back wall was lined with a long bench and small, high tables. A rambunctious group of men were gathered at one end, and bursts of laughter peppered their loud conversation. A high counter ran the length of the tavern, from the door to the back, ending at the doorway to some other room. The center of the room was crowded with tables where quieter men were eating or playing some sort of card game. The innkeeper led them to a small table close to the far end of the counter, and then hurried off to get food and drink for them.

The table was a comfortable height for Glenn; Arissa felt like a child sitting among adults. At least from her seat, she had a clear view of the room. She had her back to the rowdy drinkers, and the doorway—leading to a better-lit, enticing kitchen—was on her left at the end of the counter, behind Glenn. She saw no women in the place at all.

When the other two Wyth men came in, they went to the bench behind her. Arissa envied them for how easily they joined the drinkers' banter. The dignified stable hand came in, too, and slipped behind the counter, near the open tavern door. He set some empty glasses on a deep-sided tray and pushed that aside, and then retrieved a large book from somewhere behind the counter. A notebook followed. He glanced around the room, momentarily met her gaze before inclining his head to imply a bow, then turned his attention to his book. From her angle, she couldn't see his face as he bent over his work, occasionally writing something in his notebook. It would have been interesting to know what an out-of-place man like him was studying so earnestly.

He looked up when a young girl came in from the back room and skittered over to him. Arissa couldn't hear, but the girl seemed worried as she gestured back the way she came. The man listened and said something serious, and though the girl went away after that, the book was neglected. His shoulders rose and fell with a deep breath, and he picked up the tray and disappeared into the kitchen.

Two generous plates of food were brought to the table by the innkeeper, who was a huge, middle-aged man who looked like he had done more interesting things than innkeeping. He had a dramatic scar on the side of his face, and his hands were calloused, but he smiled broadly as he set their meals down. To her surprise, he pulled over a chair and sat down across from Glenn. "Did you have any trouble on the roads, friends?"

Glenn shook his head. "None. But we didn't expect to on this part."

Arissa looked at him sharply. "Do we expect to on some other part?"

His smile wasn't entirely convincing. "There are troublemakers on the roads closer to Ruatt. That's why you've got a full escort, Dane Arissa."

"Aye, it's a good idea these days, especially for a young lady, considering the news we're getting from up that way."

At Glenn's prompt, the man explained, "Ettori's pushing hard to speed up construction of the dam and anyone who disagrees is having a bad time of it. We hear he's even clearing people out of the Wyth valley. Whole villages."

"Don't the Hill Houses stop him?" Arissa voiced the first question that came to mind, and then wished she'd kept it to herself. Both Glenn and the innkeeper looked at her with something between amusement and surprise, and she knew what was coming next.

With a smile a precocious child might appreciate, the innkeeper said, "Well, it's more complicated than that, my lady. We shouldn't bother you with this kind of talk. You've got nothing to worry about with an escort. How's the food?"

Glenn gave her a real smile this time, before saying to the innkeeper, "She never gives up on a question, I've learned." He looked at her, and said, "House Wyth, for one, is trying to manage it directly with Lord Ettori—which means not stepping into a confrontation too soon." He took a large mouthful of food and that was clearly all she was going to hear about it.

So House Wyth likely wouldn't join the Gathering. Whether Lord Wyth was a pacifist or a coward was unclear, but either way he wasn't willing to confront Ettori. Not even to defend people who depended on the House for protection. That was a serious dereliction of a long, long tradition. In return for the Tithe and the support it represented, the Houses had always promised assistance—it was a trust going back for generations. She thought of the people who looked to Aryn, people like Petros Gibbon and the other shepherds, and couldn't imagine letting someone push them out of their homes. Wyth's abstention was a betrayal among the Houses, too. If Lord Ettori was clearing villages from another House's domain, he was depriving that House of people who worked the land and paid the Tithe.

Well, Wyth might not be willing to take a stand against Kor, Lord of House Ettori, but Arissa of Aryn would. She'd be in Ruatt by tomorrow night, and she would slip away from Glenn as soon as she could, hopefully find Gadrin, and be on her way to the Gathering.

A trio of rough-clad men pushed into the tavern and headed for the only empty table, the one beside Arissa's. They looked like field workers, she thought, with their sun-burned faces and coarse clothes. One of the newcomers noticed Glenn as they passed, and stopped, aggressively close, to leer at Glenn. His nose had healed badly from a break at some point, and Arissa thought he probably would look just as unpleasant if he smiled.

"Look," the man said to his companions. "Here's one of 'em." To rough laughter, he pushed his forefinger at the insignia embroidered on the shoulder of Glenn's jacket.

Glenn set his drink down, and sounded almost affable as he said, "I'm Glenn Treval, serving House Wyth."

"Aye, we recognize ye well enough, with that uniform." The man spat at Glenn's feet. "That's what we think of Wyth."

There were some approving mutters from his companions. Arissa hoped Glenn hadn't noticed that she had gasped when the man spat, as if she were as righteous and fastidious as her mother about manners. It had been unexpected, that was all, and a startling, crude confirmation of what kind of reputation her pledged husband had.

Glenn pushed back his chair and stood, a match for any intimidation. "Please notice there's a lady present," he said, less friendly now.

"I know her type, too," the man scoffed, scarcely even glancing at her.

Glenn was drawing in his breath and no doubt preparing to say something biting when the innkeeper stood up, stepped between the two bristling men, and dropped a heavy hand on the uncouth man's shoulder. "No need for this sort of thing," he said. "I'm Essen, and in this place you can say what you want, but I'll have no fights. What's your quarrel with House Wyth?"

Still glaring at Glenn, the man said, "The new Wyth broke trust." He spat on the floor again, and Essen stretched his arm out to block Glenn, though Glenn hadn't moved. "We pay the Tithe and we work the land just like we always done. But since the old Wyth handed on his House, we get no help, no protection."

One of his fellows spoke up. "Wyth's star-freaks took everything and burnt our homes!"

"The Starborn?" Glenn sounded incredulous. "Wyth has nothing to do with them."

The man snorted. "Wyth knows all about it—looked down from the House and saw the fires and he did nothing. Not even after. Just let it all happen and not even a word to us. Wyth let those star-freaks stay, and Ettori used them to ruin us!" Other conversations in the tavern halted at his shout.

Glenn brushed past Essen and took a small step forward. He was eye to eye with his accuser when he said, without rancor, "So is it Wyth or Ettori, then? Do you really think the Starborn—a group of deluded cultists—take direction from the Houses? Your village is in ashes, and you came to a tavern in Trint to have a drink and complain?"

One of the other men got up from the table. "We came for cheap supplies, you bastard, since Wyth isn't givin' us so much as a loaf of bread." He looked Glenn up and down, and Arissa saw the moment the idea came to him, just as he called to his mates, "Let's see what Wyth gave this one." He lunged, throwing his full weight into a shove that knocked Glenn into the table, which sent a mug of ale into Arissa's lap. She sprang up and jumped out of the way just as Glenn, in his stagger to regain his balance, kicked over a chair. As it clattered to the floor, the villagers shouted encouragements, and the noise rose even more as a contingent of half-drunk men surrounded the combatants, clamoring for a real fight to begin. Arissa stood aside and watched her other two escorts throw themselves into the group, indiscriminately hitting and shoving to get into the center.

6
THIEF

Crossroads Inn

DAVYN CAUGHT ONE glimpse through the melee of Essen, whose shouts were lost in the riot, before the brawl closed off his view again. He looked to see if the girl were safe, and saw her slip out of the tavern through the door to the back. It was a smart move, going up to the guest quarters where she could be out of sight and out of the way. What she probably didn't know was that her door was likely locked; typically, Essen or Mira would take the guests up and let them in if they wanted to go up this early. He started to follow, but was on the wrong side of the tavern, where he'd been clearing a table. He moved to skirt the fight, but a man was expelled from the scrum and stumbled into him. It was Essen.

The big man's weight nearly knocked him over; at least he was able to break Essen's fall. He saw the red bloom on Essen's arm and in almost the same moment saw a blade flash in the fight before the crowd reformed and filled the gap Essen had left. The men lurched almost as a unit toward the door as they struck and evaded and parried unaimed blows. Essen's legs sagged, and Davyn eased him the rest of the way to the floor.

"Ah, lad, I wasn't expecting that." Essen grimaced at his arm. "I'm glad Mira's not here to tell me I'm a fool." There was a gash on his left arm below the elbow, and blood was already staining his slashed sleeve. Davyn pulled the fabric away and winced in sympathy. It was a clean wound, but deep.

"Who had the knife? Wyth?"

"I think it was one of the village men—not sure. Didn't see it till I felt it, and didn't see who owned the hand it was in."

Davyn found an unstained bit of Essen's bar towel and clamped it against the wound. If he'd had more luck today, there would have been a Starborn healer here, but the camp had moved on and it had been a wasted ride up to the lake. He looked around the tavern for someone who was paying attention and could help. There was no sign of the girl, so her guest door must have been unlocked, or perhaps Elanna or Tunny had helped her. He could hear the noise from the fighters in the street, and the tavern was empty now except for Elanna, who was hovering near the door to the kitchen with her hands clamped together in front of her chest. Davyn waved her over, and together they helped Essen into a chair. Then he sent Elanna to get clean water and proper bandages and honey.

While Essen held the cloth in place, Davyn checked on the brawl outside and reported, "Looks like it's now a few different fights. The Wyth guards seem to be winning, but the villagers aren't giving up. And some of ours are in it, too."

"Just for the thrill, I reckon. Any sign of the Watch?"

"Not yet, but it shouldn't be much longer. Someone is

bound to have sent for them already, but I'll send someone to be sure."

Once the Watch arrived, the fight would break up. They were always massive, well-muscled men, and were usually able to stop troublemakers with an armlock or a shove to the ground. If there were any clear instigators, they might well spend the rest of the night cooling off in the Watch's keep.

Elanna returned, staring into the basin of water she carried while she clenched a bundle of bandages to her side with her elbow. She blanched when she looked at the now-soaked rag under Essen's hand, and when Davyn asked her to go find the Watch, she dashed off mid-sentence.

Not long after, Essen's wound was clean and dressed, with bandages wrapped and tied in place to hold a honey-infused cloth against his skin. "I didn't know you knew how to doctor, lad," he said. "Mira wouldn't have done any better. You telk farmers are full of surprises."

Davyn didn't want to explain. When he'd arrived, he'd wanted to put everything about Holden behind him. It was his best hope to keep his grief at bay, at first, and then it had become habit. So Davyn never talked about Van, or Holden, or anything about what he thought of as his first life, other than the bare facts of being fostered on a farm on the Holden estate. In the first few weeks here, he'd explained his skill with horses by talking about growing up on the farm. Neither Essen nor Mira believed him, but also hadn't pressed him. Since then, Essen had taken to teasing him about the farm whenever he had a question he thought Davyn wouldn't answer. So Davyn didn't tell him about Carthen the weapons master, who insisted that boys who played with swords—and men who joined the Queen's Guard—needed to tend wounds as well as cause them. "It's a good skill to have. When the physician comes tomorrow for Mira, we'll put some floodberry paste on it, but this will help in the meantime."

Floodberries, the fruit of the telk plant, had several medicinal purposes, but they were expensive. They grew only on second-year plants that had been drowned by the spring floods and left to decay, unharvested. Every crop of floodberries meant that a telk farmer had gambled, passing up the moderate reward of the telk leaves in the fall for the hope of well-timed floods and an abundant crop of the delicate white berries in the spring. The berries could be ground and mixed with other herbs to make a numbing and cleansing paste. Carthen had taught Davyn and Van to make it, but the paste couldn't be stored and some of the herbs were uncommon.

A few of the brawlers came back into the tavern to nurse their bruises and relive the fight, calling for ale as they reclaimed their tables and righted the chairs. Essen moved to stand, but Davyn stopped him. "I'll see to it, Essen. Sit still, and I'll bring you one, too."

He spent the rest of the evening fetching and pouring and serving. Essen drank far more than usual and drowsed off at the table; he woke when Elanna returned with the news that only the Wyth guards had been detained by the Watch. It wasn't fair, but at least it stopped the fight. The Wyth men would come back in the morning, no doubt aching and a little ashamed, and they'd be on their way.

"Just as well," Essen said. "Better not to have every room full tonight anyway. I reckon it's just bad luck to have House guests here when Mira's laid flat—she always wants to impress them. It's always straight from rain to floods, isn't it?" Neither of them mentioned the Sweep.

Davyn sent Elanna to check on the horses while he

checked on Mira and helped Essen get settled in the down-stairs room. He made sure the fires were out in the tavern and kitchen hearths, locked up, and put out the lamps. The girl hadn't come back down, even though he was sure she would be able to hear that the tavern was back to normal. If she had somehow managed to get to sleep, that was prob-ably for the best anyway. He crept past her room, careful to avoid the loudest of the creaking floorboards.

The syncopated knock on the door was Elanna's—a soft rap with the knuckles, then two quick open-palm slaps—but faster and louder than usual. It took Davyn a few heartbeats to wake up fully; when he opened his eyes the faint glow of early dawn revealed only shapes and shades. "Awake!" he called as he sat up and reached for the clothes folded neatly at the foot of the bed.

"They're gone!" There was a brittleness in Elanna's voice through the door. "Half the horses."

Davyn pulled open the door as he finished buttoning his shirt with one hand. Elanna was hardly even a step back from the threshold. She was a thin child, and small for twelve. Standing as she was, her arms crossed tight, looking up with worry in her eyes, she looked scarcely older than Tunny. "I made a mistake," she said, and looked up to see how Davyn reacted. "I forgot to check if the tackroom was locked last night."

"It'll be all right," Davyn said. He could see that Elanna was miserable with guilt. "It's not your fault, Elanna. They didn't take the horses because they could steal the saddles." Davyn checked that the sheathed dagger strapped to his right boot was secure, and felt for the good luck charm in his vest pocket. When his fingers brushed it, he was glad to feel the usual little touch of confidence.

It was an old charm, old enough that it was clearly not one of the trinkets sold as "wanderers' charms" to fashionably superstitious people in the cities. It was just a token, the size of a small coin. An eight-pointed star was etched on its surface, but over the years its various owners' fingers had rubbed the center of the charm smooth. Davyn rarely looked at it anymore, but he'd carried it in his pocket since he was old enough to have pockets. Although he'd never admit the superstition, he did feel like it kept him centered.

"Which horses?" Davyn asked, closing the door behind him.

"Essen's mare, and two of the Wyth horses," Elanna said, but then it seemed whatever she was about to say was lodged in her throat. "And...and...P-p-paladin."

Davyn's heart somersaulted, pushing all the air from his lungs as it flipped. For a moment, there was no thought at all, just panic. Then: Paladin, gone. Paladin, sold. Would someone else be safe, riding him—and would he be safe with another rider? And this would delay the continuation of his search for a Starborn healer to stop the Sweep.

"Get Tunny," he said to Elanna. "I need you both."

"Davyn...Tunny's sick. He wouldn't get up."

Davyn pivoted and dashed along the corridor to the room at the end of the hall, where the roof pinched the ceiling. Even Tunny would soon be too tall to stand straight in his nook, and the bed took almost all the floorspace. He was almost within arm's reach of the door as he lay in bed, only his ashen face uncovered. The familiar, unwelcome odor clung to the air. As Davyn braced himself against the wall, his knees suddenly weak, he heard a raised voice from downstairs—the tone of complaint and accusation was clear.

Elanna followed Davyn down the corridor and the stairs with less than a full stride between them. The men from Wyth were bruised and ragged from the fight and their night's confinement, and they were also angry. The three of them stood shoulder to rigid shoulder, glaring at Essen, who was supporting himself with a hard grip on the back of a chair. Davyn gave Elanna a quick pat on the shoulder and moved up beside Essen. "Tunny's sick," he said softly to Essen. "Mira?"

Essen's face was grim as he shook his head slightly, but he said to the group, "They'll be headed either home or to sell the horses—most likely going east in either case."

"We need to catch them before they get to Ruatt," a Wyth man said.

"Take the livery horses," Essen said. "Not the fastest, but a good rider can put the fire under them."

Davyn decided. "I'm going, too—they took my horse. Elanna, help these men. Leave Storm for me." He looked back at the Wyth leader. "One of yours is still here, but two of you will have to borrow ours." The little carriage horse wouldn't have the speed they needed.

The Wyth leader accepted the suggestion with a swift nod, and waved his companions toward the door. "Go with the girl, get them saddled." He started up the stairs, saying, "We'll have her wait here for us."

A moment later, Davyn heard the man knocking on a door upstairs. There was a pause, the man spoke, and he knocked again. Another pause. Another knock. And then the sound of the door banging open, followed by a loud oath. The man vaulted down the stairs. "She's gone!"

Her door had not been locked, he told them. Her travel cases were still in the room, and the bed looked untouched.

"Kidnapped," Essen concluded grimly.

The Wyth man spun toward the open door to the courtyard. As he strode out, he said, "We have to catch them."

Davyn pictured her, frightened and threatened—or worse—and reached for his sword before remembering that he wasn't wearing it. He dropped his hand at his side, pushing away the unexpected impulse. He saw that Essen had noticed.

"Your farmer's training again, eh?" The big man half-smiled. "Where's your sword? I'll get it—you go to the stable."

Two of the Wyth men were mounted on livery horses who had caught the riders' impatience and were pulling against the reins. Elanna was cinching the girth on the last horse while the third man adjusted his stirrups. As Davyn strode toward the barn, with Captain at his heels, he called to the Wyth men, "Go ahead—go east and I'll catch up."

His eyes adjusted quickly to the low light in the stables. The tackroom door was open. Storm, the youngest and fastest of the livery horses, was waiting in her stall with her ears pricked forward. She bobbed her head as Davyn approached, with Elanna right behind him. The Wyth pony, in the stall across from Storm, watched with interest as Davyn led the grey into the aisle and settled a saddle on her.

"Davyn, look," Elanna said. "Someone fed the pony."

"Hm?" Davyn ducked under Storm's head and glanced into the pony's stall. There were traces of fresh oats in the feed bucket—and the feed scoop was on the ground inside, as if someone had dropped it after filling the bucket through the bars on the stall. "Not you?"

"No. When I came out this morning and saw they were gone I went right back inside to get you. Who would've fed just her?"

"That question will have to wait," Davyn said as he checked the stirrups. He pulled an empty waterskin from the saddlebag and tossed it to Elanna. "Fill this for me?"

He met Elanna in the yard as she was coming back, with Essen. Elanna handed him the filled skin, and Essen handed him the belt and sheathed sword before tucking a hunk of something wrapped in a napkin into the saddlebag.

"You might get hungry," Essen said.

Davyn pulled Essen out of Elanna's hearing. "Send for the physician right away—this means I won't get a chance to look for the Starborn for a bit. Keep Tunny upstairs away from other people, too, especially if he's coughing. If it gets worse, or if anyone else gets symptoms, you need to quarantine the inn."

Davyn gave Elanna a quick hug. "Tell Tunny to rest well so he gets better quickly, and keep your distance till he stops coughing. And take care of the horses today. Rusty Bucket might come back today, and you know he'll be cranky. Coddle him or he'll take it out on the others."

Elanna was blinking back tears, sensitive as always to the tension. On an impulse, Davyn knelt and unstrapped his dagger, and handed it to her in the boot-sheath. "Here. You can use it if you need it, and you know I'll come back to claim it. So take good care of it."

"I will." Elanna clutched it in both hands.

"I'll be back soon," Davyn said. He buckled on the sword belt and swung up into the saddle.

"Stars guide you, boy," Essen said, in benediction.

There weren't many people on the streets this early: only a few people carrying baskets of fresh bread or produce, and day-servants rushing to their employers to be there for breakfast. Davyn trusted that they would move out of the racing horse's way. Storm's hoofbeats were sharp on the stone streets, percussive and even.

He urged the horse into a full gallop. The road was

paved for about a half mile beyond the town before subsiding into half-dried mud, and then the hoofbeats no longer rang. They weren't far behind the others, and Storm—with Davyn's encouragement—closed the distance easily. With the slightest suggestion of the reins, Davyn asked the horse to slow down to match the trot of the others as he caught up.

When Davyn rode up beside him, Glenn raised his eyebrows—all the acknowledgement he gave of Storm's speed—and pointed to three distinct tracks: stripes of darker, wetter mud had been churned up on the road ahead.

The horses must have been galloping, their hooves digging into the soft road. He would have been able to tell Paladin's prints by the length of the stride, but the tracks were just ruts. Three were clear and deep, but the fourth seemed to weave among them. One horse was either leading or following, and there was no way to know if that meant something good for the girl.

The muddy stripes led east toward Ruatt.

Davyn saw the horses in the distance at the edge of the road, in the shade cast by the craggy edge of a stony overhang. Paladin and the two Wyth horses were riderless. The village men were out of sight, presumably behind the boulder. The girl, on Essen's mare, was off to one side, her back to the approaching rescue.

Paladin whinnied and half-reared, and the other three stolen horses pulled against their hitches in panic as Storm and the others charged toward them. The three men rushed back to the road, cursing as they grabbed at the reins—but they were too late. Davyn and the Wyth men closed the gap before they could mount.

At Davyn's prompt, Storm plunged straight toward the

nearest thief and then reared to avoid collision as the other horses ripped away from the villagers and scattered.

As Storm landed, she danced in a tight circle, and Davyn saw that both the girl and Essen's mare had wild eyes as they struggled for an escape. The girl, gagged, had her hands bound in front of her. The mare's reins were wedged in a crevice of the rock, and the horse strained to break free. She still had the bit in her mouth. She'd seriously injure herself, might even snap her jaw, if she kept pulling. Davyn dropped from the saddle, drew his sword, and took two leaping strides toward them. He sliced through the reins near where they were caught in the rock.

The mare staggered at the sudden release, recovered, and wheeled toward the open road to the east, with the girl clinging to the saddle horn. "Wait!" Davyn yelled, but the horse had already launched into a gallop. The girl crumpled forward, low over the horse's neck, and for a moment it looked like she might fall. Davyn turned back to Storm, ready to swing back into the saddle and ride after the runaway horse—but Storm had abandoned him.

Paladin had recovered from the alarm and was watching from the edge of the scene. Davyn clicked his tongue, and the horse looked his way, though Davyn doubted that even Paladin's sharp ears could have heard him over the sounds of human and equine anger, fear, and confusion. The three Wyth men had dismounted, and the villagers were closing in to fight.

Davyn saw Glenn face the tallest of the three thieves. Knife in hand, that villager dove forward. Glenn shifted his weight, and when the man was at the extremity of his lunge, Glenn shoved him sideways. When he found himself suddenly on the ground, his yell was more outrage than pain. Glenn stood aside as he started to get back on his feet.

"Look out!" Davyn shouted to Glenn, who whirled to face the thickset man approaching from his right. Already one of the Wyth men was sprawled face down, unmoving, just behind this second horse-thief.

"You again," the man sneered, his crooked nose making him instantly familiar as the leader of the brawl in the tavern the night before. He had scored a few solid hits against Glenn in that fight, but in return Glenn had blackened the man's right eye and knocked a tooth out.

"You remember me, do you?" Glenn gave him a false grin. "Hoping to get your tooth back?"

Glenn wasn't able to repeat his dodge, and this assailant's surge knocked them both to the ground. They struggled for position, but Glenn got the upper hand and pinned the villager. A few feet away, the first thief—the one Glenn had duped—grappled with the last Wyth guard, the youngest. Both were desperate to control the thief's dagger. Davyn turned once around, scanning for the third thief.

His eyes fell on him just as the man leaned over the wrestling pair, almost casually, and drove his dagger into Glenn's exposed back.

Davyn saw Glenn sag as his arms buckled, his weight falling on his opponent. At the same moment there was a victorious shout from off to the side. The man who had stabbed Glenn straightened, and his dagger was red. He gave a half-growl that could have been a laugh or a snarl, and moved to strike Davyn. Before Davyn could raise his sword, the man collapsed, revealing the young Wyth man behind him, holding the hard-won knife—the villager who had owned it was dead. Stunned, Davyn just looked at the Wyth man blankly, and then felt Paladin's presence on his right—his ally. He pulled himself into the saddle.

As he gathered the reins, he heard a scream close to

his side. The Wyth man who had just saved Davyn now dropped, his hamstrings sliced at the knees. The man who had been pinned under Glenn had freed himself and now killed the young Wyth man with a quick jab of his knife. Davyn lifted his sword, but as the man struck forward with his bloody dagger, Paladin flung his head back and reared. Davyn clung on as, with a sickening crack, Paladin kicked the villager in the chest. The man's head struck the ground with a thump.

It was suddenly, terribly quiet. Davyn heard his own pounding heart as if from a distance, and the horse's labored breath somehow sounded like his own. He swung down and stood at the edge of the horror—six men down, limbs at odd angles and faces contorted, blood everywhere. He felt himself sway, and deliberately shifted his weight forward, as Carthen had taught him, taking conscious control of his movement. Numb, he broadened his gaze, and took in the rest of his surroundings.

The horses had scattered. Storm was far out in the fields across the road. Two more had stopped at the next bend in the road and were looking back at him. The inn's horses were some distance back the way they'd come. There was no way he could catch them all and he wished he could tell them to find their way home. Chances were good that the livery horses would; the Wyth horses might have a harder time.

The girl was gone.

He tried not to look as he stepped past the man Paladin had vanquished and knelt beside Glenn. He had been pushed onto his back, and the ground was dark and wet where he lay. His eyes were closed, and one arm was flung wide. Davyn held his breath as he placed his fingers on Glenn's neck. For a moment, he thought he might be feeling his own pulse hammering down to his fingertips, but it was Glenn's, faint.

Davyn retrieved his saddlebag, and pulled out the waterskin and the cloth that had been wrapped around the chunk of bread. He carefully wedged the saddlebag under Glenn to keep him partially lifted from the ground. He trimmed the soaked fabric away from the wound, wet the bread cloth and gently wiped away some of the blood so he could see the damage. As he pressed the cloth against the wound, there was a strange overlay of memory from the night before, tending Essen's slashed arm. But at the inn he'd had help, and plenty of water. The thought had occasionally occurred to him before, that it would be good to keep some basic healing supplies in his kit, but he hadn't acted on it.

When the flow of blood had stopped, he took a swallow of water and wiped the back of his hand across his lips. He tasted blood and saw that his hands were covered with it. And none of it was his own. He felt his throat constrict as it came to him: for once he had acted fast, without deliberation, but he had rushed in to save a horse, not a human. Perhaps he couldn't have helped Glenn or the girl. It might have made no difference, or perhaps he would have been killed. That was the trouble with what he'd struggled to teach himself to do: leap in and trust that he could improvise a plan. No point in evaluating alternatives after the fact.

He did what he could for the dead men, which was only to close their eyes and move them to the side of the road. When all five were out of the way, with some attempt to cover the indignities of their deaths, he returned to Glenn.

He wished he could move him into the shade, but he didn't dare shift him too much. He checked the wound.

At his touch, Glenn opened his eyes and issued a strange, hard gasp.

"It's all right," Davyn said, "I'm here."

"Arissa?" the man rasped.

"Arissa?" Davyn echoed. "I don't know." She was frightened but I think unhurt—her horse took off. I stayed with you."

"No, no, no," Glenn moaned. "Find her. Go…"

The man murmured something else, too garbled and weak to decipher. Davyn leaned in to hear—and jumped when the man's hand clamped on his wrist. "Go," Glenn said, more forcefully but with that same brittle breath. "Go."

It was the last thing he said.

A fixed memory of the girl's terrified eyes drove Davyn. It had only been a couple of hours, at most, and her horse would have stopped running long ago. Davyn nudged Paladin back into a trot.

The sun was high overhead when he saw the horse grazing, slashed reins trailing, just off the road. The girl was slumped in the saddle. Davyn stopped Paladin several strides away and dismounted. He whistled softly, and Essen's mare lifted her head and turned to look at him. "Easy, easy," he said, approaching slowly. She seemed to be counting his steps. "It's all right now." He reached as he got close, ready to take hold of her cheek-strap. Before he made contact, the mare swung toward him and bumped his hand. He slipped his hand under a strap and looked up at the girl.

She was unconscious, or close to it. The gag was still tightly in place, and her wrists were bound together and to the pommel of the saddle. He touched her knee and spoke to her, but she didn't respond. The horse stayed still while he untied the knotted rope around her wrists and lifted her down. In his arms, she seemed smaller and even more fragile, and he carried her to a spot where the ground was less rocky. The softness of her clothes, which were stained now, and torn, seemed to emphasize that she belonged in a gentler world.

The gag was filthy, and when he removed it he saw bruises and red pressure marks at the corners of her mouth. Her face, which had seemed so pale at the inn, was flushed in patches. After trying to make her comfortable, he checked her saddlebag—there was a nearly full waterskin. He raised her a little, cradling her head in the bend of his left arm, and held the waterskin to her lips. He was relieved that she swallowed the trickle of water. For a few minutes, he continued giving her a sip at a time as she gradually regained her senses.

When she noticed that she was braced against him, she tried to pull away and so knocked the waterskin out of his hand. Water splashed both of them. Davyn pulled his empty right hand away from her so she could see.

"You're safe now," he said. "I won't harm you."

"Why are you here?" she asked, with confusion and hostility melded in her voice. She shifted so she could see his face. Oddly, the look in her eyes didn't match her tone; she looked wary, and frightened.

He explained about the discovery of the kidnapping and the theft, and the pursuit. When he recounted what had happened after they had met on the road, she grew very still.

"Glenn?" she whispered.

Davyn shook his head. She looked down at her hands, and said nothing, and began to pick at the grass. The rope had rubbed her wrists raw. He sat quietly, wondering what he was meant to do now. The men had told Essen they were escorting her to her betrothed; she probably needed to complete that journey, but House Wyth was at least another day's journey beyond Ruatt. She needed rest, and comfort, and staying where they were wouldn't do her any good. Softly, he said, "We should move from here."

"And go where?" she said, with a note of accusation that made no sense to him.

There was no point in taking her back to Trint, Davyn thought. If they rode on, they'd be in Ruatt in a few hours, which was the sensible thing. She could stay at the Briar Inn and send word to House Wyth, or hire some men in Ruatt to escort her there when she was ready. Once he saw her safely settled under Shea's wing, he would take Paladin and Essen's mare and go home. He'd look for Starborn on the way.

"Ruatt," he said. "You need time to recover, and you'll be safe there. It's a step closer to House Wyth, so you'll be with your betrothed before much longer." He didn't look at her. He had the feeling she wasn't all joy at the thought of marrying Lord Wyth, and he didn't understand. House Aryn would benefit from the match, and House Wyth was wealthy and respected. Perhaps she was already in love with someone else.

He stood up and reached down to help her up, but when she took his hand she winced, and showed him her red, swollen palms. She tried to get to her feet without support, but she was off-balance and would have fallen if he hadn't reached to steady her. She leaned against him until she was sure of her step, and then pulled away. "I'm Arissa, daughter of House Aryn."

"I'm Davyn Ralen," he said. "Stable master at the

Crossroads Inn." He led her to the horses, and before she asked anything further, he continued, "Do you think you can ride?"

She made a noise in the back of her throat. "I can try. Help me up."

7

TRAVELER

Trint

AFTER WHAT ENDED up being six days at Peggy's, Piers had headed south through the woods again. He surprised a man who was cutting down a tree, and made himself useful. That led to a week of minor acculturation with a trio of men who he suspected weren't supposed to be timbering—but they'd been hospitable, if not exactly forthcoming. Then there'd been another small farm, with a farmer who was impressed enough with his "mending" that he'd been referred to the man's brother.

He'd had enough time with enough people that Piers felt he'd caught the dialect, and he had at least some sense of what passed for normal. Along the way he'd acquired some money, in the form of a handful of metal coins of unknown value. So far there'd been no use for them, but he was hoping that in the town he would be able to buy a new pair of shoes or boots. He also desperately needed to find local replacements for most of what was still in his pack. Things that had looked primitive on the ship looked glaringly artificial now. As soon as he could, he needed to jettison his thermal flask, for instance, and anything else that would force a revelation before he was ready. The clothes Peggy had given him had solved one problem, because at least on first impression he looked less out of place. Not attracting attention was a good thing, overall.

So far, though, he'd found no Empathic resonance in any of the people he'd met, and being so utterly alone in his head for this long was starting to make him feel insubstantial and ungrounded. Five weeks on the planet, give or take; in the three without Arthur he'd had a lot of time to think as he walked, and time to work at re-centering himself.

Now, Piers groaned as clouds coming from the east thickened with little warning while he was eating his lunch. It was the last quarter of his last, squashed sandwich from his last brush with civilization. The novelty of rain had worn off completely now that mud seemed universal. With a boom of thunder that raised the hair on his neck, the clouds released the rain in torrents. He could almost hear Arthur complaining, and he was starting to disproportionately resent being wet. It was easier than thinking about Arthur. Among other things, it seemed hard to believe that his squelching shoes could ever be dry again.

Definitely time to get back to the comforts of indoor living. And it was past time to get on with the important part of the assignment: he needed to be around people to find Empaths and find whoever was in charge. Brief consultation with the ship directed him to a new road. He had walked a mile, at most, when he saw a marker beside the road. A simple arrow was carved into a wooden post, pointing ahead, with a label in an unfamiliar font saying *Trint, 10*. Below that, it said, *Ruatt, 40*. On the opposite side of the post, he saw, *Cantrel, 22*. Distance, he assumed. Peggy had mentioned Cantrel, but he decided Trint would do just as well. He walked on, making official notes of what he saw.

As he came to civilization, he stumbled more than once as he stared. He passed a few houses at the outskirts, which were surrounded by tended gardens and trees given room to spread their limbs. A dog barked at him, and it took him a moment to spot it. It was inside a shelter scarcely larger than the animal, tucked at the side of the house. The dog apparently wanted to stay out of the rain while defending its territory. Piers saw no people as he passed.

Then he came to the more built-up part of the settlement, where the stone streets were bordered with stone buildings. The paving slabs had been cut and aligned so precisely that the gaps between were almost invisible, and the buildings seemed almost as close together. Flower-filled boxes hung from some windowsills, and through some of the windows he could see rooms furnished with domestic touches: inviting chairs; decorative bric-a-brac; even, in one case, a row of books on a table pushed right up against the window—with a cat sitting by them, regarding him with haughty disinterest.

He stayed on the same road as it wove among the houses, and eventually the tenor of the place changed. There were signs of commercial activity, and he saw people hurrying through the rain. So many strangers. Periodically he would make himself Open for a minute at a time, long enough to feel someone else Reaching—but no psi touch came. Piers stopped under an awning, just for momentary shelter while he considered where to go, and was confronted with a display of bread and pastries that made his mouth water. An old woman with a reasonably friendly countenance came out of the shop, carrying a basket, and nodded to him.

"Rain brings flowers," she said, with a bit of sympathy.

"Some good has to come from it," he replied. She seemed amused by his comment, and he felt a little of his tension ease. A pleasant exchange, that's all, but hearing another voice was wonderful. Before she could move on, he asked if she could direct him to an inn—Peggy had said there were several in Cantrel, so he hoped there was one here, too—where he might stay for a night or two and not have to sleep in the open.

The first night had been the worst. Arthur had still been battling constant vertigo and nausea, and the shelter they'd found wasn't anything like sufficient protection if anything actually had gone wrong. There had been wind in the trees, which sounded more ominous at night and led to half-dreams of damaged systems on the ship. Piers heard small rustling noises around him that weren't quite far enough away from his head to be ignored. When some creature stalked past him, and looked right at him with eerie, luminescent eyes, he gave up the pretense. He'd moved out from under the shelter, away from Arthur's misery, and tried to let it all sink in. His mind that night was full and the excitement was almost unbearable, but it had been the sky that finally overwhelmed him. He'd seen the bewildering stars for the first time, entirely from the wrong perspective. It had been unnerving that night, and it still made him uncomfortable—but rain at night was worse.

The woman's directions led him to an imposing building that dominated the plaza at the center of the town. The rain vanished as abruptly as it had started as he paused to review the words he'd need to have at the ready, but he couldn't focus. All he could think about was how much he wanted to change into dry clothes. He hoped, with some vehemence, that a hot bath would somehow be possible.

It took a moment for Piers's eyes to adjust as he stepped

into the Crossroads Inn and Tavern. The large, open room, crowded with tables and people, was dim and warm. There were lamps along the walls, and a fire burning openly in the hearth—so startling, but so welcome—but not much light, overall. Some men were playing a card game at one of the tables near him. Other than that, drinking seemed to be the primary entertainment, and the atmosphere was relaxed, soft with the blending of genial conversations. He shut his eyes, just for a moment, and let it wash over him.

He walked over to the long counter where a pretty, young woman with long, brown hair and an open face was wiping glasses with a rag. Instead of a greeting, she said, "Is it a meal or a bed, then?"

"Both," he answered, "if they're available."

She gave him a strange look, but smiled. "Oh, aye, available. It's possible." Some consolation that whatever was wrong with the word he'd used, it was apparently amusing rather than rude. She walked to the end of the counter and called through an open door, "Essen! One of yours."

Piers was still wondering about that when a giant came through that door and stepped around the counter to meet him. The man had arms that could clearly bend steel, but one forearm was wrapped in bandages. There was a dramatic scar on his face—another reminder that medicine wasn't quite the same down here—that might have made a smaller man look more intimidating. On his face, it was just a feature.

Essen sized him up with a quick glance, and said to the woman, "He's all right." Then he turned back to Piers with a grin that stretched the scar. "You're a stranger, right enough, but you don't look like trouble."

"I don't want to be any trouble," Piers quickly agreed.

"I'm just hoping to stay for a couple of nights so I can explore Trint. And dry out a bit."

"Explore, eh?" Another assessing look. "Not going to market?" There was doubt in Essen's voice, but he seemed curious, not concerned.

Without thinking, Piers Pushed a little sense of trusting to Essen, just in case the man was sensitive enough to pick up on it, and stopped his reflex before he checked the man's response. Funny how hard it was to break the habit of trying to break a habit. Deliberately, now, he lowered his screens enough to feel a reciprocal Push or Reach if one came; none did. "No," he replied. "I've got nothing to sell and I don't need much. I'm just on the road." He wanted to give a neutral reply and a vague answer, delivered in a way that made it sound like it meant more than it did. It should work.

Essen turned and a whisper of his friendliness disappeared. "Your own business, then." He motioned for Piers to follow him and led the way to a table near the hearth. "Never mean to pry," he said as Piers took a seat. "We had some trouble here two nights ago with some other strangers."

Ah. "Is everyone all right?"

That seemed to reset the big man's natural sociability. "Don't rightly know. One of ours got caught up in it and isn't back yet." He lifted his bandaged arm ruefully. "Anyway, it started with a brawl, so likely everyone's hurting some." He shook his head. "The girls reckon strangers might mean fights, and that's more my work than theirs. Now. You'll dry off beside the fire. Ale? Telik? Either one could warm you up. Food?"

He had yet to find a non-bizarre way of saying, "So, see, I have no idea what these coins are worth and no idea what things cost and no idea if I'm rich or poor..." Transactions like this were the hardest to bluff—and he had a personal rule: no outright lies. He tried, "I'm hungry, no question, but I've got to make sure I can enjoy my days in Trint. What would a gold coin get me?" He hoped his little self-conscious laugh would convey a sort of either-way doubtfulness. He nearly held his breath as he waited for the reaction.

The big man guffawed and clapped Piers on the shoulder with enough force to make his chair jump a little. It covered the burst of released air from his lungs. "Ah, my friend, does this look like the kind of place to get the king's dinner?" He chuckled. "For a silver, I'll bring you telik and a good meal you won't forget. For three more I'll give you a quiet room for the night and feed you in the morning."

Piers hoped he was reading this right: assuming that a king's dinner would be a luxury, gold must be worth more than silver and the man was telling him everything he'd get for less than a gold coin. On the other hand, the king's dinner could be some ironic euphemism and he was being told he'd need to hand over a lot more than one measly gold coin. If that were the case, more cold, hungry nights might be in Piers's near future. He poured his few coins into his hand under the table and picked out four silver ones. It didn't leave much to return to his pocket. Essen took the offered coins, patted Piers on the shoulder a couple of times, and went back over to the counter.

Piers noticed now that his hands were shaking a little, which sometimes was the only sign that he'd been playing with fire. The adrenaline was there whether he acknowledged it or not. He placed his hands on the table and tried to relax, but then he was thinking too hard about his body language and felt like a very obvious fraud. No one was paying him any attention at all, though, and he started to calm down and feel almost normal. Sure, normal. Sitting by himself, in a tavern, surrounded by people he hadn't grown up with and who didn't know a thing about him. Sitting in a *tavern* on a *planet.*

When Essen returned, he carried an enormous plate in one hand and a steaming mug in his other. He set them down in front of Piers with a flourish.

It was meat—and not synthetic, either. It was a portion that would be a family meal on the ship, and it was mixed with a vegetable he didn't recognize. There was bread with it, too, like he would need more food. He wanted to feel guilty about it, felt like he should, but he couldn't quite manage it. The savory smell alone was luxury worth paying for, and he was definitely hungry. The mug, well, that he wasn't sure about. The liquid was a deep red-purple, the color of Kath's favorite wine. It wasn't ale, so maybe it was *telik?*

He grinned at Essen. "Guess I'm glad I didn't get the king's dinner. Who would want anything more than this?"

Essen's smile was genuine this time. "Aye, bachelor's stew is my specialty. And take a taste of that telik and you'll believe the legends."

Might as well ask. "Which ones?" He went with the same self-conscious little laugh he'd used earlier.

"Immortality, friend. One sip and you'll live forever."

His filed that for later, and raised his mug to his host— even if it wasn't a gesture for toasting here, it could just mean *here goes*—and took a sip. It was too scalding to taste. He set it down, and said with polite regret, "Too hot. At home we say that means it's a social drink—you have to make conversation 'til it's ready."

"I like that—a social drink. It is, at that." Essen hesitated for a moment, then looked over at the girl at the bar, who was chatting with people across the counter. He looked back at Piers and seemed to overcome some last small reticence. "If you'd welcome some conversation, I'll pour myself some and join you. Jel over there seems to have everything under control."

Piers hoped he managed to seem relaxed and friendly—and not like he was battling the impulse to jump out of his chair and shake the man's hand exuberantly. At any rate, Essen seemed to think everything was normal enough, and he was soon sitting across the table with the two steaming mugs between them.

"So, traveler," Essen said. "Tell me some news."

News? How about: birds are kind of alarming. Horses are really big. Rain is actually kind of nice but it gets old. Or maybe: there's a spaceship over your planet right now, with about three thousand people on it who've never breathed unfiltered air. Oh, and we'll be landing soon. Hope you don't mind.

"I don't think I'm the one to ask," Piers said instead. "I've been on the road for a while and haven't seen that many people. In fact, that sort of surprised me."

Essen scanned the big room, as if taking a count. "It's not like it was, for sure. We don't get nearly as many strangers here now as we did before." There was a very subtle emphasis on the last word, so subtle Piers wasn't sure it was deliberate. "Not too many reasons to travel now." The innkeeper looked at him with a question clearly on his mind.

"Unfortunately, I didn't have a choice. I had to leave home," Piers said, then amended, "Not because I'm running from trouble. Just got too crowded and it was time to go."

"Oh, aye. I have three older brothers and it was out the door for me, too. Are you thinking to make Trint home?"

Piers figured the truth would do. "I want to see what's

here. I've never been here before and I thought it might be interesting."

"More so a few years ago," Essen said, lowering his voice. "Been getting harder even here, and there's not much to interest a young traveler now."

He almost asked, but managed not to. Whatever had happened, there was a *before* and a *now* and it didn't sound like a happy change. And whatever it was, it was something everyone knew and didn't talk about. Blundering into that line of questioning with blazing curiosity and blatant ignorance wouldn't be worth it.

"Don't know what you're looking for," Essen continued, "but if you can't find it here, you might try Soll. Or better yet, Ruatt. Unless you're coming from there?"

"Honestly," Piers replied, "I've been on the road so long I don't know where I've been."

Essen chuckled. "You'd know if you'd been in Ruatt. If you'll take advice from someone who knows, you should go that way when you go. There's even work there, if you're looking for it and you aren't too choosy." He looked at the plate of food in front of Piers pointedly. "Eat, friend. It's better warm."

While he ate, Essen told him about Ruatt. It was built at a spot where the Lentava River narrowed, and trade and people both had always flowed through the town. "Not much flowing now," Essen noted with wry bitterness, "except for the telk." With that, he picked up his mug, and pushed the other one closer to Piers. "Cool enough now. This is Tyndaran telk—ever had it?"

"No," Piers said. The way Essen said it, this was some special kind of telk, and it was apparently plausible that he'd be familiar with some other variety. "How is it different?" He lifted his mug and deliberately inhaled the rising steam with its strange, spicy-sweet-metallic aroma.

"Taste it and tell me." Essen watched him closely.

It wasn't bad. A bit medicinal, but not enough to overpower the odd mix of flavors, all of which seemed familiar and none of which he could name. He took another sip. "I've never tasted anything like it."

Essen laughed appreciatively and slapped his hand on the table. "It's the best, and no one will ever make me believe it isn't. They say the plant is the same as ours, but that truth hides the real truth if you ask me."

"I can't describe the difference," Piers prompted.

The innkeeper thought for a moment. "I think our northern telik tastes a little...harsh, I reckon is the word. Maybe almost bitter." He gave a short laugh. "Or maybe that's just my tongue borrowing what my mind knows."

Might as well, Piers thought again. He drank a bit more to cover his hesitation before he pushed himself to say, "Things are rough." He tried to sound like he was just commenting on the state of affairs, commiserating with the man's unvoiced point of view. He even Pushed his very genuine interest. *Tell me your tales of woe.*

It didn't work. Essen just murmured, "That they are, my friend, that they are." He drank more of his own telik, and lightened his tone. "But this, this is what telik should taste like." He stood and looked over toward the counter. "Now, I'd best be getting back to helping. When you're finished, let us know and I'll take you up to your room. No rush at all."

Piers tried to make sure he didn't look in any one direction for too long, and to focus on his food for long intervals between rounds. No one was paying much attention to anyone else, so he figured it wouldn't be the most prudent thing to just stare at everything interesting. And by all the shining stars, *everything* was interesting. There were probably thirty or forty people here—and not a single person he knew. On the very rare occasions on *Redemption* when he'd been around people he didn't know, there'd always been some he knew well in the mix, too. Now here were forty people who had stories and experiences he couldn't possibly imagine. How could he not stare?

He was down to the last swallow or two of the telik, which was soothing. As he tipped the mug back, he closed his eyes, braced himself and dropped his psi screens. Crowds, even just groups, could sometimes fill his mind so fast the headache came without warning. In this whole room full of seemingly relaxed people, there would surely be a few who were hiding stronger feelings.

Nothing. Not even the soft, blurry background sort of energy he always—always—felt on the ship when he was this Open. Piers Reached, indiscriminately; not too many *of Redemption*'s Empaths could do that. Usually Reaching was directed at someone in particular, a sort of Empathic tap on the shoulder. After his psi ability had been activated, it had taken Piers a while to understand that most others couldn't do what he could do, keeping the signal of his Reach focused enough to carry his own emotions toward no specific destination.

Still nothing. One last thing to try. He Scanned. This, too, he could do without a target, though it was harder, and more of a strain. There was something! Faint—feeble, even—and gone before he could Reach out to it. It was like seeing a shadow disappear around a corner, a glimpse that revealed neither shape nor source. The flat psychic silence from before settled back into Piers's awareness even as he stretched to follow the trace of someone that he was sure he'd felt. He felt exposed, like he'd just done something dangerous and maybe he still wasn't safe. Screening didn't feel like enough; he started Blocking to deliberately push away any psi touch that might come.

"Time for bed, then?"

The woman's voice jerked Piers back into the physical space. He opened his eyes and saw the woman from the counter standing on the other side of the table, her head cocked and a smile lifting one corner of her lips. It was taking him a second to get reoriented.

"Did I wake you?" she said, now with a laugh in her voice. "If you were dreaming, it must not have been a good dream—never seen anyone scowl like that in their sleep."

"Concentrating," he said. "That's all. Trying to catch a thought."

"Well," she said, "I brought more telik for you, and I'm done for tonight. I've been watching you. If you're still looking for hospitality, I'll have a drink with you." She tipped her head toward the empty chair at his table.

"Please," Piers said, "I'd appreciate the company."

She reminded him just a little of Kath, when Kath was eighteen and had just joined the scout team. It was something about the way she moved, maybe, or just her feminine athleticism. "I'm Jelellin," she said, and poured more telik into his mug. The spiced steam rose in a spiral from the swirl of the dark liquid. "It's not every day a handsome stranger comes strolling in here."

Somehow Piers had never considered the possibility of a flirtation here; he wasn't sure any of the scouts had. All the talk, all the planning, had been about how to deal with either suspicion or hostility, or just managing through the routine interactions. The people who lived down here had been sort of vaguely imagined, considered mostly for the part they would play in advancing or impeding the scouts' progress. Jelellin's open smile was hard to read, and he couldn't glean anything Empathically, either.

"And it's not every day a beautiful woman brings me telik," he said, just offering some friendly and non-committal gallantry, he hoped.

She laughed, and seemed pleased but not swept away, so Piers decided he'd gotten through that little maneuver well enough. With her sitting across from him, he was acutely aware of her sizing him up, and he tried to ignore the self-conscious impulse to deflect her gaze. He just smiled at her, and fixed his eyes on the perfect contour of her lips.

They weren't far into the conversation when she said, "I like the way you talk—it's different. Where are you from?"

Right to the hardest question, then, the one he'd been dreading, and tied to the most basic, unavoidable linguistic observation, too. Piers had his answer rehearsed. "It's kind of an isolated place—I hope I'm not too hard to understand. I haven't spent much time away from home, and I haven't had much of a chance to speak to anyone other than the people I grew up with."

Jelellin's eyes, fringed with unbelievably long lashes, widened with comprehension. She leaned toward him, and said in a sort of thrilled, conspiratorial tone, "You're Starborn?"

Piers's heart jumped. There was absolutely a propernoun ring to the way she said the word. Oh, careful, *careful*, scout, he thought. That might not mean what it sounds like. "Sounds like I shouldn't say yes to that," he said.

Color rose in her cheeks. "Sorry! I didn't mean anything. I just don't think any Starborn have ever come into the tavern before." She sat back in her chair and looked away.

To make her feel better, if he could, Piers Pushed some mild good humor toward her. "Well, it's new to me, for sure," he said. He was distracted by his racing thoughts, which he intercepted and discarded one after another. He almost asked her to tell him what she knew about the Starborn, but when he played that forward in his head it seemed likely to end with him being asked to confirm what she thought. Back to a safer topic. "Is it usually this crowded?"

"Oh, this is pretty quiet," she said. "We don't even have anybody staying over except for you."

"Essen said not as many people are traveling now."

"It's dangerous," she said. "Your people know that better than anybody."

Hm. That was even more interesting, and possibly not in a comfortable, academic way. "Do you think it's worse now?" Maybe he could find a round-about way to follow up on Essen's *before*.

With her voice softer than before, she said, "It's not just the Starborn now. There's been trouble in some villages, too." She looked at him with sympathy. "It must be so horrible for you. If you see Ettori on the road, *don't* let them know you're Starborn."

Truthful reassurance on that point was easy; he wouldn't be in a hurry to tell anyone he was Starborn, and Peggy had already warned him about Ettori. He had to just hope he'd recognize whoever or whatever Ettori was if he saw them. He looked around the room and said, "None of them here, right?"

"No. I haven't seen any for a few days." She looked into her own mug of telik; she seemed to be doing it to avoid looking at him. After a moment or two, she looked up, through her lashes, and said, "I won't tell them about you if they come here."

"I'm grateful for that," he said, quite sure that he was. Clearly better not to be Starborn around here, definition aside.

"You don't want people to know," Jelellin said.

Piers smiled. "Exactly what I was thinking." He set his empty mug to the side, and rested his arms on the table.

She was leaning forward again, and she slid her hand across the scarred wood surface and brushed the back of his hand. "I wouldn't have known," she said, "but it *is* kind of intriguing to make my bed available under the circumstances. I'd already decided I would."

Now the alarms went off. *Now* he knew why "available" had amused her. How the hell was he going to get out of this trap? "I didn't realize..." he started.

Jelellin let her hand rest against his and smiled again. "Well, I thought you might not. I was pretty sure you weren't asking, no matter what you said." He started trying to frame an apology for the misunderstanding, but she patted his arm. "I would—you are very handsome—but it's not what you're looking for. And your people keep to themselves, anyway, don't you?"

No clever reply or banter surfaced in his mind. Piers sat there, stunned, until he managed to summon up what he hoped passed for a smile.

"It's too bad Davyn's gone," she said. "He went looking for Starborn and here you are. Unless...did you come here because you sensed it? I've heard the Starborn can do things like that—know things without people saying."

The day just handed him that gift, without fuss or ceremony, like it was payment for everything that hadn't been easy. Whether Jelellin's comment was rumor or legend, it was the best lead he'd had. Any Empaths here would be descendants of *Valiant Star*, and "Starborn" was a reasonable enough moniker for everything they represented. That night, for the first time since leaving the ship, Piers drifted to sleep with an idea of what his next priority needed to be.

He was surprised by how well he slept. Not that he hadn't known he needed a solid night's sleep—that had been true since they landed, and even more so after Arthur—but he hadn't admitted that he hadn't felt safe at night since he'd arrived, until now. Even in Peggy's barn and in the relative comfort of other hospitality, he'd felt vulnerable. Here, he felt secure: there was the comfort of knowing other people were nearby, and there was no question that he had permission to be here. Best of all, there were no animals around, no sounds of an unmitigated natural night, and no confusing stars to be seen from this alien perspective. And no need to sleep with his pack as a pillow. So when he woke, the room was bright with morning light and he could hear the murmur of voices from the tavern below.

A musical tone reached Piers's brain through the implant rather than through his hearing. The ship was within range, and a message was waiting for him. It was a short clip from Jon, not much more than an acknowledgement of last night's notes, despite the reference to the Starborn, but it was comforting to think of *Redemption* circling up there. He wished he had someone to talk to about all this. The implant only worked between a scout and the ship, so without Arthur, those messages from home were the only reassurance he had that he wasn't truly alone.

After a quick wash in a tub of cold water, Piers hastily dressed in his one dry outfit: the clothes that had been inside his waterproof pack. No remedy for the shoes, though, and his dry socks didn't have a chance of staying that way. He ran a hand through his hair, bemused at how long it was getting. And wondered again if he needed to give in and learn to shave with a knife. There didn't seem to be any taboo about facial hair, thankfully, so he'd let it go, but it wasn't something he was used to. He and Jon had debated for a long time whether his pico-razor would be obviously alien tech, and they'd decided to take the safe route. With his few things stuffed back into his pack under the bed, he went downstairs and into the tavern.

Essen was there, glaring at a uniformed man who was half-braced on his hands, leaning forward as if he were about to leap over the counter between them. The man said something—Piers didn't hear what—and Essen erupted. He slammed a hand on the counter, and his voice grew louder and angrier as he barked, "Because Lord Wyth's bride was kidnapped, four horses were stolen, the stable is empty, and Davyn is away—that's why!"

The other man rocked back, and then bristled. "Doesn't change that you guaranteed that you'd have couriers. If these"—he shoved a pile of folded papers and envelopes toward Essen—"don't get there tomorrow, they'll blame me. And I'll bring that right to you! You're paid to handle this—so do it!" He pivoted and strutted out of the tavern.

Essen made a gesture toward the man's back, and Piers was pretty sure he knew what it meant. He hung back for a moment, in case Essen's temper was the indiscriminate kind. But the big man inhaled slowly and reached for the papers, and began tapping them into a neat stack, so Piers strolled over to him and greeted him casually. "Good morning."

Essen snorted. "Not today. You heard that? Aye, problems like to keep themselves company."

"Sounds like a bad situation."

That was all it took. Essen told him about the brawl, the missing horses, the discovery of the young woman's disappearance, and the decision to chase the thieves. "No word from our man Davyn," Essen went on. "Mira's worrying like only a mother can, on top of being sick, Tunny's still down, and Elanna is like a lost shadow, poor lass. Doesn't look good for the inn for the Great Houses to have trouble here, either. And now this." He pointed to the papers. "That lazy beetle you saw works for the Council and it's his job to deliver messages all over Merra. But he pays us on the side to get around doing it himself."

Piers's attention fractured: Great Houses, sickness, council, messages, Merra. Daniel Merra was the captain of the foundation ship. Piers wrested his mind back to the conversation. "Anything interesting?"

"Not likely." Essen rifled the stack without really looking. "The usual, mostly people in Ruatt. Probably some for the town guild or even the Council, and some are just people passing on news. The aldermen here have made it their work to make sure Trint is known as the crossroads for everything— you should hear them go on about it. So they put it out that they have a courier network, but it's really just the inn. Usually there's some traveler going where the news needs to go, and Davyn will make a trip if there's no one else."

"So he's the guaranteed courier?"

Essen grinned. "Aye, that's about it. That horse of his has wings, I'd swear it. Davyn can make it to Ruatt and back in the same daylight. But even if he's caught up with the thieves, he may not come straight back. He was planning to go find a Starborn healer, and maybe he's heard where to look."

"None around here?"

"Not often," Essen said. "There was a camp up by the

lake, but they never stay long. Mostly they stay in the hills. If they need something from civilization, they usually find their way to Ruatt."

That settles that, Piers thought. Go to Ruatt, seek out the Starborn. "So how far is it to Ruatt?" That one had been on the signpost, he thought.

"About eight hours riding at a good pace, for anyone but Davyn," Essen said.

Piers nodded as if he understood, but mentally slipped the answer into the ponder-later category. It was another of Jon's training games, to figure out what series of questions it would take to establish a common understanding. At the moment, he needed to figure out how to ask what he really wanted to know: how long will it take *me* to get there?

"I could take them," he said. "From what you said, it might be a better place for me anyway. I wouldn't be riding, but I can walk pretty fast." His luck was running strong, to be handed a destination and a cover story, connected with an airtight seal.

It didn't take them long to work out the details. Piers ate a cold breakfast while Essen disappeared into the inn. When he came back with the papers, now bound into a tidy packet with twine, he also gave Piers a bundle of food swaddled in cloth. He gave back Piers's four silver coins, too, plus two more, saying that was the usual deal for couriers. Then Essen told him how to get from the inn to the road to Ruatt, and told him to send word back if he heard anything about Davyn or the missing woman.

"You likely won't be there yet before dark," Essen said, as they walked together across the inn's little yard, "but it shouldn't be too long after. If you have to stop overnight, try to get off the road a bit—if you can keep going till you get there, that's better. Tell them at the Briar that you've come from Crossroads and they'll make sure you're comfortable for the night. Just be careful."

At the gate, Essen put out a hand to stop him. "Come to think of it, do you have a weapon, friend?"

Hoping Jon wasn't wrong about this, Piers just smiled, balled his fists and boxed the air.

"Ah, no, lad. If you meet someone you need to fight, you won't be trading punches. Wait here." He disappeared into the inn. A few moments later, he reappeared and handed him a knife in an old leather sheath. "Take this. It's the only decent blade I can give you, but it's Davyn's, and he's expecting us to keep it for him—so take good care of it, and make sure it gets home to us, if you don't meet up with him."

The man wouldn't make eye contact. Something was off. Bracing himself, Piers dropped his screens and Scanned, and a little pulse from the innkeeper surfaced: reluctance, and guilt. *He feels like he shouldn't give me the knife,* Piers thought. *He must really think I need it. Not the best encouragement.* "I'll give it to him when I see him," he said, and Pushed a little pretended confidence to Essen, without checking.

"Use it for your own safe-keeping, if you need to," Essen said. "May the stars guide you, friend."

Piers was caught off-guard again by that blessing. It just had to be a linguistic trace of history. "Thank you," he said. "For this, and for your hospitality. I'm glad I passed through here." He tucked the sheathed knife under his waistband and wished he had a belt. Then he stepped onto the road, resettled his pack on his shoulders, and headed east toward Ruatt.

The rain had left behind a lot of puddles, but despite everything, Piers felt more buoyant—and at one level he wondered if that were a sign of some unhealthy disregard for tragedy. Being rested and well-fed lifted his hopes, and he felt like he had found direction again. He recorded a short message for both his parents to reassure them, and a long message for Jon, Barston, and Kath about the inn. The ship should be in range soon, and he was really looking forward to hearing from home again. Among other things, he hoped that they'd send some observations from the other scouts. They had seen civilization only on this island and on the eastern coast of the mainland, so that's where they'd sent scouts. Then the ship had moved off to the other side of the world, to study the planet itself and to stay out of sight except for periodic orbital sweeps.

He'd had a few downlinks from the ship a couple days ago—including instructions from Barston, encouragement from Jon, and a few personal recordings from friends. There'd even been a message from Melody, his niece. It was a sign of Jon's paternal doting that he'd let his daughter use the official comms just to wish Piers a happy birthday and promise him a kiss when he came back. She could hardly pronounce the words, but even at three years old she had an insistent determination that Piers knew she'd inherited from his sister. He played it back a couple of times, enjoying the touch of home, until he felt the stirrings of homesickness and shut it down.

For the first few miles as he walked through the town, the road was paved. There was more traffic than he had expected, and he wondered what the population of this town was. Shops were opening, and he couldn't resist taking at least a little time to explore. He saw some trinkets that tempted him to buy souvenirs, but he knew he needed to be careful with his money, and then the practicality of carrying that stuff around for weeks or months helped him move past the impulse. Further temptation came when he saw a cobbler's shop and for a brief moment thought he might be able to replace his shoes, but then he discovered that they were all made-to-order and it took a few days. He did buy a leather belt, and it was worth every one of the precious coins he paid to not have the dagger held against his skin by the waistband of his pants any longer.

A few survival tools and upgrades seemed worth adding to his kit, so at another shop he bought a flint and steel set for starting fires, a length of rope to replace the one he'd left behind at the rapids, a small canteen that seemed better than the flask Peggy had given him, and a rough blanket that wasn't even a little bit damp. All this did start to clarify the value of the coins he had: six silvers were equivalent to one gold, and there were small, thin, irregular disks of hammered gold that were so abundant that he inferred they were worth a lot less than either of the actual coins.

Once he cleared the edge of the town, Piers stopped dawdling. It was already past noon, so as he walked he ate a filled pastry the innkeeper had packed for him. He had no real idea of how far he'd come, or more importantly, how far he had yet to go; his in-town curiosity probably meant another night outside. At least if the weather held, tonight he could try to study the stars a bit. Both moons might be visible tonight—they seemed to be on the same trajectory, and it was hard to match his perception with what he knew. The one that looked smaller was actually larger but much farther away. If he could focus on things like that, he might keep his mind busy with intellectual observations, too busy for the majesty and strangeness of the night sky to stagger him again.

From his first glimpse of the planet from the ship, he'd been in a near-constant state of exhilaration and wonder.

Kath had teased him relentlessly about his tendency to wax philosophical about the mission. When Barston had assigned him to the landing scout team, the others had been skeptical. They didn't think he knew, because somehow most Separates never really understood that with his degree of Empathy, not reading minds was not at all the same as not knowing what people were thinking. They didn't know how necessary his assignment was. They felt Barston had accepted him only because of his father; they felt he wasn't serious enough to be a scout. Too easily awed, with too much poetry in his approach. Kath, the only one who had openly expressed those reservations, was also the only one who actually understood. "You can't help it, can you?" she'd asked, one time when they were in the dark viewing room, taking a break from their studies to contemplate the silent, distant stars. "Everything always feels interconnected to you."

He'd been startled by the clarity of that insight, coming from her. She had as close to a purely practical mind as anyone he'd ever met. She'd wanted to understand, had tried with an impressive degree of suspension of disbelief to follow his attempts to describe the way it felt to him, and it was gratifying to find some of it had reached her. "Mom always said being Open is like trying to pick one conversation when everyone is talking at once."

"It must be overwhelming."

"Yes," he admitted, "it can be. You learn to shield yourself some." It was a strange conversation to be having. People just didn't talk about psi abilities. In fact, the Manifesters had it as a point of policy that they'd carried from Earth: psi was silent. Of course everyone knew the officers of both the foundation ships and the ark ships, including *Redemption*'s fifteen crew members, had been

Empaths, but by nature it was an internal, private sort of thing. Piers assumed people guessed about his ability, just because of his family history, but Kath was one of the few who officially knew.

He had stared out the viewport, trying not to feel Kath staring at him. He was Blocking as hard as he could, reinforcing his psi barriers to keep from picking up anything from her even accidentally. He'd had a crush on her since he was a kid, which had started just as she crossed that line into adulthood, when he was still a head shorter than her and waiting for his voice to change. The five years between them now didn't matter to him anymore, and he didn't want to know if they mattered to her.

"Maybe it makes you a better scout," she said. "You'll be open to understanding on a different level. I'll observe and record, you'll interpret and explain."

That had been very close to the way Jon had described it when he paired Piers with Kath: Kath's ability to focus on just the facts would give Piers the security to connect to people *despite* the facts. In a way, Piers had been assigned to the team just because he was the captain's son. It just was about genetics, not family status.

Building the New Foundation Project ships with time-drives had been a controversial decision. It meant the ships required psi energy, and a lot of it—not just for the jump but for guidance and navigation. Whatever the interpersonal hazards of it, the crews had to be able to experience and react simultaneously as a group to manage the ship. Byron Haldon, Piers's great-grandfather, had extraordinary psi ability and had been signed on as captain. He'd brought his wife, too, who was one of the few psi passengers. Shortly after they'd realized they wouldn't be alive for the landing, she'd gotten pregnant; with the psi gene from both parents, Piers's grandfather had a double dose. So he'd been a natural choice for the second-generation captain, which no one had ever expected to need. His own psi-gifted son had taken the helm from him in turn, becoming the third Captain Haldon.

"Dad always said that was why the bridge crew was supposed to lead the landing team. They thought the psis could keep things calm," Piers said.

"I guess it wouldn't have mattered too much if things went according to plan."

He'd given that some thought. "I don't know. The two crews knew each other back on Earth, but by the time we were supposed to get here, the foundation crew would have had twenty-five years of experience and aging. Even if everything was on plan, it would probably have been tense. Empaths would cut through a lot of possible misunderstandings."

Kath had thrown something at him, only half-playfully. "Yes, pity the poor Separates who live in this crazy state of isolation and ignorance. Just imagine!"

"I only meant—"

She'd kissed him then. It came out of nowhere and had completely thrown him. "I know what you meant," she said when she pulled away. "You meant that being able to understand each other's perspective from the inside would keep them from making assumptions. So what I want to know now is why *you've* been making assumptions about what *I'm* feeling." She laughed at his confusion. "You clench your jaw when you're Blocking. Idiot."

They'd had a pretty intense fling, which lasted right up to the moment when it had run straight into the wall that they both should have expected. When Piers dropped his screens, at first it was a miracle to them both. She wasn't psi, but just his remaining Open when they were close had a similar effect. He could feel her emotion when it was intense enough to shine through the wall that Separates lived behind, and her astonishment at being understood was a mutual aphrodisiac. A few months later, the imbalance started to bother her. When she pressed, he tried to verbalize his feelings, but it was never enough for her. It frustrated her that she couldn't really know what he felt, and then, by subtle degrees, she started wondering if he were telling her the truth and then suspecting that he wasn't. They ended it while there was still a chance of saving their friendship and working partnership.

And now here he was. Whether he deserved the assignment or not, it was his, and he was humbled to experience all these first-since-Earth moments. He thought of all the Manifesters who had been willing to die for this experience. When they slipped into their "induced long-term suspension" on Earth, they had no guarantee that they would ever be awakened, or that if they did wake they would find that every single one of the myriad unbearably precise plans had actually worked. His grandfather had talked about the heartbreak of his parents' realization that it hadn't all gone right. The Manifesters had grappled with the pain of it even while they set about making plans for future generations. So many people had wanted so much to have this experience, and in the end, it came down to Piers—a man who'd been born among the stars and had lived every minute of almost twenty-eight years with no real idea of what it was like to be anywhere else. He tried to record his observations with as much humility and sensitivity as he could, trying to convey the experience along with the information without too much artistic expression.

As he walked along the road, with boundless, cultivated

fields on either side and the warmth of the sun baking the mud underfoot, he still felt awed. As a newly activated Empath, when he'd Linked to the few remaining original passengers, the Manifesters, he'd felt their longing, and he realized now he hadn't really understood. Of course the lives they had left on Earth had for the most part not been agrarian ones, but they'd had the experience of sunlight and open air, and those feelings had been part of their identities. He'd dismissed it—walking past the vents on the main deck had meant feeling a breeze in his hair, and no "weather" was needed to feel hot or cold or wet or whatever. He'd thought the old Manifesters were just nostalgic.

But it was different, and now he knew. Had Arthur really been uninterested in that aspect of scouting? Maybe I should have Scanned him, Piers thought, then shoved the thought aside. Arthur's feelings, whatever they were, hadn't been something he'd wanted to share with Piers—and being an Empath wasn't license to pry. It was just that if he had Scanned, he might have really known Arthur in a way that mattered. That might have supported a friendship, no matter how different they were.

Piers almost wished it were raining. The regret, the loss, seemed distant in the sunshine, and it was hard to reconcile those once-removed feelings with the horror and guilt that dogged him. It didn't seem right to be basking in the sun and drinking in the blues and greens around him. He lowered his eyes and watched his feet scuff along the road instead. He heard something coming up behind him. A group of uniformed men on enormous horses were catching up fast. There was nothing but open ground on either side of the road; there was nowhere to duck out of sight. Running would be worse. Piers stepped to the side of the road, unsure whether he should keep walking or stand still until they passed him. It turned out to be moot, because they reined in beside him before he'd decided.

There were eight of them, riding in pairs. *Patrol,* maybe? The dark uniform was only mildly impressive, in his opinion, but the men were most definitely—and seriously—armed. He noted that with an exclamation point. Somehow the dagger he carried seemed reasonable and civilized, since knives were always useful one way or another. All of these men were wearing swords, which looked like they were only good for one thing. Thinking of Jelellin, he wondered if these were Ettori, and decided it didn't matter. They weren't friendly in any case. He was reluctant to drop his screens.

"Traveling alone?" The first rider didn't bother with a greeting, but as he moved his hand the sun glinted off his signet ring. Piers was probably supposed to recognize it.

"I am," he answered, ignoring the pang at the thought of Arthur. He tried to mimic Essen's vowels and inflection. "And you're the first people I've seen since I left Trint." He felt distinctly disadvantaged. Just standing beside a horse was intimidating enough; looking up at a man who was sitting on one made him feel bizarrely small.

"Be glad for that. Six men were murdered up ahead on this road two days ago—laid out for passersby to find them like some kind of warning."

Piers felt his heart drop—he hoped Davyn wasn't among the dead. Just in case his reaction raised suspicion, he Pushed a sense of relaxed interest toward them, but again felt no response. He started Screening again, gladly. There was enough going on without risking a headache. "That's terrible," he said. "Any idea how it happened?"

"Not yet," a second man said. "But you can be sure that when Lord Ettori learns who did it, there will be justice."

So *Lord* Ettori was an unwelcoming authority of some variety, who inspired fervent declarations from uniformed men. Piers really hoped this wasn't one of those expected-response situations. He asked, "Who were the victims?"

"Three villagers from the valley and three House men from Wyth."

Housemen from with? Is Davyn a houseman? As in Great Houses? "Terrible," he repeated. He had absolutely known that vocabulary would be the trick.

"It's a strange one," said a third man. "Don't often see attacks on House and village together."

Piers tried to look as if that had occurred to him, too, and added a few more questions to a growing mental list.

"Why are you on the road?" The man who asked was glaring at him as if he'd already given the wrong answer.

He was glad he had his excuse, but still felt like he was testing his luck. Piers said, "Taking some messages to Ruatt. I just left the Crossroads this morning." Might as well offer an alibi, before they felt like asking.

The two riders at the back were having a conversation of their own, and then one horse moved forward, apparently in response to a signal Piers hadn't detected. It stopped with its massive head within arm's length and flared its nostrils. The leather straps that were supposed to control it seemed very, very thin.

"You don't seem like a courier," the man holding those straps said.

"They didn't have anyone else to ask," Piers answered. "I was coming this way anyway."

The Ettori man turned in his saddle to say something to another rider. Piers couldn't hear what the suspicious man said, but the reply from the other included, "...not dressed like Starborn." Piers Pushed a little gratitude for

Peggy and her husband's wardrobe into the empty psychic space around him.

The rider in front evidently came to some conclusion of his own. "We passed a farmer with a cart a bit ago. If you wait, you can probably ride with him for a while. Safer for you both." Piers took it as a good sign that his personal safety was a consideration now.

"Stay on the good roads," the first man said, "And if you see anything strange, leave word at an inn. Safe journey, friend." They nudged the horses forward and trotted away.

A little shaken, and almost wanting to laugh, Piers sat at the edge of the field to wait for the farmer. *Anything strange* was a long and jumbled list from his perspective, and he'd clearly been just about to be put on their own. How significant was it that they'd decided he wasn't— quite—strange enough to worry them?

He pulled out his canteen and a piece of fruit. The water was welcome, even though it was tepid and canteen-flavored. The fruit was something like an apple. That was the thing with the terraforming. They'd sent the seed ships back in time to start the process, but evolution was unpredictable on a planet that had its own past and influences. The foundation ships had spliced in some true-Earth genes, and the ark ships were supposed to deliver the rest of the full kit, but the new home worlds were going to be different from Earth and different from each other, and an apple might not be exactly an apple.

He filed his notes for upload. This was part of what had enticed him to take the mission. He was loving the chance to explore, experiment, improvise—all the "doing" things that added up to a novel experience. It was easy to forget there was a purpose for this: the scouts were to give the planners a sense of all the native "-ologies"—techno, eco, socio, psych, and ideo—to inform decisions about how to introduce the ship's ready-made scientific advances. In any case, the intent of his particular mission certainly wasn't to contemplate how fruit had evolved.

What they could tell from the ship was that none of the technology they'd expected was present, and that there were patterns of land development that seemed to belong to Earth's ancient history. When they landed, there would be culture shock on both sides. Piers's father had decided they needed to send surreptitious scouts, not just an advance team. They didn't know what they would find, but it had been an easy guess that being a millennium late to a party might have made the hosts assume they weren't coming.

With close to three thousand people packed on the ship, and technical problems that only a few people knew about accruing, they couldn't put off the landing much longer.

There were people on *Redemption* who were pressuring the captain and the crew not to wait for the scouts' recommendations. With the planet now in visual range, discomforts that had hardly been noticed before became torments. The overcrowding, the noise, the maxed-out life support systems, even the limited menu were unbearable for a growing number of passengers. They demanded to land immediately and sort out the integration details after the fact. They didn't know the issues went deeper than that. Without psi energy from the outside, and a conduit to guide it, the engineers predicted the ship would be in freefall from the moment it entered the atmosphere, ripped loose from nav's control. From there, the models offered various disaster scenarios, none of which ended with three thousand passengers happily disembarking. Quite a few had alarming probabilities of complete annihilation.

"We'll give you as much time as we can," Barston had told him the night before the second set of teams left the ship. "For now they're listening to the captain when he says it will be better for everyone to know what we're going into. But I guarantee that once Dahlia Prethon's baby is born, that'll be it. One more baby will be the tipping point."

Piers was wondering if he should eat the core of the "apple" when the farmer's cart came into view. It was still a good distance away, so he watched the horse nodding toward him as the wagon bounced and rattled along behind it. When they were close enough that he could see the farmer's face, Piers stood up and waited at the side of the road until the horse slowed and stopped near him.

The farmer's greeting was cautious, and his gaze lingered on the pack. Then he looked more closely at Piers, taking in his not-too-clean clothes and the fruit still in his hand. It seemed to reassure him. "If you're done with that, the core would be a great treat for the horse," he said.

Show no fear, Piers told himself. Just a horse. Foller did it. He stepped closer to the horse, picturing Foller holding out a lump of sugar for Peggy's horse. Steeling himself, he tried to hold his hand perfectly still with the apple core balanced on his palm. The horse's breath was gentle, but seeing that very substantial jaw coming toward his hand made him flinch. He took an involuntary half-step back, but the horse stretched forward, and Piers felt an intense, undefined craving reach out to him. He could have fallen over from the surprise—he'd accidentally stopped Screening for a second again, and now he was feeling Empathic waves from the *horse*! Velvet lips brushed his palm and found the fruit.

Piers wanted nothing more than to sit down again. His

legs were weak. But the farmer was saying something, and he had to refocus. Still dazed, he realized the farmer had asked him where he was going. He mentioned Ruatt, and the man jerked his head toward the back of the cart. "Hop on, then, if you can spare a coin or two. I can take you as far as the crossroads and at least save you a few miles."

He tossed the pack over the low side of the cart and used the large wheel as a boost to swing himself over as well. The cart was empty, except for a few clumps of hay, an odd-looking long-handled tool, and the man's own gear. Piers fished a silver coin from his pocket and dropped it into the driver's hand. It was a relief when the man slipped it into his own pocket without comment.

Piers pushed his pack into the front corner of the cart, and leaned against it so that he was looking back at the road he'd walked. He dropped his screens, intentionally this time, but there was nothing at all, not from the horse, and not from the man. The psychic silence was disconcerting even though he was relieved. On the ship, there was always something. Did it mean that all the background emotional noise on the ship was caused by the small percentage of Empaths? Down here, other than what he'd started thinking of as "the shadow," the few psi touches he'd felt had all been from Separates—and now an animal—when their emotion flared up, suddenly, fleetingly strong enough for him to notice. Something to think about.

The man gave the reins a flick and the horse stepped forward with an equine huff.

Piers managed to keep up a light conversation, but succeeded only in learning that the man was a weaver by trade who had traveled to find seasonal work on a farm. He thought it had been about an hour when they reached a paved intersection. It seemed odd, since to his eyes it was the middle of nowhere; the fields around them were flat and empty. But the pavement was marked with pointers. Ruatt was due east.

"I'm on to Drisk," the driver said, pointing north, "so we'd best part ways here." He squinted at the sun. "You've got maybe three hours of light now. If you walk a good pace, in about an hour or so you'll come to a good place to spend the night. There's a copse some hundred yards back from the road, you'd have some cover. You'd have daylight left to get yourself comfortable, and you'll be well on your way in the morning."

The copse only counted as cover because there was nothing else to break the horizon in any direction. If there was a crop planted, it hadn't made much progress; only a thin layer of green covered the land on either side of the road, except for the stand of trees. Piers left footprints in the soft soil as he crossed.

Long shadows, including his own, stretched away from him. When he reached the edge of the trees, his shadow fell into the woods, between the straight trunks, seeming to thread through them as he moved. He didn't feel like counting the trees, but there were enough that he couldn't see through to the other side.

Piers dropped his head back and looked straight up the trunk of a tree. The dizziness he'd felt on the first day, when he'd first looked at the sky, now felt like weightlessness. The leaves spiraled against the sky, and he steadied himself with a hand on the rough bark. Looking forward was like looking into a new room. Dimmer, cooler, softer, and enclosed. A bird chattered at him and swooped to another tree.

They'd read about trees, just like they'd read about

meadows and rivers and oceans. Those descriptions had tugged at his imagination, even more than the images, but still he was unprepared. It wasn't just the physical presence of the trees, awe-striking as that was. There was a stirring, breathing feeling in the woods. Under his hand, he could feel the tree moving, a tiny sway in a breeze he himself couldn't feel.

He moved a few yards in, until he didn't have a clear view of the road, dropped his pack, and sat down with his back against a tree that was a bit larger than the others. If Kath were with him, maybe she could tell him what kind of trees these were, if they were Earth trees. And then she could give him more information than he wanted, and her voice would be comforting even when he stopped listening to her words, which she always knew and never seemed to mind. There wasn't much undergrowth, though there were tiny, blue flowers that floated on a carpet of dark-green leaves. He wondered about starting a fire with his new flint and steel. It would be reassuring, he thought. Of course it might also attract the attention of a nearby murderer that Lord Ettori has yet to bring to justice. Less reassuring. He decided against it, a little disappointed not to be able to test his practical-man-on-a-planet ability, but not sorry that he didn't have to gather wood.

At least he was armed—not that he expected he would be very effective in any sort of fight. Other than the usual scuffles and scraps as a kid, he hadn't had much experience beyond the basic self-defense moves he'd tried to learn. Having a weapon at hand did make him feel a little more secure. He pulled the dagger free from the belt and looked at it in the dappled light. The leather sheath was dark and worn, and stamped with stylized vines that twined in curves and swirls. Etched vines wrapped around the hilt and trailed onto the finely honed blade itself. Holding a well-used and well-maintained weapon made him wonder a bit about its owner. Was it a weapon or a tool for Davyn? Piers tried holding the dagger several different ways, but it felt awkward in his hand. He slipped it back in the sheath and put it down where he could reach it.

Redemption's orbit should bring the ship over his area sometime soon. He composed a long message for Kath while he ate, and couldn't stop himself from describing the splendor of late-day sunlight, and the silver-green shimmer of new leaves in the branches overhead. Birdsong echoed back from the other side of the woods, like a repeated theme in a symphony.

When the ship came in range and he heard the chime, he requested contact; she must have been online, maybe even waiting, because the connection was nearly instantaneous.

"Finding time for a little planetary poetry?" she asked, and it was a joy to hear her teasing.

He laughed. "My best ode yet. You'll love it. I wish you were here, Kath. The plants are incredible. I've seen some animals, and lots of birds, but the plants might actually be in charge down here, judging from the size of their contingent. The trees are magnificent, nothing like what I expected."

There was a pause, and he wished he could unsay it. He blathered on, "Sorry, Kath. I know how much you want to be seeing this." He hadn't thought before opening his mouth. He'd just been thinking that she'd be untethered if she could see the trees, and how nice it would be to see her enjoying it. "How is your recovery going?"

That wasn't a great topic, either; it probably wasn't what she wanted to talk about. He could picture her sitting there, still caged in the special frames they'd made for her leg and her arm. They'd been designing it for her when he left on the shuttle that should have been hers, too.

"Slow and painful," she said. "Just like I was promised. I can walk a bit now, though."

"That's good." He faltered; there would never be the right words. When he'd been there with her, it was easier, because he could Push his full sympathy to her and she'd know his intent, even if she couldn't decipher exactly all the things he didn't know how to convey in words.

"It's progress. Anyway, there's plenty to do up here— the reports the scout teams are sending has got everyone stirred up. I'm not bored."

Piers leaned back against the tree, and pictured the scouts' workroom. The big screens with the images of the planet would be filling up with annotations, and transcripts of the reports would be posted and marked up. The planners would be trying to piece it all together, and Jon would be trying to share just the right amount of it with the bridge crew—and the rest of the passengers. "What's the general mood?" he asked.

"They're going crazy. Your dad's having a time of it, trying to keep everybody calm. The scout team is being careful about what gets shared, so people are making up their own versions. People want to know the plan, and they don't like being told it's too soon. Barston is in rare form."

He could just imagine. Commander Barston's impatience was legendary, and when he was lit up he was like a caricature of himself, booming orders and demanding instant answers. It wouldn't be helping the situation, if people in general were feeling like they weren't getting the truth. Which, Piers thought, they aren't. Most people didn't know the ship actually *needed* Empaths, and no one wanted to risk the possibility of adding a flare-up of old-fashioned anti-psi hysteria to the mix by telling them. The official story was that the scouts were trying to identify a landing site, since there'd been no signal to guide them, and find help if they could. The captain had decided that *very* few people needed to know that they'd already picked a site and that Piers's mission was more critical than that. When the scout assignments had been announced, Barston and Jon had been circumspect about their rationale. Even in what should be secure communications, no one was going to mention the particular information Piers was looking for, or why he'd been assigned the most populated of the four target areas.

He was on the verge of asking more, wanting to hear about what was happening with his friends, his family, and everything. Life hadn't paused up there; it felt like the shuttle had swept him away practically mid-conversation, and he couldn't help wondering. Of course he wasn't supposed to be dwelling on that, and for the most part he was managing to set it aside better than he'd expected to, but human affections had a way of demanding due attention when given a chance.

Kath asked, "How are you doing, about Arthur?"

The implant's encoding made it a flat statement, but he knew the soft, careful way she would have said it. The subject of emotion wasn't always an easy one between them, now, ever since she'd concluded that there was no way for it to be an even exchange. And he struggled, always, with the way language could only ever be an approximation when describing feelings.

The subject of Arthur wasn't an easy one, either. She had told him too much about her stormy relationship with Arthur when Piers started training with her, when their own romance was as-yet unimagined. It had backfired when their problems surfaced—he'd made the mistake of bringing a comparison into an argument. Her explosion of rage had caught him off-guard, and unguarded, and the shock of it knocked him to his knees. That had been when she'd finally, truly realized how deeply connected to her emotions he was, and how asymmetrical it was.

"I can't talk about it," he told her, meaning it on at least three levels. What her feelings about it were, he wasn't strong enough to ask.

"Well," she said, choosing to leave it there. "Tell me about the trees."

After the sun went down, he tried to stay awake, thinking it'd be better to sit through this end of the night rather than waking up long before dawn. He worked on an official scout report for a while, and wished he had some tech with him, and thought wistfully of Arthur's communicator. Barston would have loaded the scouts up with tools and weapons and sensors, to "maximize the data and minimize the danger." Jon argued that too much tech would be a risk all by itself, and that it was more of a diplomatic mission than a scientific one. Better not to go in bristling. Their compromise had been the implant.

They assumed it would be easier for a psi to adjust to, since the experience of having external inputs arrive ready-made in the mind was familiar. And he didn't mind that part—he was used to sorting out what was authentic to himself and what came from someone else. The hard part was how formal and rigid it all seemed. There was an unnerving, detached feeling from having the voices in his head when there were no sensory inputs, just nerves being stimulated in a precise sequence that was delivered to his brain as *fait accompli*, an immutable recording—like perfectly preserved memories of sounds he'd never heard. He wished they could go beyond aural input, that there could be a fuller kind of sensory recording, but they hadn't solved that technical challenge yet. He could only send words. At least through the implant's flash memory he could hold unfinished thoughts in mental stasis and come back later to revise as much as he wanted.

Arthur's last-minute assignment to the landing scout team didn't leave enough time for the implant, and he'd carried the sole piece of observable ship-tech they'd had. It had been an unavoidable risk, Barston had insisted. That communicator could relay images and sounds, and Piers wished it hadn't been swallowed by the river. Maybe some-day someone would find it and wonder.

It was another uncomfortable night, and colder than he would have predicted. He put on both shirts, wrapped himself in his new blanket, and ended up emptying his pack so that he could take advantage of its waterproof lining against the damp ground. There must have been periods when he drifted off, because there were times when he wasn't aware of shivering. As soon as the dark started slipping away, he had bread and fruit for breakfast and repacked.

There were a few stars still shining through, dazzling against a blue-grey, slowly brightening sky. The air was fresh and cool, and there was a dawn breeze. He walked east into the day, on toward Ruatt.

8
GUIDE

Near Ruatt

ARISSA TRIED SHIFTING her weight in the saddle, but soon conceded that there was no way to be comfortable on the black mare. She waited while Davyn checked her horse's bridle and managed some sort of repair to the slashed reins with the rope that had bound her wrists. When he handed the reins up to her, he seemed composed and confident, but formal again. "You won't need to do much. The mare will follow Paladin. Just hold the reins, just in case."

He had no trouble getting up on his horse. She envied the way he swung into the saddle and dropped into the easy posture of a natural rider. There was no sign of the stiff and self-conscious stablehand in his elegant command of himself and the horse. The beautiful stallion seemed to glide into motion, and her horse rocked forward under her.

The mare's gait was especially jarring now. Arissa was developing a headache and her legs were burning. She was going to have to ask him to stop; she couldn't stand this.

Her face and hands hurt. She tried to force herself to think of other things. Why was a man with the fighting skills of a House Guard a stable hand at Trint, of all places? And what did he study by lamplight in a tavern? Of course someone who worked at a stable would be a good horse-man, but there was no way the stallion was a livery horse; he must be boarded there by someone wealthy. She directed her thoughts away from horses. What would happen in Ruatt? Where would they stay?

If she could find Gadrin, maybe all this would turn out to be a gift from the stars. She didn't have to go to Wyth now. Lord Wyth would think she was missing, and Gadrin would help her get to the Gathering. She glanced at the still-light sky, where the larger moon had already risen. Its waning crescent was pallid and low, and the small moon was starting over the horizon in pursuit. Three nights from now the nearer moon would be dark, and the small moon would be obscured behind it, and for one night, neither moon would shine.

The man riding beside her wasn't much help for dis-tracting her. He didn't seem to be lost in his thoughts, really, he just wasn't going to share them. Arissa stopped trying to think of anything to say, and tried above all not to think about how long she would have to keep riding. The rhythm of the horse's stride lulled her into a state of hazy awareness, almost dozing, more escape than sleep.

As the horses stepped onto the paved road, the change in the sound roused her. The longer rays of the late after-noon sun were just beginning to give a shimmering quality to the air, and not far ahead she could see buildings making a canyon of shadows. Her companion's horse was a little ahead of hers. "Is this Ruatt?" she asked.

He turned in his saddle and blinked into the sunlight.

When he spoke, his voice over the hoofbeats was deeper and richer than she'd noticed before. His accent, with those soft vowels and subtle lilt, made her think of music. "The edge of it," he said. "It would be best to be alert now." There was a trace of friendliness when he added, "You'll be out of the saddle in no more than half an hour, I promise."

"Then I might make it," she grumbled, and was surprised by his soft, sympathetic laugh. "I'm not joking."

"No, I didn't imagine you were. It's what I've been thinking for the last two hours."

That admission made her like him more. "Where are we going?"

"The Briar Inn. They know me, and they'll find room for us."

"I don't know what I want most—to eat, wash, or sleep."

He didn't respond right away, and when he did, he sounded drained. "For me...I just want to sit still and drink a cup of telik and forget about this day, at least for a while."

The Briar was a different sort of inn, that was clear. For one thing, there were women as well as men in the tavern, and there seemed to be more food and less ale involved—the evening meal had started. A fire blazed in the hearth at one end of the large room, and there was a small lamp on every table as well as all along the walls. Arissa stayed close behind Davyn as they went into a reception area to the right, up to a window that passed through to a brightly lit office.

The older woman who came to the window in answer to Davyn's greeting looked haggard, until she recognized Davyn and her face seemed to crack open as a smile hatched. "Davyn, you rogue. Didn't expect to see you again so soon! Atto said you were coming—he was all clatter and chatter all day. He'll be full of I-told-you-so when he sees you tomorrow!"

Davyn shifted, and put his right hand at the middle of Arissa's back, drawing her forward beside him. "Shea," he said, and Arissa saw the flush of color on his neck and ears, "My friend and I need your help and hospitality."

Shea looked at the two of them again and took in the evidence. "Stars, honey!" She bustled away from the window and opened a door a few paces away. "Come in here, come in."

Davyn steered her toward Shea, and stayed close beside her. His protective presence and the pressure of his hand on her back were more of a help than she would ordinarily admit. Shea took each of them by an arm and pulled them toward a bench against the wall.

When she sat down, Arissa felt the last of her composure wither. She tried to hold herself straight, but she couldn't keep a sob from bursting out. Davyn put his arm around her, and the tears she had managed to suppress all day also broke free. When he brought his other arm around and pulled her into the security of an embrace, the hilt of his sword was pressed against his ribs, cradled between them. For a moment she teetered between fright and comfort at the sight of it, and then she gave over and clung to him. Over her head, he murmured something to Shea, and she heard the woman leave the room.

Several times Arissa thought she was steady, only to surprise herself with another vehement sob. Even after she finally stopped, he held her. He smoothed her hair, but didn't try to make her talk. She started to drift toward sleep, and in that half-aware state she heard Shea come back in. In the warmth of his arms, she felt detached from the explanation Davyn gave for their arrival. With her head against his chest, she heard his muffled voice as a low rumble and paid no attention to the words.

Shea put a hand on Arissa's right shoulder, and said, "Honey, let's get you upstairs. A little clean-up and then you need to sleep. You both do."

Arissa woke to rain—the kind of steady, early summer rain that would make the moor a silvery, sodden mess. The patter of it against the window was soothing, and it took her a moment to remember she wasn't home at Aryn. When she moved to sit up, the aches and bruises from the day before brought reality back in a rush. She felt nauseated, and she was grateful for the warm comfort of the bedcovers even as a cold wave of doubt washed over her.

She'd made it to Ruatt. That much was good. It had been her plan all along to slip away from her escort here—it just hadn't happened the way she'd planned it. She had left the inn in Trint well before dawn, sure that she wouldn't be missed for hours. It had nearly broken her heart to leave Wisdom at the inn, but this kind of adventure wouldn't have been fair for the little pony. By the time she'd reached the edge of town, she'd realized that she'd rather be riding a pony. Sitting astride on the big mare was uncomfortable, and her legs had been aching from the unrelenting stretch. So when the terrain changed and the road-bed sank below banks that were edged with tumbled rocks and boulders, it had seemed like a granted wish. It would be easy to find a natural mounting block to help a small person get back on a tall horse. She had been intensely grateful to slide off the saddle, even though her legs shook as she landed. The horse, too, had seemed relieved to walk beside her, and the whole thing had started to feel like a good idea again.

That was why she hadn't been paying attention, and

hadn't heard the approaching horses until far too late to remount. The village thugs from the tavern had been entirely surprised to find her, but it had taken them less than a blink to decide that ransoming her to Wyth would be simple. She'd struggled, and it had been the man whose hand she bit who stuffed a gag into her mouth and yanked it into a tight knot. They'd lifted her back onto her horse—and tied her wrists to the pommel of the saddle.

She would have ended up at House Wyth, if Glenn and Davyn hadn't come to her rescue. But Glenn...It was too horrible. He had a wife who would wonder why he didn't return, and maybe she would never know the circumstances. Arissa started mentally composing a letter. The words repeated and rearranged themselves in her thoughts as she tried to find the right note of sincerity and compassion, but imagining Glenn's widow reading a note like that was paralyzing. Her thoughts slid to her own situation.

Gadrin had said she could get to House Dannpelier "discreetly" via Ruatt in a day, and she had today and tomorrow. Surely she could afford to rest today. Should she bother trying to find Gadrin? She had hoped to enlist him in helping her reach the Gathering. She could start by asking Shea about him; if he was a messenger for Dannpelier, he probably passed through inns frequently, and this one seemed to be popular. If Shea didn't know him, maybe she would at least know someone else who might.

And Davyn. He was part of this whole mess, and she owed him for bringing her to safety, but she needed to be careful. There had been scattered moments when he seemed to be warming to her, but there had been hours and hours of his self-contained silence. He had come to find her, and had escorted her here, which he needn't have done. Hoping for a reward from Lord Wyth for delivering his reluctant bride, maybe? Well, she wasn't about to go to Wyth now.

The rough-hewn wooden floor was worn smooth beside the bed, where over the years scores of people had taken the first step of the day. Arissa had a blurred recollection of getting undressed and putting on this antiquated nightdress. It was long enough to trip her, and the sleeves dangled inches past her fingertips, but it was fresh and clean. A skirt and blouse were draped over the foot of the bed this morning; also far too long, but her own clothes were gone. She folded over the waist of the skirt several times so that the hem grazed her ankles, and pushed the blouse's sleeves up past her elbows. There was no mirror in the room, which was a mercy. Her hands quickly verified that her hair was a tangled mess, and it would have to stay that way for now.

When she stepped into the tavern, now dim in the watery daylight that leaked in, it was empty except for the tall man across the room, standing with his back to her as he looked out a rain-streaked window to the street.

At her greeting, Davyn turned. He looked like she felt: disheveled and faintly ridiculous in clothes that didn't fit. For all that, he somehow managed dignity. When he reached her, he held out an upturned hand and said, formally, "Lady Arissa. Good morning."

She placed her hand lightly on his for a moment, then took a small step back and looked up at him. His dark hair was falling forward into his face, and she felt a rush of protective affection for him. "I think you should just call me Arissa, after all this."

He seemed to stand even straighter, and responded, "An honor, and I'd be pleased if you would call me Davyn." His reserve made her want to shake him; he'd carried her and held her, seen her filthy and scared and sobbing.

"Of course," she said brightly, to compensate. "Have you had breakfast?"

"Shea's in the kitchen making something now."

"She asked me last night if you were courting me." She hadn't meant to bring it up, not without some preamble, but it did break through to him—he flinched a little, started to say something and then turned away. "No reason to be embarrassed," she teased. "She said if she were younger—"

He spun back, so abruptly that she had to stop herself from recoiling. "Stop." There was force in the single syllable, an element of remonstrance, even though he didn't raise his voice. He must have seen her draw back, because he softened and said, still quietly but much more lightly, "It's one of her favorite themes. I come here regularly with messages, and she's been trying to match-make for the past couple of years."

Shea bustled in, carrying a tray. "Good! You're up and about. It was too soon for me to worry but I confess I was considering it. Come, both of you, and get some proper food in you. We'll call it breakfast, never mind the time. Davyn, I marvel that Boyd's clothes fit you at all, but you're handsome enough it doesn't rightly matter. Don't you think, Lady Arissa? And look at you...Janie's are every bit as long on you as Boyd's are short on Davyn. You look like a little waif. Well, your own poor rags will be clean for tomorrow if you want them." She set the tray on the edge of a table, and unloaded two large mugs, several bowls and heaping plates. "Sit, sit! I won't stand shy manners when I know you're hungry."

She kept up a stream of chatter while Arissa and Davyn sat down across from each other at the table. When she was satisfied that they were both enjoying the food, she gave Davyn a knowing look and said, "I'll leave you to talk."

Left with Davyn's taciturn company, Arissa felt abandoned. She looked toward the kitchen, trying to think of a reason to get up from the table and follow Shea.

"Arissa." Now his low voice was gentle and velvety again, almost a caress. When she met his gaze, the intensity in his deep grey eyes was unsettling, but his expression was mild. "The good news is, you've made it to Ruatt just as you intended—even if not the way you expected. So you can get back to your plan."

How did he know? Stars, had she said something last night about it? She tried to look grateful and relieved, and hoped he couldn't tell her heart was racing. If he knew about the Gathering, would he try to stop her?

"You can stay here for a few days, and we'll send word to Wyth. I'm sure Lord Wyth will send someone to escort you the rest of the way. You're safe now, and I need to be on my way back home."

The actual relief made her feel light—he didn't know about the Gathering and wasn't going to force her to Wyth. Then she registered on the rest. "You're leaving?" Why did her heart sink at the thought? It was better for her to be on her own, or with Gadrin, from here on.

He hesitated, and his eyes seemed to darken. "I need to find a healer," he said. "People I care about in Trint need medicine."

"Isn't there a healer in Trint?"

He sounded cautious, unsure of her reaction. "I want to find a Starborn healer."

Arissa studied his face. *People I care about*, he'd said. She thought that must be an understatement—she could see he was agonized with worry. It was almost all she could see in his face. It compressed his lips, it hollowed his cheeks, it collected on his brow, pooling above his dark eyebrows. He was a beautiful man, she realized, with those fine, sculpted features and the thick, dark hair, but everything else was second to his eyes. They were storm grey, with a ring of black at the edge of the iris, and at the moment, they were so intense and eloquent that it was hard to look away.

"I'm sorry you've lost time bringing me here," Arissa said.

It seemed to surprise him, but before he answered her, his attention shifted to something over her shoulder. She turned, and saw a teenaged boy coming toward them with a decided bounce in his step despite the water rolling off his oiled coat.

"Davyn!" The boy's voice practically sparkled with cheerfulness. "I knew you were coming. Gran didn't believe me."

Davyn stood and met him with a handshake and a hug too quick to be called an embrace. "You're soaked."

"Nah. It's stopping, anyway." The boy gave Arissa a quizzical look.

"Atto," Davyn said, gesturing toward her, "this is Lady Arissa, daughter of House Aryn."

The boy was flustered, hesitantly reaching out for a handshake and then deciding to bow instead, though he didn't really know how. If he weren't so earnest, she might have laughed. Instead, she held her hand out, palm down, in case he had the presence of mind to meet properly. Then again, why would he know to do that?

But he grinned and slipped his hand under hers, lifting it ever so slightly. Gadrin himself couldn't have done better. "Lady Arissa, I'm honored to meet you. I'm Atto Reed, and this is my gran's inn."

"Lady Arissa is on her way to House Wyth," Davyn explained.

"But you'll stay today, won't you?" Atto asked.

Davyn shook his head. "Sorry, Atto. I need to get back. Mira and Tunny are sick."

"What've they got?" Atto asked, and the way he said it implied that he knew, and dreaded, the answer.

But Davyn didn't answer directly. He just told Atto the same thing he'd told her, about wanting to find a Starborn healer. "A few months ago, someone mentioned seeing a camp somewhere around Soll," he said. "So before I go back, I'm going to try to find them. Hopefully they're still there."

"There's lots of Starborn in the valley," Atto said. "Even a group that stays put. I heard people talking about them. They actually settled down in one place."

Davyn's posture changed, a subtle adjustment of the set of his shoulders that registered his avid interest. "Do you know where?"

"I think somewhere north of House Dannpelier," Atto said. "The man who was talking about it was coming down the long road, and he said he wasn't sure if it was Dannpelier or Wyth that was generous enough to let them stay there."

Dannpelier and Wyth! Arissa's arms tingled with goose-flesh. She wished she had paid more attention to the specific geography of the Hills. She couldn't remember where Dannpelier was in relation to Wyth. Would she have to pass Wyth to get to Dannpelier? "What's the best way to Dannpelier from here? How far is it?" she asked.

Atto answered without much thought. "A day, maybe?" He and Davyn were still standing beside the breakfast table, and Atto's gaze was drifting to the thick slices of bread that she and Davyn hadn't eaten.

She invited him to join them, and he'd barely taken a seat before a piece of bread was in his hand.

Davyn smiled at her, and there was a little easing of the worry lines. "If I leave now, I can be in Soll by this evening," Davyn said, mostly to himself. "Then maybe a day to find the camp, at worst, and two hard days to get home."

Atto said, "But Soll's the wrong way, and you could spend a whole day looking for them and they might not even be there. Then would you end up going to the valley anyway?"

Davyn's eyes seemed to focus on something distant. Arissa supposed that four days, with that much concern boiling in his mind, sounded unthinkable. But the boy was right. "I know it's not my business," she said, "but Atto's making sense. A known harbor is better than a rough map, and all that." Besides, if you go toward Dannpelier, she added silently, you can take me there.

He looked at the window, flecked with raindrops. "The roads will be slow," he said. "Too bad that healer from Estend isn't still here."

"Davyn?" It was the softest tone she'd heard from the boy, all his energy packed down into a gentle prompt. "Is it the Sweep you're worried about?"

A chill started at the base of her neck and sped to her fingertips and her toes. Arissa had never been exposed to the Sweep, which was one of the good points of House Aryn's isolation. Sometimes it wasn't much more than a cold, but the outbreak a couple of years ago had been something different: people said the pain was beyond imagining, like every nerve was being pinched or scraped at the same time.

If the Sweep was on the move, and it was at the Crossroads Inn...She felt apprehension rising and locked a wail in her throat. In a strangled whimper, she said, "Is it...?"

Somehow Davyn seemed to force her to look into his eyes, and the fear subsided. "I think so," he said, with astonishing calm. "A respiratory version, so far. The Starborn have better medicine for it and might be able to stop it from spreading." His voice was gentle. "You never even saw Mira or Tunny, Arissa. You weren't exposed."

"What about you? What if you're carrying it?"

"I'm not." He said it with such certainty.

Atto leaned toward Davyn, and said, "You should go to the valley and get the healer. If it's a coughing Sweep instead of a screaming Sweep, then Tunny's probably already been there and back. But if they really have some way to stop it, you have to."

If someone forced the truth from her, Arissa would have to admit that Davyn was right. She was miserable. It wasn't raining right now, but the damp air was raw and burrowed right through her travel clothes. There was mud, every-where, and it was splattering up from the horses' hoofs onto her legs. And the horse. Why had she been in such a hurry to get back on the blasted horse?

Davyn hadn't been eager to let her come with him. He thought she should rest in Shea's care for a day or two, and then hire an escort to take her to House Wyth. Rest would have been wonderful, but the Full Dark was tomorrow, and if he left and took the mare with him, her best chance of getting to Dannpelier would leave with him. She'd been nearly desperate to persuade him to let her ride that far with him, and he had tried to talk her out of it. She wasn't sure she could trust him, and she didn't tell him why she wanted to go to Dannpelier, so he thought—well, she didn't really know what he thought. That she was just being stub-born and didn't want to stay in Ruatt, maybe. He'd painted a very clear portrait of what this ride would be like, as it turned out, and they'd been in a match of wills.

It had been Atto, again, who'd brought Davyn around. "It makes sense for her to ride with you," he said. "House Dannpelier's part way to House Wyth, so they could send an escort down to get her. You have to take Essen's mare with you anyway, so why not let her ride?"

Now she bit the inside of her cheek, to remind herself not to complain. It had only been an hour since they'd left the Briar Inn, saddlebags stuffed with everything Shea apparently thought a half-dozen people would need for a month-long ride. There was even a change of clothes in there. Shea had somehow managed to get the stains out of her travel clothes overnight, and had mended a tear, so she at least had clothes that fit today, and she would be able to put on something clean to appear at the Gathering with at least some of her dignity intact.

She wondered how far they had to go before they took a break. Davyn had made casual mention of arriving after sunset, but he didn't seem to be in a hurry. If they went faster, Arissa reasoned, they'd be able to take more breaks. They'd passed the last of the outskirts of Ruatt some time ago and were just about to enter the Wyth Valley. Going straight east, they would skim along the bottom of the valley, just a few miles north of the border. Somewhere up ahead, they would branch off and go north, but she had no idea if that was ten minutes or ten miles away.

Davyn was riding half a length ahead of her, which seemed to suit the mare. When Arissa tried to get the mare to pick up the pace to be even with Davyn, the mare just grunted. "Why won't you listen to me!" she snapped at the horse.

Davyn turned in the saddle to look back at her. "Me?"

"No," she said. "The horse. She won't go any faster." She kicked again, slamming both heels into the horse's sides, to no effect.

She didn't see what Davyn did, but his stallion paused, and the mare drew even. Davyn was almost smiling, the faintest quirk of his lips, like he had some private joke. "You're laughing at me," Arissa protested, although she supposed she probably did look at least a little ridiculous.

At that, he did laugh. "You're not the first person to have trouble getting Jewelbox to cooperate."

"I can't see why anyone even tries," she grumbled. "I don't know if I'll ever walk right again."

"Let me know when you need to stop," he said, magically getting his horse to move forward—and pulling hers along with him.

"Yes, please," she answered.

"Already?"

Arissa just nodded. Maybe she was supposed to be embarrassed, but she wasn't. She just desperately needed to change positions.

Davyn dismounted with his unthinking elegance and came around to her left side. As she tried to swing her right leg over the horse's rump, her left leg trembled. She was afraid she was going to tumble backward. Then his hands were there, secure on her waist, and he lifted her so easily she felt like she floated down to the ground. Her knees sagged a bit as she landed, but his hands held her steady. *Now* she was embarrassed.

They walked, leading the horses. She tried, for a few steps, to stay clear of the worst of the mud, but Davyn said, "When it dries, it'll knock right off your boots." She was sure her cheeks were blazing, but she didn't say anything. She just stopped trying to place her steps.

"I'm sorry," she said. "I know this slows us down, but my legs really hurt."

"The horses appreciate it, too," he said. "I doubt Jewel minds carrying you, but Paladin can use a break from me. He's been hauling me around a lot the past few days."

"He's a beautiful horse. Where did you get him?"

Davyn stiffened, and some of the grace left his fluid stride. She managed not to roll her eyes at him, but barely. "How did I offend you this time?" she asked.

He was taken aback by the challenge, and she saw color creeping up to his ears. Good. She waited for him to say something.

"I...Paladin belonged to my closest friend," Davyn said. His lilting accent was more pronounced when he spoke softly. "When my friend died, no one else could handle Paladin, so he was given to me. Three years ago." He'd guessed her question.

With a ripple of chagrin, Arissa said, "I didn't mean to imply he couldn't be yours. I just meant he seemed too magnificent to be a livery horse."

Davyn looked away. "Others have thought I'd stolen him—he's too good for the likes of me." It could have been a bitter comment, but he smiled a little. "Van, my friend, was the heir to the Holden estate. He was just an average horseman, but Lord Holden always wanted the best stable."

The pieces fell into place. "You're Tyndaran!" She had never heard of Holden, but he called it an "estate," which wasn't a Merran phrasing. "I was trying to place your accent."

They talked for a while about Tyndaris, and what it had been like for him to settle in Merra. He'd just felt like he needed to go north, he said, and Trint was the closest place big enough to have the kind of work he could do. He told her about living at the inn, and about the farm he'd grown up on, and the way horses had always fascinated him.

As he was describing the wonder he'd felt when he first saw Holden's stable of perfect horses, Paladin made a sound very like clearing his throat, and then puffed air at Davyn's ear. Davyn's laugh was open and warm, and he patted the horse's gleaming cheek. "Yes, you're the most perfect of all," he said. The stallion puffed again, and bumped his nose against Davyn's shoulder.

"I see you understand each other," she said.

"Van used to say it was my secret power. Not a very useful one, I'm afraid. Ready to ride again for a while?"

They reached an intersection and turned onto a road that led them northeast. The Lentava River raced beside the road, going the other way, gorged with the recent rain and struggling against its banks. The riverbed was level with them at first, but then gradually deepened until the road was well above the tumbling water. The last of the morning's clouds fled to the west, pushed by a spring breeze that was sweet with the fragrance of wet grass.

Davyn rode beside her now, his horse perfectly paced with hers. "I don't know much about House Aryn," he said. "I know it neighbors House Chant, and I know you're on the moors. There's a summer ford there, too, isn't there?"

So she told him, first about the moor itself, because that would always be what she missed most. She told him about walking out to meet her friends from House Chant, and riding Wisdom around the tarn while seabirds kited overhead and sheep bleated from over the ridge. She described Nevin, and Lyndi, and the dogs. By that point, she was nearly in tears.

He said, so softly she almost missed it, "You don't want to marry Lord Wyth, do you?"

"No," she said. "I wanted to stay at home, and fight for House Aryn. Nevin thinks the best way I can help is by marrying into a rich House, even though I've been more or less running things for the past couple of years. He's not a very good Head of House and he'll need help to be a good Lord Aryn—he just doesn't see that Lord Ettori is strangling the Houses."

Davyn had heard that before, apparently, and said he knew enough about Lord Ettori to imagine why she'd say that. Before long, Arissa found herself telling him all about Aryn's troubles.

"When everything is perfect, we barely have enough," she said. "I know it sounds ridiculous to complain. People think of the Great Houses and they think of the rich eastern ones like House Glay or Caladen, at least as it used to be. But Aryn isn't like them." She envied those Houses. As far as the riches went, it was all ancient wealth and all they had to do is keep it going. House Aryn had never been rich.

Arissa took a centering breath, and asked, "You know about the Council Tithe?" That was a wasted question; of course he did. Everyone in Merra paid something to the Tithe, either to their sponsoring House or through tax to an independent town like Trint. Probably a business like the Crossroads Inn had to pay promptly and reliably or Ettori would find a way to shut it down. Anything left after Prime House took its due for Council purposes was doled out to those who needed help, which was supposed to be the towns. The Great Houses were supposed to be the support system for others.

She went on, "Aryn might be the only House that gets support from the Tithe, and some years we get more back than we give. But lately, nothing is coming back." Since House Ettori had become Prime, after House Caladen fell, Kor—Lord Ettori—was using the treasury differently. "He's using the Tithe for his own purposes. But he's smart; he always dresses it up as something for the good of us all."

Davyn seemed to take time to process this. His thoughts pulled him away from her, and though his eyes were locked on the road ahead, his gaze was vague. Then he said, "Surely the other Houses won't tolerate it too much longer?"

She stared at him, but he didn't turn to her. She held her breath, and wavered, and then cast her lot. She told him about the Gathering.

After another hour or so of riding, they came to a spot where the road turned east and seemed to look forlornly at the remains of the bridge that had been washed out. Davyn reined in, and so of course the mare stopped, too. From where they sat, Arissa could see the water seethe and leap and crash against the stranded pylons.

"Well, that's not good," Davyn said. "We haven't passed anywhere to ford, either."

He spoke lightly, but from his frown she thought he must be concerned. He hopped down from Paladin and came over to help her as he had before. It was starting to feel natural to be in his arms.

"Do we have time to stop?" she asked. Without the bridge, one way or another they'd be taking a long way around. Davyn seemed to know, though, that there was only one answer to her question that wouldn't make her want to burst into tears.

They sat at the end of the missing bridge and ate winter apples without conversation, letting the sound of the river fill the space. The sun had gained confidence, and the light breeze danced through the grasses along the riverbank, perfectly balancing the sun's warmth. Time seemed suspended;

it was every childhood summer day and every remembered adventure all at once, mixed with irresistible optimism.

Then Davyn said, "This is definitely going to slow us down," and the moment splintered. "We won't get to Dannpelier tonight."

"Is there any other way to get to there?"

With an easy flick of the wrist, he tossed his apple core into the river, then smoothed a patch of half-dry dirt in front of him. With his forefinger, he sketched a map for her. The triangular Wyth valley spilled down from the highlands, cradled between the eastern high plains and a long ridge on the west that tapered down to Ruatt. He marked House Wyth near the head of the valley, the apex of the triangle. The direct road from Ruatt to Wyth stayed on the flat land west of the ridge and climbed only at the end to reach the House. The road they'd been on was a nearly straight line along the bottom edge of the valley, at first, but he marked where they had branched off to course beside the Lentava River, which flowed southwest from the plains. Across the river from where they stood, the road resumed its easterly route until it reached Dannpelier, halfway up along the eastern side of the valley.

There was another road that ran the full length of the valley, forming the east side of the triangle and continuing beyond. That long road connected Wyth and Dannpelier and eventually Estend to the southeast and Manssorand to the northwest. "We could go back to the split," he said, "and stay on the lower valley road. We'd meet up with the long road, here, and then can come up to Dannpelier from the southeast."

She knew he'd been casual about the scale of his finger-map, but even so it was obvious that they would spend the rest of their day traveling in the wrong direction.

"It'd be safe, though," he said. "And there would probably be an inn for the night. The trouble is, we'd be hard pressed to make Dannpelier tomorrow afternoon."

Arissa looked at the map, and her eye followed the wiggly line of the Lentava through the valley. "What if we leave the road and cut across?" She drew her finger to the spot where the straight line of the long road crossed the Lentava, somewhere between Dannpelier and Wyth. Assuming they could get on the long road there, they could approach Dannpelier from the northwest. It looked like it would be a much shorter route.

"Hm. It might not be easy to stay close to the river the whole way," Davyn said. "If we can, we might even find a place to ford before then and be able to cut across to the road."

Since he was beside her, she could only see his face in profile, but she suspected she wouldn't be able to read his expression anyway. He seemed to be scrutinizing something in the middle distance again, something only he could see.

"Or," he said, "we might not, and it might take even longer that way. We don't know what we'd come across."

"I don't love our choices," Arissa said.

"Still think a known harbor is better than a rough map?" He waved his hand over his sketch with a revealing flourish. He looked at her, then, and despite the rueful humor in his voice, his eyes shone.

"I might, if I knew which was which."

He swept away the map with the edge of his hand. "It's a gamble, but look at it this way: the closest thing to a known harbor is going south and probably arriving late. At least the rough map gives us a chance of getting there faster."

She stared at the road on the other side of the water,

wishing she could will the bridge back into being. If he was right about the distances—and he seemed confident—the risk of missing the Gathering was almost a certainty if they went south. No point in arriving safely if she missed the reason for going. Leaning forward, she drew an arrow in the dirt where the map had been, pointing north. When she looked over to tell him, he was grinning.

As they rode northeast along the river, deeper into the Wyth valley, Arissa tried to get Davyn to talk again, but they often had to ride single file. Her horse seemed content to let the stallion lead, but it meant that even when Davyn did speak, she couldn't hear him unless he remembered to look back at her. After the tenth attempt to start a conversation, and asking him to repeat himself for the tenth time, she gave up and rode in silence.

The valley was filled with the fresh greens of early summer, and the river chuckled as it tripped over shallows. As much as she loved Aryn's bleak and lonely scenery, with its barren swells of land and frequently brooding sky, this lush and leafy valley had its own enchantments.

The ground in the woods was bare and soft, covered with layers of decaying leaves and shaded by the dense canopy high above. They were able to ride among the trees most of the time; occasionally Davyn would follow a deer path off to the right, through the tangled undergrowth, and they would come out onto a meadowy verge beside the river. They would water the horses, and when they could, they'd ride along the bank for a while, enjoying the sun and the sparkling water.

On one of those interludes, they were riding side by side and she was surprised when he starting to sing softly, as if to himself. It was an old song, with a cheerful tune she knew even though the words he sang were unfamiliar. She hummed along, and he flashed a smile at her, and it wasn't the wry half-smile he usually gave her. He seemed to be genuinely enjoying the ride. The resonance in his low voice made her feel like the whole valley was in an expansive, exuberant mood.

This time, the verge ended abruptly where the river curved, and there was no break in the brush to let them pass back into the woods. Davyn dismounted and started to clear a path with his sword.

The sword wasn't a fine one; she'd listened to her brother talk about blades endlessly and saw that Davyn's wasn't much better than a practice weapon. Even so, that same relaxed self-command she'd seen in him as he rode was evident in the way he handled the sword, and he looked very dashing, even though he was just slicing through the brambles. The thought made her laugh. He heard her and paused, smiling quizzically at her.

"You look very heroic," she said, still laughing.

He flourished the sword and gave her an exaggerated bow, but she saw his shoulders stiffen. He turned back to hacking through the tangle with a sort of rigid determination. "Cutting weeds is about as heroic as I get." A few minutes later he came back to where his horse stood beside hers, and pulled himself up with no visible effort. In that quiet, formal tone she now recognized as his retreat, he said, "Back into the shade we go." He urged his horse forward and rode ahead of her back into the woods.

PART TWO

ORBIT

9

DEFLECTION

Wyth Valley

DAVYN SAT CLOSE enough to the fire that he could simply lean forward to add wood. He'd had to make do with fallen branches; a camp axe was one more thing he could consider keeping in his kit. How many contingencies could he prepare for without having Paladin loaded up like a packhorse every time he rode out? He also missed his dagger. Giving it to Elanna had been good for her confidence, but it would have been useful for peeling the wet bark from the wood.

He'd managed to get a decent blaze going, and it was putting out enough heat and light to keep the night at bay. The horses, unsaddled and unbridled, were tethered to a tree far enough from the fire to be relaxed but close enough that he could make out their shapes. For their sake, he had picked a spot on one of the grassy riverbank clearings for the campsite. He banked the fire near the edge of the woods, under the high boughs of the border trees.

While he kept watch and tended the campfire, Arissa

was supposed to be sleeping. Every few minutes she shifted into a new position and tried to knead her saddlebag into something more like a pillow, but it didn't seem to help. He had thought that she would be tired enough to sleep, and she had certainly seemed ready to escape from the day's emotion to a night's oblivion. When they'd stopped to make camp, such as it was, she'd been uplifted at first, and in high spirits had told him more than she meant to. Then she had crashed and was stifling yawns, so he told her to try to sleep. Apparently the discomforts outmatched her fatigue.

She gave up and came over to him, clutching her wrap around her. "It's just not going to happen," she said. "Aren't you tired?" When he shook his head, she sat down beside him and her face looked soft in the firelight. Neither of them spoke, until she murmured, "Thank you for doing all this."

He acknowledged her thanks, but didn't elaborate. She'd told him how much she resented being treated like she was helpless; in a burst of excessive candor she'd even declared with passionate disdain that she hated men who treated her like a child. It seemed wiser not to say that he was glad to help her because he couldn't stand the idea of her riding out alone. She wasn't a good rider, didn't know where she was going, and didn't seem to have much chance of fending for herself—none of which was surprising given her background, and none of which she wanted to admit.

"Do you do this a lot?" she asked.

"Not a lot, no. But I spent my whole childhood outside, and in the summers we did sleep out sometimes."

"Your friend?"

Davyn watched the flames wrap around from the underside of the logs, drawn toward the sky. It was hard to see the smoldering underneath from his angle, only the forge-like incandescence that anchored the fire. "Van was more like a brother. We met when I was seven."

That memory was still vivid. It was a warm and clear spring afternoon, one of the first good days for rambling, and Davyn was making his way home as indirectly as possible. The farmhouse stood at the edge of the nearest field, with a clear view up to the manor on the hill—but Davyn was beyond the farmhouse, in the newly planted fields that edged the western bank of the river. He was reluctant to go home, and without really meaning to, he'd wandered, following a network of deer tracks until they crossed back over the dirt road and he found himself much farther than he'd meant to go—almost past the bend in the river.

He was a week away from marking his seventh birthday, and while he was allowed to ramble on his own, there were boundaries, and he knew he'd be in trouble if his mother had started to wonder where he was. So he had just decided that he needed to hurry back when he heard hoofbeats coming fast toward him and a panicked shout.

"Get back! I can't stop him!" A large bay horse careened around the bend, skimming the ground with thunder under its hooves. Davyn froze in awe in the middle of the road, oblivious to the shouts from the boy yanking on the reins. As the horse neared, he willed it to stop so he could get closer—it was nothing like his father's field horses.

With a snort and a whicker, the horse checked just in front of him. It stamped irritably, tossed its mane, and then reached its head forward and snorted at him. "Thank you for stopping," he said, putting a hand up to the horse's face.

"You're welcome! He really did *not* want to stop!" Davyn looked up at the boy in surprise, and with a flash of disappointment understood that the horse hadn't granted his wish. The rider leaned back in the saddle and said, with a relieved grin, "You should have moved."

"I couldn't," he managed to get out. He recognized the emblem in the medallions on the bridle straps. "You're from Holden?"

Eight-year-old Van had evaded supervision and taken his father's horse from the stables. He introduced himself, and after a few minutes of basking in Davyn's admiration for the horse, he invited Davyn to come up to the manor the following morning to see the other horses in the stable. As easily as that, Van had changed his life. Visiting the horses soon turned into helping to care for them, and his mornings in the stables soon grew into whole days in Van's company. Sometime in the last days of that first summer, Lord Holden had offered to have him study with Van, too, and from that point forward they'd been inseparable.

"What happened?" Arissa's voice brought him back to the fire-lit moment.

"A riding accident. Almost four years ago." He hadn't meant to be brusque, but he had locked those memories away for good reason. Her hurt silence rebuked him. She'd only been trying to make a connection. More neutrally, he amended, "When he died, there was nothing left for me there."

She seemed to have another question ready on her tongue, but she swallowed it instead. She pulled her knees more tightly to her chest and stretched her wrap around her legs, too, so that she was bundled in the thin fabric. When he looked over at her, she didn't look up, but stared into the fire so intently that he suspected she was shutting him out.

Every once in a while, a lick of flame would escape, breaking free from the fire to launch into the cool air, only for its liberty to vanish in a blink. Davyn tossed a stick into the blaze. After a few seconds of sparks and spits, the fire resumed its steady crackling.

He had an impulse to apologize. She had a way of making her reactions seem like the only valid ones, and somehow brought him into her mercurial moods as if it would be disrespectful for him to have his own. Since her arrival at the inn, they had taken turns offending each other, yet she'd clung to him in her tears and been grateful for his help. He annoyed her, it was clear, but though she wouldn't admit it, she needed him. So he had fallen into this role as her protector or servant or whatever it was, and perhaps that explained it. She treated him like her House man, and then was confused when he didn't act the way she expected him to.

The fire was low when he saw her yawn again. "Arissa," he said, "tomorrow will be a long day. You really should try to sleep."

"It's too cold now," she said, not as a complaint but as an explanation.

Davyn retrieved his saddle bag and pulled out his extra shirt. It was sturdy fabric, much thicker than her delicate wrap. He draped it around her shoulders.

She thanked him, but made no move to go back to where she'd been trying to sleep. "Will you build up the fire again?"

He put a small piece of wood on the pile. It wouldn't do much except burn brighter for a little while, but it seemed to satisfy her. He didn't want to build a blaze that would take extra effort to put out in the morning. "Don't you want to lie down?" he asked.

Arissa shook her head, and the firelight rippled through her hair, gossamer gold. "I don't think I can sleep like that."

Davyn reached down to take her hand and pulled her

to her feet. He led her a few steps away, still close to the fire, and sat down where he could put his back against a fallen tree. He pulled her down beside him, and folded his arms across his chest. "Lean against me," he said. "See if you can sleep now."

At midday, Davyn and Arissa were leading the horses on a narrow path between the trees and the river. The mare was limping slightly, and even Paladin had lost some of the lightness in his step. It was easier walking than in the woods, but it was hot in the full sun, and both humans and horses drifted toward the shade from the trees when they could. Davyn had taken off his vest and draped it across the saddle while they walked. Arissa's wrap had been stuffed into a saddlebag early on, and she'd rolled up the sleeves of her tunic.

Long meadow grass reached up to Davyn's knees, and he felt like he was wading. The river, which was some twelve feet or so below them now, looked shallow enough to ford, but the bank was frustratingly steep on their side and vertical on the other, topped with brambles. At least they had been able to keep along the river, so they were still sure of their way.

"Can we stop?" Arissa called from behind him.

She was on the ground several yards back, tugging at her boot. The mare reached for the grass, unconcerned. Davyn walked back, letting out the length of Paladin's lead rope but holding on.

"Something in my boot," she said. "I may be sorry about this—I don't think I'm going to want to put it back on."

"Wait, before you get it off. Let's get into the shade, and we can rest for a bit. We've been making good time." He gave her a hand up, and she hobbled into the woods ahead of him. Once they were past the dense liminal underbrush, the forest floor was open again. The shade brought instant relief.

Davyn looped the horses' leads around a branch, though he trusted Paladin not to wander and Jewelbox not to stray from Paladin. He pulled his waterskin from the saddlebag and drank; the water taken from the river that morning was still cool.

Arissa sat on a rock and pulled her boot off. Some sand fell out when she tipped it. "How under the sun did that happen? Where was there sand?"

He laughed. "Probably it's been there since Ruatt, and you just noticed because of the walking. Any damage done?"

"I don't think so. Maybe the beginning of a blister. Do you think we—"

Davyn held his hand up to cut her off, but she heard it at the same time: horses somewhere ahead. There was an indistinct shout, and then clangor and more shouting. Davyn ran through the woods toward the noise, ducking under branches and weaving around the trees. Sooner than he would have guessed, he came to the woodline. He stopped with a jerk just before he would have burst through into a clearing, and crouched down into the brush just as an unseen woman shrieked.

Armed men were ransacking a scatter of fifteen or so square tents that looked like huts. Some of the attackers were some on horseback and charged and trampled without any clear direction. Others, on foot, were invading the tents and dragging people out.

Arissa caught up and knelt beside Davyn, fumbling to tie her boot. "Starborn," he whispered, though she had to know that already. They'd found the settled camp. "I think those are Ettori men."

The closest tent was fifty yards from the woods—a man and teenaged boy were forced out of the tent with a sword behind them. A sobbing woman came after them, with a younger boy at her heels. She cried out, "Please, no!"

The man with the sword whirled and struck her with his free arm, with such force that she spun as she was flung to the ground, halfway back into the hut. The child screamed, and the swordsman shoved the boy forward toward his father and brother. "Three!" the man yelled, answered by another, "Six more!"

Struggling but helpless, the Starborn man and his sons were prodded on, leaving the woman on the ground.

"We have to do something!" Arissa broke into the open just a step before Davyn, and ran toward the woman. Over her shoulder, she shouted, "Help the boys!"

His sword was already in his hand, but for an instant he was torn between following her and going after them. As he veered to follow the captives, a uniformed man intercepted him, sword raised. Davyn swung, and the two blades clashed, sending a shock through his wrist and elbow. He leapt back, and threw his body weight behind his next swing. He glimpsed the man's scowl and felt pulled by intense determination as his sword arced. The man parried, redirecting Davyn's momentum with a deft twist, and stepped to the side. Davyn tried to use the sweep of his arm to help him regain his balance as he closed toward his opponent again. His sword was met with a countering sweep. The man lifted his blade away, and Davyn staggered again, leaving his right side exposed. He felt an inexplicable spark of exhilaration and saw the flash of the other blade high in the air, swinging toward his neck, and he flung his own blade up to block it.

The shock in his arm was stronger this time, a splintering

pain that shot straight to his shoulder. He reeled and the ground lurched. He forced his eyes up and realized that he'd almost fallen against the Ettori man. Leering, the man grabbed Davyn's arm with a merciless grip and wrenched his right wrist. His sword tumbled loose and away. A powerful shove at his chest sent him straight backward; he landed with a shattering jolt that scattered his thoughts. The man loomed over him, sword poised and glinting. "Leave him!" he heard, just before a warm and terrible blackness swallowed him.

⌘

Arissa looked out the window from the room where Lord Wyth had jailed her and saw the cloudy midday sky arching over the forests, fields, lakes and streams. House Wyth was high on the ridge, and from here she could see that the valley was a collection of clearings stitched together by bands of trees. The river she and Davyn had been following glimmered in and out of the woods, but she couldn't see the road or the approach to the House. She looked down on the tops of trees that carpeted the hills. Somewhere out there was House Dannpelier, where she should have been last night. To have gone through everything the last few days had demanded only to miss the Gathering added to the injustice.

She walked the circuit of the room again. If the door weren't locked, she would have liked this room. Upholstered chairs were covered in soft colors and rich fabrics, and the warm wood walls were carved with trees and birds. The patterns flowed onto the deep rug on the floor, which had clearly been created for this room. House Wyth was certainly richer than House Aryn. She'd known it, but the proof was in every detail of this room.

The House had impressed her when she saw it, even though she'd been fighting tears and exhaustion at the time. After rattling northwest on the long road, they'd come to it sooner than she had expected this morning, and her first glimpse of the House up on its perch gave her a feeling of refuge. After the night shivering in a corner of the caged wagon with the Starborn men and boys, listening to the Ettori men as they drank and laughed around their campfire, she'd thought that no matter what Lord Wyth was like it would be a relief to be in his home. Now she resented that misleading sense of safe harbor.

After the Ettori men had realized who she was, they'd pretended that having her "travel" in the wagon was in consideration of her comfort. Miserable as the wagon had been, she wished they'd left her there. The captive Starborn had been kind—one man had even offered her his jacket, and he'd sat beside her through the night. He'd whispered to her that he'd heard good things about House Wyth and tried to reassure her, despite the fact that his situation was worse. When the Ettori man pulled her out of the cage at dawn, she promised the Starborn man she would do something for his family if she could.

The wagon had been left behind at the bottom of the hill as a contingent of men delivered her to Wyth. She'd ridden here on the same horse with the Ettori man who had captured her at the camp. He'd thought it was amusing when she shrank from contact that she couldn't avoid as he reached around her to hold the reins.

When they reached the courtyard of the House, a stable boy came from one direction at the same moment that a man came out of the imposing door and strode down the stone steps. She'd known immediately that it had to be him. Who but a House lord would have looked over the group with such possessive nonchalance? Then with an arrogant wave of the hand, he indicated that they should dismount and follow him in.

"Time to meet your husband, girl," the Ettori man whispered in her ear. "Best look happy to see him. He wouldn't want an unwilling bride." One of the other men pulled her off the horse and propelled her up the stairs. It started to rain.

"Found her tied up in a Starborn camp, Dan Owen," she heard one of the men tell Lord Wyth at the threshold of the House. *Owen.* What did it say about this marriage contract that no one had thought to tell her his name—and she had never asked? "There was a man with her. He tried to give us a hard time."

"Well?" Owen, lord of House Wyth, sounded impatient.

"Clint took him out. He wasn't a House man, but he wasn't Starborn, either."

Owen finally turned his attention to her, standing at his door, and looked her over with a flick of the eyes. His expression didn't change. Then, his first words to her: "What happened to my men?"

One of the Ettori men answered before she could. "We think her man killed them, sir. They were found dead on the road to Ruatt, along with three other men."

It was like someone had struck Owen so hard that a mask had come off. With the arrogance gone, what was left behind was a pained and bewildered expression. "You're sure?" When the man confirmed it, Owen had given Arissa a bitter, harsh look. "I doubt you're worth it."

And he'd had someone bring her here, and lock her in.

10

TREASURE

Ruatt

RAFFIC AT THE outskirts of Ruatt made it clear that it was a bigger place than Trint. As he neared the town itself, Piers started to feel like he should be wearing either body armor or a flashing light; neither horses nor riders seemed to be able to see him. There seemed to be choreography on the crowded streets that he didn't know, and several times he caused near-collisions because he dodged the wrong way.

Though there wasn't a wall or a gate, the road approached a break in a row of buildings that was clearly the main point of entry. Piers walked along a cobbled street where the top stories of the buildings pushed forward to peer into each other's upper windows. Two carriages could pass, but only with careful maneuvering, and when they did there was no good place for a pedestrian to be, as Piers discovered.

Both drivers shouted at him, but all he could do was hustle along in front of one until they were clear. He looked around for a way to be out of the traffic, and noticed a teenaged boy balancing on the raised threshold of an open doorway, watching him with a cocky grin.

"All right there, fielder?" the boy called.

Fielder. It didn't sound like it was intended as an insult, but it probably wasn't a compliment, either. "Seem to be," Piers answered, and made his way over. "I guess you can tell I'm not from here."

The grin broadened. "It shows. Always walk facing traffic—that way you can see them coming. Wherever you're from, you must have wider roads."

Not really, no. The corridors of *Redemption* weren't spacious. They just didn't need to accommodate horse-drawn carriages. "It's a different world," he said. "Can you tell me where to find the Briar Inn?"

"For a silver, I'll show you where it is," the boy said. Piers asked for directions, but the boy shook his head. "Easier if I show you." He took the silver coin Piers offered him, and then hopped out from the doorway. He pointed over his head, to a painted sign that read, in faded letters, "Briar Inn Lodging and Tavern."

The look on Piers's face must have been exactly what the boy was hoping for—his laughter was exuberant. Not unkind. Recovering, the boy held the coin out. "Here, fielder. You'll need this."

When his own surprised irritation passed, Piers laughed and took the coin back. "You should've asked for more," he said.

The boy grinned. "I'm Atto Reed," he said. "My grand-mother runs this place and she'd burn me for doing that to a guest."

Piers promised not to tell, and Atto led him inside. A woman who looked to be in her sixties met him with a wel-come that seemed genuine, introduced herself as Shea, and asked if he'd be staying the night, if he needed breakfast, if he had a horse, where he was from, what brought him to Ruatt. It went on, a stream of innocuous questions that kept him dancing on the fine line of the truth. When he handed her the packet of papers from Trint, she looked him over again with sharper interest. She was unsurprised when he explained that Essen had asked him to bring them, but in response to his next question she only said that Davyn had passed through and was fine.

When he checked, there was only the muted presence of non-psi emotions. Piers realized he'd started not to expect to find anything else, but it was odd. Less than two percent of the people on *Redemption* were psi, in the fourth generation from the original bridge crew. A higher percentage of the people on *Valiant Star* had been psi, and there should be thousands of Empaths among their descendants. Almost seven weeks in, and other than fleeting traces, so far only a *horse* had registered on Piers's psi sensitivity.

The upstairs room Shea gave him was larger than the one in the inn at Trint, but the furniture was just as astonishingly solid and handmade. In the bathroom down the hall, Piers had a shock from the mirror. As unkempt as he looked, it was a wonder she'd agreed to let him stay. The beard didn't help, and finding a razor moved up on his priority list. He soaked in a full tub of tepid water, pure luxury despite the coarse soap and the knowledge that he'd be clean only until he put his clothes back on.

He had finished the last of the rations from Trint last night, and the smell of food drew him down to the tavern. There were women, dressed in everything from practical trousers to dresses that hid their ankles, sitting with men who wore unstained clothes and had the relaxed posture of people that other people respected. (Obligatory Scan: nothing.) The tavern was airy, compared to the Crossroads, with natural light and open windows. He hesitated at the threshold, and was relieved when Atto saw him and came over.

"You're all right, fielder," the boy said. He deposited a bin of empty plates on a waiting cart.

"Why do you keep calling me that?"

"Aren't you? You act like you've never been in town before."

A healthy understatement, he thought. "I came from Trint. It's smaller, isn't it?"

That was all it took to prompt Atto to explain why Ruatt was better than Trint in nearly every regard, although he admitted that he'd never been to Trint. *Better* mostly meant it was bigger and there was more to do. Atto also liked being on the river and going down to the docks to see what was coming and going.

That was an opening Piers couldn't pass up. He invited Atto to eat a late lunch with him, and over one meal with a restless teenager he learned more than he had in the previous weeks of interactions with adults. Atto told him that before the war—over before he was born—more people traveled on the river; now it was mostly just timber from Dannpelier and even that was less than adults remembered. Piers wished he could ask about the war, but he still didn't see how he could cover for being unaware of something of that magnitude. So he asked just about anything else that came to mind.

For once, Piers was looking forward to reporting the plain facts to Barston and Jon.

"Have you been lots of places?" Atto asked him.

He was tempted to reveal too much; Atto's openness and enthusiasm made him want to respond in kind. He caught himself just in time. "I've been traveling as a mender, but I haven't covered much ground."

The boy was disappointed. "I was hoping you'd been to some of the Houses, or maybe even the south."

Piers couldn't think fast enough of a way to follow both of those shining leads, but remembered Essen's talk of Tyndaran telk. *Houses* would still wait. He teased, "Well, aren't we south of somewhere?"

"You know what I mean. Nobody ever talks about Tyndaris. It's like we're not supposed to even know it exists."

There were some tempting sociopolitical insights lurking in that, Piers was sure. "Why do you think that is?" He hoped he didn't sound like he was just trying to get a kid to do his own thinking rather than providing all the answers. His interest in Atto's perspective was genuine and he wanted the boy to know it.

Atto looked off to the side. "I dunno. I just wonder what it's like. I have a friend who's been there—actually he grew up there—but he won't really talk about it. I don't know why, though. He's been everywhere and he's really interested in different places."

In a voice that wouldn't carry, Atto added, "He's working on a book about Merra. He keeps it quiet, so people don't stop talking around him, but he travels all around and goes to taverns to hear things. He says he's trying to understand the politics of the Great Houses."

Now *that* would be a helpful connection. "Is your friend here in Ruatt?" Piers asked, oh-so-casually.

Shea bustled to the table with a kettle and interrupted to pour more telik for Piers. "Atto, don't be bothering the man with your chatter. You've got chores to do."

"I don't mind at all," Piers said, as blandly as he could manage. If there were an Empath paying attention anywhere nearby, there would be wild laughter. It was hard to imagine that even non-Empaths could miss how much not-minding he was feeling just now.

"I was just going to tell him about Davyn," Atto protested.

Hearing the name was like being pricked by a thousand micro-needles, making Piers's skin tingle and sharpening his senses. Even to him, his voice sounded almost crazed. "Davyn? From Trint?" The coincidence of it—the man he happened to be looking for also happened to be someone he *ought* to be looking for. Someone who could offer some critical intelligence that would help him get to the right authority quickly.

Atto's eyes widened. "Do you know—"

"Go on, get to it," Shea said. She slipped a hand under Atto's arm and pulled him to his feet, sending him off with a light push. Atto frowned as he left the table, and Piers suppressed his own disappointment. "He'd sit here and talk all day," Shea told him. "He always wants to hear about every place anyone has ever seen. It's kind of you to talk to him like that, but now you won't get a moment's peace from him. He pesters Davyn constantly."

"Essen's worried about Davyn," Piers said. "I'm glad to know he's all right. Did he say anything about a young woman? He rode out after someone he thought might be in trouble." Shea's earlier reticence about Davyn might have been partly concern for the girl, Piers thought. For all she knew, he could be trying to capture the girl himself.

Either he hit the right note, or Atto's acceptance of him was enough of an endorsement for Shea. With clear affection and admiration, she told him that Davyn had rescued the girl and brought her here to recover. She had been bruised but all right, but since she had no one to protect her, Davyn decided to escort her as she rode on to her destination. "She's Lord Wyth's bride, and she'd be a pretty target for other troubles, too. And Davyn can handle himself with House people; he says he's met too many of 'em to be impressed."

Piers managed—barely—to keep himself from diving headlong into that tangent, and just nodded to encourage her to continue.

"They just left this morning for Dannpelier," she said. "He said he'll come back this way and take the west-bound courier packet if there is one. Atto will be closer than his shadow when he gets back, wanting to hear all about it."

He's not the only one, Piers thought, and decided he'd just found a good reason to spend a couple of days in Ruatt.

Breakfast at the Briar Inn was even heartier than at the Crossroads Inn. Shea prepared eggs for him, which he had learned to like early on, and sausage, which he hadn't. Once again, a loaf of bread was sitting in the middle of his small table, apparently just for him. Other foods he wasn't sure of appeared in steady procession, and he gamely tried them all. Most were fine, and a few he really liked. There were also some in the other category, even one that caused a gag. He'd have to tell Kathleen, who had teased that the reason he'd be a good scout was because he'd eat anything. No one on *Redemption* had much experience with culinary variety.

Atto appeared, and helped himself to the bread, this time semi-apologetically explaining Gran's was his favorite. He offered to show Piers around Ruatt for two silvers, but didn't hold his negotiating position very firmly, fortunately. It didn't seem likely that Piers would be able to earn anything as a "mender" in town.

"Whatever needs to be fixed, there's someone around who does that exact kind of thing," Atto said through a mouthful of bread. "Menders just patch things up until the real repair gets done, don't you?" Piers was going to have to find some other way to get paid—or figure out how to get by without money.

The first step outside after being inside for any length of time had become a moment Piers relished. Fresh air. Weather. And variation. When the door opened that first time, the temperature could be a surprise or even a shock, so there was a momentary, repeatable sense of discovery. Atto looked up at the sky, and said, "Looks like rain is blowing in. Come on, if we hurry we can probably get there before the wind comes up."

Piers saw only white clouds being swept along by a breeze. There was moisture in the air, but the sun was shining. He didn't know where Atto was leading him, but the boy was sincere about hurrying so he picked up his pace. If he fell behind, he'd be out of luck entirely. After a few turns, curves, and dog-legged alleys, Piers lost his sense of direction. It reminded him a little of the times he and his friends had hidden from each other in the warren of empty crates, bins, and boxes in the cargo bay. A little kid had once gotten so turned around in there that they'd had to use a fly-by bot to find him. Who knew what help there'd be for a lost kid here?

He would have liked to take his time on the uneven cobblestones, but they rushed past shops and sights. Atto moved faster and faster, and by the time they stopped at a decaying dock, Piers was more winded than he cared to admit.

The detritus of abandoned commerce was all around, and the wooden dock certainly wasn't usable now. Rotten planks were disintegrating atop thick wooden posts that stuck up from water like monuments. A few yards out the water was flowing fast and boats were moving in each direction. Here, the water lapped at a border of pebbles and made no effort at all to sweep away the posts. In fact, this seemed to be some sort of forsaken side channel of the river.

Piers felt his stomach lurch.

Beside the dock, a small boat rested upside down. Atto rapped on it with his knuckles and said, "This is my rowboat."

His stomach sank.

The boy was beaming, and looking at him with bright, expectant brown eyes. There was no sign of any trepidation, and Piers wished he had paid more attention to the descriptions of the different kinds of boats. It just hadn't been a focus. The idea of it—needing a way to float in the middle of a deep body of water—had seemed too ludicrous. "You go out on the water by yourself?"

Atto rolled his eyes, and Piers supposed he deserved it. He sounded like a scold, and he couldn't explain what his incredulity actually represented. The boy just said, "Help me turn her over and I'll take you to see my cave, if you want."

Face the unknown, scout, he told himself. You're here to learn, not to be safe. Piers clenched both hands, swallowed against the rising nausea, and took a steadying breath. Feeling like he might have left his common sense at the breakfast table, he helped Atto flip the boat and position it on the pebbles. Is it called a beach when it's on a river? he thought. Mirroring Atto, he helped push until the front half floated and the boat seemed to cling to the land with a tenuous grip.

Atto grinned at him, said, "You push," and climbed into the boat and scrambled to the front. *Bow? Prow?* Piers wondered what the right word was, a distraction. Atto sat down on a cross-wise bench with his back to the river. The boat dipped and rocked, and Piers reached to grab the back before it floated free. He focused on detailed observation, and tried to ignore the water.

There was no way to disguise his discomfort or his ignorance, but that added to Atto's fun. The boy made a few teasing jokes, and laughed Piers through the process of launching the boat while simultaneously getting in it. Piers managed, with only a few splashes and a bruised shin, to get himself onto the other bench, facing Atto. It was a strange sensation, like he was losing his balance even though he was sitting down, but the bottom of the boat was relatively flat, so it probably was more stable than it felt. He ignored his queasy misgivings. "Now what?" he asked.

In answer, Atto picked up the oars at his feet, and slipped them into brackets on either side of the boat. He began to row, with his back to the direction he was going, out past the end of the old dock. It seemed like a patently bad idea, and Piers helpfully pointed out hazards until Atto finally told him to "damp it." Context is meaning, Piers thought, and kept the next warning to himself. Atto angled the boat before they left the calmer water, and rowed hard against the hastening current.

The riverbank was punctuated with docks, many not much larger than the one they'd left. Some rowboats and some even smaller boats bobbed in place, but there were also covered boats big enough for several people to walk around on, and even some long boats that had full-size huts on top. The people Piers saw were just as varied, going about whatever it was people did with boats docked on a river. Atto greeted some of them, but never broke the rhythm of his rowing.

A few minutes later, they reached a place where the river widened slightly. Wooden walkways and platforms that extended from the bank created a network of crowded docks. "This is the wharf," Atto said. "It's more interesting in the afternoons. Sometimes if you go at the right time, they'll pay you to go find whoever's waiting for whatever they brought. Or maybe to help them unload, if they're really in a hurry and it's nothing valuable. Once I got a gold because they didn't want anyone to know what they had." His eyes sparkled. "For a silver, I don't ask questions. For a gold, I don't answer them if anyone asks, either."

"So for free, will you answer: how much farther is this cave of yours?"

It was just on the other side of the wharf, as the river started to curve to the north. It wasn't what Piers thought of as a cave, but there was a spot where the river had carved away enough of the bank to leave a shelf of rock jutting some six feet out and four feet over the water. Atto rowed into the torpid water close to the bank, now, right up to a large tree growing low and almost horizontally in front of the hollow. He ducked to dodge the guarding tree, and Piers leaned back. Atto nosed the rowboat into the dark alcove. Two more strokes of the oars and the boat bumped against stone.

"Your eyes will adjust," Atto said. "Give it a minute." He tied the boat to a branch of the sideways tree.

Piers began to make out ledges in the stone, each several inches deep, that formed natural shelves. An assortment of objects was distributed on the higher shelves, unidentifiable shapes in mismatched sizes. Atto found a match and lit a candle stub, then dripped some wax onto the stone to hold it in place. "It's mostly stuff I've found," he said. "Some of it Davyn gave me. I brought him here, once, but you're the only other person who's been in here." Atto's forehead wrinkled at some uncomfortable thought.

Probably wondering why he trusts me, Piers thought, and had a moment of reflexive guilt before he remembered that he hadn't, in fact, tried to influence Atto's feelings. Atto had judged him trustworthy without a prompt. Guilty conscience for past transgressions. He shook it off.

"It's amazing," Piers said as he looked around. Most of it looked like junk, the kinds of odds and ends that only a kid would think to treasure.

Atto had a story for each piece in his collection, and each story revealed another fragment of information that Piers collected just as avidly. He learned that the river they were on started somewhere high in the hills to the east, and came through a watergap which Lord Ettori controlled even though it was on House Caladen's land. (Something Piers was evidently supposed to know about had happened to Caladen years ago and it was no more—but Atto had a metal button stamped with the defunct House's tree emblem.) Piers knew the eastern part of the island was higher elevation; Atto explained that the high plains were planted with telk to make syrup but that the telk grown in Tyndaris produced floodberries for medicine. (He had a delicate, curved knife no longer than his palm, which was a "berry knife" that had accidentally been shipped with a crop Atto had helped unload.) The lake at the northern end of the valley was called New Lake, and House Wyth reportedly had an ancient drawing of the valley showing no lake at all. (A smooth pebble with a vein of brilliant blue-green had come from New Lake, brought by a visitor to the inn who had eyes that same color.)

Amid the clutter of trinkets, some items had clearly been given pride of place. "What's your best find?" Piers asked.

"That's easy," Atto said. He took something down and handed it to Piers. "I don't know what it is, and nobody else does, either. I think it's really old."

It was a disk, slightly convex, that Piers could just hold

in one hand. As he took it, he felt light-headed. Oh, he absolutely recognized it. The rim was missing, the edges were somehow chipped, and the plexi-composite material was cloudy, but it was unmistakably part of a light fixture—the same kind used on the shuttle that had brought him to the planet. "Where—" He was hoarse. "Where did you find it?"

There was a sandbar a good distance upstream from the wharf, Atto explained, which was the farthest he had ever rowed. He'd been there for a second time on a day last summer to explore, a week or two after heavy rain, because one of the rivermen had said the sandbar had shifted in the high water and he'd found some coins. The curved edge of the half-buried disk had caught Atto's eye. He brought it back to show Davyn, the most well-traveled person he knew, but Davyn didn't know what it was, either. They'd even taken it to a glassmaker who had also never seen anything like it—glass that wouldn't break.

Piers managed to avoid the dreaded question of whether or not he'd ever seen such a thing by preemptively asking, "Have you gone back?"

"Twice. Haven't found anything else. It takes me hours and hours to get there and Gran starts smoking if I'm gone too long. It's not worth it because Mom'll burn me to ashes when I get home if I worry Gran."

Piers turned the disk over in his hands, and tried to breathe normally. Was it really a thousand years old? Manufactured on Earth and carried through time and space, only to be destroyed in some catastrophe, and no one knew. He handed it back to Atto, and tried to let it go, mentally, too. An ancient remnant of a long-gone ship didn't solve anything for him.

The candle stub burned down until it wasn't much more

than a pool of wax with a wick that was defying physics to remain vertical and lit. When the last flicker came,
the abrupt dimness was disorienting and the sound of the
water seemed louder. Reflections of the sunlight on the
river bounced into the alcove and Atto's pale shirt seemed
to shine. Atto sounded disappointed as he announced that
they should go back. He untied the boat and pushed off
from the stone riverbank with one oar. The rowboat spun
a quarter-turn around and drifted toward the current. Atto
used the oars to keep the boat under control but didn't
bother to row for momentum.

Piers watched the oar make dimpled eddies, and looked
into the deceptively calm, murky water. A fish dodged
around the boat near the surface, and darted toward the
faster channel, and then down, and he lost sight of it as it
faded into the silty depth.

"You've really *never* been in a boat before, have you,
fielder?" There was mischief lurking behind Atto's smile.

With a few strong pulls on the oars, Atto propelled the
boat into the river's full current, and the little boat picked
up speed. The breeze was maturing into an adversarial
wind that pushed them even faster downstream. Terror
spiked, but Piers clamped his jaw and grabbed the sides of
the boat. They arrived at the derelict dock in a small fraction of the time it had taken them to reach the cave. Piers's
legs shook as he stepped out of the boat.

As they pulled the boat out of the water, a gust of
wind shoved at them. "We're going to get caught in it,"
Atto said. As if it had been waiting for his signal, the rain
started. Well, his shoes would never be dry again. Piers
answered Atto's what-can-you-do shrug with a wry smile.

The skies cleared just as Piers was finishing his evening meal. He was grateful for something to eat that was almost familiar, although the wild fish, caught from the river that morning, had more flavor of its own than the tank-grown fish on *Redemption*. He ate his meal as slowly as he possibly could, mesmerized by the conversation around him. Even the small talk was interesting. It seemed every conversation began with some comment or complaint about the weather, just the way on the ship people would ask if you knew what mood the captain was in—a mindless social protocol rather than a meaningful topic. He knew he was the only listener who really wanted to hear the answer. He ought to record copious notes, but right now he didn't want to commit to the level of concentration needed for coherent observations.

A pair of men who looked to be in their late thirties or early forties ambled in as he was finishing his second mug of ale, and took the table beside his. Both were dressed in clothes that looked too fancy for physical work, and neither carried a weapon that he could see. The taller of the two acknowledged him with a shallow nod without interrupting his friend's conversation. "I've seen her," the other man said. "She's a pretty one. I say he's made a good match."

"But what good does it do to be tied to House Aryn? They've been living off the Tithe for as long as they've been there."

Piers registered on the name and wished he could ask them to speak up.

"You're not looking at it like they do," the first man said. "She's a House daughter, and that means their children could be granted Caladen—that's why he agreed to such high bride gift. She'd be a good match for him just for that, but she's beautiful as well. And Katia says she's not too lofty, and has a temper." The man chuckled. "Maybe our new Lord Wyth is getting more than he bargained for, but I think he needs a wife who will bring a little fire to it."

An arranged marriage?! Piers almost said it out loud. No wonder she tried to run. Atto hadn't mentioned it and obviously these two didn't think there was anything unusual about it. Incredible. That hadn't been part of *Valiant Star*'s mores.

"That may be, but he can't be happy about it. She's already cost him Glenn and his lieutenants."

The shorter man seemed to notice Piers's interest, and he lowered his voice as he replied. He was still audible, just: "Maybe. We don't know for sure what happened. For all we know, the man who was with her murdered the House men to try and get her. Though the girl told Dan Owen he was protecting her."

The other man said, "Not very well, if you believe what they are saying. Couldn't even fight off the Starborn."

"I doubt that's what he was doing. It was the Ettori guards who took him out. I'd wager Ettori's men were the ones who captured her in the first place, not the ones who rescued her. I just can't see the Starborn taking anybody captive, can you?"

"It'd be a new thing in the world, if they did. At any rate, she's safe enough now. Katia says Lord Wyth plans to marry her before the end of the summer, and he's keeping her with him."

"As soon as my girls hear about that, they'll start begging me to take them up to the Wyth summer fair to catch a glimpse. And with every breath I hope this Aryn girl isn't 'fashionable' or that'll be the end of my peace completely. Three daughters... You and Katia should hope for sons."

Their conversation turned toward their own lives then—wives, children, health—and Piers swallowed the last of his ale and tried to fit the pieces together. Was their talk of a protector a reference to Davyn? Now Piers recalled the Ettori patrol he'd encountered, talking about a fugitive murderer—hopefully not also a reference to Davyn. He wondered if Davyn was a killer, or if he had been killed, or both. He thought of the worn grip of the dagger he was supposed to give to the man if he found him.

This little round of eavesdropping had revealed some choices to make, too. It sounded like the Starborn might be near here somewhere. Could he afford to wait a bit longer in Ruatt, in hope of making that connection? Or should he take time to look for them? Or did he need to head straight for Ettori, who was clearly someone the ship would need to reckon with? Maybe he should follow the woman to House Wyth. She could tell him where she had seen the Starborn. And maybe Lord Wyth was influential enough to advocate for *Redemption*?

Threaded through all of his thoughts was the awareness of time passing with nothing to show for it. Commander Barston hadn't reached the boiling point of his impatience, yet, and Piers was still within the timeline of the plan, but he needed to make real progress soon. If he couldn't find the Empaths, then he needed to get some other allies of some kind. He needed to verify, too, that the landing site they'd picked was suitable for a safe landing but also remote enough to limit the human cost of disaster, if it went that way.

He filed a report for the ship, and sent along a ping to see if anyone was online. The chime that sounded through the implant came soon after, signaling that the ship was in range, but no one responded to the ping. There'd been no response yesterday to the report he'd filed the night before, either, despite passing along that first long conversation with Atto. Last night he'd uploaded the report about Atto's treasure cave and the ship light. He'd expected to hear that little falling tone this morning, when the ship passed over, letting him know that a reply was ready for download. Since there hadn't been one, Piers was really looking forward to a long discussion with Jon. Now he also wanted to consult about his next move. When he turned off the lamp beside his bed a few hours later without contact, watching the little flame sputter and then smother as the wick was cut off from the oxygen, it was with uneasy disappointment.

When he saw Atto the following morning, Piers asked how long it would take to get to House Wyth.

"Why?" Atto seemed to brighten at the unexpected question.

Piers wanted to kick himself. It was an obvious question in reply, and he'd blundered into it without having an appropriately vague answer ready. He didn't want to tell Atto what he'd overheard—didn't want to share the devastating speculation about Davyn. "I just wondered how long it should take for Davyn to get back if he went all the way," he said.

The universe was in a merciful mood: Atto didn't pursue his curiosity. "Probably a day or two," he said, "if you take the road up the hills on the west side. Or a bit longer if you go across the valley and up the long road, but they say that's easier. Not as steep."

"I wish I had a map," Piers said.

Atto laughed. "I thought menders never use maps."

"I guess some don't, but I wish I had one all the same."

"Stay here." Atto was gone for only a few minutes, and returned with a massive book. There was no title on the front cover, and Piers couldn't see the spine.

"Davyn gave it to me," Atto said. "His tutor wrote

it." He flipped to the center. Spread across the two pages was a map, in full color, with symbols for hills, forests, and plains. Inset on the left page was a small image of the whole island, with a box drawn around the northern part. With an effort to mask his distraction, Piers called to mind the images they'd taken from the ship and tried to compare them with what he was seeing now. The rivers and roads were familiar from the hours he and Kath had spent studying their destination. Now, at last, he could see the place names, and the geography of Merra solidified in his imagination.

They looked at the map together, and Atto seemed to enjoy being the tutor. He pointed out the Twelve Houses in Merra and explained that there were three more south of the border. That prompted the brief history lesson Piers had been craving about the Border War, some eight hundred years ago, when there had been a violent disagreement about which House was to be the Prime House. Things had been more or less stable until the last thirty years or so, when Merra lost one House to the south in a war and another House was tragically destroyed. So now Merra had just ten Great Houses.

The fifteen ancient Houses went as far back in history as anyone knew, Atto said. When Piers saw the names on the map, he came close to blurting out a truth he wasn't ready to share, not yet. It wasn't just Captain Merra's name that had been preserved. Several of the Houses were named after Merra's bridge crew.

The Manifesters, his great-grandfather included, had delighted in the coincidental nomenclature of the foundation bridge crew, and they'd joked about the names so often that it was history everyone memorized by accident. Of the fifteen members of that team, there had been four Daniels and a Dana. Like every child of *Redemption*, Piers could recite them in his sleep: Daniel Merra, Daniel Lin, Daniel Manssorand, Daniel Pennington, and Dana Janoval. From Atto's history lesson, it sounded like they'd tried to set up a distributed power structure, but somewhere along the line, the Houses had become the aristocracy. There was definitely irony in that, since the crew had been chosen in part because none of them had been power hungry.

Was it possible, Piers thought, that *Valiant Star*'s descendants had passed those Houses down through generations...and the bridge crew's genes with them?

Through the afternoon, Atto stayed close while they waited for Davyn, just as Shea had predicted. At first Piers was careful to structure his questions to hide his ignorance, but as the conversation went on it became harder and harder. Finally, he gave up and told Atto that he knew his questions were strange but he really didn't know anything at all about this part of the world, which Atto, grinning, said he'd already figured out. "Either that or Gran's paying you to see if I was listening when she told me all the stuff about the war and everything."

"No," Piers said, "I genuinely don't know. Where I grew up, it just wasn't something we had to learn."

"I wish I lived there, then. What'd you have to learn instead?"

Navigation systems, Earth history, genetics, basic engineering, historical and predictive linguistics, a little ecology... "Practical things, mainly."

"So that's why you're a mender?"

He needed to push this conversation in a different direction, or he was going to end up having to lie outright. "It gives me a reason to travel and talk to people."

"I want to travel," Atto said. "Maybe that can be my

work." He talked a bit about his ideas about work he might like, and it turned out to be another lesson. The integration planners would be fascinated. "Sometimes I think I'll be a pilot on the river," Atto said. "But most of them end up just going back and forth between a few places, and that would be boring. And anyway Lord Ettori wants to build a dam so he can flood the whole valley to grow telk for floodberries, so that'll ruin the river."

That raised some agricultural questions Piers wanted to ask, but he picked up the political thread instead. "Can he do that? Wouldn't Wyth or Dannpelier have something to say about it?"

"Gran says they can't because House Ettori isn't acting like Prime House should act. She says Kor is pushing them all down so he can be a king, more like how the Tyndaran Queen is. He's already pretty much acting like it."

A passing sense of rivalry caught Piers off-guard. The landing scouts in the southern part of the island shared that part of his mission, and a queen meant they'd have a clear authority to negotiate with. But that was beside the point. The ship had to land in Merra, because if he couldn't find the Empaths, he was going to have to try to balance the full force of the ship's Empaths on his own. He might never be Captain Haldon, but he was still key to bringing *Redemption* home.

11

TRUST

House Dannpelier

THE STUDY AT House Dannpelier was a showcase for its owner's collection of rare books. Since it was also where Tarken, Lord of House Dannpelier, chose to entertain his friends, there was also an impressive array of bottles, cruets, and decanters. In some ways, the room reminded Rane of the library at House Wyth, except that Dannpelier presented a certain degree of cozy clutter. It was a comfortable room, and the hours that he spent here with Tarken were generally happy.

This morning, Tarken had invited him to stay when the other House lords had left after the Gathering. The two of them sat in their accustomed places, reviewing the previous evening's discussion and this morning's dissolution. They were drinking telik, and the aroma was starting to soothe Rane.

"Maybe that's why people say it makes you live longer," he said. "You feel like nothing bad could possibly happen."

"Don't fool yourself," Tarken said. "We have all kinds

of opportunities for things to go wrong. Especially if your brother finds out."

Rane shook his head. "I'm sure he doesn't know, and he won't." When he'd left Wyth to call the Gathering at the western Houses, he had been followed—at his brother's behest, he assumed—but had slipped them in Trint. After that he had adopted a series of disguises and had taken indirect routes as a precaution. Owen would have to be more determined than that if he wanted to control Rane.

When Tarken had first made mention of a Gathering to Rane and his brother, Owen had emphatically refused to countenance the idea. He had even tried to forbid Rane from having anything to do with it. They had argued, the kind of argument that they were having more and more often as Owen felt the increasing weight of becoming Lord Wyth. Their father's illness had devastated both of them; he had come down with the disease shortly after their mother finally succumbed to it. Now he was seldom able to get out of his bed, and his mind was taking leave of his pain-racked body. Owen had started taking over the affairs of the House a year ago. With the healer telling them that their father's time was limited now, Owen's transformation into Head of House was almost complete. That was as it should be, but they had differing opinions about what the House needed. So Owen now set spies on Rane—denied, of course—to make sure that Rane wasn't undermining his new authority.

"If Owen knew," Rane said, "he would have stopped us. So that's one less worry, isn't it?"

From the four Houses where Rane had called the Gathering, only two lords had come. Lord Manssorand had needed some persuasion, but decided he couldn't ignore the threat on his own doorstep. The western Houses had been hard to predict; Rane had never met any of them, and he didn't know how much impact Lord Ettori was having there. Lord Janoval had refused so vehemently that Rane worried he might be an Ettori ally, though Tarken was sure he wasn't. Lord Chant had said no, but then he'd come—and Arissa of Aryn's *yes* had been erased. She was on her way to Wyth. Rane tried to shove aside his lingering disappointment, along with a buzzing worry that perhaps somehow his brother had heard about this Gathering and was neutralizing Aryn's involvement by sending for her early.

The other two House lords that came were ones Tarken had approached. Lady Andali, on the far north coast, had given a half-convincing *maybe* and hadn't shown up. The lords of Lin and Glay, though, had both been eager; since the Estend War, the two remaining Houses on the high plains had been wary allies. Both mistrusted the signs of ambition from Ettori. House Estend's greed had led to losses in both Houses, as well as a war that had torn Merra apart. Lin and Glay had better cause than most to remember the cost.

Instead of replying, Tarken got up and walked to the window. He stood there, holding his cup of scalding telik loosely and looking at the garden that was just starting to bud. Rane waited.

The Gathering had been an airing of grievances, and the six House lords had been eager to compare the ways that House Ettori was ruining them. The pattern was the same: he throttled their livelihood and then hit them with fines or fees. When their traditional resources started to dwindle, so they couldn't pay, House Ettori—as Prime House—would take over management.

Tarken had, at first, wanted the Gathering just to test

the air. Then Rane had learned, from Owen, that Ettori's Truolt River dam would be more significant and further upstream than most people knew—and work was progressing faster than anyone had realized. Instead of damming the river for minor irrigation, which was the justification Ettori had offered, he was going to dam it above the Caladen Pass, before the Valon fork. Ettori was now conscripting people, mostly Starborn, as laborers and the diversion tunnel was nearly done. The location for the cofferdams had been marked. When the dam was completed, the reservoir would drown part of the Great Forest, and Ettori would be able to flood the valleys—including Wyth—at will. It would make the valleys suitable for growing the kind of telk that flourished in Tyndaris. Merra would have no more need to trade with its southern neighbor.

The men at the Gathering understood; it was easy enough to see how all the pieces fit together. Ettori would have total control. It was harder to decide what to do about it.

They discussed and debated and agreed—in principle, at least—to coordinated defiance. They would each refuse to pay the Tithe at harvest, which would be provocation, but it was within their right as equals to revoke Prime status from House Ettori. It might be more symbolic than effective, unless there would be some benefit from drawing Ettori out. If Ettori retaliated, he would be showing his true intent.

House Wyth was the obvious first target of Ettori's wrath if it unfolded as they expected, though there was that small chance that because of Owen's general cooperation, Kor would spare them. He might attack another House first. It would be House Manssorand or perhaps even Dannpelier, because they were also close. If their neighbor Wyth didn't help them withstand Ettori's aggression, and one of them fell, it would mean the certain collapse of the plan and might start an implosion of the entire network of Houses.

Lord Lin had advocated for more overt insurgence. "If we're going to end up fighting, we should make it count," he said. "We should do something about the dam, even if it means starting a war in order to end Ettori."

That was going too far for Lord Chant, who made a passionate appeal for caution. House Chant didn't have the resources to defend itself, he argued, much less to instigate something—and neither did the other western Houses. Besides, Merra couldn't bear another war less than a generation after the Estend fiasco, when people were already strained and barely getting by. Chant insisted there had to be a nonviolent way to unseat House Ettori.

They'd cycled through the reasoning several times, and in the end, Chant's dissent divided them. After arguing for half the night, they'd each spent sleepless hours in their own agitated musing. This morning, they'd reconvened and when each of them had declared his position, it was clear this Gathering had resulted in little more than a general agreement to refuse the Tithe—and to meet again at midsummer Full Dark.

Rane's frustration and disappointment were slowly dissipating with each sip of telik.

At last, Tarken turned back to Rane. "I still have plenty of worries that start with your brother. I worry for you, when he hears you went behind his back. I worry for House Wyth if Owen pays the Tithe and the other lords feel he's on Kor's side. I worry for Wyth if you *don't* pay the Tithe and Owen faces Kor's accusations. And I worry for all of us, because we don't know which way Owen's going to go."

"I'll talk to him," Rane said. "He's got to understand."

"Rane, my friend, he may understand perfectly and still not agree."

He wasn't in a hurry to have that conversation with Owen, and Tarken was a willing accomplice in his procrastination. They filled the rest of the morning with a walk up to the highest part of the ridge behind Dannpelier, where the top of a stone outcropping provided a view of the Wyth Valley to the west, the Great Forest spreading to the east, and—on a clear day, when the trees were bare—the Caladen Gap to the north, where the river cut through the ridge. The treetops below them swayed and creaked in the wind that pushed from the northeast to follow the course of the river.

From here, it was easy to see the charred area on the distant hill, around the village that had been attacked a week ago. He and Owen had seen the smoke from the burning thatch that day, not long after Glenn had left to go to House Aryn. Whatever was happening over there, it was dire; Rane called in a servant and ordered the Guard and the horses made ready. In an unanswerable tone, Owen had countered it. Ettori had told the villagers to leave, he said. They were gone, and the empty village was being destroyed as part of the plan for the dam. When Rane said he was going to ride over just in case help was needed, Owen had told the grooms to lock the stable and not let Rane take a horse. It was as close to a physical fight as they'd come in years. Looking at the gap in the trees, now, he said to Tarken, "I still need to go over there and see for myself."

"I've heard there are some people blaming the Starborn camp by the river for that."

"The Starborn? They wouldn't attack anyone."

Tarken said, "I don't think they'd attack unprovoked, but who knows what they would do if they're fighting back? I know the villages have given that camp some trouble, and they might be tired of waiting for help from us—even though they're the ones who want no part of any House pledges."

Tarken sat on a slab of rock that made a natural bench, while Rane alternately paced across the bare stone and stood too close to the edge. Directly below him, there was a pile of boulders that had once been part of the ridge; he dared himself to see how close he could get to looking straight down to the base of the cliff-face. Every few minutes a stronger gust of wind would shove at him, not enough to threaten his balance, but enough to inspire the illusion that if he stepped off into the air he would fly.

When, with tolerant concern, Tarken asked him to step back from the edge, Rane settled beside him on the rock. "I need to get through to Owen," Rane said. "He's changed so much. I need to help him get free of Kor."

"You need to come to terms with the fact that it may be too late," Tarken said. "Kor doesn't let people go."

The wind intensified, and the two of them watched the low, racing clouds coming toward them, just skimming the forest. The diaphanous grey-white veil of it blurred the scene. A few moments later, cold moisture blew against their faces and then they were engulfed in the cloud itself. It wasn't quite rain and it wasn't quite fog, but a force of air bearing the essence of water that seemed to soak them without actually touching them.

It made the walk back to the House less pleasant. As they descended the ridge, the cloud became rain, and their drenched clothes trapped the cold water against their skin. When they reached the House, Rane saw no need to leave until after the rain stopped and both he and his clothes had dried by the fire for a while. So it was mid-afternoon before he ran out of excuses that let him avoid going home.

For most of the three-hour ride back to Wyth, Rane

tried to prepare for the conversation with Owen. He considered simply not bringing up the Gathering at all: if Owen didn't know, he couldn't interfere, at least not on purpose. The trouble was that not all of the House men would fight without Lord Wyth's command, even if they wanted to. There were some, like Glenn Treval, whose loyalty to their House lord would trump all other principles, even their loyalty to the House itself. So for Wyth's House men to stand firm, the acting Lord Wyth would have to do the same, which gave Rane no choice but to try to convince him. If he failed to bring Owen around, there was a risk that he would tell Kor, or take steps to ensure that there was no resistance from Wyth.

But he knew Owen. They had been close, before their parents' consecutive illnesses shattered their family and Owen started to be crushed by the pieces. Owen had once saved a terrified fox from his own dogs—but he'd done it at the last possible minute, when it was clear no other intervention would come. He'd always been reluctant to choose sides, but the two of them had always ended up in the same place. Rane just got there first.

Rane reached home at the usual time for the evening meal, if there were no guests, so he looked for his brother in the family dining room. The room was dark, with no sign that Owen had eaten and no sign that the staff had a meal ready. Uneasy, Rane went to the kitchen to ask about the lapse; the cook said Owen had told the staff he wasn't eating tonight, and only asked for something to be sent up to Oterin, the healer who was tending their father, if he asked. Rane checked the library and then the study, but both rooms were dark and no fires had been lit.

He eventually found Owen in the training room, stripped

to the waist and gleaming with sweat. From the doorway, Rane watched as Owen threw himself full-body at the tackling dummy, and kicked, punched, and wrestled with it until Rane wondered what kind of monster he thought he was punishing. When Owen backed off, panting, Rane started to speak, but his brother launched at the dummy again.

He watched Owen do this two more times before he crossed into the room and stood where Owen would see him when he paused.

"Not now!" Owen growled the word as he stalked over to a waiting tankard of water.

Never had he seen his brother this fierce. "What happened? Is it Father?"

That shoved Owen into a different emotion. "What? No, not that, not yet."

"Then what?"

Owen rubbed his face with a towel and stood rooted to the floor. It was terrible to watch him battle for self-control. "Glenn is dead," he said. He didn't look at Rane. "Along with the two House men he took with him to escort my future wife." Before Rane responded, he added, "And my betrothed is here, delivered not as a happy bride but as an angry woman rescued from a band of Starborn by a trio of Ettori's protectors."

The words didn't make sense. "The Starborn kidnapped her?"

"I don't know. It's hard to imagine. And I don't know why they would."

A sick feeling rose in Rane's throat. "Oh, stars, Owen— the village. The Starborn might be blaming Wyth," he said. "Getting back at us."

In that moment, his older brother seemed almost unrecognizable, victim of a sudden, evil metamorphosis. His eyes glittered and burned in his flushed face. Every muscle in his body was taut; his jaw was clenched as tight as his fists. "So it's my fault?"

Rane backed toward the doorway, keeping his eyes locked on his brother's. "No..." he said, not sure whether to be soothing or firm. He tried both. "No. We'll find out what happened." He escaped into the corridor, and all but ran until he had shut himself in his own chambers.

Rane knocked softly, eased the key in the lock, and cracked the door. "Dane Arissa? Are you all right?" There was no answer. "May I come in?" He heard movement and pushed the door open far enough to see inside.

She stepped out from behind the door, ready to bash him with a candlestick that was as thick as her wrist.

"Gadrin?" The carpet muffled the candlestick's fall.

He slipped into the room and pushed the door shut. "Please," he said, "Don't use that name." This was exactly why he needed to see her before Owen tried to introduce them. If Owen had heard her react like that, it wouldn't take him more than a minute to start puzzling out how they knew each other. He turned back to her, ready to tell her, and saw a bruised and bedraggled version of the woman he'd met at Aryn. "Oh, stars, Arissa. What happened?"

She wavered, and then took a few deep breaths. "Why are you here?" she asked in return.

It was his turn to steady himself. "Fair question. I'll explain. But listen, Owen doesn't know we've met. Please, please don't give me away. Promise me."

The rope burns on her wrists looked vicious. "Promise?" he repeated. Raw spots marred the corners of her mouth. She nodded, slowly. "Good. Before I get to that, are you all right?"

"I am," she said, chin raised. But then a quiver started to tug at her lips, and tears welled in her eyes. "No one else is."

He moved over to her, and put his hands on her shoulders, skipping the protocols and niceties of their new acquaintance. He ducked his head a bit so that he could make eye contact with her. "It's all right now," he said.

"It's not!" She broke away from him. "Davyn's dead, and it's my fault!" Then the tears broke through, and the sobbing started. He guided her to an upholstered chair, and knelt facing her.

Between the sobs and the self-recriminations, he wasn't entirely sure he understood everything that had happened. "Who is Davyn?" he asked.

Tears were still rolling down her cheeks, but she managed, "He was at the Crossroads Inn and rode out after me. After...after Glenn died, Davyn took me to Ruatt. Then he was bringing me to Dannpelier. We tried to help the Starborn and then he—they killed him. Ettori killed him." That set off another round of racking sobs that left Rane feeling vacuous and useless. He couldn't think of anything to say; he didn't know if giving her space would be kind or rude. She wept a while longer, then finally took a shuddering breath and said, "I don't know why I'm like this. I didn't even know him that well."

"He was with you through a trauma—makes sense there'd be a bond." One dark thought hovered in the corner of his mind, and he asked, "You told him about the Gathering?" He didn't think he sounded accusing, but fury sparked in her eyes through the last traces of the tears. He rushed to adjust the tone of the question by adding, "You must have trusted him." Really, it didn't matter now. The man wasn't going to tell anyone and the meeting was over.

"I was sorry you weren't at the Gathering," he said. "Did you convince Lord Chant to go in your place?" he asked.

"He went?" She clearly hadn't known, and it distracted her from her anger. "He was completely against it. We argued about it."

Rane thought he heard footsteps in the corridor, and sprang away to stand behind the door with his heart pounding. The footsteps passed by, and he let out his breath. He went back to her and offered her his palms. It was past time to go.

"Will I see you later?" she asked as he started to leave. "You haven't told me why you're here."

With her hands resting lightly on his, he tried to smile, but felt false. "Yes," he said, "we'll see each other." He faltered, but it was better to get through this reacquaintance without Owen standing there. He forced himself to say it: "I'm Owen's brother."

The blue eyes snapped wide open and she snatched her hands away. "No!"

"I'm afraid so. He—Wait, listen!" She retreated behind a chair, like she was afraid he'd attack. He needed to explain, or they'd never get past this moment. "Listen! That's why he can't know we've met! He doesn't know about the Gathering and he can't find out. If he knows I went to Aryn, he'll be suspicious."

"He's helping Ettori!"

"Sometimes, yes, but it's not like you think!" Rane hoped that was true. The echoes of Tarken's caution were hard to ignore, but he couldn't believe Owen would really be actively helping Kor.

"No? When they brought me here, they said they

were taking the Starborn men to Ettori. They said Wyth wouldn't interfere."

That, unfortunately, did sound plausible. Owen might stay on the sidelines even for this, to avoid having to take a stand that would make their powerful neighbor angry. "I don't know what that's about," he said. "I know some people are blaming the Starborn for something that happened. Ettori might be going after them."

Arissa's mouth skewed into a frown, and her eyes narrowed. Rane didn't want to notice that the way the expression distorted her features emphasized how sweet her face really was. The thought was out of place, and one he couldn't afford to entertain. He reiterated his belief in his brother, along with the plea not to give away the Gathering.

"Don't you think it's a huge risk, you going behind his back like that?" she asked. The note of challenge was mixed with scorn.

"Did you tell *your* brother about it?" The retort was out of his mouth before he knew that her comment had needled him. He went on before she could reply. "It is a huge risk, Arissa. All of it is a risk. But if we only did what was safe, there'd be no hope of stopping Ettori."

He left it at that, and his last glimpse before he shut the door behind him was of her frozen in the middle of the room, looking at him with doubt, but no scorn.

The small fire in the hearth was noisy but did nothing to make the room welcoming. The lamp on the table wasn't lit, even though the night was pressing against the windows, and Rane figured that if anyone glanced into Owen's study, the shadow that waited for him would scarcely be noticed.

Rane lounged in the only comfortable chair, an old-fashioned piece that hadn't been in style for a hundred years, despite periodic new cushions. His legs were stretched toward the fire, ankles crossed, and he rolled Owen's penknife through his fingers over and over. It had only been a couple of hours since he'd seen Owen in that murderous mood.

After he'd re-locked the door to Arissa's room, he'd gone back to his rooms and tried to reconstruct Arissa's experiences in sequence. None of the staff would tell him what had happened between Owen and his bride; they said they didn't know. Owen had been looking forward to Arissa's arrival, in the infuriatingly taciturn way of his, and Rane knew he'd been hoping to make a good start. Locking her in a room made no sense.

On one level, Rane thought Owen might have done Arissa a favor. He had never seen Owen in a real rage—his brother hardly even had the family temper. But Glenn had been their father's most trusted advisor, most reliable ally, and best advocate, and he was Owen's link to the fading Lord Wyth's experience and even judgment. To Rane, Glenn had been an avuncular friend; to Owen, he had been a lifeline. Arissa was probably better off at a distance for a while, and maybe Owen had thought so, too.

It was a time when a brother should be a friend, but Rane knew Owen wouldn't seek him out. So he waited in the dark room with his rambling thoughts and worries, prepared to wait all night if he had to.

The door had a creak that no one had ever managed to cure. When it was opened slowly, as it was now, the sound stretched into a complaint. Rane stood up and stepped closer to the fire so that he wouldn't seem to be hiding. Owen seemed unsurprised to find him there.

"If you're hoping for an apology—" Owen lit a lamp on the sideboard.

"I'm not," Rane said. "I just...I'm sorry about Glenn."

Owen held up both hands. "I'm not in the mood for a heart-to-heart, Rane. I just told Glenn's wife, and I didn't have answers for even the obvious questions. How do I live with that?" His face was drawn, and the shadows from the lamp deepened every crease.

When their mother had died, Owen had been slow to grieve. He'd held himself apart from the aftermath, dutifully doing whatever was needed, but doing it by rote. At the time, Rane had tried to crack the shield because he thought it would help. It hadn't. Owen had simply pulled away from Rane, too, and that had left them both isolated. Now, Rane let Owen's question linger until it dissipated on its own. He just stood in silence by the hearth, watching his brother pretend to adjust the lamp and idly flip the pages of a book lying beside it on the table.

After the quiet, Owen said, "I let him convince me that he should escort her, rather than going myself. He told me I ought to stay here, to be near Father. He knew I didn't really want to do it and he was giving me a way to avoid it."

Rane stayed still.

"They think the man they found with her at the Starborn camp was the one who killed them," Owen said. "They said he seemed to be protecting her. So what does that mean? Was she in love with him, and he tried to keep her from coming to me?"

It was hard to say nothing, knowing things he couldn't legitimately know.

"This match is the right thing to do, and I like the idea of marrying a daughter of a House. But if she is—or was—in love with someone else, she probably hates even the thought of me." Owen faced Rane. "What gives me the right to move people around like game pieces, sending

Glenn and the others on an errand I was too much of a social coward to do myself, and dragging a woman I haven't met away from her House and friends?"

Rane thought the eye-contact was the cue. With a fleeting qualm at the disingenuousness, he asked if Owen had talked to her about any of it yet. Owen confessed to avoiding her, and to locking her in their mother's sitting room.

"If her man killed Glenn and the others," Owen said, "how can I be sure it's safe to trust her? Until I know what happened, I want her accounted for."

"I understand," Rane said. "But Owen, you can keep an eye on her without keeping her caged. If you don't talk to her and set this all in order—soon—I don't know how she'll ever trust you. You've got to give her a chance."

Owen resumed the disinterested page flipping, and took his time. He kept his eyes on the book, and said, "I can't face her."

"Then write her a note, or let me take a message to her. Tell her you're sorry for the poor beginning and say you hope she'll join you for breakfast tomorrow so you can start over. You don't even have to explain it all now, just let her know you made a mistake. And unlock the door."

"Not going to be that easy," Owen said.

"Of course not," Rane answered. "But it'll be even harder if you don't even make that much of an effort."

12

INTENT

Ruatt

P IERS WATCHED ATTO drift toward the street door yet
again. As the late morning passed and Davyn failed
to appear, Atto's disappointment shifted to concern
and then agitated distress. His grandmother's worry was
more philosophically expressed; she said that since worrying about Davyn wouldn't have any effect on how well
he could take care of himself, it did nothing to help her,
either, and it wouldn't make him arrive any sooner. She
tried sending Atto home to his mother, but he insisted on
being at the inn so that he wouldn't miss Davyn's return.

"It'll break his heart if something has happened to
Davyn," Shea said to Piers as they watched Atto pace to the
tavern window. "Atto doesn't have many friends his own
age, and Davyn means the world to him." With a shake of
her head, she added, "He'll wear a hole through the floor."

By early afternoon, Shea was losing patience with Piers
as well as Atto, though she thought she was hiding it. She
pointed out that Piers was in Ruatt for the first time, and

could be seeing the sights. Then she suggested a few people who might have work for a mender. Finally, she sent Atto to the market and suggested that Piers would be doing her a tremendous favor to keep an eye on the boy.

He could take a hint.

When Atto protested that he wanted to stay at the inn in case Davyn came, Piers took Shea's side and wound up pleading with Atto to show him the market. Atto grumbled as they stepped into the street. "She doesn't even need anything."

"I know," Piers said, "but we were annoying her. And she's right about one thing—I don't really want to sit inside all day when I could be exploring Ruatt. There's a lot to see."

"That's it!" Atto clapped once and jigged a couple of steps. "You can see everything and we can still watch for Davyn. Come on!" He took off, sure that Piers would follow, and rushed along the cobbled streets. Piers thought they were moving away from the river, thankfully, but the haphazard streets were just as disorienting as they'd been yesterday.

Just steps behind Atto, Piers rounded the corner of an imposing stone building, and turned his ankle as he stumbled to an unexpected stop. Atto started to scale the wall, using the uneven stones for purchase. He balanced on his toes on inch-wide ledges and gripped the corners of rough stones with fingers curved like talons. He grinned down over his shoulder at Piers. "You can see for miles up at the top. We'll see Davyn before he even gets to the edge of town, no matter which way he's coming."

Piers bit back the questions that would annoy Atto—after all, whether or not he was breaking a law, regulation, or courtesy against climbing up buildings, Atto had done it before and had no hesitation now. No point in asking, *Are you sure this is a good idea?* The kid was sure, even though it really, really didn't seem like a good idea to Piers. He tipped his head back to look up the wall. Several stories up, the edge of the roof was stark against the overcast sky. "I'm not going to climb that," he said.

"It's easy." Sure-footed Atto was already a full body-length above Piers's head. "I've been doing this since I was little."

That still didn't make it a good idea. "Is there some other way up there?"

"Never looked! I can climb anything."

It didn't take Atto long to reach the top. He took two last steps against the wall, hoisted himself and swung his legs onto the roof. By the time he leaned over the edge, grinning, Piers was imagining Commander Barston's reaction to an injury report.

"You coming?" Atto called.

"You can tell me what you see," Piers answered. He was a bit embarrassed to be standing there, safe and steady on the ground. When he'd been Atto's age—a shining decade ago and then some—he'd have been the first one to take the dare.

Atto was disappointed twice over. He didn't get to show off the panoramic view of the town, and Davyn was not approaching Ruatt on cue. Atto stayed on the roof just long enough to scan the horizon on all sides, then clambered back down the wall the way he'd gone up. He dropped the last few feet.

"Tallest building in Ruatt," he told Piers. "I wish you could climb. It's a great view."

"I can climb. I'm apparently just more wary of falling than you are. So. Which way to the market?"

The market was a marvel. Piers was glad Shea had

pushed him out the door. Among the profusion of consumables, there was a staggering variety of goods and services on offer. Several times, he lingered so long in fascination that Atto had to backtrack to retrieve him. He tried to pay attention to the transactions going on around him, to get an idea of how far his dwindling handful of coins could take him. Four silvers in Trint had gotten him two meals and a good night's sleep, but Ruatt was more expensive. He handed over one of his few silver coins for a primitive-looking razor, and he didn't care if he was overpaying. He dropped it in the pouch Shea had loaned him, which he was wearing on his belt, satisfied with the clink against the remaining coins.

On the ship, a barter system had sprung up only a few years into the voyage—not for things the fabricators could make, but for people's time and talents. Here, of course, nothing was free, and nothing was fabbed. Everything—everything—had to be created or prepared by human hands. He wondered if Atto would be just as amazed to see a machine produce goods like these on demand.

The debate about how to introduce the ship's tech had been a hot one, and unresolved when he left. Hide it, control it, share it, or destroy it. Every option had consequences they'd all have to live with. Piers was glad it wasn't his decision.

Atto tugged on his arm. "Stars, fielder, spark it up and let's get this over with. I don't want to spend all day here."

Atto guided Piers to a particular vendor at the outside corner of the market's central square, where he started bargaining with the merchant for some apples. Standing beside him, in the shade from the cart's faded awning, Piers could look back into the heart of the market. It was crowded, and there was a festival atmosphere. In the warm sun of a bright spring day, with a gentle breeze carrying away yesterday's rain, people were smiling and intent on enjoying themselves.

Nearby, a young woman was perched on a stool beside a cart, weaving together long strips of some supple material. Sunlight splashed over her almost artistically, brightening her hair with copper-colored gleams as she bent over her work. She seemed to glow, Piers thought, and on a whim, Reached to her. Of course there was no response, but again he felt a feather-touch of something, not from her, something that made a knot tighten in his gut. He Blocked, but kept watching her.

Three men in dark uniforms were closing in on her. They started calling out, and from where Piers sat it looked like they were stalking her. She didn't react to them, but her movements became more studied, more mechanical. Piers Pushed his interest to her, just to say *I'm keeping an eye on this, you aren't alone.* Maybe some would get through.

One of the men was a step ahead of the other two, and getting close enough for mischief. Whatever he said made her hunch forward and turn away on her stool, trying to ignore him. Rude laughter carried clearly.

"I'll be right back," Piers told Atto, and didn't wait for acknowledgement. He hurried as he cut through the crowd, but slowed to a normal pace as he approached her cart from the side.

The men paused in their game for a second to look at him, but then the closest man reached out to the woman to touch her.

"Hello," Piers said, intentionally loudly, but with an upbeat inflection. The woman looked up, worried about what new torment he represented. He smiled. "I'm wondering how much these are?" He looked now at the wares on her cart, which turned out to be reed mats and baskets. He picked up the closest basket.

She stood up, quickly, and came to stand beside him with her back to the trio. "That one's four silver twenty." In a cutting whisper, she added, "What are you doing? They're *Ettori*."

With a confidence that Piers thought Atto would approve, he started to haggle. It was absurd, because he had no intention of buying the basket and even more because he was just randomly making counteroffers. After a few minutes, the Ettori men retreated, though Piers was aware they didn't go far.

Sure that they were out of earshot, Piers said, "It looked like they were bothering you."

"You shouldn't have gotten involved. They'll make you pay for interfering." Her voice jittered.

"No chance they thought I just happened to want a basket?" He was trying to downplay his confusion.

"Definitely not, especially when you're haggling over chippers," she said.

"I don't have much money." Piers figured he'd keep the real explanation to himself. *Chippers* must be the hammered gold bits. He was still holding the basket in question. Looked like it might be watertight despite being woven, and he wondered how she did that. His mind did that: it slipped off to chase some tangential idea when the main topic was uncomfortable. "I don't really need the basket anyway."

"You're mad," she said. "It was kind of you, but I don't know what they'll do to you." She looked at him, maybe actually *seeing* him for the first time. "Don't you know how foolish it is to bring attention to yourself?"

Starting to get an inkling, he thought. He supposed this

might be exactly why the people at the Crossroads Inn had been so adamant in their cautions to him. And Jon had told all the scouts, more than once, not to blindly jump into situations they couldn't possibly understand. So maybe it hadn't been his smartest moment, but she'd needed help, and it had been a simple intervention. "I had to try to help," he told her. "Will they come back?"

She was putting the various baskets into nested stacks and gathering the mats into a pile. "I'm packing up." Piers offered to help, and she said, "No, please, just leave. While you're here they are still watching me!" He tried to hand the basket to her, but she pushed to toward him. "Take it. Go away—get away while you can."

Piers turned to go back to Atto. The three Ettori men were standing off to the side, and he knew they saw him. He risked dropping his screens, wanting to get a sense of intention if he could. It was so odd to be fully Open and yet feel nothing at all—then the same peripheral shadow he'd felt before swept through his awareness, too quick to Reach for. A ripple of nausea followed, not dissipating until he was Screening again. Atto was standing where Piers had left him, holding a bag and looking around for Piers.

He was halfway back when the Ettori men surrounded him, broadcasting menace so clearly anyone could pick it up. Piers stopped mid-stride. "Hello again," he said calmly. He lifted the basket a bit, as if to show them. "She did lower the price in the end."

"Had just about enough of your kind," one man said. "You Starborn freaks can't just mind your own business, can you?"

"What makes you think I'm Starborn?" That wasn't really what he'd meant to say, but maybe it was good that had slipped out. It wasn't too weird of a thing to say, under the circumstances, and maybe he'd get a hint or two.

The man spat on the ground. "Look at ya. Rags and dirt and wild eyes."

"Take him?" a second man asked.

"Nah. Lord Ettori will never miss him. Let's have some fun."

Two of them lunged for Piers at the same moment. He threw the basket at their faces and darted past them. Atto was ahead, yelling. A strong hand grabbed his arm and jerked him back, and a fist drove into his stomach. Piers doubled over, but another man pulled him up, holding him to face the other two. Another blow landed, and Piers struggled but couldn't break free.

"Fielder!" It was Atto, shouting. Piers looked over, in time to see Atto fling his bag at the man who'd just hit him. It hit the man's back with a thump, and apples spilled out, tumbling and bouncing on the pavement. The grip on his arms weakened, and Piers broke away. Atto leapt forward, clamped a hand on his wrist, and hauled him clear of the apples.

They ran.

The Ettori men shouted and charged after them as Atto led them all on a dodging chase through the town.

Atto knew every alley, every corner, every obstacle. Piers ran as hard as he could, trying to get enough air in shallow gasps, desperate to stay at the front of the race. The men behind them were gaining. "Atto! I can't!" Piers knew the next time he stumbled, he'd be down for good.

Atto glanced back. "One more!"

That turned out to mean one more block, one more sudden change of direction, and then the sudden appearance of the busy wharf in front of them. Atto slipped between some hulking cargo crates and pulled Piers after him. Despite Piers's raucous breathing, the Ettori men lost the trail.

After hiding behind the crates on the dock long enough to be sure the Ettori men had lost interest, and to stop panting, Piers followed Atto back to the Briar Inn through other slipways and shortcuts. They came in through the side door, straight into Shea's kitchen, and she was not happy when she heard what had happened.

"They didn't follow us here," Atto said. "I promise."

"It doesn't matter," she answered. "If they see either one of you again, you won't likely get away."

Piers hated the thought of Atto having to be wary because he himself had not been. "I'm so sorry. I had no idea." The feeling of rock-hard fists driving into his stomach wasn't fading.

"I'm not worried," Atto said. "Mostly the Ettori people don't come to Ruatt. They take the long road down to Estend, or go straight west to Manssorand. I can stay away from them."

"It was a rash thing you did, young Piers," Shea said. She laid a hand on his shoulder. "It was generous, though, and it's a shame to us all when kindness is repaid this way." She fetched a bottle from a cupboard and poured something into a metal cup that she heated at the fire. She wrapped a kitchen cloth around the cup and handed it to Piers. "Drink that, and both of you stay here and stay quiet. I need to see to the tavern." With a heavy kettle in one hand, she banged through the swinging door into the tavern.

Piers looked at the dose of dark, syrupy liquid in the cup a little skeptically. "Doesn't look too enticing."

"It will help," Atto said. "It tastes awful but telk syrup helps when things are wrong on the inside."

Well, there wasn't much of it, and absolutely it would be good if this brought any relief for his bruised abdomen. Piers downed it in one swallow, and the taste made him shudder. It was a plant extract, there was no way to miss *that* in the vegetative saltiness of it. He hoped it worked fast.

"That is *really* foul," he said.

"Yeah, I know. Gran got it from some Starborn a while ago—they do all kinds of stuff with telk for medicine. That's why Davyn was going to find a Starborn healer."

That seemed a good opening to ask the question that the Ettori man had partly answered. It hadn't been the first time someone had assumed Piers was Starborn, and it clearly wasn't a good thing. If he could find out why, he could work to correct the impression. Atto didn't know much about the Starborn, which was informative in its own right; a proper education didn't include learning about that subculture. He'd never been around them, he said, because they didn't interact much with anyone else. Even when they turned up in town, they just went about their errands and then disappeared again. "Plus," Atto said, "my mother doesn't like them. She thinks they're insane, but I think she says that because they live in tents instead of houses. Gran just calls them 'mystics' and says not to bother them."

As to why Piers might be mistaken for one of them, Atto had a ready answer. "You sound different, like you learned to talk somewhere else. And you *do* look like you live in a tent. You should let Gran give you a haircut."

The two of them ate their meal in the kitchen, out of sight in case anyone was looking. Shea came in and out through the evening, each time telling them with relief that there were no Ettori men in the tavern. Atto washed dishes episodically, and in between taught Piers a card game that "everyone" knew. He seemed happy enough to have an evening when he wasn't clearing dishes from tables or running back and forth from the kitchen. Piers thought it was a pleasant evening, unexpectedly. The syrup had eased the pain of his bruises, and the telik they'd been drinking had relaxed him completely.

When the tavern closed and the overnight guests went to their rooms, Shea dropped into another chair at the kitchen table. "I missed your help," she said to Atto. "Busy night."

"I don't need to hide, Gran," he said. Then he grinned at her. "But anytime you want me to keep somebody company instead of carrying heavy tubs of slimy dishes around, let me know."

Shea didn't answer, and Piers wished that he could get some emotive signal from her. She seemed to be weighing her thoughts, and finally said, "This business with Ettori has me worried."

Ah. Well, Piers could put that together well enough. She wasn't comfortable with him staying at the Briar, now, and was thinking about what would happen if he were discovered here. "I think I need to be on my way," he said. "For one thing, I need to find work if I'm going to keep staying in inns." That was true, even if it was barely in the top ten reasons why he needed to go. He had counted out his coins and had unhappily confirmed that he was going to be destitute very shortly. It made a polite reason that they could all hide behind, so that she wouldn't have to feel that she made him unwelcome.

She didn't protest. "Where will you go?"

One thing today's encounter had done: Ettori was no

longer on the list. Piers would find the Starborn or he would see if Lord Wyth was a friendly type, but staying clear of Lord Ettori seemed wise.

"I'm going to head toward Wyth," Piers said, deciding on the spot. "I'm hoping I can talk to the Aryn woman and see if she knows anything about Davyn, since I promised his people I'd try to find him." Among other things.

Atto blazed with abrupt energy. "I'm coming with you. I want to find Davyn."

Shea took hold of Atto's hand. "No, my boy, you're staying right here and safe. Tomorrow you can stay with your mother and see what she needs you to do."

Atto grumbled and resigned himself. But as he turned away, he met Piers's gaze. Whether it was something he saw in Atto's eyes or something more internal, Piers was nearly bowled over by the boy's obstinate determination. He knew he wouldn't be going to Wyth alone.

13

HOSPITALITY

House Wyth

BORROWED CLOTHES AGAIN, but this time they were finer quality. Arissa decided against wearing them, as a pointed snub to her surly host. She'd worn the shift as a nightdress, but that was different than letting him see her beholden to him. After she'd been alone in the dark room for hours, a woman had brought her his note last night and led her to an exquisite bedroom. Then she'd brought a full meal and the clothes, filled the wash basin, laid the fire, and been so kind overall that it triggered Arissa's cynicism.

When she'd woken in the night, shaken from dreams of Davyn's death, she still saw the wreck of the Starborn camp. It was more disarrayed than destroyed, but amid the havoc there had been a child by herself, crying, and a dog whining beside her. A group of women huddled over other children, turned inward among themselves like a crumpled rose. Older men stood at the edges, stunned. When her captors pushed her toward a group of men and boys surrounded by uniformed men and horses, she stumbled on something. Davyn's sword. And only a few feet away, Davyn himself lay still on his back, his face turned away, with a dark stain on his right shoulder.

Just like that, it was over. She had admired him and trusted him, and had started to like him despite his bristling pride, but they had barely started a friendship. Admittedly, there'd been moments when she'd felt her heart skip when he smiled, or when he'd done some little kindness for her. Now that possibility was gone. His smile, gone, and the music of his voice. Because he'd tried to help her. Even though he'd been an unwilling champion for her at first, he hadn't complained about the difficulties, and he'd been determined to get her to Dannpelier. All for nothing. She had missed the Gathering, she was stuck at House Wyth after all, and Davyn was dead.

The water she splashed on her face was cold, and the shock of it was welcome. Somehow she had to get through this day.

Nothing about going to Lord Wyth appealed to her. His note had dampened her anger, but hadn't reversed the effects of their first encounter. She could see his face, the coldness in his eyes and the way his mouth had set into a hard line, crooked down at one end. His words kept taunting her. This man she was supposed to marry hadn't even pretended sympathy for what she'd been through. Nothing he could say now would erase those words. *I doubt you're worth it.*

She thought of her sister, Lyndi, and the way her husband-to-be looked at her with love and longing. There'd once been talk of Lyndi marrying into another House, but whoever her father had approached had apparently not been interested in a long betrothal and it had come to nothing. After their father died, it had been too complicated. Lyndi had taken over the maternal role that their mother abandoned; she'd said she wouldn't marry until Nevin was ready to be Head of House and Arissa was old enough to marry. When Caleb met Lyndi, she'd been resolute in refusing to even consider his courtship, but he persisted with such genuine kindness, admiration, and devotion that she softened—and now they were about to start their bride month.

Until Lyndi's engagement, Arissa hadn't really thought much about what would happen when Lyndi left. Then she'd realized that her own romantic prospects didn't amount to much. She'd thought Aryn was too poor, and Nevin was too young, for any House lord to see a gain in the match. As a young girl, she had wished that the heir of their nearest neighbor, at House Chant, would look her way, but he had married someone else when Arissa was still too young to catch his eye. With Lyndi's engagement, Arissa had decided that she would stay at Aryn, working around both her mother and her brother to keep the House functioning properly, at least until Nevin married. With no real chance of meeting someone for a love match like Lyndi's, and expecting no interest from another House, she'd been content to devote herself to Aryn.

And then Lord Wyth had swooped in with all his arrogance and snatched her out of her plans. She wondered if he'd even let her travel to Portsay to witness Lyndi's wedding.

Her own clothes were lying on the chest at the foot of the bed. When she picked up the tunic, she saw that the embroidery had been ruined, and the fabric was torn in several places. Even Shea's mending was undone. The trousers were in worse condition. With a longing thought for the clean clothes in the saddlebag she'd left lying in the woods, she dressed.

There was a large mirror in the corner of the room, and it was the first proper look at herself she'd had since leaving Aryn. Her eyes were swollen. Her hair was drab and limp, and the fading bruises on her face made her look like her lips reached halfway to her ears in a mocking smile. In her ragged blue travel clothes, she looked like a beggar child. Whatever Owen might think when he saw her, it wouldn't be that she was an independent and resourceful woman. With a second, deeper, sigh, she reached for the loaned clothing.

No one was guarding her door and no one was waiting to guide her through the House. Lord Wyth's note had simply asked her to meet him in the breakfast room, and the House woman had given her an idea of where to find it—but Arissa had assumed someone would be escorting her. What did it mean? Was she supposed to think he suddenly trusted her completely?

The corridor outside her room was wider than she'd noticed when the woman led her here. The wood floors were inlaid with intricate, geometric patterns that led to each of the doors spaced along the hall. To her right, the hallway ended in another door. So she turned left, and found a long staircase that wrapped two stories down and one up around a huge stone column. Down two flights and across a landing to a short hallway with a brace of steps halfway along it, she came to the room on the right, where sunlight was reaching through the open door to the hall.

Lord Wyth was seated at the end of the table, positioned to face the door. Even so, he didn't see her, because he was turned to one side, giving table scraps to a dog. In the cheerful light, she saw that like his brother, his face had a boyishness that made it hard to guess his age. He was half-smiling at the dog, and there was a hint of a dimple on one side. Dog and master noticed her at the same moment, and Lord Wyth almost tripped in his hurry to stand up and come over to her.

"Dane Arissa," he said, holding his palms out. "Please forgive my behavior when you arrived."

She ignored his hands. "Does that include arrest?"

He let his hands fall at his sides, and looked away. The dog, who had followed him, nosed his arm. Reflexively, he rested his hand on the dog's head. "It does," he said. "It was a terrible beginning and I hope you will forgive me for it." He met her eyes, then bowed slightly to her. "Arissa, daughter of Aryn, welcome to House Wyth. I'm Owen, acting as Head of House in my father's illness, and I am extremely glad that you arrived safely." He held his hands out again. "Please let me try again."

His eyes were the same hazel-green as his brother's, and he was looking at her with an earnest eagerness that nearly made her tell him everything was forgiven. As she met his hands with hers so briefly and so lightly it was a rebuke, she said, "You can start by hearing this: I didn't want to come here. I don't want to *be* here. Getting here was a series of the worst experiences I've ever had, and when your pet thugs dragged me up to your door, you barely acknowledged me except to insult me and treat me like a criminal. So let me assure you, I have no doubt—*you* are not worth it."

After all that, his gaze didn't waver. He just nodded. "I know. I handled it poorly. Glenn was a close friend and I was knocked sideways by the news, and I mistreated you because of it."

She had expected a rebuttal or denial or at least some

defense. The complete acceptance threw her off balance. Grasping, she said, "That's it? That's all you've got to say?"

Owen turned away, and the dog whined. He went back to the chair he'd left and seemed to deflate into it. "I'm sure we could both say plenty," he said, "but I don't want to make things worse. Please, sit down and have something to eat."

Feeling deflated herself, Arissa took the nearest seat at the table, and noticed that all the plates and water glasses had gold-leaf on the rims, where at Aryn there were chips and cracks. "I'm sorry about Glenn," she said. "He was kind to me."

"He was a good man." Owen rang a small bell that was on the table, and a House maid appeared in the doorway. "Do you drink telik in the morning, Dane Arissa?"

The conversation over breakfast alternated between superficial and stiff, and she was exhausted and raw. Arissa was more and more certain she was going to say something rude just to change the tone when Gadrin breezed in.

"Good morning, brother," he said to Owen. Then he turned to Arissa and bowed. "You must be Arissa of Aryn." Nothing in his expression gave anything away. "I'm Rane, Owen's brother." There was a minute shake of his head and a warning look in his eyes as he gave his name. *Don't say anything.* He offered his hands, and she accepted the gesture.

He pulled out the chair next to her, angling it toward her as he sat down. "You arrived yesterday?"

It was bizarre to play-act the introduction and small talk, but Owen was watching them with a strange, suspended-judgment look. "Rane" was charming, full of the same social perfection he'd displayed to her mother at Aryn. He paid her easy compliments and kept a lively conversation going. He told her that this part of the House was the oldest surviving section, and that House tradition was that only family and close friends were received here. The view, he told her, had once been clear from the House to the lake in the valley, but their grandfather had loved trees and refused to cut them even as they started to obstruct the view. He introduced her to the dog, with obvious affection for the animal, and told her there were puppies in the stable. As he entertained her, he would occasionally direct a comment to his brother, but Owen would not be drawn in. He would respond with a word or two and then lapse back into his calculating observation. Finally, Rane glanced over at his brother and said, "Owen, you should take Dane Arissa out to see the puppies. It's a perfect morning and she ought to see the grounds."

Owen frowned and hesitated. Rane shot him a look that served as a kick under the table, which Arissa saw, and Owen said, "Yes, if you'd like to, Dane Arissa."

She agreed, less enthusiastically than she might have if he hadn't needed to be shoved into the offer. It would be worth the tedious company to be outside, though, and to get a better sense of how House Wyth was situated—and what the best possibilities for a quiet departure might be.

The curtains were open and the bedroom was bright. A tumbler of water had been placed on the nightstand, and a robe was laid across the foot of the bed. One of the House women must have come in without waking her, which was a bit disconcerting. She'd meant to be on guard.

Once again there was a folded note propped on the dressing table. This was Arissa's fifth morning at Wyth, and each day she'd had breakfast with the brothers in the small dining room before spending most of the day with Owen. Odd, she thought, how few times something had to be repeated before it felt routine.

"*Dane Arissa,*" this morning's note read, "*I hope you slept well. I enjoyed our talk yesterday and was hoping to continue today, but unfortunately I've been called away. It looks like it will be a fine day, and you might want to spend time outside. Darletta has promised to find boots for you, and I know my brother would be pleased to walk with you if you want company. Breakfast is waiting for you, or just ring if you'd rather have something brought to you. I look forward to your company when I return tomorrow.*" He had simply signed "*Owen,*" in a tight script.

From this window, too, trees and more trees were all she could see. They were in full leaf now, and the shocking spring green was mellowing toward its summer hue. Birds soared over the branches, across a cloudless sky. She would welcome the fresh air.

More new clothes were hanging beside the dressing screen, and a pair of boots that looked small enough for her had been set below them. Owen had told her yesterday that he had sent to Trint for the travel cases she'd left behind, but in the meantime the House women had continued to find clothes for her to borrow. Today, it was a pair of buff-colored, suede trousers and a soft tunic woven of light wool. Once again she had to roll the hems, but the clothes fit well otherwise. Despite herself, she took pleasure in them.

As she stepped into the sunny breakfast room, Rane looked up from something he'd been reading. "I didn't know if you'd come to breakfast, knowing Owen isn't here."

"His company isn't really the motive," she replied. She felt mean as soon as she said it. Owen had been hospitable and respectful ever since his apology for their first encounter. If they'd met differently—and if she wasn't supposed to marry him—she thought she might like him.

Rane laughed. "Poor old Owen. He's not the most out-going person, but he really means well."

She felt herself blush. "I know, I shouldn't have said that. I'm—I'm still getting my bearings." There was a place set for her, and Rane set a fresh cup of telik in front of her. His smile was warm and inviting. Trying to sound neutrally polite, she said, "He said he had been called away?"

Something passed over Rane's expression, dimming the smile for just an instant. "Just a little House business," he said. "He'll be back tomorrow." There was the briefest pause, enough for an unguarded thought to slip through and flit across his face. Then he arched an eyebrow at her. "So the cat's away and the mice can play. Want to see the 'secret' passageways of House Wyth? Or do you really want to just walk around the garden?"

The ancient House had been built and rebuilt in sections, and it was riddled with false walls and blocked rooms. Rane led her through hidden doors and narrow tunnels to dark and empty rooms that smelled of dust and secrets. His lantern cast light only a few feet around them, making a small world just for the two of them.

On the main floor, dead-end passageways ran between rooms, allowing eavesdroppers to monitor both sides while providing a false sense of soundproof privacy for the occupants of the rooms themselves. Many passages were just wide enough for them to walk side by side, and Arissa found herself distractedly aware of how often they were almost touching. He didn't tower over her as much as Davyn had, and when they stood close together she couldn't help thinking that his shoulder would be just the right height to rest her head against. This recurrent, unhelp-ful observation tempted her to daydream, and more than once she had to snap herself out of it.

Rane told her dramatic ancestral stories of intrigue, from wartime espionage to clandestine romance. He also made her laugh with his memories of childhood games and pranks. Discovering the tunnels was a Wyth rite of passage: each generation pretended to know nothing of the passageways until the children discovered them, and then the tales were passed on.

"There's one room almost no one finds unless they are told about it," Rane said as he pushed open a plank door and let Arissa pass under his outstretched arm. The constricted tunnel in front of her curved to the left, and intersected an equally narrow staircase that spiraled upward. He handed her the lantern and told her to go ahead. "Don't know if you remember seeing the tower from outside?"

"Is that where we are?" She'd seen a tower that rounded the northwest corner of the House and rose a single story over the roof.

His voice followed her up the stairs, close behind her. "The House used to only have three stories, and the tower was two stories higher. When they added the top floor, for some reason they just blocked off the tower—I have no idea why. Eventually someone built proper walls and squared it off, so from inside you'd never know the tower was there."

"Don't people imagine there must be some way into the tower?"

"One of the tower windows is level with the roof now, so you can get in from there, which of course children do, and it feels like you've found the secret. They built a floor in the tower when they closed it off, so now it seems like it's just one story, over the roof."

Arissa reached a wider step, where a door hung on battered hinges to her left. Rane stopped two steps below her, and said, "You can go in—just don't tell Owen I showed you this."

The lantern revealed a small, circular room with stone block walls and a low wooden ceiling. It was furnished with things that wouldn't be missed. Rane took the lantern and set it on a small table that had one leg replaced by a stack of tattered books, and waved Arissa to a misshapen sofa. He sank into an enormous pile of cushions and blankets on the floor and leaned back with his fingers laced behind his head. "I haven't been up here for ages. Owen and I used to spend whole days camped out here." He gave her a thoughtful look, and added, "I don't think we ever brought anyone else up. You're our first guest...don't judge the housekeeping."

She laughed. "You and Owen are close?" It was hard to imagine many more unlikely friendships.

The merriment leached out of his face. He told her about their mother's death and father's illness, and how he'd seen Owen change. "It was like watching the life drain out of him," he said. It wasn't that Owen hadn't been ready for the responsibility, but their mother had been the soul of the family and the heart of the House. "We've always been very different, and he's six years older, but we were close all the same. After our mother died, he just withdrew from everyone, and when our father got sick, Owen put up walls. I don't feel like I'm really myself without being able to talk to him."

He kept his eyes away from hers, but loss hollowed his expression. He made no effort to mask his vulnerability. "I miss him."

"I'm sorry," she said. "My father died a few years ago. My mother never really recovered from losing him, so my older sister ended up holding things together for me and our brother, until Nevin was old enough to take over."

Rane said nothing, and for a few minutes each of them

sat alone with their thoughts. Rane drummed his fingers against his knee and Arissa wound a few strands of her hair through her fingers.

Then Rane said, "This room has this effect. I can't tell you how many times Owen and I had deep conversations up here. I guess it's because it's a place apart." He got up and pushed a cushion back toward the pile with his foot. He held a hand out to her and pulled her to her feet. As she stood, she found herself face to face with him, and too close. They paused there, and she felt like they were truly seeing each other for the first time, with no flirting, no posturing, no pretension. Rane whispered, "Damn. I really want to kiss you."

Her stomach fluttered, and heat brushed her face. This couldn't happen. In the dim room, his eyes almost seemed to be a source of light, shining straight into hers. He was close enough that she could feel his breath. If she swayed forward, just a bit, his lips could be on hers. His arms could be around her. "No," she whispered. "I can't. Owen…"

He stepped back abruptly, and she felt disappointment soak through her. "I'm sorry," he said, and it almost sounded more like regret than apology. Then he added, "Thank you."

Arissa couldn't let herself look at his face. This feeling needed to vanish; she needed to have him as a friend. "Let's go get some of the sunshine while we can," she said. "We haven't had much of it lately." She picked up the lantern and held it out to him.

He seemed surprised, but the smile he gave her was softened with gratitude. As she followed him out of the tower room and back down the stairs, she tried to feel relieved.

14

HEALING

Wyth Valley

THERE WAS A single lamp glowing when Davyn woke, which lit the tent well enough that he knew where he must be. He could hear people talking softly outside, but he was alone. As he took his bearing, he lay still. His throat was dry, his wrist throbbed and his shoulder burned. When he moved, the burning flared into searing. He turned his head to see what he could without sitting up.

He was on a narrow cot, set in a corner of canvas walls. Clothes—his—were folded neatly on a stool beside him. His saddlebag was propped where he could easily see it, with Arissa's beside it, and his sword rested against the bag. So he wasn't a prisoner. A stack of rolled cloth strips, a mortar and pestle, and small piles of leaves were arrayed on a narrow worktable just at the edge of his line of sight. No drinking cup or jug.

There was no power in his voice when he spoke, but a woman appeared in an instant. She came toward him, and said lightly, "Welcome back." She pulled over another stool and sat by his shoulder. "Do you remember what happened?"

He did, more or less. For the rest of his life, he'd be able to recall his opponent's expression—the sharpness of his jaw and the broad, flat planes of his face, and the malevolent satisfaction—in the instant when they both realized Davyn was vulnerable. The woman watched his face and waited sympathetically. He nodded without lifting his head.

"That's a good sign," she said. "You've been hurt, but it's a clean wound and I think you'll heal well." She reached down and lifted a small wooden cup that he hadn't been able to see. She slipped her arm behind his neck and lifted his head, just enough that she could tip some liquid into his mouth. The brackish tang of telk syrup, barely diluted, spread along his tongue. "You've been asleep for about three hours."

Davyn tried to speak again, but she seemed to answer his thought before the words were formed. "You want to know about your friend," she said. "I'm sorry to tell you: she was taken by Lord Ettori's men. But she wasn't hurt when they left, and we think they were taking her to Lord Wyth, not the dam."

If Arissa had been taken to House Wyth, Davyn thought she'd be unhappy but unharmed. He'd promised to get her to the Gathering, though, and he tried to think about what he should do, but his thoughts slipped away from him, like water flowing over stones. Perhaps he should try to go after her, or take word to House Dannpelier, or...

When he woke again, the night was quiet. Through the canvas wall of the tent he could hear only the pulsing hum of the nighthoppers. Inside, the lamps had all been extinguished and he could see nothing at all. Pain was with him, but he didn't move and for the moment it was an evenly spread pain rather than the spikes he'd felt before. He wondered where the woman was.

"You're awake again." Her voice rippled toward him from somewhere in the darkness to his right. A single candle bloomed, bright as sudden daylight to his eyes. He turned his face toward the room. The woman was sitting on a low bench directly across the tent from him, the candle in her hand. It illuminated her face from below, so that her own shadow hid her expression and her eyes gleamed.

Again she helped him drink, and then she adjusted her seat so that she faced him. The candle was set off to the side now, and half her face was softly golden. One candle didn't reveal much, but he could see that she was curious, and concerned for him.

"Thank you," Davyn said. He tried to clear his throat, and said more strongly, "You're very kind."

He could see the left side of her face smiling, and she said mildly, "I'm a healer." She reached for the candle and brought it closer to cast its light on his bandaged shoulder. "Nothing soaking through," she said. "I'll leave it alone for now, then, and change the bandage in a few more hours. Staying still is the best thing you can do for the moment. The telk will help."

A Starborn healer. He felt a surge of recognition a moment before his mind caught up, and he shifted to sit up. Instead, pain cinched tight around his torso and he froze, hoping that the spinning sensation would stop.

"Do you need something for the pain? I can send you back to sleep."

He didn't want that. There were too many questions, and his mind was clearing. "I can manage," he said. "I've been looking for you."

"For me?"

"A Starborn healer. We need you. Will you come with me, to Trint?"

She adjusted the bandage with cool, light fingers. "I'm quite sure you're not going anywhere for a while."

"I have to get back." His attempt to sound resolute only resulted in his voice cracking. "My family is caught in the Sweep."

"Drink," she said, and offered him the cup again. "You aren't covered with House emblems, so I think you're not a House man, but I don't think you're Starborn and you don't look like a laborer. So a town man? Who's sick? Your wife?"

It was awkward, introducing himself when he was unable even to offer a hand, much less sit up. "Davyn Ralen, from Trint. The family I stay with is sick. Lady Arissa—the woman I'm with—needed an escort to Dannpelier, and I'd heard there were Starborn close by. The bridge over the Lentava was out, so we were trying to cut across to the long road. We heard the noise and—" Davyn broke off and bolted up, his injuries forgotten as he remembered the horses. The pain exploded and he fell back, gasping.

She gave a short cry and sprang from the stool to lean over him. "What is it?"

"My horse—our horses—in the woods—"

"They're fine, they're fine." Her voice was soothing as she repeated the words, with a faint tinge of amusement. She pulled a blanket back into place over him, which was the first he noticed his skin was bare. "We found them this afternoon, and they're taken care of." She laid a cool hand against his cheek and smiled. "The black one was worried about you. We couldn't do anything with him until he stuck his big head in here and saw for himself that you were alive."

"Paladin," Davyn said, trying to recover his breath. "He's a friend."

That made her smile again. "Well, Davyn Ralen, friend of horses, you need to believe me when I tell you that you need to stay still."

"I do." He gritted his teeth as if he could block the pain that way.

"Good." She righted her stool. "I'm Tienna," she said. "We'll give this a few minutes to see if the pain subsides a bit for you."

While he lay there, she talked to him, and he concentrated on her words rather than the pain. She told him that twelve men and boys had been taken, out of the fifty-two people in her group of Starborn. They'd set up their camp here about fifteen years ago, and they stayed despite the tug of the wanderer's life and the risk of the attack that had finally come.

When he'd first heard of the Starborn, Davyn's imagination had been captivated. In fact, he and Van had spent hours building out elaborate and mystical scenarios based on what little they knew of the Starborn's beliefs. They said there'd been a time before humanity, the first age, and then the ancients had arrived from the stars. They'd built civilization, and the world was still in its second age. A third age would begin when people came from the stars to usher the world into peace and prosperity. Van had considered it all absurd, but their tutor, Ger, believed there was truth in it, and his conviction eventually became Davyn's. If humankind really had meant to take root here after traveling through the stars, then the Starborn were eccentric for still waiting, but perhaps not mad.

Tienna explained further. The founders had expected the third age to begin in their lifetimes, but whatever had gone wrong for the founders had not only obliterated the traces of their past but had wrenched their future into a new and unplanned course. Some people had simply tried to start over, but others thought it was a cosmic punishment for some human sin. Someday, the Starborn believed, redemption would come and whatever order there was meant to be would be re-established. It was why they didn't build anything permanent: to them, permanence felt like apostasy.

"Why did Ettori's men attack you?" he asked.

Her face tightened. "He's been taking men to work on the dam. Every Starborn crew we know about has been raided; people told us we needed to move from here, but we thought—foolishly—that because of Dannpelier and Wyth we'd be safe. We didn't think he'd come for people in their lands. But some villagers upriver are blaming us for trouble that came to them, and we think that may have been the excuse he was looking for."

No doubt Ettori could find some people who would take the work for the right compensation, but not too many could sell their hours when there were fields to till and fish to catch and children to raise. Nor could Ettori enlist men from the Houses without their lords' permission, and as far as Davyn knew, no other House supported even the idea of the dam. But like the villagers at River's End, the Starborn belonged to no House, and weren't part of the Tithe cycle. They had no one to object on their behalf.

"We've talked about moving," Tienna said. "It's a hard decision. We like it here, and our elders think this is the right place to be right now. There are some who think the third age is about to begin, and this valley has always been associated with the legends."

The Starborn woman turned aside and busied herself at

her bench. When she turned back, Davyn saw reluctance and worry in her eyes. "But it's not safe for us here now."

"Where would you go?"

She checked his bandages, and gave him another swallow of telk syrup. "That's the question," she said. "This is happening to Starborn all over Merra, so some of us want to try to make it over the border. But there's the question of leaving people behind—do we really just leave our men in Ettori's clutches and flee to Tyndaris? Assuming we even make it."

Davyn felt the telk push his thoughts out of the way. He wanted to tell her he could help, that he had contacts in Tyndaris, but he drifted. Time skated past in flowing, falling drifts that he couldn't quite catch. He may have slept. He blinked as the sweet trill of a river lark drew his attention to the light that was gathering outside the tent.

"I love the river larks," Tienna said. "I always think they seem like they are trying to describe the sound of a stream." She blew out the candle. "I'm going to leave you in peace for a little while I go see how everyone else is this morning. Rest, and don't move your arm if you can help it."

The tent flap split open near the foot of Davyn's cot and bright sunlight rushed in, along with fresh air that tried to billow the heavy canvas of the tent. Above him, the ceiling rippled. To his right, he could see that the room was crowded with furnishings that it seemed his cot had displaced. The worktable that held the accoutrements of healing was near the center tentpole, inconveniently bisecting the space. The wooden bench against the other side of the tent was partly barricaded by a low table and some chairs. Now he could see that the canvas wall behind him was a curtain that spanned the tent. Through a gap at the side, he could see the end of another cot. Another room, then, with more privacy.

Tienna slipped into the tent from outside, her slim figure resolving from silhouette to form as his eyes adjusted. She tied the flap open, then came close to him. Her movement was graceful and her long skirt seemed almost elegant to him, out of place here, despite the practical tunic that she wore over it.

"How is the pain?" Tienna asked. When she leaned over him, her dark hair fell forward over her shoulder and she pushed it back reflexively.

"I had almost forgotten," he said, although at the mention of it he felt the burn in full.

"Until I reminded you." With light hands she pulled away layers of bandage from his shoulder. He felt the tug as it loosened from the dried blood, and then a sharper blaze of pain in response.

He tried to imagine himself elsewhere.

"The cut on your shoulder nicked the muscle," she said, "but it's not too deep. I think it will close well enough on its own, if we can keep it clean and you don't move it too much."

She dabbed at his shoulder with a damp cloth. The rasp of the cloth at the raw edge of the wound added another texture to his pain, but he tried to suppress every wince. With a touch like a butterfly's wings, she pressed something into the wound. There was an instant of excruciation and then a welcome, spreading numbness, recognized from a boyhood of skinned knees and years of nicks and cuts from sparring. "Floodberry paste," he said as he felt the pain reduce to a tingle. "A thousand mercies for the person who discovered it."

"It will block infection," she answered, smiling at his relief. Her eyes were the pale blue of an early morning sky. "And it stimulates healing, so if it does its work well, we won't need to stitch the wound." She laid the cloth over it, to keep the paste from drying too soon. "I wish we had something as good for your wrist. I don't think it's broken, just badly sprained. We'll splint it when the swelling goes down."

His wrist was padded with a poultice and resting on a folded blanket. She wrapped a fresh bandage around his arm and shoulder. "It'll be a few weeks before you can wield that sword of yours again."

Davyn tried to focus on the fact that it could have been worse. He could manage a few weeks of left-handedness, even with the sword if needed. The real question was how long before he could ride—he needed to get back to Trint, with a healer.

Tienna laid her hand gently against his cheek again. "I know you want to get home, but you need to rest for a few days."

"You seem to read my mind," Davyn said. He couldn't interpret the oblique look that she gave him before she turned away.

She bent down beside his cot and picked up a bowl. "I'm good at reading people. It's a good gift for a healer," she said. "You can rest, Davyn. We sent word to another camp, asking their healer to go to Trint." A bloody cloth was bundled in the middle of the bowl, tinting the water. She saw him look. "It looks like a lot, but it's just from cleaning up. You've stopped bleeding, though it's still raw—keeping still as much as you can now will help you heal faster." Tienna moved to the tent's opening, still holding the bowl, and said, "Jemma."

A small girl burst into the tent. "What, Mama? Oh, he's awake!" The girl darted over to him, and stood close to his shoulder. "I'm Jemma," she said earnestly. "Everything's all right now." She seemed about Tunny's age.

Davyn wished he could keep the soft smile Tienna gave her daughter as a talisman for strength. The girl couldn't even see her mother's face, but Davyn thought the light in her eyes gave truth to the girl's words. He reached across his body with his left hand, as far as he could without shifting. "It's an honor to meet you. I'm Davyn."

Jemma placed her small hand lightly against his, despite the inconvenient angle, and turned toward her mother. Before the girl spoke, Tienna said to Davyn, "She'd like to stay with you for a while, if that wouldn't bother you. If you don't feel like talking, she won't mind, and if you feel like you can sleep, you should. But if you need anything, she can get it or come find me. I'll bring you something to eat in a little while."

So Tienna left, carrying the bowl, and the girl perched on the stool beside the cot. With eyes very like her mother's, she studied Davyn's face with unabashed curiosity. After a few moments, she said, "You're going to be good for us."

15

COMPANY

Ruatt

PIERS HAD SLOWED a bit to admire a pair of shoes displayed in front of another cobbler's shop. They looked like they might fit—and they looked waterproof. Or at least, they looked like they weren't perpetually soggy, which would be a nice upgrade.

"How much money do you have?" Atto was grinning as he came up beside Piers, with a pack hoisted on his shoulders. His question was apt.

He shook his head. "Not enough to spare any for new shoes," he said, and readjusted his own pack. It was heavy now, with everything Shea had insisted he take. The telk syrup had kept the pain of the bruises from his market encounter to a minor discomfort, but didn't help with the pinch of a twisted shoulder strap. "I've got one gold and six silver, and a handful of the little ones, and that's it."

"I've got one and twelve," Atto said, "and twenty chippers. And I bet Gran gave you enough food that we could both be full for days, if you don't mind sharing. I brought some, too. So we won't have to pay to eat. Can you sleep rough?"

"It's an art I've been learning," Piers replied. Being outside in the dark still put him on edge, but he was getting better at coaxing himself to sleep. Inns would be out of the question unless he found some work soon. He hadn't expected Atto to contribute resources to this adventure—he'd have been glad just for the knowledge and company, but a little extra money brightened the prospects for sure.

He wondered if he were obligated to try to send Atto back to the inn. What's the age of autonomy here? Or the age of rebellion, for that matter? Atto said his mother was fine with him going, but Piers had plenty of personal experience with parents who were obliging only because they hadn't been asked. And Atto's grandmother's point of view had been very clear. On the other hand, he would be the beneficiary of Atto's disobedience, so he had a conflict of interest. "Atto, are you sure you want to do this? Your grandmother didn't want you to, so she's going to be worried and probably pretty angry. I don't want this to cause problems for you—plus I can't promise that it's going to be safe. There are some bad things happening on the road these days."

Atto rewarded him with a perfectly executed look of teenage disdain.

It made Piers think of the verbal shrug his own friends had used at that age, to brush off unwelcome advice: *It's my airlock.* In other words, I have the most to lose if I don't check the seals before I start. He swallowed a laugh—it sounded so absurd juxtaposed with this context. "Just asking the question. Did you at least let someone know you're going?"

The sigh Atto gave conveyed all of his disappointment that Piers was *that* kind of grown-up. "I told you, my mother said I can go. She and Gran had a huge fight a few years ago about who I had to listen to, and after that they decided that if they don't agree on something to do with me, Mom's got the last word."

Even if he'd lost some status in Atto's eyes, Piers was glad he'd pressed the point. Knowing that this was a sanctioned adventure alleviated one concern. There'd still be plenty of potential for a guilty conscience if something went wrong, but at least no one would think he'd abducted the kid. He started walking away from the cobbler's, with purpose in his step, and said, "Well, then, let's get moving. I'm not getting new shoes any time soon."

They didn't make very good time. Atto had proposed they take the road across the valley, cross the Lentava at the turn for Dannpelier, and then take the "long road" to Wyth, rather than the less used and less maintained hill road. It also meant they had to walk through the city, and Atto was seeing his hometown with fresh enthusiasm. He kept pointing out landmarks and telling Piers bits of trivia and history, and Piers had neither the heart nor the inclination to rush Atto along. So they were just coming to the edge of town when Atto announced that he was hungry and it was time for lunch.

Eating a somewhat smushed sandwich while sitting in the sun with decent company was actually a pleasure. Piers let himself set aside the assignment, the challenges, the thoughts of Arthur, even the worries about Kath and the ship; it was a healthy thing, Piers thought, to relax and enjoy Atto's cheerful commentary. Even in the first two weeks, when he'd had someone to share observations with, Piers hadn't really been able to think of it as fun. Now the sense of adventure and wonder was trickling back.

After lunch, they set a faster pace. A quarter of an hour

later, when the last stone building at the eastern edge of Ruatt was starting to shrink in the distance behind them, they came to a cluster of three huts gathered around a well and a trough near the side of the road. Atto went straight up to the old woman sitting behind a cart beside the well and handed over a silver coin. Without saying a word, she poured two large mugs of ale, nodded to Atto, and gave him a ladle. "Travelers' last chance to fill up," Atto said, as he led Piers over to the well to fill their canteens. It was also, he added, probably the last water closet they'd see until they got to Wyth. Piers was even getting used to that reality.

Mid-afternoon, as the light was just starting to shift into the long-rayed, golden glow that Piers had decided was his favorite phase of the sun's progression, they came to a makeshift bridge across a surging river. A series of planks had been placed on top of damaged pylons, creating a catwalk not much wider than a foot and a half. Even more unnerving, the planks didn't seem to be secured in any way, and simply rested on the posts. The water bashed against those same posts, frothing and foaming.

An acidic burning in his throat warned Piers. He managed to get a few steps away from Atto before his lunch was expelled. Images in his mind blinded him: Arthur's face, Arthur's boot sole, Arthur's wrecked body.

Atto's hand was light on his shoulder. "Want some water?"

Piers shook his head and wiped at his mouth, still doubled over. He shuddered, and a dry heave raked his lungs.

"Take a deep breath," Atto coached. "Are you going to be all right?"

Concern brushed at Piers's awareness. With a panicked sense of exposure, he slammed the psi barriers back in place. It was another reminder that Screening wasn't autonomic, no matter how practiced he was and how little attention he gave the effort. The strength of Atto's concern surprised him—for a non-psi's emotions to reach him that clearly, without him Scanning, was vanishingly rare.

Piers braced his hands against his knees and took three shaky breaths. The ground, at least, had stopped tilting. He straightened, and looked to the sky, trying to draw his senses back. He tried a smile.

"Sorry," he said. "Rough water brings back some bad memories."

Atto cocked his head, considering, and then said, "Glad it wasn't Gran's sandwich."

They turned back to the bridge. "Is there another way across?" Piers asked.

"I think there's one more bridge between here and House Wyth, but it's somewhere north and we'd have to go a long way around through the woods."

Five planks spanned something like sixty feet from one steep bank to the other, with the river fifteen feet below. On their side, the ground was flat and bare north of the road, the nearest trees a few minutes' walk behind them. There were traces of stone pavement close to the bridge, half-buried by the dirt road. To the right, the ground sloped away from the roadbed, to a brushy clump a few yards away. The opposite bank of the river was overgrown with the same kind of brush. At the foot of the bridge over there, the road flared to the sides before narrowing back into its straight line and carving a path eastward through the overgrowth.

Side by side, the two of them considered the crossing. "Can't believe that's the best they could do," Atto commented. He nudged Piers. "You should fix it, mender."

Of all the times to call my bluff, Piers thought. "I don't have the right tools with me."

Atto squinted at him, the unasked question in the air like a storm on the way. He studied the bridge for another moment, and then said, "I guess maybe a mender already tried. Except not a very good mender. I wonder how long it's been like this."

To their left, a track led north through the grass along the riverbank, parallel to the road. Maybe someone had found a better place to cross. Piers commented on it and took a few steps, as if testing the ground. Atto didn't reply, and Piers turned to look at him.

The boy had stepped onto the plank bridge, his pack slung diagonally across his back. He was going slowly, with his arms out to the sides but held low, as if keeping his ability to balance in reserve. Below him, the water leapt, desperate to nip his heels.

With the aftertaste of his fear still tainting every breath, Piers stood at the end of the plank bridge and watched Atto risk his neck.

When Atto reached the other side and turned around with an exhilarated grin, he waved, and that seemed to push a beat of triumphant glee back across the bridge. It felt—almost—like a psi Push. Piers tried to Link, but there was no response.

"It's not bad," Atto called. "More stable than it looks."

That was beside the point. "I can't swim," he said. Neither could Arthur. He couldn't move, didn't want to. Getting lost in the woods, however far out of their way, seemed like a much wiser course of action.

Atto laughed. "Me neither! Come on."

If you can throw yourself at a planet in a cobbled-together shuttle, Piers thought, you can zip up and get across this damn river like the intrepid scout you are. Piers took an enormous breath, checked the distribution of weight in his pack, and set his left foot on the end of the first plank. He didn't want to see the river, but he also didn't trust his feet enough to stop watching them as they bore him out over the water. Through his concentration, he heard Atto shouting encouragement, but the words didn't penetrate.

It's plenty wide, he told himself, and tried not to notice the slight movement of the board with each step. *Hold the rail, Piers, hold the rail.* That had been Dad's favorite admonition when he wanted Piers to keep calm and stay balanced. What he wouldn't give for a rail now. He held out his arms like wings and slid his foot forward. The first plank ended on a pylon a fifth of the way out, end-to-end with a second plank that took him across the same width again. The planks were thick and felt solid, but only their own weight held them in place on the bridge supports. As he stepped onto the second plank, it wobbled a bit and Piers wobbled with it. He leaned to the right and caught his balance easily enough—but his heart pounded and his vision blurred. He froze, until his breath was no longer shallow, then inched forward.

The step that brought him back onto solid ground released a sob. He forced a laugh over it.

Atto swung a playful punch at his arm. "You did it! Not too bad, right?" They looked at the plank bridge, which now seemed quite substantial. Piers's sense of victory trickled away. His stomach was still complaining.

With the bridge behind them, they started walking again. After a few minutes, they could no longer hear the river. Piers's skin stopped crawling and his knees seemed to strengthen. The sun pushed at their backs. There were a few more hours until dusk, but Piers doubted they'd arrive at anything like a destination before night fell. He thought they had come about fifteen miles since leaving the inn—if they kept going at this pace, he would burn through Barston's patience before he even got to Wyth. At least they had made better time once they were clear of Ruatt and its distractions.

They found shelter for the night in the woods, away from the road. Atto proved to be even less of an outdoorsman than Piers—he confessed that while he'd slept outside on a few occasions, it had been in town. So Piers sent Atto to gather kindling and fuel for a fire while he cleared an area down to nothing but soil and built a ring from stones and dirt. He'd done this several times now, practicing this procedure while knowledge from the ship slowly turned into experience on the planet. Atto watched with close interest while he struck a spark with the flint and steel, and Piers felt he'd managed to redeem himself somewhat when he got a small blaze going. It would be enough to provide some comforting light in the tree-surrounded darkness. Trees, he knew, made quite a lot of noise in the middle of the night. Something about rustling leaves overcame his rational mind when the sun disappeared.

He opened his pack and took out a couple bundles of food. Atto took one, but he hardly even glanced at it. He said, "You're not carrying any tools at all, are you? Are you really even a mender?" He was looking at the open pack.

Piers didn't see how Atto could be sure that there weren't tools at the bottom of the pack, but it must be obvious that whatever was in there wasn't a complete set of things a mender would carry. He'd been waiting for this question, or some form of it, for weeks, and had avoided it partly by avoiding extended company. All the same, he'd been careful along the way not to say anything that the truth would contradict, because at some point he was going to have to come out with it and being discovered as a liar wouldn't help his case. For most people, learning about *Redemption* was likely going to be a test of their credulity anyway, and he needed to be seen as an honest man.

Atto was the only friend he had—maybe this was a chance to test his explanation. "No," he said. "I have been fixing things when I can, though, to earn a little bit of money as I go." Deliberately, Piers dropped his mental screens entirely, leaving himself completely Open for any hint of another Empath's presence. He didn't bother Reaching; he didn't expect to get any sort of response. He just wanted to dial up his sensitivity, to have a better chance of being able to read Atto's reactions to what he was about to say. That was, after all, the supposed advantage of being an Empath.

As he drew a breath to speak, Atto asked, "Are you in trouble?"

"Nothing like that. I'm…" Piers stopped. Involuntarily, he'd resumed Screening. It was a self-protective instinct, like shielding himself from an object hurled at his face. Hm. He wondered why, but he'd learned early, with his prodigious psi talent, that his own emotions could provide guidance long before his mind even registered on a situation. So, his intuition was reporting that it wasn't the right time to tell Atto—whether because Atto wasn't ready to hear or because he wasn't ready to say, he wasn't sure. "I guess it's a little bit like what you said Davyn does. I'm learning everything I can about this area, to help people make informed decisions. I need to meet the people who are in charge." Stopping short of the full explanation felt like an evasion, but if Atto asked who needed his decision-enabling research about Merra, he'd be stuck with half-truths that would shade very close to lies.

"That's why you want to go to Wyth?"

With relief at being able to postpone the conversation,

Piers said, "That, and I really do want to see if we can find out anything about Davyn."

"You don't think he's dead, do you?" It was a plea for reassurance.

Piers was taken aback by the reminder that Atto saw him as an adult. He showed him Davyn's dagger as evidence that he hadn't given up hope of being able to give it back to its owner. "My grandfather often said, 'Don't let what-if distract you from what-is, and don't let I-wish deter you from I-will.' We just have to do the best we can with what we know, and not let our worry hold us back."

Atto looked up at him, his young face earnest. "We'll go faster tomorrow," he said.

Piers smiled at him, and stood up, brushing dust and dry leaves off his legs. "It's been a long day and we've got a long way to go," he said. "Traveling takes stamina, so we should get rest while we can."

"How long have you been traveling?" Atto asked as he imitated Piers and started looking for a sleep-worthy patch of ground.

A trick question. "On this trip, just over forty days."

"This is the first time I've gone anywhere," Atto said. "How long do you think we'll be away?"

"Always hard to know. You start a trip with something in mind, but things happen that change your plans." Like discovering that your ship's timedrive is broken and you're going to miss your rendezvous by a thousand years.

Atto sat down in the middle of his chosen spot, stretched out his legs, and said, "I'm glad you came to Ruatt."

"So am I," Piers answered, meaning it. "And I'm glad you came with me when I left."

They started the day early. Atto was impatient to be on the road from the first trill of the first bird, and he had his pack on before Piers had finished shaking out his blanket and rolling the kinks out of his neck. The road raced ahead, straight into the morning sun, with tall grasses and weedy flowers swaying on either side.

"Atto, pace yourself. Running yourself breathless and collapsing by noon won't get us there any faster."

Atto grinned. "Can't keep up, fielder?" He trotted ahead a few yards, then turned around and kept going, backwards.

Piers kept his stride to a comfortable pace he knew he could sustain. "I'm sharing my hard-earned wisdom," he said. "And just so you know, I won't carry you." Atto jogged in place until Piers caught up. He was a head shorter than Piers, and couldn't match step for step, but he kept the pace, too.

"I wish we had horses." Atto said. "But I guess we wouldn't have gotten them across the bridge anyway."

"We barely got *me* across the bridge."

"Are you afraid of heights? Is that why you wouldn't climb up to the roof?"

"No, it's not a phobia. I just...need to be careful. And as you probably noticed, rivers intimidate me."

"If you're scared of the Lentava, you should hear Davyn talk about the Truolt. It's twice as big and a lot faster. I want to see it someday."

It led to a reprise of their earlier conversations: the places Atto wanted to see and the things he wanted to do. His enthusiasm for exploration reminded Piers of his own at that age, but with a difference. Atto knew his options. Piers had imagined a thousand lives for himself, but the looming event horizon of his lifetime—the landing—had in a strange way restricted his dreams. No one knew what opportunities would exist for any of them. The only certainty was that the world he knew, *Redemption*, would be left behind and he would not be the fourth Captain Haldon. He half-listened as Atto rambled, and let his mind roam over past and present. It made the miles slip by, so much faster than when he had trudged into Ruatt on his own.

"Where are you from?"

The question jarred Piers back into the conversation. Atto had been talking about where he might want to live, with endless references to things Davyn had told him about various places. Piers had been thinking about things he wanted to ask Davyn, if he got the chance, since it sounded like Davyn wasn't unlike a scout himself—a scout who had already been on this assignment for years. He'd been so far into that line of thought he hadn't been paying attention to the cadence of Atto's monologue. Usually there were cues that someone was about to hand over a conversation, but he'd missed them.

"Far from here," he said, which was more or less what he'd said before, though Atto hadn't asked so directly.

"I know that. I've never heard an accent like yours before. Are you from overshore?"

"Farther than that." He stopped Screening. Atto's curiosity was piercing, much stronger than Piers expected to feel. He stayed Open. "Atto, have you ever heard legends that more people are traveling through the stars to get here?" It was, he thought, a decent opening gambit.

With a half-laugh, Atto said, "Is that what you've been thinking about? I knew you weren't really listening." But he seemed unoffended, and answered, "Sometimes."

"Why only sometimes?"

"I believe it when I'm talking to Davyn, but Gran thinks

it's ridiculous. I mean, we don't even have proof that any of it really happened, and there's nothing about a second landing. I don't know. It seems crazy, but it also doesn't seem any weirder than the other stuff people come up with, and Davyn says there's evidence if you know where to look." Atto scuffed at a loose stone and it rattled a few yards ahead, still in his path. When he reached it, he kicked it again, and it rolled to a stop several steps in front of Piers. Piers sent it on its way, aiming it so it was set for Atto. After kicking the stone a good distance ahead, Atto said, with a certain amount of diffidence, "You know that disk I showed you? The one I found on the sandbar?"

Piers felt like his lungs might burst. "Yes."

"Davyn thinks it could be part of whatever they landed in." Atto was confiding a treasured secret and was braced for scorn.

Deep breath. "I think so, too," Piers said. It was his turn to kick the stone.

There was a change in the undercurrent, one that made Piers expect to feel a psi touch. At his affirmation, Atto had dropped his last barrier of reserve—no doubt without knowing it. To an Empath, the moment was a familiar part of establishing a friendship. Automatically, Piers Reached to Atto, an Empath's reflex, and it was disorienting when no response came. It was like finding that the thing you wanted to grasp was just a hologram. Atto's psi-like attributes were so convincing that Piers couldn't quite stop hoping.

"Really?" There was an edge of excitement in Atto's voice that his affected skepticism couldn't mask. "What do you think it is?"

Piers stopped and let his pack down at the edge of the road. They had seen no one this morning. "Let's rest for a minute," he said, partly to buy time to sift through the kaleidoscopic tumble of his thoughts. He sat down, letting his legs stretch into the road. The weeds and grass seemed to stand guard over him, and crushed stalks stuck out from underneath.

Atto sat beside him, his pack cradled on his folded legs. He took a gulp of water from his flask and repeated his question.

"I've seen things like it before," Piers said. "I grew up with them."

With a force that made him catch his breath, Piers felt Atto's surge of wild curiosity. So much stronger than a non-psi signal should be. "Where?" Atto demanded. All his longing for adventure, his imagination and ambition, and an earnest wish for the world to be more than it seemed was compressed in that small word.

"I grew up on a ship like the one your ancestors arrived in."

A flash of confusion, and then Atto was guarded again. "What do you mean? A ship?"

Sitting beside a dirt road, with his face shaded by the tall vegetation that surrounded him, Piers hardly trusted his memory of *Redemption*. He looked up at the few soft clouds drifting northward, and the brilliant sky filled with sunlight that blocked the stars, and took a full breath. Then he told Atto about the ship, about the journey, about the three thousand people desperate for a sustainable home. Atto's eyes narrowed, then widened, as the revelations accreted. Piers watched closely, and tried again to Reach Atto Empathically, but his friend still seemed unaware. He could almost feel Atto struggling through doubt and even suspicion and knew the boy's mind was beginning to construct barricades against further shock. So he stopped talking.

It wasn't silent; the small sounds of insects and hidden creatures in the grass and the faint music of birds in the distance were as loud, in their own way, as the hum and purr of the ship's systems. But as Piers waited for Atto's reaction, he felt as if he were being pushed along with the clouds, cut off from the tangible world and unable to alter the course of the wind.

This was the longest he'd stayed Open in ages, and the nausea was beginning to bubble. Before he let himself take refuge in Screening, Piers decided to take the more active step and Scan to see what he could pick up from Atto's feelings. It wasn't polite to pry, but even a psi-sensitive Separate would feel only a slow, creeping discomfort. If he tried it on an Empath without first Connecting, it would prompt something closer to outraged confusion. Atto's current mix of complex emotions would probably mask the intrusion.

Piers Scanned, and found all of Atto's emotions on the surface, unmasked but also unoffered. The strongest was a trembling, wistful doubt. Atto wanted to give in and believe, but resisted because he dreaded disappointment. Good enough, Piers thought. At least he doesn't think I'm crazy. A headache was now seeking a place to set up shop, so Piers gratefully hid behind his psi screens again.

"I don't know if I believe you," Atto finally said.

"I can imagine. I know it sounds bizarre."

Atto laughed, a short, dry laugh that made him sound years older. "There must be a better word. Bizarre's just the start." He stood up, and paced a few steps up the road, then back, several times while wrapped in his thoughts. He stopped in front of Piers. "So were you born up there? Is that what 'Starborn' means?"

"I'm not sure that's what they mean by calling them-selves that. But yes, I was born on the ship. It wasn't supposed to be like that—the ship was supposed to get here in my great-grandfather's time."

Another moment or two of speechless thoughts, and then Atto said, "Well, 'fielder' doesn't really cover it, then."

With his own laugh, Piers acknowledged the point. "No, not quite."

"It explains why you don't know anything at all," Atto said. He paced away again, and returned. "About here, I mean. I know you know all kinds of other stuff." Another there-and-back pause, and then the questions flooded out. He wanted to know what people on the ship did all day, if they had windows, what they could see, what they ate, what they did for fun. He wondered what was different and what was the same. What was the strangest thing for Piers about being on the ground? What did he like best? What did he miss most? And the ship itself: why didn't it fall to the ground, what did it look like, how did they steer it, how did they build it...

They started walking again as Piers did his best to handle the barrage. There were things he couldn't answer to Atto's satisfaction because Atto simply didn't have the background to make sense of it. Beyond that, he wasn't sure there was any way to explain the timedrive that wouldn't be gibberish to Atto—it wasn't clear if Atto had even rudimentary understanding of physics, much less metaphysics and psionics, and overall it seemed kinder not to get sidetracked into education even if it meant leaving some of his explanations unclear. With each round of questions, though, Atto's incredulity weakened, and Piers knew the fluency of his answers helped, even when they weren't entirely comprehensible.

"Do you think I'll get to see it?" Atto asked.

"The ship? I hope so. I'm here to make sure we can

land safely." He didn't want to go into the more subtle part of his mission. "Assuming we do land, three thousand people and a lot of new technology will suddenly appear, so we want to know that we won't be causing problems with awful consequences. So that's what I meant last night when I said I need to find whoever is in charge. It sounds like maybe that's Lord Ettori?"

Atto frowned. "Not really in charge, even if he is Prime House now. The Great Houses are supposed to be equal, except when they made up the Council they all agreed that one of them would have to be sort of in charge of the Tithe. House Caladen was Prime for ages and ages—since the Border War, I think, Davyn would know—but when Caladen fell, Ettori just took over."

Piers thought back to Atto's lesson. "So would I need to get all the Great Houses help us, not just Ettori?" So much for fast negotiation.

Only the Council would matter, Atto thought, but whether or not they would all need to be consulted was a question for someone else. He was sure, again, that Davyn would know, and of course Lord Wyth *probably* would. They kept walking.

16

CURIOSITY

House Wyth

RANE STRETCHED LAZILY in his bed and looked over at the window. All he could see was grey and silver, a dark-clouded sky and the glinting threads and streams of rain on the glass. He had always liked rain. His mother had told him that it had been raining the day he was born, and that rainy days were his lucky days. She also insisted that she had chosen his name irrespective of the weather, but he'd always liked the association.

Even for him, though, there'd been a little too much rain this year. Spring was always wet, but this year it was lingering and encroaching on summer. Every few days, more rain came, and the mornings had been cool even when the sun appeared. In a way it was too bad he'd shown Arissa the passageways already—it was the perfect thing for a rainy day. He wondered when Owen would be back.

Owen's frequent absences these days weren't all bad, because everyone unbent a little when he was gone. Breakfast didn't have to be at eight o'clock sharp, the chores didn't have to be done immediately, the servants didn't have to tiptoe about their business for fear of disturbing the quiet morning hours that Owen insisted he needed for managing House affairs. The routines weren't unreasonable, and there was nothing tyrannical about the way Owen treated the servants or Rane. He was just so miserably serious all the time, and seemed so seriously miserable, that no one wanted to cross him.

What bothered Rane about Owen's excursions was that they were usually at Kor's bidding. Kor used Owen like he was part of Ettori's House guard, sending him on errands or demanding his attendance. And Owen went along with all of it.

"I can't antagonize him, Rane," Owen explained every time Rane pushed him to assert his own authority. He reasoned that if Wyth could stay on Ettori's good side, Kor would keep pretending that they had a choice in going along with him. Owen didn't want to force Kor into overt dominance, because the House would suffer for that. Kor wasn't a friend, but Owen didn't want to make him an enemy.

So Owen hadn't refused the summons this time, either, and Rane was left to be host to Owen's bride-to-be for another day. He got out of bed and washed at the basin, and then dressed with—he admitted it—more care than usual. Yesterday had been a revelation. As he'd been sliding into sleep last night, he'd thought about the fact that he felt closer to Arissa than he had to most of the women he'd spent far more time with. He had to stop it here. Had to get his feelings in check, or at least be much, much better at hiding them. His lapse yesterday was unforgivable and unfair to all of them. Owen had enough troubles, and for that matter, so did Arissa.

He left his room feeling as ready as he could be to face her. He'd slept later than he'd meant to, and it was well past nine, and he'd promised to see his father first thing. Arissa had probably eaten her breakfast alone anyway, so he'd seek her out after visiting.

His father was fading. It was hard to reconcile the attenuated figure on the sickbed with his boisterous father, and the wheezing that convulsed the old man's body made it painful for him to talk. He had little memory of his sons. Owen and Rane had fallen into a routine of frequent, short visits, letting Father know he wasn't forgotten but not demanding much of his energy. On this visit, Rane rambled about little things going on, but his mind was occupied with gnawing thoughts of Arissa and worries about Ettori.

Rane gently closed his father's bedroom door behind him as he left. It was a reasonable hour to knock at Arissa's door, though he hadn't yet thought of a way to entertain her today. As he crossed the landing that overlooked the entrance hall, he heard a servant call to him, "Dan Rane, sir, a moment." It was Douglas, the senior House man whose unerring competence kept the House functioning. Rane paused and met him as he came up the wide stairs.

"There's a man here who says he wants to speak with Lord Wyth. He has a boy with him; they're both soaked through. I put them in the small receiving room while I came to find you." Douglas held his sheathed dagger out to him, hilt first. "Just in case, Dan Rane."

"Any guesses?" Rane asked, tucking the dagger into his belt without comment. It was the kind of practical precaution they counted on Douglas to think of. He'd have to find Arissa later. He started down the stairs.

"Hard to say," Douglas said. "They came on foot—the boy said they've walked from Ruatt, and they look like it. Polite enough, though."

They reached the heavy oak door to the receiving room,

and Rane asked Douglas to bring telik, something to eat, and some towels. The door swung into the room, and Rane saw the man and boy standing in puddles in the center of the flagstone floor. Beside each dripping figure was a pack surrounded by its own little pool. As Rane entered, both visitors turned to face him and the man took a half step toward him. With what was supposed to be a subtle gesture, the boy knocked the back of his hand against the man's arm. Rane held back a smile as the man stopped short and made what was probably the most inept attempt at a bow Rane had ever seen.

"Lord Wyth," the man said, "I'm Piers Haldon, and this is Atto Reed." The boy ducked his head, a child's gesture.

Rane acknowledged the man's bow, and then offered a handshake. "In fact, I'm the younger son, Rane. Welcome to House Wyth."

The small receiving room was rarely used. Guests to House Wyth typically were greeted in the hall these days and then whisked off to wherever the visit began. This room had once been elegant and used when receiving guests on informal occasions. Now it was usually used as a staging area for luggage. The comfortable chairs had long since migrated to other rooms, but there was a wooden bench beside the door, and a quartet of carved chairs facing the disused hearth across a low table.

"I've asked Douglas to bring telik and some towels for you," Rane said, waving to take in the chairs and the bench. "It's fine if you'd like to sit. I apologize for receiving you here, but Douglas thought it'd be a better place for your wet gear. It's miserable weather to be on the road."

The boy said, "Sorry we're dripping all over everything." He had the broad accent of a Wyth Valley native, and the direct casualness of a town dweller. Ruatt, then.

The man was harder to place. He spoke with studied precision, but it wasn't an accent Rane recognized.

"Not worth a thought," Rane said. The man might be in his late twenties or early thirties, with only a few faint creases at the corners of his eyes, and no sign of grey in his hair or the stubble on his face. It was hard to guess what shade his hair would be when it was dry, but it was long enough to curl around his ears. There were some small tears in his clothes, and his shoes were nearly worn out. The drenching didn't do anything to counter the vagabond impression he made.

Rane wanted to stick to small talk until they were more at ease, and they gamely answered his questions about their journey until Douglas returned with a tray and a helper who was carrying a stack of towels. With telik poured and cooling on the hearth table, and Atto eyeing the food, Rane excused himself for a few minutes to give them a chance to dry off a bit and feel more composed before the conversation turned to anything more serious.

The wooden chairs weren't very comfortable, but it did feel good to be off his feet. Piers thought longingly of his dry clothes, but looking at Atto's pack he knew there would be no way to explain why everything in his own pack wasn't just as waterlogged. At least there was no longer water streaming or dripping from him; he'd dried his hair most of the way with the towel and had wrung the rain out of his shirt.

The telik was welcome, both for the heat of the mug in his hands and the soothing warmth of the beverage as he drank. He'd learned to appreciate it, though he still couldn't decide if he liked it. It seemed to be a mild sedative, with a touch of a psychotropic effect that made everyone around seem to be as familiar as friends. At least that's how it affected Piers.

Atto, however, was not noticeably sedated. He'd eaten two of the breakfast pies—sausage and egg in a pastry crust—and was ebullient, thrilled about being in one of the Houses. He stayed in his chair with verbalized reluctance, but every few minutes he repeated some version of the hope that they'd be able to see more of the House.

The door opened, and in his relaxed state, Piers took the measure of their host more deliberately as he joined them by the hearth. He was a good-looking man, close to Piers's own age, and dressed like he was used to luxury. Piers particularly noticed his shoes, but everything he was wearing was quality. There was a dagger at his hip, though he didn't look like a brawler. No, this was the kind of guy whose confidence came from knowing he had a reserved seat on the escape shuttle.

For a moment Piers wondered if he'd made a mistake in not keeping Davyn's dagger on him—but Atto had been adamant that it should be hidden away, and had buried it deep in his own pack. "They'll check you first," Atto had said. "And if they don't find any weapons, they will probably figure we're both safe." He'd grinned. "They'll think that since you're the grown-up, you'd be the one worried about defending us." Cheeky kid.

Rane motioned for them not to get up, and he pulled a chair around to face theirs. He picked up the third cup of telik that the servant had poured, took one of the breakfast sandwiches, then sat back and looked at Piers expectantly.

Piers dropped his screens, hoping for a subconscious cue from Rane that would help him navigate. He felt Atto thrumming with nervous energy at his right, like a vibration felt through the air. It was the clearest and most sustained sense of Atto he'd had. He Pushed some reassurance to him, and was gratified to feel the nervousness tip toward curiosity. Whatever else, Atto was the most psi-sensitive Separate Piers had ever met. Then Piers trained his Empathic attention on their host.

At first there was nothing. He kept his focus, in a trick he'd once compared to letting his eyes adjust to the dark. And like dark-adapted eyes that can distinguish a shadow in the darkness by its deeper, smoother blackness, he found Rane's wavelength because it was being dampened. It was not walled off by natural Separation. It was a psi barrier, as solid as any Piers had ever encountered, but different. Instead of the shimmering, energetic barrier most Empaths could learn to hide behind, Rane's was dense and smooth and inflexible. It was like scar tissue, Piers thought. His next thought ripped through that one as the real import hit him—Rane was psi.

Piers started, his body betraying his surprise. He slammed his own screens back in place and his physical senses rushed back in. The man was regarding him with a neutral gaze and a hint of a smile. Was it a knowing smile? Or just a cordial expression? Very cautiously, with the lightest touch he could manage, Piers Reached again. But there was no change in the hazel eyes, and no Empathic response. Piers left his screens down, now, but tuned out Atto's buzzing.

"So you've come from Ruatt to see my brother," Rane said. "Would he know what this is about?"

Piers struggled to hold himself in the conversation, rather than diving back into the attempt to Connect. He replied, "Atto tells me that Wyth is the authority here."

And there it was—a flare that broke through Rane's control: suspicion, doubt, and a shred of alarm. The flecked green eyes showed all of it, though there was no other change in his expression. It was gone just as quickly, and Rane said, "One of several."

Piers felt his stomach start to seethe, Blocked, and backed away from the topic for now. If it was going to be a tricky conversation, he'd rather wait to have it with the right person. "Atto and I are searching for a missing friend, and the last person known to have seen him is the woman he was traveling with—Arissa of House Aryn. We were told she is here."

"You're looking for Davyn?"

Ah. Redirection achieved. "Yes. His friends in Trint are worried."

That earned him a sharp look, but Rane's response was a heartbeat late. "I see," Rane said.

"Is he here?" Atto asked.

With a look Piers didn't quite catch, Rane turned to Atto and said, "No." There was remorse, or at least regret, in the way he said the word. Then Rane looked at Piers, adult to adult, and Piers understood. Damn.

Unfortunately, Atto understood as well. "No. He's not dead," Atto declared. "I'd know if he was."

Rane's gentle look of pity was genuine, but he only said, "I hope you are right."

Piers put an arm around Atto's shoulders and Pushed a bit of slightly artificial calmness. Given the intensity of Atto's denial, and the nearly disabling disappointment he himself felt, Piers imagined that he wasn't going to be very effective in managing either of their emotions.

"My brother will be home later today," Rane said, changing the subject with no attempt at subtlety. "You'll need to talk to him about Lady Arissa. If you'd like to wait, you can be more comfortable in the guest quarters.

You both look like you could sleep for days and I suspect you'd be glad for a bath as well." He barely raised his voice to call for the servant, and the door opened immediately.

Piers and Atto followed the servant back outside. The rain had stopped, though there were still heavy clouds loitering above the House. The guest quarters apparently didn't have internal access to the rest of the building. Interesting security choice, Piers thought. Wyth guests might run off in the night or get up to no good outside, but the House, its inhabitants, and its riches would be perhaps that little bit safer. Daggers and locked doors. Maybe the Wyth way of thinking wasn't the best hope to welcome *Redemption*'s passengers home—but Rane was undeniably psi, and Piers had to build on that.

The door opened into a sitting room, which was small but furnished with upholstered chairs, a thick rug, a few tables, and even art on the walls. One whole wall, to the right, was a floor-to-ceiling bookcase, entirely filled with leatherbound, gilt-lettered books of various sizes. Piers could hardly wait to take a closer look. The opposite wall had a small window that was barricaded by iron bars.

Across the room from the door, a stone fireplace interrupted the far wall, and a corridor led past it on the left, offering a row of open doors. After watching the servant, Douglas, light a fire in the hearth with a simple strike of a match, Piers made a mental note to ask Atto if stealing matches would be a criminal act or just bad manners. The back of the firebox was metal, and Douglas explained that it was the side of the water tank for the bath. The water would be comfortably hot within half an hour, he said, and then showed them how to drop an insulating panel in place to keep themselves from being boiled. Piers thought it made a decent metaphor for the way his psi screens worked.

Atto was uncharacteristically quiet after Douglas left, and stood rooted in the middle of the sitting room. Piers stopped Screening, again, to pick up any emotion that Atto might unknowingly evince. He could now pick out Atto's emotional state without effort, like a path had been cleared between them. It wasn't his imagination. It was absolutely more than the effect of Piers being Open to a Separate, because Atto's presence was so distinct and persistent—but it wasn't like Linking, because Atto didn't seem to be aware at all of Piers's presence, and certainly wasn't Reaching back to pick up any reciprocal emotive information. It also wasn't like Scanning, because he didn't have to pry to get the full sense of Atto's feelings. What Atto seemed to be feeling now was nothing but resolution.

"He's not dead," Atto said. "He's just not here." There was unshakable conviction in Atto's voice. He seemed to have decided what he wanted to believe, and what's more, he believed it without any reservation at all.

There were stories about people who had that sense about someone else, though it mostly happened with family or lovers. It happened, certainly, to Empaths who had been Connected for a long time. There seemed to be different psi patterns here, as if the ability refused to be managed. Atto had Empathic ability, Piers was sure of it, but the boy had no idea. He felt Pushes but never Reached, never Screened, never listened. There wasn't even the accidental flailing that afflicted newly triggered Empaths on the ship. It was almost like he'd achieved the psychic saturation of Connection accidentally—maybe Atto really could tell that Davyn was still alive.

Or maybe Atto had just decided not to believe an assumption. No one had explicitly said that Davyn was dead, and no one had explained what had happened. On one level, Piers wanted to say that to Atto, that perhaps Rane had it wrong. But he had no particular reason to offer that hope. There was no evidence either way—and Davyn's death seemed more probable.

"I still want to talk to Arissa," Piers said. "I want to hear what she knows."

"Yeah," Atto said. "Maybe she saw what happened."

"Atto, I understand some of what you're feeling, and I hope Arissa has answers for us. Just protect yourself a little, all right? It might be bad news."

Atto cocked his head and considered Piers. There was no question that he wanted to say something like, *How can I possibly make this any clearer?* Instead, he said, "I told you. I know he's fine." He ran a hand over the patterned silk on the back of a chair. "Look at this place. You have no idea how rich this is."

They went from room to room, with Atto explaining whatever caught his eye. Piers walked after him and made his own notes. There was just a single door to the outside and three heavily barred windows with a view to the wet courtyard. House Wyth really didn't trust guests, but apparently there was a hospitable interest to see to their comfort. And to make sure they knew where they were: the House emblem was carved or embroidered everywhere, an elaborate W styled to look like the folds of a paper fan. An arrow pierced the folds, straight through all four strokes of the letter.

Atto pointed out what was exotic and what was expected, and where House Wyth was showing its history and its wealth. Both were evident in the furnishings—Atto told Piers to sit in a narrow, plain wooden chair and said it was probably the oldest thing in the House, probably hundreds of years old. The fact that furniture like that had survived epochs when other people were using whatever they had for firewood was also a sign of Wyth's wealth.

The more obvious riches included the luxurious fabrics and the abundance of exotic wood. The timber from the forest around Wyth wasn't good for carving, Atto said, so the fact that even the walls were covered with carved panels meant someone had paid a lot of money to bring that wood from somewhere else.

When Atto had concluded his thorough inspection of the suite, he flung himself backward onto a bed despite his still-damp clothes. "It's better than I imagined, and we haven't even seen the real House! They probably never want to leave."

Piers leaned against the door frame to the bedroom, his thoughts now well beyond the rush of fascination. "What do you think, Atto?" he asked. "Will they believe me?"

"Doubt it," Atto said cheerfully, propping up on his elbows. "House Wyth has been right here for hundreds and hundreds of years, and I bet they think they've seen it all." He sat up. "But you'll try anyway, won't you?"

"I have to. The ship can't support us much longer, and we've got to land. If we could just land in the middle of nowhere and keep to ourselves, we would, but we're going to need help." That was truth, but such a small part of it that Piers's guilt pushed him to elaborate. "The ark ships, like mine, aren't equipped to start a civilization from scratch; the foundation ships were supposed to do that. And at this point, none of us have any idea how to go about it."

"Ships? More than one?"

Oh, good move, Piers thought. He hadn't intended to go that far. "There were three pairs. Three different planets."

Atto was quiet, taking that in, and then he smiled. "Well, maybe you should see if there's a teller here. He could tell one of the legends and then you could just say, 'That's true, by the way.'" Atto laughed, but Piers wasn't sure he was entirely joking.

"A teller?"

"People who just wander around and entertain people with stories. Kind of like menders. Sometimes one of them will stay at a House for a while. I wasn't serious, though."

"I know, but it isn't the worst idea."

"Ha! They'd just say you're as crazy as the Starborn and throw you out. I think you have to work up to it, like you did with me. They'll start realizing there's something a little off about you—yes, I did! I just didn't know what—and then when you tell them, they'll feel like everything's been explained."

"So how are we going to get them to let us stay for a few days so I can convince them I'm strange?"

Atto grinned. "Oh, it won't take that long."

∽

Although Owen was standing by his chair and looking cool and commanding, Rane knew he wasn't feeling that way. He'd been in a foul mood when he returned from his Ettori errand with the last of the daylight, but he'd insisted that it was his obligation to greet the guests as soon as possible. None of Rane's sensible advice to wait until he was better rested had made any difference.

Arissa was near Owen, and she looked like she was trying to overcome some anxiety. It was good that she was here. If the stranger really did just want to talk to Arissa, then he could do it with an audience. If there were some deeper purpose to his arrival at Wyth, Rane was pretty sure he'd be able to detect a false note when the man encountered Arissa. She'd been less sure that it was a good idea. She didn't want to talk about Davyn, she said, and didn't want to talk about what had happened at the Starborn camp. She said Owen had reacted badly when she told him how the Ettori men had treated her. So it had taken all Rane's deliberate sincerity to persuade her to be here in the room, and now the three of them were posed in the grand receiving room, Lord Wyth, his bride, and his brother, waiting for the stranger.

Douglas returned with Piers, and the Ruatt boy had come, too. Owen was never comfortable with children, and there was a comedic exchange of first impressions: Owen reacting to Atto's presence and glowering at Piers, and Piers reacting to Arissa's presence and tripping over his own feet. In other circumstances, Rane would have laughed. He understood, though. In this room with its dark and masculine furnishings, Arissa's bright hair, sapphire eyes, and luminous skin made her look even more exquisite.

Owen introduced her as Lady Arissa of House Aryn, and added, with a cool possessiveness, "My betrothed." Arissa looked a little miffed at that, but walked up to Piers with her hands out, palms down. There was a flash of alarm in his eyes, and then he took her hands in his, folding his fingers around hers, and bowed over them. Arissa snatched her hands away.

At that, Rane did laugh—just one little sputter before he caught himself. Atto giggled, too, and Rane grinned at him before he glanced over and saw that Owen was stone-faced, and his rigid posture would have made their old tutor proud. Briefly, Rane wondered what the stranger was up to, but then he saw the man's stricken face. The poor man was utterly bewildered.

"I'm sorry if I've offended you, Lady Arissa," Piers said. "I'm not familiar with the customs here."

"So I see," she said, recovering somewhat, though she was blushing.

Rane winked at Atto; he couldn't help himself. He was glad someone else also found humor in the fact that right after Owen had staked his claim on Arissa, in a rather high-handed and charmless way, the stranger had inadvertently proposed to her—with an old-fashioned, formal, and romantic gesture that was what girls supposedly daydreamed about. And Piers was handsome enough for the role, now that he was dry and dressed in better clothes.

"I beg your pardon," Piers said to Arissa with a rueful smile. "I just meant to greet you courteously, because I am honored to meet you."

That wasn't bad for admitting a gaffe, especially since he obviously knew he'd embarrassed her and didn't know what he'd done wrong. Rane was sure Atto was looking forward to enlightening him when he got the chance.

The interactions after that were stilted for a while. They sat in chairs that circled a Wyth medallion on the carpet. Owen leaned back, feigning blasé confidence. Beside him, Arissa perched at the edge of her chair, her hands tucked under her as if to hide them. Directly across from Rane, Piers sat like he had fossilized himself to keep from fidgeting. Atto did fidget, and seemed to be appraising everything in the room. Rane ended up as the facilitator, and more or less managed to keep the conversation going until Owen finally decided to take hold of the moment.

He leaned forward, his eyes at their most intense. "And where are you from?" he asked Piers. "You sound like you're far from home."

"He's a mender," Atto said before Piers could answer. "He wanders."

Owen gave the boy a look that would have made most people quail, but Atto was unfazed.

"We have no need of a mender." Owen directed his annoyance to Piers. "Why have you come here?"

Piers took a very deep breath and flicked his gaze to Atto. Rane saw the boy shake his head, slightly, and saw Piers make the same gesture in reply. Then Piers said, "Davyn was expected back at the Briar Inn in Ruatt several days ago. When he didn't arrive, Atto wanted to come after him."

"He's not here. He's dead," Owen said, apparently without even a passing thought that it might be painful news to the visitors.

As the boy drew his shoulders back and prepared to argue, Piers put a restraining, brotherly arm around him and cut in, saying, "I have another reason for coming to you."

Rane saw Atto tense, and saw Piers weighing his words. With a strange cadence in his voice, as if he were beginning a tale, Piers said, "I have traveled all my life, and I've seen both more and less than you could imagine. I have more in common with your ancestors than with you."

"And I have no patience with riddles," Owen grumbled.

Piers inclined his head, an acknowledgment and apology in one gesture. "I don't mean to be cryptic. I just honestly don't know where to begin." He seemed to wander into his own thoughts, and Rane saw Owen growing impatient as the silence spun out. Owen was on the brink of real annoyance when Piers began again. "I'll start by saying that I know this is going to be hard to believe."

17

PERSPECTIVE

House Wyth

I T WAS A relief when Rane and Owen stopped snarling
and started to glower silently at each other in that
way that only siblings can. Arissa recognized it for
what it was: a brief boiling-over of a simmering dynamic
between the brothers that had little to do with the situation
at hand. But she wanted them to stop sparring over Rane's
history of pranks so that they could talk about what the
stranger had said.

"Are you done?" she asked the brothers. Neither one
looked at her, but Rane gave his brother one more emphatic
scowl and then flung himself into his chair. Owen muttered
something she couldn't hear and stomped over to the sideboard and poured a glass of wine. He tossed it back and
refilled the glass. He offered her a glass, then, but pointedly
did not offer to pour one for Rane. She shook her head,
and said, "Come sit down, Owen."

She took a seat opposite the two of them, and waited
for one of them to say something. Owen's lips were still

compressed and his jaw tight, as if that were the only way to keep from saying something he'd regret. Rane, though, exhaled sharply and adjusted his position so that he was no longer slouched in the chair like a sullen teenager.

"What if it's true?" Arissa asked, to break them out of the obstinate silence.

Rane chuffed. "If it's true, things are going to get very interesting around here."

"Don't be ridiculous," Owen said. "Three thousand people in the sky, looking for a place to live? That's a town the size of Drisk."

"We know it's happened before," Rane said. Owen's furrowed brow worried Arissa. She hoped Owen wasn't one of the people who denied history. They had all kinds of alternative explanations for how people came to be and why there was no sign of history going back further than the Houses.

"We *suppose* it has," Owen countered. "That's all we know."

"The ancients came from somewhere," Rane said. "No sign there was anything here before the Houses."

"No sign of a landing, either," Owen insisted. "Even if they just came down a few at a time on a 'shuttle' like his, someone, somewhere, sometime, would have found at least part of it. Metal lasts a long time."

Sitting here in House Wyth's formal receiving room, they weren't going to be able to answer a question that people had been asking for generations. There was no new evidence—unless the man's oilcloth pack really was something else, like he said—to prove either argument. As Arissa saw it, they would have to decide what to do without knowing what was true. If three thousand people were about to arrive in search of safe haven, it would be good to have a plan.

"That's true, brother," Rane said. "But personally, I'd rather be prepared and wrong about them coming than *un*prepared and wrong about them *not* coming."

He saw her take a beat to parse his words, and grinned that charming, irreverent, irrepressible grin of his. "It sounded very profound in my head," he said.

"Your head is profoundly asinine," Owen muttered.

"Ah," Rane said. "Now we're friends again." He turned to Arissa. "When he starts muttering insults at you, you know he's not really peeved anymore. When he's angry, he's very, very articulate."

Owen gave his brother a hard look and then laughed despite himself. He looked more like Rane when he smiled. In a way, Arissa thought, seeing him lose his temper had made him more likable. At least it was a sign that he had emotions. "Peace, then," he said to Rane. "I'm sorry I accused you of setting this up."

"I only wish I *had* thought of a prank like that," Rane said. "But Arissa's right. If there's any chance that it's true, the Houses are going to want a say in how it unfolds. We should call a Gathering."

Owen sagged. "The damn Gathering again? Rane, no. For the millionth time, no."

Disingenuously, Arissa asked, "Why not?" Rane's hazel eyes were fixed on her face, a plea for caution. Owen truly didn't know the Gathering had happened, which must make Rane happy, but how would he explain his opposition?

Owen pulled back into his shell, and, as if another person took his place, the stiff, mirthless Lord Wyth reappeared. "I'm not discussing it. Rane knows my thoughts on the matter."

Her own temper ignited. "Well," she said. "I guess there's no reason why you should share your thoughts with *me.*" That acid edge, the one her mother said she should never let a man hear, seemed to sting him a little. Her first reaction to the flicker in his eyes was satisfaction, but then the rush of guilt swept in. Well, it was better he learn now that she wasn't going to simper in the background while men discussed and decided everything interesting.

Her betrothed didn't reply. He set his almost-empty wineglass down and got out of his chair. He dipped his head toward her, very coolly, very properly, and said, "I've had a long day. No doubt in the morning we'll be able to address this more productively. Good night." And he strode from the room, leaving Arissa alone with Rane, whose grin was now infuriating.

There was no note this morning, and Arissa tried to swat away the slight pang of disappointment. Had he stopped trying to win her over already? Because she'd angered him last night? How could she possibly marry a man who was that thin-skinned? As she washed her face and brushed her hair, the last question was the one that persisted. Thin-skinned, obdurate, boring, and rude. She couldn't, wouldn't, marry him—no matter how rich, handsome, or well-positioned he was.

The servant's knock at the door startled her, but she called that it was open. She hoped Darletta was bringing telik as she'd done the previous morning. She kept her focus on the mirror, adjusting her hair, and brightly said good morning.

Rane answered, and she could hear the smile in his voice. She turned, feeling oddly foolish, and saw him standing just inside the room looking perfectly at ease. He was holding a small lantern, and a cloth sack hung from his shoulder. "I've had a devilish thought that I just can't ignore," he said, with mischief gleaming in his eyes. He rocked back on his heels. "Owen told me last night that he's going to talk to the man on his own this morning, and that you and I have to stay out of it. In fact, he *forbids* us to talk to the man again, and he's going to decide on his own what to do about this. Apparently he thinks we're not skeptical enough to be trusted even to listen."

That nearly started her seething, but Rane was still smiling. She said, "I imagine it will be an interesting conversation."

"Oh yes, it will be. I brought breakfast for us. Come with me..."

The passageway beside Owen's study was one of the narrow ones, so they sidled in, half-turned toward the wall of the study, not quite able to walk but not quite limited to shuffling sideways. Rane led the way, and she stayed close to get whatever benefit she could from the lantern.

They heard the low rumble of man's voice. Arissa tapped Rane's shoulder. He craned his head back, and she pointed to the wall and shook her head—she couldn't make out the words. Rane held up one finger, then moved a few steps further.

When Owen spoke, his voice was muted but not muffled. He must be right on the other side of the wall. No wonder Rane had warned her that silence—not just quiet—was essential. "No," Owen said in answer to the rumble. "Not here. I'll go there. He might be more at ease." Another rumble, and Owen said, "Please go tell him I'm on the way. I'll give him a few minutes to get himself together."

Rane stepped toward her, nudging her to hurry back. She reversed her angle to face back the way they'd came, but with the lantern behind her, she was feeling her way cautiously. Rane misjudged her pace and bumped into her back. He caught her as she stumbled, and she bit her lip to stop a giggle, and tried not to be so aware of the warmth of his hands. When she was steady, he let her go with a light tap to tell her to move ahead, and held the lantern higher.

When they were back in the hall, Rane took her hand and pulled her after him, looking back over his shoulder once to flash a smile at her. At the far end of the north wing, where she hadn't been before, the gracious hall was lined with massive wall hangings that were at least fifteen feet wide. Halfway along the wall to their right was a pair of closed, carved doors. Rane glanced around, and then lifted the nearest hanging away from the wall.

That stubborn giggle resurfaced as they moved behind the curtain. The fabric rippled around them, and they must look like two moving lumps—a snake swallowing prey—as they edged along the wall. Near the middle, Rane pushed his foot against the wall, and a board tilted away from its neighbors. He slipped his hand into the gap and pried open an entrance. When they were inside, he pushed the board back into place.

They stayed close to the wall on their left, and walked single-file almost to the far end. Rane whispered, "We're between the banquet hall and the guest suite. They took half the hall to make the suite, and they left this passage on purpose." It ran the full length of the hall, perpendicular to the north end of the House. One of the windows that used to grace the eastern end of the banquet hall had been turned into the door to the guest quarters.

When a vestibule was added for the door to the guest quarters, the architect had extended the outside wall for symmetry. Rane stopped just short of that pocket space between the former exterior and the new one. There was a vertical seam in the wall, and a small notch at waist height. "It opens into the guest room," Rane whispered, so close in her ear that a shiver ran through her. "The wall is thinner here."

A moment later, they heard a knock and the visitor said clearly, in his strange accent, "That must be him. Wish me luck, Atto."

The boy's lighter voice was harder to hear.

"Lord Wyth," Piers said. A pause, then a pleasant laugh. "I wasn't sure if I should propose or not."

In the dark passageway where they stood side by side, Arissa could feel Rane's suppressed laugh, and her cheeks burned. She elbowed him vengefully.

"A handshake will suffice," Owen said, and Arissa could picture his wooden expression.

"Not a good beginning," Rane said. Another shiver danced along her skin, not entirely unpleasant. "The man can't read Owen at all."

They heard the boy's voice, and then for a few minutes, nothing. Then Owen said, "I want you to explain it again."

The stranger's explanation was no different—and no less bizarre—this time. No detail had changed. Owen asked more questions, and Piers answered freely. In the near-dark of the passage, Arissa and Rane sat down against the wall, close together. They ate the pastries Rane had brought in the sack, and stared at the solid wall of the guest suite as if they could see through it. She looked over at him a couple of times, and was aware of him looking at her when he thought she wouldn't notice.

"And your three thousand, do they want to settle here together? Or are we being invaded?" Owen asked, and his voice was very clear.

The pause was the length of a sigh, and Piers answered, "If things had gone as planned, they would have stayed together because there would only have been one settlement.

Since we're late, I think we have to do whatever is best for the existing community—communities. But it will be hard. We won't fit in very well."

"You've managed, haven't you?"

"I trained hard to be ready for this," Piers said. "My great-grandfather should have been the one, but we...we got lost on the way here. We had to do a lot of guesswork to try to prepare. We must have done pretty well if you think I'm managing to fit in."

"These references to getting lost and being late...What do you mean?"

A much longer pause this time. Then, "Your ancestors and my great-grandfather were the same generation. They—we—have technology that lets us move through time. They left Earth within weeks of each other, and they were supposed to be transported directly here at a precise moment. So my ancestors were supposed to arrive here twenty-five years after yours. Your ancestors would have started to build a civilization, and our ship was supposed to bring the rest of the population and more supplies. But our technology failed and we were transported to the wrong time and the wrong place. Instead of twenty-five years, it had been nine hundred and some. And we were far away from here, and our ship couldn't jump through time again. So we had to move in real time, and it has taken us eighty-two years of traveling through the stars to reach you."

Owen's response came after a long silence, and Arissa held her breath to hear him. He meted out his words. "And after the stars, your people need to land. Here." Even through the wall, Owen's mistrust and incredulity was blatant.

"Yes," Piers said. "We need to land soon, desperately. We need help. It's why we sent scouts—to find assistance. And to try to ease the shock."

"And if you're not welcome?"

There was flint in Piers's voice. "We have no choice. We have to land, and we're not set up to carve a place for ourselves in the wilderness like your ancestors did, so we need to be near civilization—near people who know how to live on a planet. It will be better for all of us if we arrange for this together."

"It's quite a tale," Owen said.

"It's not a tale," Atto protested, and it sounded like he was standing right beside Arissa, as if the wall weren't there. "It's the truth. Piers actually never lies."

"It's all right, Atto." Piers's strong tenor carried easily. "I know it's a lot to process."

Owen went back to the interrogation, and asked Piers about everything from food to family life, some of which he'd already talked about. Arissa thought Piers was more tolerant and more candid than she would have been, and he didn't sound put off by Owen's skepticism. In fact, there was humor in a lot of his answers.

Piers talked about growing up on the ship, about footraces in the corridors, sneaking into forbidden areas as a teenager, and trying to evade his studies. His education had been thorough and tedious, and it made an unremarkable recollection of childhood scholastics, except for the subjects. When he talked about his parents and sister, it sounded ordinary, familiar. There was a sense of home, and of homesickness, when he spoke, just like any traveler. He had a niece, he said, a little girl of three. Her fascinations were pretty colors and animals.

"What animals?" Owen asked. "You said you'd never seen a horse until you were here." Arissa thought there was a note of challenge in his voice. Beside her, Rane flipped his hands up and rolled his eyes at Owen's tone, then smiled at her.

"All Earth animals," Piers answered. "She looks at the pictures and asks for stories about them. We do have a few small animals on the ship, and she constantly wants to chase them down to pat them."

Earth. In the archives at Aryn, the oldest document they had was a fragment of a family tree that had supposedly been started on Earth. And yet...Yet Earth was little more than legend, too far removed to have meaning.

Owen asked about Earth. Rane cut back the flame of their lantern to extend the oil, and Arissa tried to hold her breath so she wouldn't miss a word of Piers's answer.

Piers paused. Atto's coruscant curiosity was almost distracting. He'd found no way to read Lord Wyth, other than through whatever physical expression of his thoughts he didn't bother to conceal. Unlike the younger brother's psi-protected feelings, this man's emotions were stifled by something more unyielding, battered into submission by inexorable will. Whether psi energy was involved or not was surprisingly hard to tell.

The room felt far too warm. The heat from last night's fire was taking a long time to dissipate. In the old wooden chair with his back to the fireplace, his elbows on his knees, Piers could swear it felt like there was still a fire burning.

Despite all the information he'd shared, his host still didn't seem convinced. Piers didn't know what else he could do, short of having the ship land. The man was looking at him now with such strong skepticism that he was glad—relieved, even—that he couldn't actually feel it.

"Understand, everything I know about it has been passed

down," he said carefully. "There's no one alive on the ship now who was there. But it sounds like Earth was very much like here, physically. This planet was chosen for the New Foundation Project because they could make it Earth-like."

"Ridiculous," Owen said. "No one 'made' it like anything. It evolved."

"Yes," Piers said. "But that evolution was intentionally set in motion. A seed ship landed here, hundreds of thousands of years ago, with the technology for accelerated terraforming." He stopped. Did Owen know the word? Did he have any knowledge of bacteria, or ecosystems, or DNA? Asking would be taken as condescension, he suspected. He changed tack and simply described what he knew about the climates on Earth.

Lord Wyth listened, and seemed interested but still dubious. Atto drank it in.

"Tell me about this 'New Foundation Project,'" Wyth said.

Piers wished he hadn't mentioned it. He didn't want to try to explain Earth politics from a thousand years ago, and didn't see how any mention of psi abilities could possibly be helpful just now. The NFP had been controversial from its inception, and the unimaginable cost of the program had staggered Earth. But there had been enough people, sick to their souls at the wreck they saw coming, willing to pay to give humanity another chance. The persecution of the psis had been a piece of the mosaic for some. When it was leaked that the bridge crew were psi, some people had suspected that the Empaths were manipulating people into supporting what amounted to an escape plot for themselves. That canard had lasted surprisingly long, even to the point of signs being held up on launch day, well after all the money had been spent.

He told Owen the simple version. "There were people who felt humanity needed a fresh start. The project was to create three new home worlds, and rebuild only the best parts of the civilization they were leaving behind."

The questions didn't stop. For another hour, Owen grilled him about the rebuilding plans, and asked the hardest question of all: why hadn't the plan worked here?

"I wish I knew," Piers answered. "When we learned about the time-slip, we were excited because we thought we'd get to see how technology evolved. When we got here and found the planet silent, it was a blow."

"And by 'silent', you mean…?"

"Non-communicative. If nothing else, there was supposed to be a signal here, something that would guide us in. There wasn't, and when we scanned the planet we found nothing we recognized." He tried to stay away from any phrase that would seem like a judgment. The truth was that when they'd determined there was nothing down here that generated a signal, not even radio, it had been crushing. It was his generation's equivalent of the Manifesters' realization that the ship had missed its timemark. All expectations had been erased by that one new fact.

"So without this signal, how are you going to land?"

Piers hesitated. It was the most salient question, by far, but he was sorry Lord Wyth had gotten to it so quickly. He wished he'd told Atto about his psi ability—wished he'd tested the reaction to that truth. This man, whose incredulity was almost hostility, didn't seem likely to welcome another revelation. Atto was watching him closely, seeming to recognize a moment of deliberation and apparently counseling caution. It was probably wise, but he couldn't ignore that particular question.

"I can communicate with the ship," Piers said. "I can guide them."

Lord Wyth parroted his words, testing their flavor. And then he threw his head back and barked a laugh that provoked an angry glare from Atto.

"I see," Lord Wyth said. He rose. "So. You are going to land an invisible ship that is large enough to hold a town, bringing us thousands of people who need charity, who want to settle here on your imitation Earth. With or without welcome." He rubbed the back of his neck and inhaled slowly. Then: "I will consult with Lord Ettori about this, and we'll determine how we should deal with you."

Piers felt ice slide down his spine.

When the door shut behind Lord Wyth, Atto said, "For what it's worth, I don't think you sounded any crazier than before."

18

EXPLANATIONS

House Wyth

Huse Wyth's version of hospitality for strangers made sense now. The guest quarters seemed noticeably less gracious when Piers heard Lord Wyth lock the door as he left. Amazing how that simple, mechanical sound could have such an outsized psychological effect, but the rooms seemed dimmer, smaller, and far less comfortable now. He'd jumped in too soon and too abruptly, and the reaction had been exactly what Atto had predicted: they thought he was crazy. Atto hadn't predicted that their opinion would lead to confinement, though.

"It'll be all right, Piers," Atto said. "He just has to have some time."

"I don't know. You saw his face."

"I think Rane and Arissa believe you. They'll talk to him. And anyway, you'll get what you wanted—you'll get to see Lord Ettori, I bet."

That night, Piers forced himself to give sleep a chance, and managed to doze a bit. It was still deep dark outside his barred window when he was awakened by the faint two-note chime, like tinnitus in his left ear, that meant the ship was in range. They would have picked up his last message.

The protocol was that it would be up to him to initiate any real-time contact, unless there were an emergency on their side. Even though the exchange would be subvocal on his part, the concentration required was unnerving to witness, even for people who knew why he had become a zombie with glazed eyes. He was behind a shut door, and Atto was asleep in another room, so he sent a ping, then closed his eyes—and opened the channel.

In seconds, there was a response. Piers skipped the lead-in. He said, "I am so glad to hear from you! I thought my reports were interesting enough to merit *some* response."

"Sorry about that. Are you managing?" It was Jon's encoding. His brother-in-law's words were clipped. Anger? Distraction? It was so strange not to have access to the underlying emotion.

"So far," Piers answered. Some part of him wanted to give another answer, and it was a strange battle of wills, self against self, to keep that part from subvocalizing. "They're holding me while they figure out what to do with me. Only bad thing is they're holding Atto, too. Guilt by association. But it's all very civilized and I'm not hurt. "

"In that case, my bet's on you. You always find a way out of trouble." Jon's nonchalant confidence was reassuring, at least to the victor of the inner debate. Jon went on, "Captain says we'll stay on this orbit for a while. Not that we can really help, but we'll be in range for you every two hours or so."

"Good to know," Piers replied. "So what's going on up there?"

There was too long of a pause, and Piers felt an unwelcome intuition begin to stir. He'd been so deep in the labyrinth of his planet-side concerns since Ruatt that his uneasiness hadn't registered, till now. The fact that communications with the ship had been decidedly irregular was a significant sign of *something* not being right. The reports he'd uplinked hadn't even drawn questions from the planners, which was not the way that was supposed to work. "Jon?" he prompted.

Jon's sigh was encoded as little more than static. "No point lying to an Empath, is there?"

"What's happened?"

"There have been some...political complications," Jon said. "Let's just say there's a fine line between disagreement and mutiny and some people are crossing it. The captain's still got the helm but people have done some unbelievably stupid things that we're all going to pay for."

Piers realized he'd just dropped his screens entirely, and was trying, without conscious intent, to pick up Jon's emotions even through the encoding. The impossibility of it was like a slap in the face, like someone trying to bring him back to his senses. "Skip the understatement, Jon. Tell me what's going on."

Jon's silence was shorter this time. "Some lunatics destroyed the greenhouse to force the landing. But look, Piers, it won't do any good for you to spend your energy worrying about us. The last harvest was already in, and we can get by for a little longer on that as long as the fabricators keep working. We're fighting to stay the course and you've got to do the same."

There was no chance of sleep on the other side of that conversation. Jon flatly refused to go into it, but with every deflection Piers's concern cinched tighter until it was strangling him. If destroying the greenhouse was the least of what they'd done, the ship was in serious trouble already. Beyond the strain that put on already scarce resources, it meant that there were people who were willing to make their shipmates suffer to force the bridge crew to change the plan. From a few things Jon would not answer, Piers gleaned that there had been other incidents, even violence, and Jon wasn't sure that there wouldn't be worse.

Piers struggled to reorient his awareness after they closed the channel. He stayed so still on the bed that he could feel his pulse throbbing throughout his body. Logic was clearly on Jon's side; there wasn't a damn thing Piers could do to help them, other than get them down here *soon*.

Restless, he slipped out of the room and back to the front room. Low light from a slow-burning lamp gave his eyes something to work with, enough to make his way carefully over to the console table where a large carafe of water and two glasses, all etched with the distinctive *W*, had been left for them. Piers poured half a glass and sat on one of the upholstered chairs just in front of the built-in wall of books. The thought occurred to him that having the books behind him was like having ancient knowledge at his back as he sat staring into the dark and wondering what was coming.

Scuttling, scraping noises came from the wall behind him, sounding like something was right over his shoulder. He jumped and the water sloshed violently in the glass. The noise stopped and he tried to calm his nerves, but he was listening with prey-like avidity. From inside the wall he heard a faint tapping. Rodents, maybe? Or insects? Piers skin shrank at that thought. Could insects be heavy enough to make that noise when they crawled?

There was a soft rap and more tapping, and then another scrape from near the floor. Piers sprang out of the chair and turned to face the bookshelf, heart pounding, ready to defend himself—from what, he hadn't consciously determined. Wishing he'd turned up the lamp, he took a step toward the wall, listening now like a predator. Something was softly hissing in there.

And then he heard, distinctly, "It's moving!" Now a louder scraping at the floor and the wall shuddered.

Piers backed away, and slunk into the darkest corner of the room where he could see the chair where he'd been sitting. Part of the wall behind the chair intruded into the room, splitting the bookcase apart at a vertical join. A gap appeared, and a lantern emerged from the darkness behind the wall.

Piers held his breath as two people followed the lantern into the room, edging in behind the chair where he'd been just seconds ago. First was Rane, trying to peer past the lantern into the darkened room. The second man was tall and angular, and his preternaturally white hair was just about luminescent.

"Now what?" the second man whispered.

"We'll wake him," Rane whispered back, and moved into the center of the room.

There was no sign of malicious intent, but Piers dropped his psi screens just a little, just to see if he'd pick up a trace of anything alarming. All he felt was sharp excitement and driving curiosity, muted through his mostly-in-place self-protection, before he closed himself off again. He stepped out of his shadowy nook. "I'm here," he said, keeping his voice low but not whispering.

Both men jumped and Rane swung the lantern toward Piers.

"I'd apologize for startling you," Piers said, aiming for a light tone, "but I think you startled me more."

"Sorry about that," Rane said, still quiet. "Owen's actually got a guard outside the door, so sneaking in was our only option." He gestured toward the hallway past the fireplace. "Let's get away from the door."

Rane moved into the corridor, and Piers followed. The white-haired man came behind him, and for a moment he was uncomfortably aware of being trapped between them. When they stopped, and turned to face each other, the unfamiliar man smiled. "Quite the traveler," he said, and offered a handshake. "I'm also a visitor to House Wyth, but I only crossed a river and a border to get here, not time and space."

He's not bothered? Piers thought as he shook the man's hand. "Piers Haldon."

"Yes, yes, so Rane tells me. I'm Oterin, Lord Wyth's healer."

Guessing at Piers's confusion, Rane explained, "My father. Owen is Head of House right now, acting as House Lord during our father's illness."

It was perhaps the strongest temptation to unbridle his full psi abilities that Piers had faced since landing. Even if there were some socially expected words he was supposed to say in response, and even though Rane's expression told him nothing, he knew the plain facts were laid over the deeper truth. He Pushed compassion, and stopped Screening to check the effect. The waves of Rane's worry, grief, love, and fear hit Piers like blows. He almost lost his balance.

The old man took hold of Piers's arm to steady him, and Piers shut out Rane's emotion. "Not steady on your feet, eh?"

Behind Piers, a door opened in the hallway. Atto said, "I heard voi—I know you!"

Rane hushed the boy, but with a quiet chuckle that could polish stones, the old man stretched his hand toward Atto. "Good to see you again, young Atto."

Atto returned Oterin's amused courtesy with an enthusiastic handshake and his broadest grin, but he kept his voice quiet, too. "I knew I'd find out who you were tending."

With a few gestures and nods, Rane ushered them into the windowless guest room at the farthest end of the hallway and shut the door. He set the lantern on the vanity table, and the four of them settled in. Atto and Piers sat on the bed, while Oterin sank into the single cushioned chair and Rane pulled the vanity stool closer.

Oterin explained how he and Atto had met in Ruatt when he was on his way to House Wyth. He talked about his journey, and Piers had to bite the inside of his cheek to keep from asking the question that was building up pressure in his mind like steam in a kettle. The introductory pleasantries didn't explain why Rane had brought Oterin here, at night, in secret, nor why Oterin was watching Piers sharply even while he traded travel notes with Atto.

"There have always been stories," Oterin finally said. "People used to believe a ship from the stars would land any day, bringing everything we needed for peace, health, longevity, and anything else people thought was good. Now the Starborn are about the only ones who are still waiting, but scholars like me have been looking for evidence—for explanations—all along. When Rane told me about you, I knew what this must mean. You must be careful, Piers Haldon."

Oterin leaned forward in his chair, and his eyes bore into Piers. "Your arrival changes everything, and not everyone will want that change."

In the conversation that followed, the warning was repeated but not clarified, much. Oterin wanted to hear about the ship, and was eager for information about the founders. Glad for the scout program's required study of NFP history, Piers answered as well as he could.

He shared what he'd learned about the Houses of Merra being named after the original bridge crew or their families, and Oterin confirmed the connection. The Houses had all been founded after "the cataclysm"—details unknown—but any record of the foundation ship's arrival and technology had vanished. Most of the families in the Great Houses went that far back, but history stopped short of their origins.

"All we have left are legends," Oterin said. "Science beyond our imagination, they say, and magic, too—there are stories that some ancients could read minds."

At that point, Oterin looked at Piers with hope and dread. Instead of trying to explain, Piers just shook his head. He couldn't read minds, and going into the nuances of psi ability just now didn't appeal.

"There have been efforts over the years to rediscover that ability," Oterin said, "and also efforts from others to make sure that never succeeded. Most people seem alarmed by the possibility."

It was like the early days of psi ability on Earth, then. It had taken almost a century for the misunderstandings to be quelled and the persecutions to stop. The ferocity with which people defended that last sliver of true privacy, their own thoughts, made sense to Piers; the tragedy was that the defenders hadn't learned how psi ability really worked before they launched the witch-hunts.

"From the ship, we can see the ground," Piers said, hoping to just slip past the other topic, at least for now. "We want to arrange a landing that doesn't cause trouble, but we have to land soon. I need help—if I can get people from Houses there, it will help keep anyone from getting hurt." *Please, please let that be reason enough, until I can be sure of them,* he thought.

His answer started a rush of questions from Atto, unrelated to Piers's line of thought, and somehow that led to Piers revealing that he had an implant that enabled him to communicate directly with the ship. He wouldn't have intentionally chosen that as the first technological marvel to reveal. Far too esoteric. He said, "It's not the source of the mind-reading legend. It's technology that wasn't even developed yet when your ancestors landed."

It probably wasn't a totally satisfactory answer, Piers realized, even though his listeners wouldn't likely be thinking about where to draw the line between a natural phenomenon and humanity's technological advances. Empathic psi ability itself was a result of bioengineering, after all. Maybe in a thousand years, the abilities provided by the transneural network implant would simply be heritable telepathy.

There were hints of daylight by the time the conversation turned back around to the present situation. "Owen's waiting to hear back from Lord Ettori about you," Rane said. "He knows Arissa and I didn't want him to do that— he actually told the House Guard that neither of us is allowed to come talk to you. I'm afraid he'll do whatever Ettori decides." The frustration and indignation simmering under Rane's calm tone was hard to miss, and obvious from the way he set his jaw after that statement.

"Ettori and Wyth are supposed to be equals, right? I know Ettori is House Prime and all that, but Wyth has status, too, don't you?" Piers said to Rane.

Rane seemed surprised by the question. Before long, he and Oterin were telling Piers about Ettori's transgressions, and then about the restive Houses and their intended act of rebellion. From Rane's description, it sounded like it was rebellion twice over for Rane, since it wasn't his place to direct the policy actions of House Wyth.

And it wasn't Piers's place to intervene in the power structure of Merra. All he needed to do on that score was find out what it was, so that the integration planners could give his father and the officers reality-based advice. He needed to connect with the Starborn somehow, or find a way to activate Rane's psi ability. And he needed to make sure *Redemption* landed on the right side of whatever power struggles were going on here—they would be defenseless on their own. House Wyth, or at least Lord Owen, didn't seem to be shaping up as protection. Making a bid for Lord Ettori to support the landing, though: would that be firing the wrong thruster? If Ettori had the de facto power, but no support from the other Houses, should *Redemption* seek alliance with authority or with popular opinion? Ettori was the one with the army.

"Do you think I could get House Ettori to help us?" he asked.

Oterin's eyebrows twitched, and Rane sat back abruptly. Both stared at him.

"So I take it you don't think it's likely," Piers said. "Why are you so sure?"

Oterin leaned forward in his chair, and said, "There are many who say he destroyed House Caladen because he thought they threatened him. It's not hard to imagine how he would feel about your ship's arrival."

"I just have to convince him that we aren't a threat, then."

19

CONNECTIONS

Wyth Valley

THROUGH THE RECURRENT haziness of the first few days, Davyn was aware of an old man passing through the front part of the tent, for long absences during the day and frequent short ones overnight. The man spoke to him with vague kindness.

Jemma hovered near him more often than Tienna did. The girl had taken over some of the healer's tasks: she kept fresh water within reach for him, brought food to him, and changed the poultice on his wrist. Her small hands were as gentle as her mother's, and she hummed to herself as she went about her tasks.

"You're good at this," he commented to her late on the fifth morning. She had unwrapped his wrist deftly and had arranged a pillow to support his arm so that his hand and wrist were above a bowl. By wringing a wet cloth above it, she sluiced the dried paste away with mild water. As she dabbed his skin dry, her touch was so light that there was no flare of pain.

"I don't want to hurt you," she said as she inspected the swelling. "Is it getting any better?"

It was hard to tell. Any movement of his wrist or hand sent shocks up his arm, but when he kept still, the pain seemed to have become a familiar part of him. "It must be," he answered. "I know it will take time."

Davyn wished he knew how much time. Each time he sat up, he felt the room roll away from him momentarily, and walking jarred his shoulder until he learned to slide his right foot to avoid the step. It would be weeks or months until he could move freely, and he knew his recovery would take effort as well as time. For now, he would have to fumble through with only his left hand.

"I don't think you should go home too soon," Jemma said. It was the same trick her mother had of seeming to read his thoughts.

"Well, right now I can't even bear the thought of riding, so I think I'm at your mercy for a while." He felt despicable for the pleasure he felt at the realization that he would have to stay. He needed to go home, even if the healer Tienna had sent had already countered the Sweep. Even if Mira and Tunny were already recovered, even if the Sweep had moved on, he had chores and obligations—and people—that he needed to get back to.

Tienna heard his remark as she entered, and replied, "I don't think your Paladin would be happy to hear that. He's impatient. Your visits aren't enough for him."

Davyn had shuffled out to see the horses as soon as he was able to get off the cot, shrugging off protests from Tienna. The stallion had greeted him with a puff of warm breath, forgoing the usual nudge, and had tolerantly let Davyn stroke his neck. There was consolation in leaning against the sleek and solid animal, the living memento of Van and the link between Holden, Trint, and even this. Paladin seemed to be proof of Davyn's ability to adapt and endure.

"He needs exercise," Davyn said now. Tienna took her daughter's place beside him and inspected his wrist, while the girl moved to the bench to spread fresh paste on clean bandages. Davyn hissed when Tienna turned his hand to the right. Through clenched teeth, he went on, "Is there anyone who could ride the mare?"

"The swelling is much better," she said. "And I don't think the poultice can do much more for it. We'll apply one more, since Jemma has it ready, but then we'll splint it. Then it's just a matter of the time to heal." She tied the poultice in place, then answered, "If the mare is as gentle as she seems, I'm sure we can find someone. But I don't think your stallion will let anyone else ride him."

"Better not to," Davyn said. "But if she canters, he will run with her."

She promised to see to it, and sent Jemma out. Tienna helped him sit up further and pulled the blanket out of the way so that she could tend his wound.

"There are things I want to know," she said finally. "You haven't said much about yourself—or about anything—and I know you haven't felt like talking, but you're awake enough for conversation now."

There was nothing accusatory in her manner, but Davyn cast about for explanations that wouldn't sound defensive or evasive. He hardly knew where to begin.

She smiled gently. "You can start by telling me where you're really from. You talked about Trint, but when you speak, I think you have spent more time somewhere else. Tyndaris?"

While she sat beside his shoulder, her hands folded in her lap, he told her about Holden. She listened with compassion that spurred him to share deeper memories, and the tilt of her head or the expression in her eyes was enough to lead him to the next point; he wanted her to know. For the first time in a very long time, he let himself feel the loss of Van, and he found himself sharing even the long-ignored anger he felt toward Lord Holden for cutting ties.

When he fell silent, she said, very softly, "You've been alone with your grief for too long."

I didn't know, he thought. The strength of those feelings, and the ache of those memories, had been set aside and neglected. He hadn't known they were still so potent.

She leaned over him, and brushed his hair back from his forehead. Although she didn't seem to mean it as an affectionate touch, he felt an upwelling of answering tenderness for her. He caught her hand with his left hand, and for a heartbeat held it to his temple.

"You've lost someone, too." He didn't know why he was so certain.

"Jemma's father," she said, and extracted her hand from his. "We fell in love young, and married before a year had passed. He was with me only for four years. Illness," she said, before Davyn asked. It was the first time he had heard anything bitter in her voice. "Despite being a healer, there was nothing I could do. I don't really blame myself, but some others did, and I worry that Jemma will, when she's old enough. We lost six people, including my parents. I know I'll always wonder if I could have done something more."

Davyn wished he could say something to comfort her, not just sympathy in the specific moment, but something deeper. He could imagine the pain and helplessness she had felt when caring for her parents, husband and the others, with clarity that made it feel like something remembered. "I understand."

Her head was bowed, and her hands rested in her lap. He was still waiting for her to say something when a shriek from outside pierced the tent.

Tienna was on her feet and at the door-flap as a man shouted, "Hold on, Jemma! Just hold on!"

"She's on the horse!" Tienna spun back to Davyn. "She can't ride!"

Ignoring the dizziness, Davyn pushed himself up from the cot with his left arm. He staggered to Tienna and out into the day beside her, barefoot and incongruously aware of the air on his bare chest.

The mare was plunging around the meadow at the edge of the camp, galloping and wheeling, with Jemma flattened against her neck and howling with terror. The saddle was slipping to the side, and there was no bridle, only a halter. A few men lunged at the horse whenever she came near them and tried to snatch the lead rope in her wake. Paladin trotted just beyond the outermost tents, in a zigzag pattern that roughly paralleled the mare, but it was as if he were corralled by the camp.

Tienna pressed both hands over her mouth and seemed to be on the verge of running toward the horses. Davyn pulled her back with his good arm and stepped in front of her. "Jemma!" he called, hoping to cut through the clamor of overwrought voices. "Jemma, grab her mane!" The child was too panicked to try shifting her hand forward.

To the men, he shouted, "Don't try to catch her! Stop!" His repeated directions finally reached them, and they abandoned the chase, gasping and clutching their sides.

All he could hear were frantic pleas from Tienna, and Jemma's wailing; the sound seemed to overwhelm his thoughts. He seemed to be dream-walking toward the edge of the camp, his shoulder and wrist forgotten, and Tienna's voice receded from his attention much faster than he was moving. The people gathered at various points throughout the camp seemed to be frozen in tableau while the mare raced back and forth beyond the farthest tents, with Paladin keeping pace along the perimeter. Davyn whistled for the stallion, and was surprised when his request was ignored; Paladin only paused long enough to strike the ground twice with his foreleg before jogging on.

Jemma was no longer screaming, but her face was contorted with fear and her mouth was open in a soundless cry as she clung to the wild horse. The mare pivoted again, her trajectory now bringing her straight toward the camp at reckless speed. Davyn mentally begged the mare to stop, with every spark of energy he had, but she showed no signs of slowing. Then Paladin's massive presence appeared in front of Davyn, his broad side presented to the mare as a deterrent. She veered away, still racing with her ears pinned and her neck stretched, and Paladin jogged off in the same direction.

Davyn called to her, and she flung her head toward him as she ran, which made her jerk sideways. Jemma shrieked. Paladin now stopped and stood beside him facing the mare. At Davyn's second call, she turned toward him. He called once more.

The mare flung her head again, and then came toward him—the galloping strides shortening to a canter and then a trot. Her sides were heaving as she came to a stop right in front of him.

"It's all right," he said to the mare, and to the sobbing little girl. "It's all right now."

Tienna ran to her daughter, and Jemma slid off the horse

into her mother's outstretched arms. Together they folded to the ground, both sobbing now and clinging to each other. Davyn took hold of the mare's halter as several of the spectators arrived with their voluble excitement and relief, and without replying to the several grateful comments, he led her back to the camp. Paladin placidly came along.

Five days later, Davyn's shoulder felt less raw. The floodberry paste was doing its work and the gash had started at last to close properly. His wrist was splinted, and as long as he didn't jolt it there was only a clamping ache there, without the bite. He'd managed to get his shirt on without agony, and he felt clearer than he had since he'd fallen at the Ettori man's feet.

Now Davyn held the mare's right cheek-strap with his left hand while Tienna boosted Jemma into the saddle from the other side. The girl had apologized gravely for scaring the horses, but it had been clear to Davyn that she was still frightened herself. In a quiet conversation, he'd persuaded Tienna that Jemma needed to push past it now so that she wouldn't end up with a lifelong fear. Jemma's stubborn refusal had backfired, because it made Tienna certain that Davyn was right. In the negotiation that followed, Jemma finally agreed she would do it, if Davyn was there with her. Her condition was easily met—he wouldn't have even fleetingly considered letting her get on the mare if he weren't there.

The mare wasn't happy about it. When Jemma approached, the horse snorted and flicked her tail with decided annoyance. A few treats from Davyn's hand softened her mood, and he'd been able to soothe her and bring her around to the idea. So she stood still while the girl squirmed into the saddle, and only one twitching ear expressed her displeasure. She gave Davyn a long look to let him know that he owed her something significant for this.

Paladin watched the preparation with supercilious amusement. Davyn had given him some treats, too, and scratched the spot between his eyes where the short hair swirled as if it had been licked. The horse had sighed as if he were resigned to the inactivity, and then gently nudged Davyn's good shoulder to show that he knew it wasn't Davyn's fault.

When Jemma was still, Davyn started to lead the mare on a sedate tour of the camp. The girl was tense and stiff, as if resisting the horse's movement proved she wasn't going along with it. Her mother walked beside her and gave constant encouragement, but when Davyn looked back he could see that Jemma was fighting tears. He halted the mare and moved back to Jemma's other side. She looked down at him with her eyes brimming.

"Can you do something for me, since you're up there?" he asked.

She seemed skeptical that he had a real request.

"I don't know if you can tell, but the mare is a little nervous, too. She doesn't remember the way you do, but she remembers how she felt. So I'm glad you're riding, because it's good for both of you to know that it won't be like that every time. You understand that, but I'm not sure she does. I'm a little worried about her."

Jemma's blue eyes were locked on his as if she were listening by staring.

"If my shoulder was better, I would be riding, too. And I wish I could, because you can tell things about how a horse is feeling from up there that you just can't from the ground. So if you can, I'd like you to tell me."

He gave her two tasks. He asked her to tell him if she thought the horse was stepping harder on one side than the other, and to let him know when both ears were turned either forward or back. Jemma sat straighter. Within a few minutes, she was lighter in the saddle, swaying with the horse's gait as she tried to decide which hoof struck harder. And she looked straight ahead, between the mare's ears, concentrating not on the ground but on the animal. Every few minutes, he asked if she'd noticed anything, and soon she was blithely reporting everything she observed.

When Tienna helped her down from the saddle, Jemma moved up to Davyn's side. She put out a hand and touched the mare's soft nose, and said, "It's all right now, Jewelbox." She looked up at Davyn. "Can I ride her again tomorrow?"

He hesitated, then promised that she could ride in the morning. He felt Tienna's astute gaze and her knowing silence almost like physical pressure. That pause had apparently been as telling as the words he hadn't wanted to say. She knew he was preparing to leave.

That evening, after Jemma was asleep, Tienna and Davyn sat on a long log beside the fire in front of the tent. The summer sky had deepened through turquoise into velvet indigo, with a smudged thumbprint on the horizon where the sun had just vanished. A handful of brighter stars were coming into focus, and the nighthoppers were starting their hum.

Their conversation had been light over supper and as they lingered. They'd slipped into silence now. Every now and again sounds would drift over from another firepit, but the camp was subdued and the voices were quiet. The river's susurration and an occasional breeze among the trees in the woods nearby were soothing whispers, and the warmth from the fire caressed his face. Beside him, Tienna was looking up at the stars.

"The woman you were with when you came—Arissa," she said. "What is she to you?"

He didn't answer right away; it was a question he'd asked himself repeatedly. Tienna asked with a purpose, but there'd been no preamble, and he didn't know what kind of answer she was looking for. Finally, he said, "I'm not sure."

The answer didn't seem to satisfy Tienna, but she didn't press. Davyn was restless in the silence now, and so he went on, "We met in Trint a few days before we got here. She was in trouble, and I tried to help." He picked up a twig and scratched a few haphazard lines in the dirt. "You see how that turned out." To shake off the feeling of uselessness, he stood up and said, "I can add some more wood to the fire. The woodpile is just around there, isn't it?"

Her hand brushed his, and he looked down. She had reached up to him, and her eyes gleamed in the light from the fire. "Stay," she said.

He didn't know if she was trying only to keep him from escaping the moment or if she meant something more. When he didn't move to sit, she stood up beside him, with grace amplified by the way she kept her eyes on his.

"What you did today, with Jemma," she said. "I hardly have the words to thank you."

Bemused, he stood there while she looked at him with some depth of feeling, and he tried to fathom the leap from Arissa to Jemma. "I needed her to think about something other than being afraid of being on a horse," he explained.

She laughed lightly, and it reminded him of the river lark's song she liked—a pure and sweet, floating ripple of sound. "I know," she said. "But I love that you didn't make her feel like a silly little girl. Not many people would be so careful with a child's dignity."

She walked toward the river. Davyn followed, confusion

and curiosity tugging at him equally. Tienna said nothing more until they were standing on the bank, with moonlit water at their feet. She stood so close beside him that when the breeze blew, her skirt tangled around his legs, too. Staring into the water, she said, "So you're not in love with Arissa?"

"What? No. No, I..." He didn't know how to explain. "She just needed help. I don't think she even likes me very much."

That soft laugh again. Then she slipped her right arm around his left and hugged it to her while she rested her head against his left shoulder. He stilled, suppressing his breath, in case it would bring her back to her senses and scare her away, like a skittish wild thing that ventured too close. And she laughed again. "Davyn, this moment isn't as fragile as you think."

Even so he felt almost shy as he pulled his arm free and put it around her. She stretched up and kissed his cheek, and then leaned against him. As they stood like that, between the shining dark of the river and the night sky, Davyn had the fanciful thought that everything he'd felt before was being swept away by the river.

In the muted morning light that seeped through the canvas of the tent, Davyn sat on the edge of his cot and paused in his one-handed effort to knot the laces of his boots. He leaned to look through the gap in the curtain, into the family's sleeping room. On the cot just on the other side of the curtain from his, Tienna still slept. One of her hands curled close to her cheek, her slender fingers cupping the air in her palm. Her breath stirred a wisp of dark hair, and her lips, so familiar to him now, were slightly parted and almost smiling. He considered kissing her awake, but decided that last night's joy and tenderness deserved to linger in her dreams as they had in his. When she woke, he would have to try again to take his leave.

He had already overstayed. Days ago he'd sent a message with a trio of merchants who passed on their way to Ruatt; if it reached Shea, he knew she would get word to Essen and Mira as well. He wanted them all to know that he was alive and would return when he was well enough to travel, and now he needed to keep his word. There was still pain, but it was evolving from the agony of injury to the sharp discomfort of healing. As long as he didn't raise his right arm, he could almost forget about his shoulder. The wrist was harder to ignore, but was past the point of needing a healer's active attention.

After spending another full day yesterday with Tienna, heart soaring just from the chance to be with her as she went about her day, he could no longer pretend to himself that he was lingering here because he needed to rest. A few days of rain had been an excuse; he wasn't going to ask Jemma to take her second ride in that kind of weather. Yesterday had been dry, so Jemma had ridden in the morning, and then Davyn had let himself be swept along in the day until it made more sense to wait until the following morning to go.

When they walked beside the river at moonrise last night, he'd asked Tienna to come with him to Trint. She had to know that it wasn't just a request for a Starborn healer. "Let me sleep on it," she told him, and then pushed the topic aside while they talked of other things. By the time they'd returned to the tent where her grandfather and her daughter were sleeping, they were well past needing words. They had tarried outside, relishing the privacy and postponing the last kiss as long as they could, and then bid each other goodnight with a last gentle touch.

He managed to secure his second boot, and got to his feet. Tienna had mended his shirt with neat stitches that were almost decorative, and he tucked his shirttails in and buckled his belt with his good hand. He picked up his vest, and had to reposition it with a flip to get it over his left arm. It dangled from his shoulder, and his wanderer's charm slipped out of the pocket.

It bounced against his toe and landed on the thin rug that covered the dirt floor. The metal gleamed, vivid against the dull colors of the rug. He shrugged into the vest and bent to retrieve the charm. When it was in his hand, it glowed as if it had some light source of its own. The crossed lines seemed to be etched from light, but there was no warmth. It seemed to pulse and Davyn felt as if he were being pulled into the air. A sound like the rush of wind through trees teased his hearing. He sank to the cot, staring at the charm on his outstretched palm.

The curtain rustled. Tienna came through, careful not to let too much light slip into the room as she slipped out. "A star charm," she said. Her voice was soft with awe. In two steps she was beside Davyn, and she sat down next to him. She brushed the charm with a finger and drew back when it pulsed. "It's beautiful."

He couldn't take his eyes from it. "It was in the basket with me. In Tyndaris, they call it a 'wanderer's charm.'" It had always seemed apt as a keepsake for an orphan, and then even more so for an immigrant. He was glad Tienna knew those stories now. "Now I think 'star charm' makes more sense."

"It looks like starlight," she said. "I've never seen one. I didn't know they did this."

It never had, before now. They stared at it until the afterimage of the crossed lines blazed in their vision. After a few minutes, the strange sensation of being drawn toward the sky faded, and the pulsing diminished. Disappointment edged his curiosity as the light subsided until the metal was just metal again, a dull silver disk centered in Davyn's hand, and he could doubt that he'd really seen anything else.

"What do you suppose it means?" she asked.

He shook his head, equally stunned. When it seemed clear that the radiance was truly gone, he dropped it back into his vest pocket. "I wouldn't have believed that if I hadn't seen it. I'll have to ask Ger if I see him again."

Tienna laid her head on his left shoulder, and let her hand rest on his thigh. He kissed the top of her head. "Davyn," she started.

"You're going to say you can't come," he said. He wasn't sure how he knew. Maybe something in the way she said his name made it clear, or maybe it was only self-protective pessimism.

"You wanted a healer for the Sweep," she said. "We sent one, and I can't do anything more than she could. There are only a few who have the talent as well as the training."

"I thought it was a kind of medicine."

"Yes, but more than that. The best of our healers can...I don't know how to explain. They can help a person from inside. They help the medicine work faster."

"Come with me. Please." It was all he could think to say. He didn't want to leave, despite the myriad calls of home. He wanted to be here, with Tienna and in this place, with a pull so strong it felt like inevitability. The Starborn had accepted him, even Tienna's grandfather, who had told him that no man had gotten so close to Tienna since her husband had died. The other Starborn healer would have arrived in Trint days ago.

"You should stay, just for a while longer," Tienna said. "It's not the time to leave."

He covered her hand with his. "You're saying what my heart wants to hear. But no matter when I leave, I want you with me. Say you will."

Jemma's voice came from the back of the tent, high and sweet, breaking her mother's hurting silence. "We will, right, Mama? But we have to wait. Somebody's here."

20

PORTENT

House Ettori

THIS TIME, KOR woke from the nightmare with a cold weight in his lungs that was more ominous than his usual panting and shaking. The tangle of his bedding proved that the dream's familiar drama had been as vivid as ever, but the emphasis had changed; the dream had gone past its previous ending. It didn't stop with the fire. He'd woken with images of a landing. *The* landing.

It was morning, but barely. His curtained room was still monochromatic, the light still not quite strong enough to force color in. It was easier for his eyes. His vision had changed in the last twenty or thirty years, and dim light was more comfortable than the glare of the sun. He lay still for a moment, recovering.

Then, as he always did after that dream, he slid his hand over to the pocket he'd had sewn into the drapery at the head of the bed and fingered out the small token. This morning, it glowed in his hand. He stared at it, feeling every nerve tingle. This was the nightmare in daylight.

He flung the disk across the room, unaimed. It shattered the delicate glass globe of a wall lamp with a bell-like ping and flipped to the floor. Kor could still see it, bright on the carpet amid the shards. He swore and hurled a small pillow after it, willing it to land on the charm and hide it from his sight.

A messenger from House Wyth arrived mid-afternoon. Kor had him brought to the receiving room, and watched him cross the polished floor with exaggerated confidence. It was one of the Wyth boy's trusted men, one who had been here before. Kor probed, not bothering to be subtle. If the man even noticed, he'd just attribute the strange feeling to Kor's stare. He was nervous, and dazzled, and wary to the point of paranoia.

Kor rose from his chair and met the man halfway. "Everson, isn't it?" He held out his hand and Pushed relaxed welcome at the man. The tightness around Everson's eyes eased. "What can I do for House Wyth today?"

"Lord Ettori, sir. Dan Owen sends his greetings and asks for your counsel."

A far more interesting turn of events than he'd feared. He was cultivating Wyth, because the young man was pliable and House Wyth's lands would be a convenient expansion one day. The boy had unusual resistance to Kor's psi influence, which was interesting in and of itself—in recent years only active Empaths had been able to fend him off. Kor had taken casual precautions to reinforce the boy's Separation, but he had no need to force the issue just now, and he enjoyed the challenge of relying only on his non-psi skills to direct Owen. The boy didn't trust him, that was obvious, but had decided it was advantageous to keep that to himself. He was unfailingly cooperative. For him to initiate something, though, was something more, and a welcome distraction from the relentless torture of Kor's thoughts.

Everson explained. A stranger, at House Wyth, was telling tales of an ark ship that needed assistance to land. The ship had supposedly arrived a thousand years late—a broken timedrive—and had been approaching through the stars for eighty years. The man had no proof to offer, but seemed entirely genuine. He was being held, at his ease, at House Wyth. What, Dan Owen wondered, should be done?

Bitter, bitter bile rose in Kor's throat. He sent Everson out, with assurances that he would consider what to do and send a man with instructions. Then Kor sank into his chair and steepled his fingers. It was confirmation of the token's activation and the dreams of the past few weeks. He'd felt a change, a new presence, but his men hadn't yet brought any news or rumors. The ship had arrived, and an advance party had somehow landed without his knowledge. Destroying the beacon had somehow not been enough to silence the signal.

The Ettori lords through the centuries had waited and watched as diligently even as had House Caladen, the House founded by the communications officer. The Caladen lords had dutifully watched for *Redemption* far longer than reason would suggest. For decades, they'd literally watched the stars, with psi senses Open all the while, ever ready to greet the ark ship. Then someone had the idea to build a beacon, one that would activate when—and they had never changed that to *if*—the ship began to orbit. It was sensitive enough, they said, to detect the psionic energy of the bridge crew once the ship was close enough. The watchers could wander, then, carrying tokens that would relay the signal from the beacon, calling them to convene when they were needed.

The tokens, thankfully, had been silent all this time. His father had distributed several thousand sham tokens, which had effectively diluted their significance. People's collective belief faded remarkably quickly when prophecies went unfulfilled. The Starborn, with their pernicious mysticism, required more subtle discrediting, but their unsubstantiated belief eventually looked like foolish eccentricity. And lately Kor's dam, wonderful multipurpose project that it was, provided a way to accelerate the dissolution of their way of life. It might take another fifty years, but Kor was confident that the Starborn would vanish—taking with them the last legends of a second ship and the final vestige of psi awareness.

Kor's dreams, around the time of Caladen's last heir being born, had alarmed him. He'd had the occasional dream before then, a manifestation of his subconscious anxiety about an influx of active psis, just when he was on the brink of finding a solution to that problem. Something had changed, twenty-one years ago. There had suddenly been an onslaught of unambiguous and compelling visions. When he'd heard that Lord Caladen, too, believed the ship was approaching, it had forced his hand.

It had been a simple matter to destroy Caladen, both the beacon and the family with their strong psi genes, but the fire and the loss haunted him still. It had been necessary, but wasteful. Caladen had been a friend to Ettori, generations ago, and the family had been the keepers of the scraps of history that had survived the early disasters. All of that was lost in the utter ruination of the House.

He'd thought that since no ship landed then, he'd succeeded. To learn now that the ship still had found its mark after all was a new horror. Perhaps there was some small hope left, if the advance party was looking for assistance.

Perhaps he could still find a way to prevent the collapse. If the ship landed...if the settlers brought their technology, their knowledge, their psi talents...this reset of humanity would fail. He would fail.

He sent for a Guard. "Bring the stranger to me."

PART THREE

LANDING

21

DEFIANCE

House Wyth

"LOOKS LIKE ANOTHER day inside," Rane commented at the breakfast table. No one had spoken since his last attempt, and it seemed to be up to him, again, to try to keep some semblance of civility going. He glanced out the window. An army of dark clouds was mustering over the valley. "We are definitely going to get a storm." It had been clear yesterday, but by late afternoon there had been hints that a change was coming. The sporadic wind had become more persistent, and the new leaves of the maple trees that shaded the garden were turned upward.

There had been a pressure system in the House, too. Arissa was furious with Owen for treating Piers and Atto as captives, and Owen was bristling. There'd been some biting words on both sides, several times, and now they were in a truce where they ignored each other. Rane was determined to talk to Owen and convince him to let Piers go, but he knew any attempt to persuade Owen right now would be worse than fruitless, because Owen was nowhere near being in the mood for reasonable discussion on any topic. Owen disappeared into his study.

Within an hour, the first crack of thunder boomed in the courtyard, ricocheting from the surrounding walls on three sides. Rane and Arissa were deep in a card game in the library, where the windows looked out to the valley. Arissa jumped at the next discharge, and went to the window.

Rane joined her. "I've always liked storms from here. We're not that high up, but it still gives you a good perspective." They were just under the clouds, and for the moment they were outside the perimeter of the storm. Bars of lightning flashed in the clouds just above their eye level, with streaks toward the ground every few minutes. "Looks like it's heading south."

Rane watched her lean close to the glass to peer at the clouds. She certainly wasn't daunted by much. Eighteen years old, traveling for the first time, her escort killed, herself abducted, and ending up at House Wyth with a contracted husband who wasn't making a very good start... Other women he'd known would still be fragile from what she'd been through and witnessed. If she found it overwhelming, there was no sign of it now. The marks on her face had almost disappeared, and she looked completely at ease here. As she should, since she would be Lady Wyth, he reminded himself. Owen's wife.

Noon passed.

The storm's drama subsided but the stinging rain continued, with the invading clouds now thick over the valley and the hills. Over the sound of the rain striking the window, they heard dogs barking, and then voices outside. Arissa went to the window again and craned to view the courtyard. "There's a wagon," she said.

Douglas found them. "Dan Rane, your brother is with

your father. I thought perhaps you would like to see to the new arrival, rather than disturbing them?"

Rane followed him to the entrance hall, with a look back at Arissa to tell her to wait. He expected to be led to the receiving room, but the front door was open, and one of the stable hands was standing just outside.

"It's Dane Arissa's luggage, sir. A girl brought her cases from Trint, but she won't come in. Says she's not staying but wants to know how to get to the nearest Starborn camp."

Rane turned, and Douglas was holding his raincoat out to him. He lifted it above his head and dashed into the rain.

The lanterns in the stable were lit, but it was still dim. A small, well-fed horse, still hitched to a small wagon, stood trembling and restive just inside. Water dripped from its mane and tail, and steam rose from its wet coat in the warmth of the barn. The wagon wasn't much more than a cart, and a tarp had been pulled off to reveal the load it had kept dry.

A slim, dark-haired girl was lifting down the travel cases. Her clothes—neatly patched trousers and a boy's tunic— were steaming slightly, too. Seeing Rane, she set a case down, and bowed her head. "Lord Wyth, sir, I'm Elanna from Trint, I've brought Lady Arissa's things as you requested." She said it in a rush, on one breath, looking at her shoes.

"I'm Rane, second son of House Wyth." Rane lifted down the last case. "I hear you're eager to get to the Starborn. I'm afraid it's farther than you think—you wouldn't get there before night. And the roads must be a mess." Rane wondered how the girl had managed the horse through the storm. Both of them seemed a bit traumatized.

Elanna from Trint looked like she was about to protest, so Rane made it formal, "House Wyth is pleased to offer you hospitality."

The girl's lower lip trembled, and her eyebrows scrunched together. She scuffed her foot on the stable floor, then glanced at the pile of luggage, and out at the driving rain. She stammered as she said, "Sir, I've come from Trint and the Sweep is there."

Despite himself, Rane shrank back. From beyond arm's reach, he said, "When did it start?"

"Ten days ago. They think it's almost over."

"How bad?"

The girl's expression crumpled. "It took my mother, and my little brother has it."

Rane winced. He knew, stars, he knew the feelings. Why had the girl come—why had they sent her—when she'd just lost her mother? And did she know about Davyn, or would he have to tell her? Would that be more than she could bear? And what rules of hospitality governed a grieving stranger who was also a child from a diseased town? "I am so sorry," he said. "May the stars guide her home."

Elanna sniffed, and she studied her shoes again. Now he saw her tears, but she was crying without drama or even acknowledgment. "I-I can't stay," she whispered.

That couldn't be right. Rane considered: surely the girl would have symptoms by now, if she were infected; the fact that the disease had taken an adult might well mean it was a year when children were spared; they could avoid physical contact. He'd have the healer look for signs of the infection, to be sure, before letting anyone else see the girl. "No, House Wyth welcomes you, Elanna. Stay the night, take your comfort here, and we'll send you on in the morning."

Half an hour later, Douglas escorted the girl to the library, with Oterin's assurances. Drier and much steadier, Elanna nonetheless froze just inside the threshold.

"I remember you," Arissa said. "You were at the inn at Trint."

The girl's reply was whispered, and she kept her eyes lowered. "Yes, lady. My family owns the inn."

The girl seemed uncertain, and when Rane invited her to sit down, she stayed at the edge of the chair, as if she were afraid to trust the hospitality. Rane poured some telik for her and refilled the other mugs before dropping into the chair across from her, intentionally casual. Elanna was out of her depth. She couldn't be more than twelve years old, and maybe not even that. For her to have made the trip, by herself, through the storm, through her grief, said something about her courage that nothing in her bearing suggested.

So Rane chattered, and told stories to amuse them, trying to offer that as respite from the storm and the sorrow. Arissa was soon laughing so hard she was complaining that she couldn't breathe. Elanna listened and concentrated on her telik. Rane kept at it until the girl finally started to relax, and then went further until at last even Elanna couldn't keep a straight face.

They were all laughing when Owen strode into the room. Arissa saw him first and choked off her giggle. That made Elanna look up, and the look that spread on her face was something closer to fear. Rane, at that moment, felt sorry for his brother. Owen's shoulders were rigid and his lips were thin—the look that meant he was holding himself in.

Elanna stood, but stared at the ground. "L-lord W-wyth. I'm Elanna from T-trint."

Owen stared at the girl, decoding the stutter. Rane stood up beside Elanna, and explained, "Elanna brought Arissa's things from Trint."

"I expected you days ago," Owen said.

Spots reddened on Elanna's cheeks, and she bowed her head still further. Rane glared at his brother. "I'm sure she came as quickly as she could." He saw Owen register the declaration of support with a cool glance, and felt Elanna take a deep, steadying breath.

"The merchant brought your message three days ago," Elanna said, stammer-free but not much louder than a whisper. "We were going to just send the cases, because of the Sweep, but then we got Davyn's message, too, so I came as fast as I could."

There was a charge in the room, as if a flash of lightning had just stung the air. Arissa gasped, "Davyn's message?"

The girl's head snapped up, and she glanced anxiously at both Arissa and Owen before she looked at Rane and let the words tumble out. "He said he was at a Starborn camp near House Wyth, recovering from a bad wound. Some men came and captured a bunch of the Starborn and Davyn thought Arissa had been kidnapped again—he doesn't know you made it here. He can't ride, so I came to take him home."

When the stunned silence passed, Arissa sank down into her chair and started crying.

The afternoon passed without the right moment to speak to Owen, and Rane was debating whether he should risk it despite Owen's mood, but it seemed likely to be counterproductive. He visited his father briefly, in part to confer with Oterin, who counseled patience. Even if Ettori sent word back to Owen immediately regarding Piers, nothing would happen until tomorrow. There was time to sleep on it, and to catch Owen in the morning if the opportunity didn't come before then. Then, Oterin said, if Owen was immovable, the healer himself would help Piers and Atto escape through the passageways and into the woods, and point them to House Dannpelier, leaving Rane closer to blameless.

"But Owen wouldn't let you back to help our father," Rane said.

Rane wanted Oterin to explain why he was confident that Owen would let him resume treatment. Instead, he said, "There's no more help I can give him, Rane. I am able to give him draughts to dull his pain, that's all."

Rane went back to the library, but couldn't focus even on the simplest of games. He sat by the window, watching the rain and listening to Arissa and Elanna as they played "Crash" with a set of Wyth's monogrammed cards. Elanna talked about Davyn with adoration, then about home, and twice was overcome with her strangely silent grief as she thought of her mother and worried for her younger brother. Nothing was said about Piers or the starship or Ettori.

Midway through the main course at the evening meal that night, Douglas interrupted to say that a messenger had arrived from House Ettori. It was too soon! It meant Ettori had sent a man back hard on the heels of Owen's own emissary. Owen left the table to greet him, though Rane knew any other messenger would have been asked to wait in the receiving room until after the meal. He was relieved when Owen came back alone.

As Owen took his place, he said, "He's come to escort Piers to House Ettori. He accepted hospitality, but said he'd prefer not to intrude on our meal, so he's settling into the blue room."

Rane felt Arissa tense beside him, and he drew a breath to say something before she could. Elanna startled them all by whispering, "Piers is *here*?"

"Not for much longer," Owen said. "Lord Ettori wants to speak with him."

Elanna's dismay bordered on reproach, and Owen snapped, "The lord of Prime House can summon a stranger if he chooses."

Elanna's cheeks went red again, but in her eyes Rane now saw the mettle that her shyness masked. She said, "I heard he makes people work on his dam. They don't come back."

As Rane tried to reassure the girl, he ignored Owen's warning signs and made a pointed remark about Lord Ettori's assumed authority. With the subject of the dam open, Rane and Owen got into a sharp discussion that made Arissa and Elanna shrink in their chairs and try not to attract Wyth attention. Their discomfort, obvious even in his peripheral vision, sharpened Rane's irritation with Owen.

It ended with Owen spitting out, "Damn you, Rane! You have no right to judge!" He stormed out of the room, and Rane heard him growl to a surprised servant in the corridor, "Ask *him* if everything's fine!"

The three of them stared at their plates, their hands, the window—anything to avoid eye contact.

"Forgive us," Rane said finally, with a sigh mingled with remnants of his frustration. "We have an ongoing disagreement about our obligation to Prime."

"Why does he defend Ettori?" Elanna asked.

Hearing it from a child, asked without the rancorous judgment Rane himself felt, it was easier to answer. "He's afraid of what might happen if he doesn't. He thinks it's safer to keep the peace—safer for House Wyth to stay out of Ettori's way."

Arissa's own frustration with Owen spilled out, then,

full force and frothing. "Safer for Wyth! *Wyth* can defend itself! Who's keeping the Starborn safe? Ettori sends them off to be slaves and no one lifts a hand! And Piers—he comes for help and instead he gets thrown to Ettori. That's not 'keeping the peace'—that's turning your back on people who count on you."

She left the table and swept out of the room, brushing past the hesitant servant who was entering with a tray laden with sweets and telik.

Elanna looked over at Rane with wide eyes, and got out, "I'm sorry, Lord Rane. I didn't mean to make everyone angry."

Rane rubbed his face with both hands. "You didn't. Everyone was angry long before you got here."

The clock in the library was counting out the seconds with a resonant beat, and the firelight tossed shadows onto the walls and the ceiling. The rain had stopped, at least for now, but the air was heavy with moisture that brought a bit of chill into the room, even though the fire was blazing. Two of the dogs lay nearby, stretched out and limp but with ears still tuned to their master's voice. Arissa was quiet, seething, and Rane tried to find a way to meet her halfway. They'd been in this conversation for almost an hour and neither one of them had given ground. He'd just raised his voice a little, which hadn't helped.

He stood by the fireplace, soothed by the warmth on his legs. "I want to help him, too," he said again, with less heat. "But he's under guard and Owen is watching us. He would never get over it if we went behind his back."

Again, she said, "If we don't let them go tonight, we're as good as sending them to the dam. Piers has to be free so he can help them land!"

He turned slowly from the mantel to face her. "Arissa, listen, I'm going to talk to Owen tonight, see if I can persuade him not to do this." Should he tell her about Oterin's offer? He shied away from it, because even now he wasn't sure if he could bring himself to go against Owen. It was one thing to play at disguises and call the Houses to a Gathering, in defiance of Owen's wishes, and quite another to deliberately intervene when Owen had already involved Kor. And it wasn't just the sad thought of Owen's irreversible anger if he were discovered, bad as that was. If Owen suspected him of working against him, there'd be no hope of meeting up with the others at the midsummer Full Dark; no hope of House Wyth joining with the others to bring down Ettori.

"You'd rather condemn them than make Owen angry with you?"

He came back over to his chair. The clock's ticking seeped into his awareness again, the heartbeat of time. Eventually, he said, "We've got to do something about Ettori—and right now I need Owen not paying any attention to me. The best plan from the Gathering is half-formed at best, and I've got to work out Wyth's role before Owen has any idea that there's something brewing. I need to seem to be going along with him."

"Isn't that exactly what he says about why he cooperates with Lord Ettori?" Her tone was pointed and the barb landed. Rane tensed and one of the dogs stirred. "If you won't even stand up to your *brother*, I don't see how you're going to—"

There was a soft knock at the door, which opened before Rane could respond. Douglas entered. He didn't acknowledge the tension, if he noticed it, but said that Owen wanted to talk to Rane as soon as convenient, and asked if they needed anything else before he retired for the evening. The interruption was enough to cool them both down.

When they were alone again, Rane said, "I don't want to argue with you—we're on the same side."

"If we don't agree then we aren't really on the same side, are we?"

The retort surprised him into a laugh, despite her fervor. It was the kind of arch comment that he often used to knock Owen out of a snit. Of course his laugh irked her, and he made a half-attempt to control his smile.

"You think this is funny?" Arissa was outraged. "You're just going to sit up here, safe in the House, and let Ettori just do what he wants. Well, I'm not. *I'll* get them out if you won't!"

That brought his alarm back. "No, Arissa, please don't. Let me handle Owen, keep him unsuspecting so the Gathering can bear fruit." He had to keep her out of Oterin's plan. Her innocence when Owen discovered the betrayal was going to be the only protection she would have. Owen being Owen, he'd marry her anyway because he'd made a pledge. If he knew she'd thwarted his arrangement with Ettori, it would be an unbearable marriage for both of them. "I'll go talk to him now, and I'll make him change his mind." He wasn't at all sure he could do that.

Owen hadn't lit the fire in the study, and the dark furniture swallowed the light from the lamps. Usually Rane found this room inviting and even cozy, but not tonight, not with Owen's heavy mood filling the air. His brother was in the comfortable chair by the hearth, folded forward with his forearms on his legs, looking down at his loosely clasped hands. He said nothing and didn't look up until Rane was sitting in the other hearthside chair.

"I wish he hadn't come here," Owen said. "I wish I didn't know." His voice was flat, and Rane felt a rush of sympathy.

"About the ship?" he asked.

"About the ship, about their problems, about Earth— all of it. I can barely manage what we were already dealing with, the ordinary issues."

"You do believe him, then."

The shadows across Owen's face hid his eyes. "I don't know. I don't want to, but I don't know why someone would invent all that."

Rane leaned forward, closing the space between them. "Then help him, Owen. Help them."

Without expression, Owen leaned back, and exhaled with measured breath. "It's not that simple. I know you don't like it, but Ettori is Prime. If he thinks a Gathering is needed, he'll call one, but he wants to talk to the stranger first. That's reasonable."

There was nothing in tradition or law that said only Prime House could call a Gathering. In fact, the whole point of a Gathering was for the Houses to come together as equals, to discuss matters that affected all of Merra. Kor was redefining what it meant to be Prime, and every time Owen accepted Kor's terms, it bolstered Kor's autocracy. It was another reason why that second meeting had to happen. Every passing day meant House Ettori was more secure as Prime. The other Houses had to do something soon or full-scale war would be their only option.

"Hard to picture Kor just having a chat and then sending Piers on his way," Rane said. "I think Elanna is right. Kor will send him to the dam."

"Don't interfere, Rane. He'll be all right."

Even Rane's exasperated growl didn't seem to register

against Owen's steady certainty. Can't you see what you're doing, brother? he thought. "What about his people?"

Owen shook his head, but didn't look at Rane. "I don't know. I don't see what they would need from us, if they have all that technology he talked about. And if it's real, if they land, there will be plenty of people rushing to help them."

"Just not Lord Wyth," Rane said, and the words were sour in his mouth.

"Not without Ettori's guidance, no."

A sunny morning was somehow not what Rane had expected. After he and Owen had talked in circles for hours last night, 'round and around on the subject of Piers, he'd been so worn and weary that he'd left defeated. With a sick feeling at the back of his throat, and a block of ice in his gut, he told Oterin he'd been unable to sway Owen. Oterin had blinked once, that was all, and then told him to go to bed. He hadn't thought he would sleep.

The water in his wash basin was frigid, shocking the last dregs of drowsiness out of his system. He passed his hand over the stubble on his chin and decided he could skip the cold-water shave. Within minutes, he was dressed and heading to the breakfast room, forcing himself to whistle as if all was right in the world.

Rane wasn't surprised not to find Owen there, but he waited at the table for quite a while before eating by himself. It wasn't unusual for Oterin not to come to breakfast—he took his meals at odd intervals, when his patient could spare him. Neither Elanna nor Arissa came to breakfast, either. Misgiving started to trickle in, and Rane sent a servant up to check on them. When she brought back the news that both rooms were empty, misgiving became foreboding.

He went to the guest suite, and found a guard sitting with his back against the locked door. When they went in, there was no sign of Piers or Atto, and no sign of the secret entrance except for a few unsettled books that no one would notice unprompted. If Arissa had helped Oterin do this, it might be even harder on Owen than if Rane had.

The guard was beside himself, flummoxed by the disappearance. Rane told him about the passageways, though this man wasn't part of the House Guard and by rights wouldn't know. He was relieved when Rane assured him that it wouldn't be held against him, and even more so when Rane said he would handle it with Owen. The last thing Rane wanted now was for this man to raise a hue and cry with the Guard or with Owen. Whatever had happened—whatever reason Oterin had for involving Arissa—Piers had gotten away. It would have been a wet walk through the woods last night, but by now the starman should be on the road to Dannpelier.

Walking back across the courtyard to the House, Rane decided his best plan was to stall the Ettori man and keep Owen uninformed for as long as possible. Once Piers got to Dannpelier, Tarken could officially grant him sanctuary, and he'd have Tarken's—House Dannpelier's—full protection. Ettori would have to either convince Tarken to turn Piers over, or resort to outright attack.

He asked a servant if Owen was in his study. "No, Dan Rane," he said. "I saw him and the healer go upstairs a while ago."

"Oterin hasn't left?" he sputtered, then tried to cover it, saying, "I thought he was going to go with the House Ettori man."

"No, sir, leastwise not that I know. I think the Ettori man's already gone."

Oterin still at Wyth, but the Ettori man and Piers were gone, yet the guards knew nothing? One scenario: the Ettori man had gone to collect Piers, discovered he had fled, and had gone after him. Second possibility: Arissa and Elanna had gone with Piers and Atto and now the Ettori man was riding after them. Worse still: the Ettori man had already caught up with them.

In the back hall of the House, Rane snatched his riding jacket from its peg, took his sword from the rack, and told the first person he saw that he hoped to be home before dark. He strode across to the stableyard.

The barn door was open, and he saw that the little wagon was still there, and the horse that had arrived with it was calmly munching in a stall. The Ettori horse was gone, though. Since no one had called for the House Guard, he must have wanted to go after Piers without alerting the House. The first stall, where Owen's mare, Breeze, was kept, was empty. Perhaps the servant just hadn't noticed that Owen had come down. Rane was going to have to ride hard, but he had one advantage in that he knew what direction to go. If he could intercept Piers and Arissa before the Ettori man and Owen did...The stall beside Breeze's was also empty—Rane's brindled chestnut was gone, too.

"Damn!" His oath startled one of the horses and a dog whined somewhere nearby.

"What's wrong?"

He whirled. Arissa stood behind him, with a wriggling puppy cradled in her arms. In the light spilling in from the yard, her hair was almost white, and she was wearing a light blue tunic that made her eyes seem to be the deep blue of a mountain lake. He was annoyed that he noticed. Her eyelashes fluttered, all innocence. He snapped out the first thing that came to mind, "Someone took my horse."

"Atto, I think. Elanna had the grey one. They put Piers on the gentlest—I hadn't thought about it, but of course he doesn't know how to ride! He'd never even been on a horse." She fondled the puppy's ears and kissed the top of its head.

"You did this?" His mind was refusing to take this in. Oterin hadn't helped them escape under the cover of the woods; Arissa had sent them clopping off from the stables.

"Of course," she said. She dropped the false innocence and met his gaze. "I knew you wouldn't be able to convince Owen. Frankly, I wasn't even sure you were going to try."

Rane's jaw was slack. It was like the air had been knocked out of him, along with all the words he knew, and he could only stand there stupidly while she told him she'd found where Owen was keeping the strangers' packs and had returned them. Atto had concealed a dagger before his pack had been taken, but since that was the only weapon the three fugitives had, she gave them hers, too. It wasn't much, but she wanted them to have at least some hope of defending themselves. She'd enlisted Elanna to get the horses ready while she found her way back to the secret door from the passageway.

There was a swelling moment, but before Rane's disbelief could manifest as anger, Owen and the Ettori man stormed into the barn.

"You!" Owen shouldered past Arissa and seized Rane, hands clamped on Rane's upper arms, and shook him. "How dare you!"

He released Rane with a shove that sent him reeling backward. Rane tried to keep eye contact, tried to will Owen to calm down. From the corner of his eye, he could see Arissa, still a glowing figure in the dimness of the barn. The Ettori man loomed behind Owen, and Rane had the impression of a grin.

"You knew that Lord Ettori sent for that man." Owen's words were clipped and sharp, edged with warning.

Rane felt his own temper stir. "I did. Yes." He drew himself up, shoulders back, and took a deep breath.

"And last night, I told you not to interfere."

"Yes. But you know it's not right." He hadn't meant to raise his voice.

Owen's face was flushed, and his eyes glittered. "You told me you wouldn't." There was hurt, beneath the anger. "You lied to me."

"Ettori didn't send for Piers so he could have a friendly chat and you know it," Rane said. He took a step toward his brother. As adults, they were almost the same height, at last; Owen was still broader and stronger. Rane leaned forward, and started softly, but his voice soon rose again. "What are you doing, Owen? You let Ettori command you, pull you around like a dog on a leash. You do things he asks even when you know better. Why? *Why?*" Rane shoved his brother.

Owen returned the shove, more forcefully. "Because Lord Ettori is our Prime!"

Something bright flitted between them, blocking Rane's next strike. Arissa. Rane barely managed to redirect his momentum to one side, barely avoided slamming into her.

"Stop it!" She looked to Owen. "Rane didn't do it. I did. I couldn't let that happen to Piers."

The brothers stared at her. It was the Ettori man who broke the suspension. "Lord Ettori will not be pleased. He was eager to have that man's help at the dam. Dan Owen, you may want to think about who can take his place."

Owen blanched. "We'll find him."

22

REFUGE

House Wyth

ARISSA SAT ON the battered sofa in the secret tower room and clutched a pillow. It had seemed like a safe refuge, when she fled the barn, but the isolation was beginning to put her on edge. There'd been loathing in Owen's voice when he ordered her to go back into the house; in the next breath he'd told Rane to saddle some horses. She'd been rattled, as much by her own anger as the violence she'd interrupted.

She hoped Piers and the children were making good use of their head start. They'd left well before dawn, and it had been hours after that when Rane and then Owen discovered their departure. If they could just make it to the Starborn camp first, she was sure Davyn would help them. The only trouble was that Rane certainly knew where they'd be going, and she didn't know if he'd hide that from Owen or not.

Rane's face. She'd never be able to forget the apprehension in his eyes when he found her in the barn. Far worse was the stricken look when Owen accused him. All the color had drained, like the sudden fading of the Aryn moor when the racing clouds swept by. The idea of Rane going against Owen's wishes had been a dire thought for both brothers; something other than the stubborn sibling contrariness she knew from her own family.

Even when the sparks caught and the argument blazed, Rane hadn't given her away. He'd answered Owen's charges with literal truth, neither accepting nor deflecting the accusation. It seemed that Rane was fighting about Ettori, not about Piers, and the brothers were getting close to doing real damage when she barged in.

The look on Owen's face when she made her confession would also linger in her memory. His first reaction had been astonishment—as if the most impossible thing in the world had just happened. She didn't know whether it was because she'd stepped between them, or because she'd let Piers go. Or both. Whatever Owen might have said was lost because the Ettori man had picked that moment to make his oily observation. The finer details of it really didn't matter, though. The facts were that Owen had just cause to be angry with her, and he didn't seem like someone who would forgive easily.

Owen and Rane returned late in the afternoon. From her vantage at an upper window, Arissa heard men's voices and the clatter of horses approaching before she saw them gather in the courtyard. Piers and Elanna were on horseback, in the middle of the group. Piers's head was bowed. She couldn't see Atto. Owen said something to the Ettori man, and then to the two House men who'd ridden out with them. At the back of the group, Rane dismounted neatly and tossed his reins to someone. He turned toward the house and walked out of Arissa's view.

She rushed through the House, to the hallway she knew he'd come through.

"Rane," she said, as soon as he was in sight.

"We got him. And Elanna." Rane didn't look at her.

"I know." She caught his arm as he started to walk past. "Rane, I'm sorry."

He shook her off. "Are you?"

"Rane, stop. Talk to me."

He whirled toward her. His fists were clenched, at his sides, and his eyes were hard. "What do we need to talk about? They'll be taken to Ettori tomorrow and they'll end up at the dam. There's nothing we can do."

"I was trying to help."

Now the fierce eyes bore into hers, and he drew a breath that would fuel a tirade. She tensed, and he checked himself. "It's pointless," he said through gritted teeth. "And I don't know how you get Owen's trust back now. That's ruined."

Arissa wanted to plead with him—it wasn't Owen's trust she cared about just at the moment—but Rane pushed past her. He wasn't going to hear her.

A few hours later, just as the evening star appeared, Arissa tried to reach into the saddlebag to get the packet of food she had stolen from Wyth's pantry. That was the least of her crimes: Arissa of Aryn, horse-thief, would have a lot to answer for. The little horse she had stolen from Wyth was easier to handle than the mare she'd stolen from Trint, but she was regretting her impulsive departure after only an hour or so of riding. She almost hoped that Rane would come after her. No matter how angry he would be, he could save her from going through with this ill-advised idea.

It had been a rash decision—not her first—to leave

before she had to speak to Owen, but Rane was right. It was pointless. She couldn't help Piers, and she couldn't expect the Wyth brothers to accept her after this. Rane was probably glad she'd left, if he'd even noticed yet. It would be better not to see him again, so she wouldn't have to see him look at her without the warmth and comfort of his affection. She was sorry, too, for the hurt she'd caused Owen. Surely he would nullify the contract, but in doing so he would lose the possibility of a birth-tie with a re-founded House Caladen. At least if she didn't marry Owen, she wouldn't have to face Rane.

There wasn't much daylight left, but there was only one road that went toward Davyn. When the Ettori men had carted her off from the Starborn camp, she'd tried—at least for a while—to pay attention to where they were taking her, and they had only turned once, to go north on the long road. That had been a few hours after leaving the camp, before they stopped for the night. In the morning, it had been a few more hours before they got to the turn for Wyth. She hadn't seen any other turns or intersections.

If she rode straight through the night, she would be at the camp before morning. With luck, that would also be before Davyn left to go home. Davyn knew her, and knew her situation. He would help her. Maybe together they would even be able to think of a way to help Piers.

She urged the horse to go faster, and let the tears come.

She knew she dozed in the saddle, despite herself. Dismounting, which she put off until the need was no longer sufferable, brought the challenge of finding something to use as a mounting block. That made her think of the awful events on the road from Trint. Twice she walked for long stretches before she found a way to get back up on the horse, and she missed the small stature and good nature of her pony.

Hours had passed, maybe, when she heard running water. She turned the horse into the woods to find the stream. Before they reached it, she found herself looking out on a meadow. The pre-dawn breeze was gliding through grass that was tipped with silver in the last bloom of moonlight. The woods curved around it on the east side, and the black gloss of the water swung out from amid the trees to run parallel to the woodline for a while before it swerved east again and disappeared back into the trees. Just before it turned, there was a bridge—it had to be the road that went past the camp, the one the Ettori men had taken. If she angled across the meadow from here, she would intercept the road west of the bridge, and could follow it away from the woods until she found the Starborn, and Davyn.

The horse trudged through the meadow grasses and flushed out a few night birds. Arissa felt a nighthopper carom against her leg and heard the whir as it beat its wings to right itself. She tried to put the superstition out of mind. If they weren't eaten by birds or crushed underfoot, nighthoppers lived for one moon cycle. Blind and flightless, they spent their short lives listening and hopping toward the sounds they made to guide each other. With luck, a hop would bring them close enough together that they could crawl the last inch, drawn together by the vibrations of thrumming wings. After mating, the females stopped thrumming. Being touched by a nighthopper was said to mean love had ended—or a loved one had died.

The elevated road formed her horizon, separating the spangled sky from the waving shadows of the meadow. She had to test her stubbornness against the horse's to get the mare to scramble up the four-foot slope. As they came to the top, she saw that the sky was brighter, the pearlescent softness that promised a clear morning.

She could see the Starborn's tents up ahead, outlined in moonlight. The woods she and Davyn had traveled through made a solid curtain of shadow beyond the camp. Thin streams of smoke were rising from firepits, and a few people were moving among the tents. The camp seemed smaller, more compact, than she remembered, and there were no fallen tents to show what had been lost.

A sentry stopped her as she reached the perimeter. "We come from the stars," he said, and waited for a reply. The password.

"I'm sorry." Her voice cracked. "I'm not Starborn, but I'm here to see Davyn. I'm Arissa of Aryn."

The man whistled a short, melodic phrase. A moment later, the phrase was returned; a second figure emerged from the shadow of a tent and the two conferred. The first man took hold of her horse's bridle, then, and said, "You'll wait here with me. Bando will see." The other man loped toward one of the farther tents.

Most of her hair was hanging in long tangles around her face. That had happened when she dismounted the first time and pushed through some brush to gain the privacy of the woods; she'd had a rough encounter with an aggressive bramble. The twining branches had picked apart her braid as she disentangled herself. Now, the scratches on her arms were red and swollen, and the ones on her face felt like they were sizzling. Her borrowed clothing was torn and there was a verdant smear of grass stain at her knee. She was tattered, hungry and exhausted, and didn't feel at all like minding her manners. She was glad there was no one here to judge her by House standards.

When the Starborn sentry had led her toward this tent, she'd been longing to fall into Davyn's arms. She remembered the way his arms had felt around her, that night when they arrived in Ruatt, and the warm, solid strength of him. But when he stepped out of the tent, there was something in the way he stood that made Arissa sure that his thoughts and attention were lingering behind him. He looked thinner than she remembered, but maybe it was just the way the light caught the angles of his face. She had taken no more than a hesitant half-step toward him when a lithe, dark-haired Starborn woman followed him out.

When Davyn recognized Arissa and said her name, with surprise, she almost started crying. "I was so sure you were dead!"

"For a while, I thought so, too." His rich, lilting voice, and the soft amusement, were almost an embrace. More soberly, he had asked, "Are you hurt?"

She shook her head, but before she could answer, another familiar voice, lighter and crisper, said, "Arissa!" Atto was just at the tent's flap. "You look awful!"

The Starborn woman came forward, smiling kindly, and said, "Looks like a wash and some clean clothes might help. I'm Tienna. Let's see what we can do. Atto, would you bring some water, please?" The woman exchanged a look with Davyn that seemed to be the continuation of a conversation.

Atto disappeared around the back of the tent, and Tienna held the tent flap back and ushered Arissa through.

The tent was larger than she'd expected, and the far end was screened off with a curtain. She was in a front room, which was furnished as an all-purpose living space, with a handful of chairs ringed around a small table, and a few stools, some tray-tables, and a bench. It was crowded but it all looked neat, welcoming, and unassuming—in that, Arissa thought it befitted her hostess.

A cot, pushed against the side of the tent, seemed out of place. Arissa noticed a man's shirt hanging there, and a saddlebag half-stowed underneath. It was Davyn's. He was living here.

Her own saddlebag was propped beside a tentpole. It was reassuring beyond reason, like finding a friend in a crowd or a recognizing a landmark after wandering lost for hours. If she were lucky, the coin purse she had stuffed down to the bottom would still be there.

"The day you were taken, a couple of the men overheard that they were taking you to House Wyth," Tienna said. "When Davyn found out, he said you didn't want to go—I think he would have ridden to your rescue if he could have. He was very concerned for you."

There were undercurrents in Tienna's mild tone that made Arissa take note. She had used the same technique often enough to decipher it: a superficial observation that was really a subtle probe for reaction. *Davyn cares about you. Do you want him to?*

She was surprised Tienna even had to ask. Davyn had been kind and glad that she was all right, but he'd barely looked at her for more than two seconds at a time. His whole being was directed toward Tienna—surely the woman could feel that? "I was lucky," Arissa said. "I was safe and comfortable at Wyth." *Until I ruined everything.*

Tienna gave her a sisterly smile. "Atto says Piers said you risked a lot to help him. He was impressed."

Clean, in the wrinkled clothes from her saddlebag, and with a cup of telik already at work, Arissa felt stronger. She sat on the edge of the cot, with Tienna beside her. Atto and Davyn were both across from her on a bench, contemplative and concerned. Davyn was studying her, and she wished the light were good enough for her to see his eyes. He'd been still while she recounted the series of departures from House Wyth, but there was no question that he was distressed. If she could see his eyes, she'd know if he were upset with her.

With a brittle voice, Atto had explained that when they'd seen Owen's men closing the gap on the road, Piers had told them to scatter. Atto rode into the woods. Elanna kicked her horse into a gallop—when Piers's horse had tried to follow, Piers had been thrown. Elanna went back, and tried to help him up, so the two of them had been on foot when Owen's men caught up with them. Davyn said nothing other than that he was glad Arissa was all right, but there had been bleakness in his voice.

It was just further evidence that she couldn't live up to their expectations. No one blamed her, but only because they didn't need to. The facts were obvious. Rane had been right, back at House Wyth, when he'd said she had ruined everything. Atto's wretched guilt magnified hers, and Davyn's tacit forgiveness was worse. The Starborn woman, Tienna, was all sympathy and kindness, and if she hadn't been so sincere Arissa might have found it easier to bear.

23

ALLIANCE

House Wyth

THE GUEST SUITE was guarded twice-over now, and the passageway blocked. A House guard was just outside the door, and another was in the front room. He was pleasant enough, all things considered, and had been curious about Piers—apparently just because House Wyth didn't usually have suspicion-inducing visitors. It seemed no one had told him about Piers's wild tales, and Piers decided to leave well enough alone on that score.

So Piers sat in one of the comfortable chairs and tried to be grateful it wasn't worse. He ached all over, mostly from falling off the damn horse. He knew he was lucky—broken bones would have been a reasonable result, and probably would be a horrific injury without the ship's medibay. Pain was pain, though, and these bruises would be with him for a long time. He would gladly drink any amount of Shea's briny syrup if he had the chance.

Elanna had hardly spoken to him after their capture, although he suspected that might be nothing to do with him. When Arissa had come for them, she'd taken them out through a maze of passageways, through the silent house, then into the shadows behind the house to the barn. Elanna had been so keyed up when they met that she couldn't manage a single sentence without a stammer that made her truly incomprehensible.

Introductions had not gone smoothly, though Atto had been affable and there'd been some warmth when Elanna realized that Atto shared her admiration of Davyn. Talking to adults—and Piers had forgotten again that he was one—was apparently more intimidating. The girl from Trint only calmed down when she started saddling the horses. Piers stood beside her, Pushed some encouragement, and tried to make sure his expression was friendly.

The girl had guileless, brown eyes that divulged her thoughts. In one moment of eye-contact, Piers knew that Elanna was frightened and homesick, and then a stab of pain, a fierce flash of a headache, made Piers shut his eyes and Block.

"Are you all right?" the girl whispered, without a stammer.

He didn't have an answer. It felt like another version of the odd half-Link he felt with Atto. It was nothing like what he might get from a Separate, but the raw energy of Elanna's emotion was also unlike an Empath's nuanced power. The headache vanished as the contact faded, leaving behind a tingling that felt like ripples in water. "I think so," he said. Elanna's concern was soothing. And here I was trying to make *her* feel better, Piers thought.

He pulled himself back from the confusion, downshifted to Screening, and turned to a lighter topic. He made himself put a hand on the horse's smooth shoulder. "I think horses are amazing," Piers said.

There was a pulse almost like a Reach that vanished before he could respond, and Elanna's expression eased. "Davyn says horses understand people better than we understand them."

If that actually had been a Reach, he had just missed a major breakthrough because he'd been hiding from the headache. Not good. He forced himself to drop his screens a bit, and braced himself, but it didn't come again.

"Sounds like Davyn's pretty wise," Piers said, Pushing a little sense of admiration to her. Appreciation of Davyn seemed to be a shortcut to trust with a surprising number of people. Everyone in the sun's shadow was devoted to the man, apparently. Oh, Piers absolutely wanted to meet Davyn, to find out why. "I know you miss him."

"He went to get help," Elanna said, whispering again and with such distress that Piers felt petty for resenting Davyn's ubiquity. "I came to bring him home."

Now, Elanna was shut away in one of the bedrooms, and had fallen asleep. At least while the girl slept, Piers was safe from the untrammeled emotion. Comfort on one front, anyway. He shifted in the chair, trying to find a way to not put pressure on his bruises.

The guard gave him a sympathetic nod. "You're in bad shape, friend. I'll ask for telik for you." He passed word to the guard outside, and then said, "At least there's a healer up at the dam."

"Really? I thought they were prisoners."

"Oh, aye, they are," the man answered. "It's just that Ettori needs them healthy enough to work." Piers noticed a slight curl of his lip when he said *Ettori*.

"Not much consolation, considering everyone was ripped out of their real lives," Piers said.

The man's expression hardened, and Piers saw anger

shaded with guilt on his face. "That's the truth," he said. "The Starborn don't have an easy time of it."

"Because they believe another ship is coming?" Piers asked. He Scanned, just a touch, to see if there were any traces of scorn, or of hope. The man was blank.

"They wander all over the place and go on and on about how redemption is coming if they just keep their hearts pure and their minds open. Hundreds of years, they've been doing that. They're an easy target."

Piers wanted to leap up and demand to be taken to the dam immediately, to the Starborn. Oh yes, *Redemption* is most definitely coming. They just don't know it's the name of the ship! As casually as he could, Piers asked, "Do they ever talk about a homing signal?"

At that, the man seemed to sink into memory. "You know, I'd forgotten about that. When I was a boy, I made friends with a Starborn lad, until his camp moved on. He talked about going into the Caladen Forest to look for some kind of beacon when he was older. He said it's supposed to signal when the ship is close. Legend says that if people are near it, they'll have visions of the ship."

Piers's blood raced. He tried to remember the map Atto had shown him. Where was the Caladen Forest? He pressed for more information, but the man had none. While a Starborn elder somewhere might know more, his boyhood friend had nothing except elaborate speculations about what the beacon did, not where or what it was. In one version of the story, the visions would cause death because the beacon was supposed to protect the ship; in another, the visions would cause ecstasy, because it was supposed to prepare people to welcome redemption. The beacon was a natural formation in a rock, or a manmade thing, or a person, or maybe a state of mind. The only part of the legend that was consistent was that if the beacon existed, it was in the Caladen Forest.

The guard said he'd figured it was long gone, if it had ever existed. Piers tried to let go of the vague hope. After all, if the beacon had survived the centuries, why hadn't they received the signal?

Piers pretended that he wanted to check on Elanna and slipped into the room beside the one where the girl slept. Through the barred window, he could see a few stars. When he'd boarded the shuttle, he'd had the fleeting thought that he would probably never be back on *Redemption*. It had given him a pang of something like prescient nostalgia, and he'd wondered if he would be himself after giving up the stars. Billions of people lived and died without ever seeing the stars from any other perspective, yet all of them were bathed in the same ancient starlight. It occurred to him now that no one could ever truly leave the stars behind. The stars went first.

Up there somewhere, Jon and Barston and Kath and all the others were going about their days. There'd been no contact yesterday, and he couldn't remember the last time he'd heard the in-range chime. There should be a fly-over soon. They tried not to pass over the heavily populated areas too often or too regularly, since pre-space humanity had a tendency to react unpredictably to unexplained celestial phenomena—or at least that had been the case on Earth.

He leaned against the wall, and composed an update for Jon and Barston. He told them about the guard's conversation and the beacon, and hesitated. It would worry all of them, but he needed to be realistic here. He went on.

I hate to say this, but things aren't looking too good for me being able to be there when you land. Long story short, I'm being sent to House Ettori for an audience. I'm not looking forward to it, and I'm right, to judge from the fact that Rane, Arissa, Atto, and Elanna all seemed distressed about it—and Lord Wyth has locked me up, comfortably, to make sure it actually happens. No one started eulogizing, though, so I take that as somewhat reassuring and I'm awaiting my fate with trepidation but not dread. I'm going to try to get Rane to meet you, in case I don't make it. The crew might be able to get him to help, somehow. Tell Kath and my folks I'm all right.

Rane brought the telik himself, and told the guard to leave them. The man hesitated, but Rane gave him a look that Piers associated with parents and commanders who were completely out of patience, and the guard excused himself.

The drink was still too hot. Social drink. Piers almost laughed, a little desperately. He held the cup between his hands, and watched the way the syrup writhed like smoke in the water as it dissolved. As it unfurled and bled color into the beverage, the aroma was released. Either he had already developed a conditioned response, or even the fragrance was a sedative; he felt the relaxation seeping through him.

"I wanted to apologize," Rane said. He sat on the loveseat and leaned forward as if confiding. "If it were up to me, you wouldn't be here. Arissa was right, you need to be free so you can help them land."

It was genuine. Piers tried again, offering a Link, but again there was no response. He wanted to probe, and even to try asking outright, but if Rane knew he had psi abilities, he did an astonishingly good job of hiding it. "Thank you," Piers said. "I know you'd have let us get away, if I hadn't fallen."

Rane grimaced. "That was a bad fall. When I saw you hit the ground I was afraid you might have been headed for the stars." He paused on a breath, and the words hung. When he met Piers's eyes, they both laughed.

"It sounds different, now that I know," Rane said.

"On the ship, when people die, we do send the body out—we say 'give him to the stars.'"

They talked about language, and Piers was so fascinated and engaged in the conversation that he felt like they were colleagues, or even friends. Rane told him, directly but kindly, that not only was his accent strange, but he didn't always have the grammar quite right. Sometimes he used archaic phrasing, and sometimes he made childish omissions; other times it was just oddly formal. Well, it wasn't much of a surprise—some syntactic change in the language was almost a given. Maybe he could take it as a compliment that his speech was only *sometimes* quaint and eccentric.

Then Rane asked him what it was like, seeing the stars from up there, and what the planet looked like. Piers tried to describe it, and then had the thought that he'd just proved wrong all the people who'd said his poetic tendencies would be a disaster for a scout. But then, this wasn't the scouting part anymore. This was closer to diplomacy, except that as a doom-bound prisoner, he wasn't a very credible ambassador.

"What will happen to Elanna?" he asked.

Rane's forehead creased and he sank back into his chair. "I don't know. I'm trying to convince Owen to let her go, but Owen's afraid of how Ettori would react, and he's also not in much of a mood to listen."

Rane got up and started pacing. He was shedding emotion as he moved, like the stuff was a virus and he an unwitting carrier. Once again, Piers Reached, offering a

Link that now he himself wanted. Rane didn't react, but Piers was aware of Elanna's presence—the girl was awake now, and not wanting to interact with the adults.

"He's in a hard position," Piers said.

"He makes it harder than it needs to be. He thinks people won't take him seriously as Lord Wyth, and that he needs Ettori's backing. But I think he weakens his position by trying so hard to keep Kor happy."

Politics. Piers knew enough about that to count it as a plus that he wouldn't be Captain Haldon. People weren't at their best when they were scheming and posturing and defensive all at the same time. It was heartbreaking, too, when he had a glimpse of what even the most jaded and self-serving people were really feeling. Most of the time, sometimes at a level that they weren't even aware of, they knew better and wanted better. Owen wasn't the kind to thrive like that, Piers thought. It was the sensitive people who often put up the most formidable walls.

When the House guards who scraped him off the road presented him to Owen, there'd been real concern in the man's eyes, though he'd said, "Lord Ettori is expecting you. So we'll go back to Wyth and try this again."

Piers had bowed to fate as soon as he'd heard the approaching thunder of the horses. There was no chance of him riding or running fast enough or far enough to evade professional riders, so he stopped his horse and just sat in the middle of the road to wait. He told the kids to get away and get help; Atto gave him a profound and rather sweet conversation-in-a-glance and then disappeared into the woods like he was riding a ghost horse. Elanna, on the other hand, had been torn. She hadn't wanted to desert Piers, but she knew just as well that Piers was as good as captured. Piers had finally shouted at her, and the girl had looked shocked and hurt—but she'd also turned her horse and galloped away.

It didn't matter that Piers's plan was to wait for the Wyth men to collect him. His horse thought galloping off with Elanna's would be more fun. The horse had pivoted and leapt forward, and Piers had tumbled off and sprawled on the road. When he'd collected his senses enough to find Elanna standing over him, he'd snapped at her, which wasn't the response Elanna had expected or deserved.

Owen had been sincerely sorry to find Elanna. He'd almost, almost let the girl go, but the Ettori guard had been hovering, judging. Piers had looked him in the eye, and said, "I understand, Owen." It startled the man, but he covered it with a gruff order to his men and they were soon on their way back to Wyth.

"Would Ettori really take Elanna to the dam?" he asked now.

"I don't know," Rane answered, pausing to study a small painting displayed on a shelf. Piers felt Rane's effort to keep his voice calm. "I don't know what he would do with her."

That opened a terrifying line of thought. Physical labor on the dam would be a much kinder fate than what Elanna might face. Piers felt a rising panic, like it was filling his lungs.

"If he takes us both, I'll try to keep her safe," he said, trying to ignore the disheartening thought that he probably wouldn't be able to do much for her. "If I'm not free to help the ship, will you do me a favor?"

His host was guarded, wary of a request that might put him at odds with his brother. He drummed his fingers on the mantel and regarded Piers with a masked expression. "If I can," he said.

"The ship is going to try to land in the open space north of Drisk—not too many people around. Like I told you, the plan was for me to find some help and meet them there."

"I can't get you out," Rane said, and there was raw misery in his eyes.

"I know," Piers replied. He was out of time to find an Empathic welcome committee, and he wasn't going to be able to try any singlehanded heroics while he was locked up, either. The only hope he could think of, since escaping was clearly off the list, lay with Rane. Rane's unacknowledged psi ability lent some plausibility to the idea that the gene had been passed down among the Houses. Maybe if enough House people gathered at the landing site, the Empaths on the ship would be able to tap into that feral psi energy somehow. Not much of a plan, but he couldn't count on getting out of here.

"The thing is, even if it all goes well, they will need help," Piers said. "The first few days are disorienting, at best." Piers thought of Arthur, incapacitated by nausea and vertigo for days after landing. It had hit the moment they stood under the open sky.

In those first few minutes, he himself had stood as still as he could, and tried to commit every sensation, however fleeting, to vivid memory. It had thrilled him to realize that the warmth on his skin was actually from the *sun*. Directly. The fragrance of all the vegetation around him, baking in that same warmth, had surprised him. It was sweet but with a tang of decay, like cut flowers from the greenhouse. The light breeze that tugged at his clothes and played with his hair also made noise in the trees. Whistles and chirps came from the trees, too: birds. Birds! He hadn't thought about there being birds. When he'd turned to Arthur to comment, he'd seen his fellow scout frozen in place with a yellow-green tint to his skin and a look comprised of horror and confusion. Yes, they absolutely would need help.

"I was supposed to meet the ship," Piers said. "Partly so that I can explain what they can expect and help them learn how to navigate, and to make sure our arrival can be managed the right way. If you could get other House lords there, it could make all the difference."

Rane got it, or thought he did, without the request being formally made. "I will make sure someone is there," he said. "Someone sympathetic. But how will we know when to meet them?"

Giant fireball in the sky heading toward an open field... "You'll see them. I just need people like you, people with authority, there when they arrive." *Authority* was not a synonym for psi ability that Piers had ever considered, but if the genetic heritage of one came with the other here, that was good enough.

24

ALLEGIANCE

House Wyth

AFTER HE LEFT Piers, Rane rapped on Arissa's door, waited, and rapped again. "Arissa, it's Rane." When there was no reply, he knocked harder. He almost turned away, thinking she'd decided to ignore him, but he tried one more time. "You were right, Arissa."

He lingered, impressed and annoyed at her stubborn refusal to acknowledge him. He told her he was coming in, then tried the door. Unlocked.

Most of the cases that had been delivered from Trint were still arranged neatly against the wall, but there were signs of a hasty departure. There was a heap of impractical clothing on the bed as if it had been dumped out, and a dresser drawer was open. He knew where she had gone. Knew it with his breath catching in his throat and his heart racing. Dreading what he knew he'd find, he went to the stables.

It was late enough that the horses were settled and the grooms were elsewhere. Rane slipped around the outside so he could go in without drawing attention and entered from the back. The roan was gone. He stood utterly still and made himself focus on his breathing until he felt like he wouldn't collapse.

There was light coming from the library. Rane hesitated. It was unusual for Owen not to already have escaped to his private rooms by this hour. Then again, it had been an unusual day. Owen wouldn't want to have this conversation, not now, but tomorrow morning would be too late. He pushed open the door.

Owen was lounging in his preferred chair with a book he seemed to have no real interest in reading. When he saw Rane enter, he set the book aside. "I thought you might come." His voice was mild. "Are you here to lecture or apologize?" He shifted so that he was lying back in the chair, crossed his ankles, crossed his arms, and closed his eyes.

Rane went to the sideboard and poured something strong for each of them. "Here," he said, holding a glass out toward Owen, who opened one eye and then the other. "You'll want a drink."

His brother's wry smile appeared. "Aren't you the one always telling me I drink too much?"

"Trust me, you'll want it."

He waited until Owen took a sip, and tried to gauge his mood. There were dark smudges under his eyes, and his brows seemed lower, like a permanent frown had set in. His shoulders were hunched and he seemed to be moving as if he were in pain. Clearly he was battered by the day, and not at all rested, and whatever self-reflection he'd done hadn't put him in a better mood.

Owen had always been good at staying silent, with

that mild, inquisitive look on his face, and it was always as if he asked whatever question Rane most dreaded. Rane pressed a hand over his eyes, rubbing his eyebrows, and drew a long breath.

"You won't like this," he said.

"I gathered that much," Owen said, still nonchalant, but Rane felt the impatience building.

His thoughts were too slow, and he couldn't sort through the whole mess of bad news to select what he needed to disclose, or in what order. He said, "She's gone."

Owen knocked back the rest of his drink.

"She was upset when we brought Piers back. She wanted to talk about it, but I was angry."

Owen leaned forward in his chair, and seemed carved from granite except for the drumming of his fingers on the armrest.

"We both needed to cool down, so I wanted to give her some time, but I just went to try to smooth things over." Rane was trying to explain unemotionally, but found himself talking too fast, like he had as a child when he'd known his father was angry with him. "She must have gone back out to the stable and taken the roan."

They were both standing now. Rane shifted his weight from foot to foot, but Owen stood with his feet shoulder-width apart and his hands clasped behind his back. There was a white edge around his lips, and a glint in his unblinking eyes. When he responded, he enunciated with staccato precision. "You were angry. And she's gone."

"Yes, but—"

"You thought she was sulking so you left her alone." Owen's monotone delivery twisted the statement into an accusation.

"Well, I—"

"And she escaped."

"Escaped?" Rane's appalled challenge pushed Owen off-balance and the military posture crumbled. "You're supposed to be her bridegroom, not her jailor!"

Chagrin shimmered in Owen's eyes, but Owen couldn't—wouldn't—back down. He threw his shoulders back and lifted his chin. "I have to be cautious when the safety and future of this House are at stake."

"If you can't tell that Arissa's not the threat here, our safety and future are really in trouble," Rane said, feeling the distance expand between them as an upwelling of grief stuck in his throat. He was losing Owen, too. "She wanted to save Piers from your dear friend Kor, because she's got principles and she's not afraid to do the right thing. She's not willing to let innocent people suffer while she plays it safe."

Owen moved toward the door, and the darkness on his face made Rane take a step backward despite himself. "That's enough," Owen said, with equal darkness in his voice. Behind the anger and menace, Rane thought he detected pain and confusion, like the complex snarls of a trapped animal. "Get out of my way."

Rane asked for food to be brought to his room, and the kitchen sent up a plate of leftovers. Dust or wood chips would have served just as well, since nothing had much flavor to him. When he set the empty plate on the tray by the door, he didn't sit back down. He crossed his room, from window to door, hearth to bed, over and over, with his mind on a similar path among his various worries, until finally he dropped into a chair and tried to be still. He should calm down, clear his head, and get some sleep.

Stopping the motion didn't stop his restless mind. Had Atto reached the Starborn camp? Had Arissa? If so, maybe they were already plotting a way to rescue Piers and Elanna. Stars, he hated the thought of the girl being in Ettori's reach.

Arissa had been right to try to spare Piers and Atto. It was bold of her, to defy Owen like that. It hadn't worked, and might have made things worse, but Rane couldn't stop himself from being impressed with her audacity. He wondered, though, if Owen would ever stop thinking of it as a betrayal. Owen likely thought his future wife should have taken his side on principle; it was like Owen to expect things too soon. By the time he had arrived at a conclusion or made a decision, he had given a situation so much thought that he was certain he knew what the outcome would be. Everything between decision and outcome then was just a formality. He tended to expect others to have reached the same conclusion independently, and he was always surprised when he discovered otherwise. It may have been obvious to him that eventually Arissa would support him, and if that were a foregone conclusion, why wouldn't she just do so from the beginning?

She would have been good for Owen, with her principles and opinions. Owen needed to be challenged, and needed a true partner with a mind of her own. But she'd made her choice and stormed off, leaving Rane to deal with the aftermath. Owen was hurt and didn't want to admit it. It had surprised Rane beyond words when Owen said he was contracting with House Aryn. His brother had always been self-contained, and shy with women, and since becoming head of House he'd been more and more walled off. Marriage was his duty, he'd told Rane, and a liaison with a House was a political need.

Duty and politics. That was what consumed Owen these days.

Rane was pacing again. He didn't remember getting

back on his feet, but somehow he found himself at the window, and the reflection of his room in the glass floated over the darkness outside. His own ghostly image was disconcerting, with his face moon-like and disembodied because his dark clothes vanished against the night.

He had made promises he didn't know how to keep. First, to the Gathering, promising not to cooperate with Ettori—which was Owen's decision. And that House Wyth would serve as a shield for the others, letting Lord Ettori blunt his army's will to attack on Wyth's own men—which also rightly would require Owen's command.

If he could have Owen's help, it would be different. Of course, if he and Owen were on good terms at the moment, a lot of things would be different, so that wasn't a fruitful line of thought. There was no possibility he could see of the refusal happening without Ettori lashing out at the nearest Houses, and Wyth would be first in line. Unless... unless somehow House Wyth didn't take part, and Owen's obliging cultivation of Kor's favor protected them. Rane had sworn an oath with the others who had attended the Gathering, though, and that needed to count for something.

He'd given his word to Piers, too. There would be plenty of mistrust and probably even fear when his ship landed. Even if his people eventually integrated into existing patterns, in the beginning there would be three thousand people who needed tolerance and assistance all at once. That much help wouldn't be spontaneously offered when people were already close to the breaking point from House Ettori's demands on them. Someone was going to have to advocate for the strangers and create some way to organize their arrival and guide the settlement.

And he'd pledged to Arissa, although she didn't know that he'd silently promised to help her find happiness—again dependent on Owen—while vowing that he wouldn't let himself love her. He wasn't sure how he would manage, when she would be part of his every day. He would need to be away from House Wyth often.

None of these oaths and commitments had been made impulsively, but neither had he quite considered the fact that he would have to keep them without Owen's knowledge or help. Nor had he thought of the implications that were tangled up with each one: the resources he needed somehow to acquire, the plans he needed to make, the people whose lives would be affected by his success or failure in keeping his word.

Those thoughts swept aside any chance he'd had of settling down. Hiding in his room would solve nothing. He thought of his father, and wished he could seek advice from the brilliant mind that was now trapped and waiting for the end.

The House was quiet, and he made his way to his father's sickroom without seeing or hearing anyone else. He cracked the door gently and saw Oterin asleep in a chair beside his father's bed. A lamp burned on the side table, softening the shadows that seemed like another presence in the room. Rane moved to the bedside, without waking the healer, and looked at his father's sallow face. He was glad his father's eyes were closed—he hated seeing the lost and vacant look that had replaced bold confidence and wit.

The healer slept quietly, his slow, deep breathing occasionally sighing out in a soft snore. Sleep was less peaceful for Rane's fading father. Shallow breaths rasped and caught in his throat, and his eyes fluttered but did not see. One hand was on top of the covers, and the fingers occasionally clutched and curled and twitched. Rane took that hand in his own, but his father didn't wake.

He stayed for only a few minutes, wanting to talk to his father but unwilling to break his sleep and the respite it offered. After he left the room, he wandered through the slumbering House. The darkness felt heavy. In the secret room in the tower, he drowsed for a time, and woke hungry. He went to the kitchen to find something to hold him until breakfast.

Bread in hand, he strayed into the courtyard, relishing the mild chill of the small hours of an early summer morning. The stars were bright and clear, and the nightbirds were warbling among the trees. The waxing moon was low and golden. He saddled Ambler, and rode along the familiar trail to the overlook, trusting the horse's night vision and sure footing.

He wasn't ready to face his brother quite yet, though he was drifting closer to his peace-making mood. He'd be ready to reconcile before Owen was, so there was no point in rushing. So Rane watched while the valley mist burned off as the sun rose. A stiff breeze started and carried scents of blossoms and new leaves. When the trees bent, he caught glimpses of the early sun dazzling on the water of New Lake; he decided to ride to the next overlook for a better view before going back to the House and trying his skill in persuading Owen to let Elanna go.

The stillness in the courtyard was tinged with emptiness. Rane thought the air itself seemed to be holding its breath, and the horse's hooves on the stones sounded loud and merciless. No one came from the stable to greet him, so he swung down and walked the horse into the barn.

One of the older stablehands was sitting on a hay bale, flask in hand. When he heard Rane, he looked up with dull eyes. "Dan Owen will be glad you're back," he said. He didn't rise, and didn't take the horse. He just took another swig and then held the flask toward Rane. "I'm sorry, lad."

He knew. Rane dropped the reins and reeled to the door, dashed across the courtyard and barreled into the House. He took the grand stairs two at a time, and raced through the corridors to arrive, panting, at the open door to his father's sickroom. The sunlight angled into the room in a concentrated beam that blazed on the bed. The empty bed. His heart resisted what his mind registered in one glance, and when the feeling came it was piercing. He gripped the door frame for support.

Owen spoke from the unlit corner of the room, where he stood so that he could look out the window without being blinded. "A few hours ago," he said, without censure. Without much emotion at all, Rane noted with concern. When Owen retreated emotionally, he did it far, far too well.

As he crossed the room, the empty bed seemed like a reproach. His father had been dying last night and Rane hadn't known. He should have wakened him. For six months his father had lain there, oscillating between suffering and exhaustion. Their father had mourned for their mother during the early stages of his own illness, when his mind still could grasp at his memories. They had watched as their father began to forget, first his loss, then his life. Rane had told himself that knowing this moment would come had prepared him, that he'd grieved with his father and for his father simultaneously, that when his father was released from his pain it would relieve all of them. None of that, now, made sense at all. Rane stopped beside his brother, and put a hand on his shoulder; Owen didn't react.

"Brother," Rane said, needing the affirmation. "The stars will guide him."

There was no reply, and they stood side by side, staring passively at the scene outside. Owen finally stepped away, and Rane let his hand drop.

"He was alert when I visited before breakfast," Owen said, "and seemed comfortable. He didn't know me, but he talked about the trees and seemed coherent, and then told me he was tired. I left him to rest. An hour later, Oterin came to get me but by the time we got back he was gone. They've moved him so they can prepare him—told me that was not for us to do."

"I'm sorry I wasn't here."

Owen shook his head slowly. "It makes no difference. He was alone at the end. I suppose we all are."

When they saw their father several hours later, the House Guard had started the vigil. They circled the body that lay on a raised pallet in the large receiving room, draped with a heavy white cloth redolent of herbs. A medallion bearing the emblem of House Wyth rested over the stilled heart. Rane could hardly bring himself to enter the room, but Owen placed a kiss on their father's forehead and said, "May the stars guide you home, Father."

As the two of them stepped back from the pallet, Owen turned to Rane and said, "Now you'll get your Gathering after all, if they will come."

"Why wouldn't they? At least the closer Houses. They'll witness the Transference—they all knew he was ill, and they all know you. No question of it being contested."

With a restrained smile, Owen said, "So you're not interested in being Lord Wyth?"

Rane returned the smile in kind. "You really haven't done a very good job of convincing me that *anyone* would be interested." He sobered. "Seriously, though, Owen.

You're ready. You'll be a good one." Once again he put a hand on his brother's shoulder.

This time, Owen clamped a hand on Rane's arm. "Thank you, little brother." He paused, letting his thanks expand, and then lifted his hand. "Help me write out the notice?"

Tarken arrived after the evening meal, so soon that Rane suspected he'd saddled his horse within an hour of reading the notice. He spent the evening with them, reminiscing about their father in his younger years and sharing their loss. It was heartening to have their closest friend and nearest neighbor with them—and to have one of the required witnesses already accounted for.

For Owen to be properly invested as Lord Wyth, House-born representatives from six Houses needed to personally witness the transfer of the emblem to the new lord. If fewer came, it meant Owen would need two Writs of Transference to compensate for each absent witness, acknowledging with signatures and seals that they would accept the validity of the new Lord Wyth, despite not being there to witness first-hand. It was all meant to ensure that Houses had connections outside their own region, but circumstances had changed in ways the first Council of Houses hadn't foreseen.

The other House of the hill region, House Caladen, had fallen when Rane was a boy, leaving only Wyth and Dannpelier. Only two Houses remained in the high eastern plains, too, since House Estend had been ceded to Tyndaris after the war. With only ten Great Houses in play, the two-for-one rule would complicate Owen's situation very quickly. If only three Houses sent representatives, he'd need six writs—meaning he would need unanimous support.

With an acidic thought, Rane amended that. House Aryn probably wouldn't respond at all, since they would think Arissa was here, so the numbers wouldn't work at all for Owen if there were fewer than four witnesses. In that case, even unanimous support wouldn't yield enough writs, and Rane didn't know what provisions the law made for that. It was unlikely that anyone would contest the transfer, but there was no requirement for them to respond at all. Owen was sure House Ettori would send someone, but there was no way of knowing what the other Houses would do.

Alone that evening with Owen, after Tarken had retired, Rane said, "It'll be all right, Owen. They'll support us." He was thinking that House Glay and House Lin, surely, would respond as co-conspirators if not as allies.

Bitterly, Owen said, "If Arissa were here, it would be a lot better. We're not married yet—she'd count for House Aryn."

Rane swallowed the impulse to blurt out that he knew where she was. Owen probably knew already, and if he didn't, nothing good would come from Rane admitting that he did. "Ettori will come," he said, "and Manssorand and Chant might. There's no reason to think the others wouldn't at least send writs."

With a sound that wasn't quite a laugh, Owen said, "Lin and Glay, yes; Andali, maybe; Janoval, unlikely. You were too little to remember. After Caladen fell, and all the Houses were anxious, Father tried to call a Gathering. The response he got from House Janoval could've started a war."

"What? A Gathering?"

"Yes—Father and Tarken both thought there was something suspicious about the fire at Caladen. They thought if they held a Gathering, they'd be able to figure out if someone had blood on their hands."

"I take it Janoval didn't come?"

Owen snorted. "He sent back a message to the effect that the hill Houses were power-mad, double-crossing tyrants who hadn't defended House Estend in the war because they wanted to weaken the plains Houses; that the Gathering was an attempt by Wyth and Dannpelier to deflect blame; that he was glad Caladen had fallen; and he'd never, ever support any of the hill Houses."

Rane pulled in a deep breath, thoughts racing. That was why Lord Janoval had seemed hostile when he tried to call the Gathering—it was a good thing he hadn't used his own name. It also explained Father's strange attitudes toward the western Houses, which had made Owen's betrothal to Arissa of House Aryn seem strange. And perhaps it was also why Owen was so touchy on the subject of Gatherings in general.

"What prompted that? Who crossed Janoval?" Rane asked.

"You don't know? Mother was betrothed to Rick Janoval. She was young and the contract was for marriage when she turned twenty. The year before, she met and fell in love with Father. They applied to Prime House, which of course was Caladen then, to nullify the contract. Dannpelier seconded the application. Janoval has never forgiven any of them." Owen frowned, and the line between his brows deepened until it seemed like a scar. "And now I suppose this thing with Arissa means House Aryn will hate us, too."

With an exhalation that made the candleflames waver, Owen put down his empty glass and announced that he was going to bed. Lord Ettori would probably arrive midday, and if there were riders from the west they might arrive any time. If he didn't have enough support by the end of the fourth day, House Wyth would have to hold the funeral before the Transference. That would be one more complication for Owen, and Rane could see that having one more worry wasn't helping his brother's confidence.

Heavy weather rolled in that night, adding to the anxiety in the house; storms through the night stole what little sleep Rane tried to get.

The following morning was clear and sparkling, but House Wyth was surrounded by littered branches and leaves. Despite the groundskeepers' objections, Rane and Tarken spent the morning with them, clearing away the storm's detritus—it was better than the strange mix of agitation and emptiness in the house, and gave them a chance to talk.

After hearing about Piers's revelation, escape, and recapture, Tarken said, "He's still here?"

"For now. The Ettori man was going to take them yesterday, but wanted one of ours to go along. Then all this happened, and Owen couldn't spare anyone. So we've still got two prisoners in the guest suite." It made his stomach churn. House Wyth didn't do things like this.

"I suppose Kor will take them with him, then. The only good thing about it is that he'll be with the Starborn once he gets to the dam. For all we know, they have some legend about landing plans and they can tell him what ought to happen."

Through the day, Rane and Tarken tried to keep Owen from chafing with worry about the Transference. Gerrid, Lord of House Manssorand, arrived that afternoon, as ill at ease and dutiful as any neighbor could be. He had done the calculations, he said, and wanted to help. A fast glance at Rane and Tarken was the only allusion to the other calculations, but Rane was sure the double meaning was intentional. There was no chance to discuss any of that, of course, since the three of them couldn't very well exclude Owen from conversation at dinner or through the long evening.

Late the following day, Lin and Glay rode in together, along with the Wyth courier who had taken the notice to them. The trip down from the plains wasn't trivial, and Owen was surprised to see them. For their part, Rane thought they must have been taken aback by the forcefulness of Owen's gratitude for their presence. They didn't know—and Owen didn't want to tell any of them—about House Aryn's inadvertent abstention from the Transference.

With witnesses from four Houses now present, and Ettori still expected, one source of Owen's distress eased. It was still unsettling to know that there was no margin, given that House Janoval wasn't very likely to be helpful. Now it was all down to House Andali and House Chant, and if neither came, both writs were necessary.

Rane lay awake that night musing over the unpleasant truth that he was counting on Ettori.

Every lamp was lit, and extra candles chased off any stubborn shadows. The five witnesses—the lords of Dannpelier, Glay, Lin, Manssorand, and Ettori—faced Owen and Rane across the pallet; they stood by their father's left side. Rane held writs from Chant and Andali, which had arrived not long after Ettori and his entourage swarmed in this afternoon, barely in time, and watched Owen's expression harden as the brief ceremony ended. His brother's hands trembled when they lifted the House emblem from the shrouded body. "The privileges and obligations of House Wyth are now in my hands," Owen said. Each witness signed the ancient record and stamped his seal at the bottom of the dated page where Owen had neatly written his name below his father's name and an arrow pointing down to his own. The two writs were attached with a drop of wax at each corner. And it was done.

The Wyth Guards carried the pallet to the pyre they had built in the courtyard. Rane stood next to Owen, holding the torch that he'd lit from the fire in the receiving room, and tried not to let his thoughts spark his grief—not yet. He tried to match Owen's detachment, impressed by the sober maturity of his brother's expression. Atop the pyre, his father's body was thankfully above Rane's gaze, but he could see one corner of the white pall trailing over the side of the pallet. It made him want to pull the shroud away and let his father's empty eyes look toward the stars, but he adjusted his grip on the torch and held still.

After Lord Ettori's unctuous eulogy, Rane had to count to ten to stifle his annoyance when it was his turn to say his words of blessing for his father. In his effort to neither rail at Ettori nor choke on suppressed feelings, he spoke too fast, and his rush of words sounded insincere. Owen managed his blessing with more dignity. The House Guards sang "The Last Journey" as Rane passed the torch to Owen, who lit the pyre at each cardinal point. The fire, carried from the heart of House Wyth, shot through the prepared wood, and before the last verse ended the entire pyre was blazing.

Breakfast was spread as a buffet in the formal dining room, and Tarken was there along with the other four guests; Owen apparently hadn't come down yet. Rane caught a sympathetic look from Tarken when he hesitated in the doorway.

"Ah, young Wyth," Kor said, as he stood and came around the table to grasp Rane's hand. Unlike the other lords, Kor had chosen to wear his House coat, as if he were presiding over some formal occasion. Just at the moment, Rane thought the crimson fern of House Ettori embroidered at his collar looked like an insect. Kor laid his other hand over Rane's, as if he were sealing the handshake. "I hope you were able to sleep. Are you hungry? Come, eat something."

Rane wanted to wrench his hand free.

"We've been taking full advantage of House Wyth's generosity," Tarken said, a diplomatic diffusion that neatly blocked Kor's arrogation of hospitality. "Your cook always amazes me."

The kitchen staff had prepared nearly every breakfast dish either Rane or Owen had ever claimed as a favorite, and Rane was sorry the meal was tainted by the circumstances. The others were doing justice to the cook's offerings, though, and Rane sat down with a plateful of eggs he would ordinarily enjoy. A servant came in with a carafe of fresh, hot telik.

"Fine telik," Lord Lin said, breathing in the aroma. "House Wyth always was willing to pay for the choicest. Maybe it's some of yours, eh, Terrance?"

Lord Glay beamed, but let the compliment pass. "I suppose, Rane, that you don't remember much from before the war. Your father had a special arrangement with Estend back then. I never knew—never wanted to know—the details, but Estend made sure Wyth always got the best of the syrup. Of course back then it wasn't half so expensive."

The telik was perfectly prepared, and Rane welcomed the way the spices seemed to seep into his raw nerves. Even his irritation at Kor faded. Kor had begun explaining how his dam was going to solve not just the price of telik but a long list of complaints. Questions from the others kept him on the topic long after Rane was bored with it, but then he noticed that Tarken was directing his curiosity with a purpose.

Tarken leaned toward Kor, absorbing every word. "If it really delivers all that," he said thoughtfully, "it'll be worth all the effort." He gave Kor a measured look of admiration. "It's ambitious—far-sighted, even."

Kor's black eyebrows rose in unison and his eyes, disconcerting and dark, drilled into Tarken as he searched for hidden meaning. Tarken looked back with no sign of the uneasiness Rane knew he would have felt under that hostile gaze. "A lot could go wrong," Tarken said, nodding to Glay as if acknowledging his point of view. "But think what it will mean if it goes right!"

The eyebrows relaxed and Kor sat back in his chair, as if he had decided Tarken was genuinely coming to this conclusion. Rane, impressed, had to stop himself from winking when Tarken turned to include him in the conversation. It was alarming, in a way, to watch Tarken in action and see how easily he made others believe in his sincerity. There was every possibility that Rane had been swayed once or twice by the same facile connection.

"Exactly," Kor said. "Worth a risk and some sacrifice."

"Yes," Tarken said, as if tasting the word. Then more definitively, "Yes, yes, I think it would be. How long do you think it will take, all in? Work has already started, right?"

With prompts like that, Tarken drew more information from Kor—while Glay, Lin, and Manssorand stared at Tarken like he was dancing with a wildcat. They already knew the dam was being built across the Great Gorge, where the Truolt River had sculpted a path through the granite foundation of the Caladen Plateau before the land flattened into the expansive and fertile valley. Kor explained that the steep southern bank of the Gorge was riddled with cave systems; the workers were enlarging and connecting the hollow spaces to form the main diversion tunnel for the river.

After the tunnel was done, Kor said, they'd need more men. They would build cofferdams and strip the riverbed of all its silt until the firm, dry ground was ready for the construction of the real dam. The design would allow a range of controls, from intentional floods to engineered cataracts.

"It will really be something," Tarken said. "It's hard to picture how that can be. Of course, I'm not familiar with that part of the river." How does this help? Rane thought. Tarken seemed to be avoiding looking at him.

Owen stepped into the room, then, and for a while the talk turned to condolences and reminiscences. Then Tarken steered back to the dam. "We were discussing Dan Kor's Truolt dam. Fascinating project." It was odd to hear Tarken say Kor's name politely.

Fingers steepled, Kor said nothing, but he looked at Owen with such controlling will that Rane felt a chill. Owen blinked, and said mildly that he understood the project was going well. He drank his telik as if unaware that Kor's predatory stare lingered, and reached for some toast.

"Dan Owen has seen the site," Kor said. "He's been an obliging neighbor. The access road goes through Wyth land."

Nothing in Kor's tone implied anything beyond his words, but Owen's head jerked up as if pulled by a puppet-string. The deferential look he gave Kor made Rane's heart sink.

"It's not easy to get to," Owen told the others. "It's so steep where the worksite is that the road actually wraps around the hill to the summit, and the equipment has to be lowered to the site with pulleys."

Tarken whistled through his teeth. "Project like this will keep the engineers going for years." As if inspired, he swiveled in his chair to face Lord Lin. "You know, Dan Chao, you could easily visit on your way home. Actually, you and Dan Terrance both could." He sounded excited and slightly envious.

Kor pounced on the idea. The others had been planning to start for home mid-morning, but Kor unceremoniously changed their plans and decreed that the entire group, including Owen and Rane, would visit the dam site. "It will do you both good," Kor said. "It's a good time for you to think about the future, about what kind of leadership House Wyth will provide."

It would be too late to set out today, by the time everything could be organized. So, Kor decreed that they would ride out tomorrow morning. He made light of it, but he requisitioned food and two of the House Wyth kitchen staff for the trip. The accommodation was somewhat basic, he said with false apology, but the group could stay overnight before dispersing to their respective Houses the day after. He pretended that Piers and Elanna would be his guests at House Ettori, and would ride with them.

It was, after that, a strangely suspended sort of day. For Lin, Glay, and Manssorand, it was lost time, when they had intended to be on their way. Less so for Tarken, who might well have lingered anyway. Kor wanted to meet the strangers, and somehow twisted his visit into an official look-around in his "right" as Prime. He kept Owen, the new Lord Wyth, occupied with questions about the House's vitality and prospects. How Owen maintained his equanimity was beyond Rane's imagination. Even if Kor truly did have the right to that detailed accounting, there was nothing fair about demanding it now. A more humane man would have given a grieving son some time before asking him to defend his late father's decisions.

Rane spoke with the servants and put things in motion for the morning, and then felt very much at loose ends. He did what he could to be hospitable to the conscripted guests; they did what they could to be no bother at all. A lengthy game of cards in the library seemed to suffice as entertainment, though no one was particularly interested in winning or losing.

After losing a second round, Tarken leaned away from the table, and looked out the window at the sun-struck garden. "Nice weather." Tarken rarely relied on banalities; more of the peculiar social maneuvering from breakfast, Rane supposed. The others politely concurred, and Tarken turned to Rane. "We should have lunch outside, enjoy the open air. Since Lord Ettori and your brother are deep in House affairs, the rest of us might as well take advantage of the weather and surround ourselves with nothing but flowers and trees."

It clicked into place, then. Rane agreed to Tarken's suggestion, and if any of the others hadn't put it together, still they were unlikely to counter their host's decision.

And so a table was set under the arbor in the center of the garden, shielded from the sun but with nothing around them but the lawn and the flower beds that edged it. Tarken kept up a patter while servants brought sandwiches and fruit, poured drinks, and made sure all was in order before they withdrew to the House. As soon as there was no one in the garden other than themselves, Tarken broke off his blathering mid-sentence, and exhaled with a short laugh.

"Now," he said, his tone business-like even though he reached for a sandwich with casual manners. "We can talk properly, at our impromptu little half-Gathering. We should be able to see anyone before they are close enough to hear us."

"Ah," Manssorand said, the only admission of belated realization. "We can be seen, though."

"Exactly," Rane said. "No cabal here, just Wyth's guests enjoying the breeze."

Tarken raised his glass to them. "So just eat and drink and be easy. We'll skip the formalities, I think. Very few picnics begin with oaths sworn on House insignia."

That brought a nervous titter from Glay and a bare hint of a smile from Lin, who was never very convivial anyway.

It was an unexpected gift, this chance Gathering. Without Lord Chant, there was less dissent; the five Houses here were close enough to House Ettori to feel the effects much more than the western Houses did. The conversation quickly sharpened to a precise focus—and yet Tarken leaned back in his chair, draping his arm over the back of it, and managed to project nothing other than relaxed comfort. Rane tried to do the same, but his attempt only made him admire Tarken's art of dissembling even more. It was hard enough not to let his voice carry the intensity of his reactions, much less maintain a physical pose that was so completely dissociated.

They repeated much of the first conversation, though Tarken thought the chance to scout the dam site might offer new possibilities. When Manssorand asked if it were still worth refusing the Tithe, Rane admitted that he hadn't yet come up with a way to keep Owen from paying.

"I always thought that plan was foolish," Lin said. "I tell you, we need a coup."

"If by 'coup' you mean 'assassination,' I still say that

would be the end of our peace." Tarken swirled the crushed ice in his glass, a study of pensive indolence.

How by the shining sun does he look so calm? Rane thought. "It could still work," he said. "Even if Owen pays the Tithe, it doesn't mean you have to. If we act together—"

Lin's agitation threatened the illusion of an amicable lunchtime chat. "Oh, *there* it is. If House Wyth pays the Tithe, you could sit back and watch what happens to the rest of us, is that it? Ettori is hardly likely to take issue with you. The question is, what will Wyth do after that...when Ettori is dropping the hammer on one of us?"

A hand on his forearm—Tarken's—kept Rane's temper from taking flight. Rane took a deep breath, and shook his head. "We'd help. I'd come to you, with any men who would follow, but—"

"Meaning no offense, Wyth, how many men do you think would follow you against your brother?" Manssorand's interruption came with a pointed, skeptical look.

Against his brother. He hadn't had that specific version of the thought that the House men might not fight on his command. Once the action started, surely Owen would step out of Kor's shadow. If he didn't...if Owen paid the Tithe and stood by House Ettori, it would mean a division of House Wyth. Rane reached for his glass, buying time with a long sip of iced wine. He couldn't take up arms against Owen. "I won't," he heard himself say into a sigh.

"Won't?" Lin pounced. "Won't commit yourself? Won't fight Ettori?"

"Won't make Owen choose sides!" His temper took over, and the words burst out.

"Calm, calm," Manssorand murmured, and then leaned forward to take up the pitcher and refill Rane's half-empty glass.

He fought past the blaze, and with smoldering heat said, "I can't ask Owen to choose between House Wyth and Merra. The Great Houses *are* Merra, and we've lost enough."

There was a pause, and the other men were looking at him thoughtfully. It was the first time he'd thought about the fact that except for Manssorand, all the others were his father's generation; he suddenly felt naïve and ridiculous. "I sound like Chant," Rane admitted, hoping to deflect their scorn.

Tarken held his own glass out to Manssorand for a refill, and then lifted it to Rane in salute. "I think Dan Rane just saved us from ourselves," he said. "It was a mistake to think a half-Gathering would save Merra. It would have been Estend all over again."

That brought a quiet suffused with dismay. Manssorand looked up into the leaves of the arbor, as if he expected to find something to say dangling from a vine. The expression on Lin's face was dawning contrition as he stared at Tarken. And Glay was avoiding eye contact altogether, which was nearly an admission of shame.

With Tarken's words in his ears, Rane said, "It's already like Estend. One House trying to take from the others. Estend just wasn't as subtle as Ettori."

"'Subtle' is hardly the word Caladen would use," Lin said drily.

"Rane is right," Glay said. "Every time a House turns against the others, the cost cripples us." He glanced at Lin. "Our Houses lost influence when Estend went, which strengthens Ettori's hand. Merra lost the cataracts, and lost Estend's people."

"And with them, a large part of the Tithe," Manssorand added.

"Then we lost Caladen's people," Tarken said, "and their part of the Tithe."

Not all of House Caladen's people had been killed, if Rane was remembering his history lessons correctly. There was no physical House now—only the burned shell of the ancient building still stood. The family, the House Guard, and a host of Caladen's citizens had been lost in the fire, but not all. Most of the survivors had drifted away. Some had sought association with Dannpelier or Wyth, others had scattered to towns and villages where they paid taxes instead of contributing to a House's Tithe.

Ettori had taken advantage of the unguarded riches of Caladen. He had control of the water gap, and Rane had no doubt that plenty of Caladen timber had fallen to Ettori axes. If Owen and Arissa managed to make it to their vows, and their marriage bed, Caladen could be refounded. But a new Lord Caladen—eighteen years from now—would hardly have the old Caladen's riches or influence, especially if there were no people to support the House. A House like Caladen needed thousands of people, and they were scattered to the four winds, far from home.

Far from home. Thousands of people. Rane tried to take a sip, wanting time to frame his thoughts. His hand shook and the pale wine sloshed over the rim of the glass, trickling around his thumb and down his wrist. He set the glass down with more force than he'd intended, earning Tarken's concern and curiosity from the others.

It took a few sentences before his voice settled and his words were coherent, but Rane told them about Piers and *Redemption* and the three thousand people who would be arriving soon. The others' reactions, at first, were muted. Manssorand seemed unable to stop nodding, although Rane couldn't tell if it were anything more than a pensive habit. With Glay, it was more obvious. He had a hand cupped around his chin and was tapping his finger against his lips. Tarken simply ate another sandwich.

Lin, though, picked at something invisible on his sleeve and at last scoffed again, "Children's tales."

"No," Rane said. "You'd believe if you had heard Piers."

"And yet your brother doesn't."

"I think he does believe—he just couldn't let himself trust it. He's sending Piers to Lord Ettori, I think telling himself that Ettori will listen fairly."

"And so now he's in Ettori's hands," Manssorand said. "If it's true, this second landing, it could be a disaster. Especially if this scout isn't able to guide them."

"You may be right," Rane said, "but maybe not. Maybe we can help them. They came expecting—or at least hoping—to be welcomed into a society that had been built for them. This might be an opportunity to reset the balance in Merra. The scout told me that they were willing to split up, but suppose they don't? Suppose instead that we help them stay together. Suppose we help them establish themselves as a new community."

"All well and good, young sir," Lin said, "but I don't think Ettori will be undone by the fact that we made friends with the newcomers."

The corners of Tarken's eyes crinkled, and Rane knew he'd put it together. He smiled back.

Glay said, "Besides, the three thousand includes children, doesn't it? Helping a thousand families set up house isn't really going to tip the balance, Rane."

And now Tarken's eyes danced. "It depends on the house, doesn't it?"

Glay gave Tarken a blank look. Rane prompted,

"Restoring a certain House would definitely change Kor's equation."

"Caladen!" Glay's voice was sharp with surprise and his wineglass slipped from his hand. "You mean House Caladen."

25

INSIGHT

House Wyth

ELANNA HEARD THE men approaching the guest quarters before Piers did, and Piers felt the girl's hope flare and then fizzle when her reason overtook her optimism. Small chance it'd be good news; it had been days, and they'd expected to be taken to House Ettori yesterday, and another reprieve didn't seem too likely.

Lord Wyth—now official, a guard had told them—ushered two other men into the guest suite. One was the Ettori man from before, looking as displeased as ever. The other, a stranger, made Piers think of black glass. Owen looked terrible, Piers thought. Like a man whose whole world was spinning backward. He moved like gravity had increased, or like he'd contracted an illness that was destroying him from inside.

The man behind him was more than intimidating enough to cover Owen's unexpected debility. He was almost dazzling with darkness, with razor-sharp edges and unbending will. Piers was aware of Elanna shrinking into herself, her presence folding into something easily overlooked.

"Dan Kor, this is the man who says he's from the ship. The girl is from Trint, and we believe just happened to have fallen in with him." Owen's voice was flat.

Piers braced himself, and offered a handshake. "Piers Haldon."

Shadowed eyes stared at him; the man's expression was concealed by a black beard. He twitched his fingers dismissively, and said to Owen, "I suppose one can't expect a madman to be polite."

Piers felt his blood surge, a disproportionate response to a mild cut. Daring, he dropped his screens, exposing his anger. He felt a feather-light tickle at the edge of his mind and nearly staggered as he slammed his screens back in place. It was the shadow presence that had been skulking around the edges for weeks, and it left a familiar trace of nausea as it passed.

No change in the way anyone was looking at him, no change in posture or expression to give away the psi who had just Scanned him. It had been careful—masterful, even—but Piers knew the technique and knew exactly why he'd felt a tingle on the skin at the nape of his neck and a squeamish ripple in his gut.

The man's deep eyes rested on Piers's face.

"So. You're Starborn," the man said. Piers expected a grating voice, but the sneer was delivered in a smooth baritone. "You may call me Lord Ettori. The long-awaited ship has arrived, I hear. Tell me."

Now his blood froze, but he couldn't fall apart. Not after all this. This man was clearly not going to be an advocate for the ship. "I'm not Starborn, but I'd be glad to answer your questions if you tell me what you want to know." His tone was mild, but he felt tension rise in the room. Owen and the guard stiffened, and Elanna actually put a hand out as if to hold him back. So no one talks to this guy like that. Good.

Lord Ettori didn't seem to notice. He was solid and tall, so sure of himself that he seemed to swagger while standing still. He came toward Piers. Up close, he had a peculiar scent Piers couldn't place. His black hair was groomed back and oiled to hide the grey. The skewed black eyebrows dominated the broad forehead; right now one was raised, and it seemed to be trying to upstage the other.

"Of course you're welcome to be enigmatic," Lord Ettori said, and the unspoken rider *but I don't advise it* was conveyed by a twitch of that same eyebrow. "But since you apparently are seeking favors from the Great Houses of Merra, I do think you might indulge me. Tell me, why are you here?"

Careful, don't push it too far. "I was sent to find help for my people and a place to call home, and to try to arrange it so that it isn't too disruptive when they come."

"Ah, yes. The settlers." Mockery, undisguised now. "Wyth tells me the starship has a deliciously allegorical name, too, sure to impress us all with how badly we've treated the Starborn."

"Hardly. It was named after the Earth ship that won the second psi war." Piers realized, too late, that he'd taken the bait.

Lord Ettori's laugh was the harsh sound Piers had been expecting. It wasn't humor; it was triumph. To Owen, he said, "There's no end to it, is there? Earth! The Starborn are getting more imaginative with their fantasies." Then he locked eyes with Piers and said, "You are not welcome here."

Panic stole a breath from Piers, and he fought to get it back. He knows it's true, he thought. It wasn't a question of this man having believed what Piers had told Lord Wyth. With all the skill and concentration he could channel, Piers opened a small gap in his screens and Reached the tip of a psychic finger toward Lord Ettori. He needed to know. He had to be sure.

The man threw back his head, exposing his throat above the crimson embroidery at his collar, and laughed. "I think not, boy."

With that, he turned his back on Piers—intended rudeness—and turned to the door. "You want to know what I'm feeling? I'll gladly tell you. You are mad, and I will deal with you accordingly."

He turned to Owen and added, "I have something that will help our friend, Dan Owen, if you will allow me." Then he motioned for Owen to follow him toward the door, and said, "Take the girl away. She shouldn't have to be around this." And to the Ettori man, "Send Benino to me, and tell him to bring the box."

Kor shot Piers a sly look, and said to Owen, "I believe I can ease this man's delusions, but for his sake, I'm sure he'd rather you not be present for the treatment. It can be rather embarrassing."

Piers watched Owen battle a misgiving or two before he beckoned Elanna to go with him. Elanna's confusion and hesitation were almost a fluttering presence of their own, and Piers Pushed reassurance he wasn't feeling to her as the door closed behind them.

"That was kind of you," Ettori said. Something about the man's tone—or maybe it was the corvine eyes—chilled Piers. He couldn't break free from the man's gaze. He was peripherally aware of the heavy door shutting behind the others, and of Lord Ettori guiding him to a chair. Ettori sat facing him, with a low table between them. He poured something and set a cup on the table in front of Piers.

"Telik for you, settler," the man said. "Drink. And tell me about the ship."

Piers didn't want to have this conversation, not when both undercurrents and overtones of malice were thick in the air. Even though he was Blocking with as much determination as he could, the feeling persisted. It felt like something clawing at the edges of his mind, gnawing and prying. Ettori gave the cup a nudge, and his expression seemed to shift.

"Ah, you are so young," Ettori murmured. "Tell me, young Piers, do you think I don't know what you are?"

"I'm a man far away from home," Piers said. "And apparently a captive."

The scratch of laughter seemed genuine. "No, my friend. Don't be coy."

The room seemed to dim, and Piers's head swam. A sensation like an ice-headache stabbed at him, and then he felt his psi barriers seem to shatter. The force of another presence displaced his thoughts. He felt the bleakness of the space between stars expand within him. It shoved him, his psyche, aside.

As abruptly, the presence withdrew. Piers felt his stomach rise; he reached for the telik, eager for the spices and the sedative. He tried to Block, but his mind was sluggish and his barriers were too flimsy now. And he felt a compulsion—which he recognized as inauthentic—to answer Ettori's question.

The realization lanced through him. "You can Direct!" As strong as he himself was, Piers had never been able to do it, to forcibly replace someone else's natural emotions with his, and he'd never been sure he'd want to.

A Push of pleased approval, so strong it was more like a thrust, reached him. Ettori smiled. "Very good. Now that we've settled that between us, let's dispense with all the psychic games, shall we? It takes considerable energy to do that, I'm sure you can imagine, and it will be much more pleasant for us both if you simply cooperate."

Cooperate with what? Piers tried again to restore his barriers, and he felt a little stronger.

Ettori lunged across the table and struck his face. In the shock of it, the barriers dropped again. "Enough of that," Ettori said. "Don't waste your energy, either."

What the hell is happening?

"What's happening, young Piers, is that you have met an Empath stronger than yourself. Don't be too distressed—you have impressive talent, but you haven't had as long to develop it as I have. I've been at this for over two hundred years."

The man's words seemed to fade in and out, like a door opening and closing. The question Piers felt his lips form was different from the one howling in his mind, and his own voice seemed to be on the other side of that door. He thought, two hundred? How? But he asked, "What do you want from me?"

"Three things. First, the pleasure of your company. Second, the satisfaction of a little psi touch after all these years."

The unspoken remainder dangled; Piers started to count backward by threes from two hundred, to keep himself from giving Kor the satisfaction of being asked. Kor tapped his steepled fingers together, and waited. One eyebrow crawled up.

Piers felt he won the round. He reached ninety-two as Kor chuckled and said, "So your pride overcomes your curiosity. One hates to be this cliché, but it really is useless to resist."

The darkness, Ettori's presence, seized Piers. His cheek

was still stinging from the blow, and now he couldn't breathe. Then he felt a sudden acceptance, and calm, that he wanted to resist. It was as if his own emotional core betrayed his mind, which ineffectually insisted he should feel horror and fear. It felt like he was drugged. It felt like he was being separated from himself.

By the time Benino arrived, Piers wasn't quite sure why he thought he should be upset. The man Kor had sent for had a round, mild face that was in no way sinister. He blinked rapidly, and cleared his throat every few minutes, and seemed unhappy and uncomfortable. He set a wooden box on the table beside Kor, and stepped back hastily, as if trying to stay out of reach.

Kor stroked the lid of the box with his fingertips. "You see, Piers, there is so much you don't know. This box holds one of my dearest secrets, one I have shared with very few people over the years."

Piers felt the advancing shadow of Kor's psi encroachment, and this time could do nothing to rally against it.

"Yes," Kor said, "I know how curious you are. Drink the telik, and I'll tell my secret. And then you'll know what I want from you."

Kor raised the lid as if beginning a ritual: slowly, carefully, with both hands and a subtle flourish. He lifted out a smaller object from within, and as he set it on the table, the gleam of it claimed Piers's attention. A cube: hinged lid, platinum-bright metal, transparent top. Etched on the lid, upside-down to Piers as Kor opened the cube, was the Staff of Asclepius—and the New Foundation Project logo.

As Kor pulled a series of instruments from the cube, he talked. He directed Benino to roll up Piers's sleeve and bind Piers's arms to the chair. Enervated, Piers submitted. He stared blankly at the array of vials and syringes and listened.

"My great-grandfather was an astrobiologist on *Valiant Star*," Kor said. "Dederick Ettori. Sometime after the landing, he married the ship's botanist. You likely wouldn't know her name, either: Laura Telk."

The two of them, Kor explained, had found the secret of longevity. The botanist had tinkered with a native plant, and found that the fruit had astonishing healing properties when consumed if prepared correctly. It also created profound psychotropic effects in people with the psi gene. Dederick parsed the biochemistry, trying to understand, and discovered that certain molecules in the plant would bind to psionic DNA. The altered gene expressed a novel protein that was very similar to one that had long ago been theorized to slow cellular deterioration. It was missing only a single amino acid.

Piers felt the words were flowing around him. He felt like he was fading into the air. In this setting, hearing this man speaking a language of science that had seemed forgotten staggered him, but he couldn't speak. Nor could he resist when Benino, with shaking hands, tied a tourniquet around his bicep.

"The poetic thing," Kor said, "is that the missing ingredient is itself part of the expression of the psi gene." A little blood from an active psi, mixed with the plant's sap, completed the protein. A person with psi genes, when exposed to that compound, would age at roughly a fifth of the normal rate.

"Regular doses are required," Kor continued, "and as the body ages, more is needed. For most of my life, there have been so few active psis around that I've simply used my own blood. It wasn't a terrible problem when the doses were a few months apart, but it is getting more challenging."

Benino slid a needle into the vein in Piers's elbow. Blood filled the first vial; Benino exchanged it for an empty one.

"Of course it's partly my own fault that actives are so hard to find these days. I've had some success in eliminating the scourge. It's taken some extended effort, but Benino here is perfecting the Sweep. It targets the gene and changes the protein—though unfortunately the difficulty has been limiting the virus to affecting only that gene. But Benino thinks the latest strain, which we're testing in Trint, may finally be discerning enough. Soon I will be the only one able to activate a psi, and I will be able to control their existence."

As Benino attached the fourth vial, Kor picked up a filled one and swirled it in front of the light. The dark blood glowed like cut gems. "So you see, this is the third thing I want from you. I'm grateful for your gift."

The darkness retreated. Piers felt his will strengthen. "Now what?" he asked, with bravado he was sure fooled no one. "You kill me?"

"No, no, dear boy. I need to keep you where I can find you when it's time. Your gift today will last for a few weeks, but I'll need you again, so I certainly want your blood to keep flowing. But you don't need to think about that. I'll make sure you won't feel a thing." He laughed. "Let's free you from this burden, shall we?"

Kor put his hands on Piers's temples, with a steady pressure, and the cold eyes locked on his. Then there was stabbing pain in his head, and ice dripped through his veins, and his vision shattered into prisms. He shook so violently that the bindings around his arms cut deep into his flesh and his chair danced in place. It felt as though he were being scraped out of his body, and sand was pouring in to replace him. A curtain of red fell over his eyes and then melted to black.

26

DIVERSION

The Great Gorge

AS THE HORSES paraded, two-by-two, along a narrow stretch of road between a sheer drop to the left and unforgiving rock face to the right, Rane found himself riding alone, the odd man, with Tarken and Lord Manssorand paired behind him. Piers rode beside the strange Ettori "physician" who had arrived with Kor, and Elanna was under the watch of the Ettori House guard who had first come to Wyth. Neither of House Wyth's unfortunate guests were in good shape. Piers was dazed and mentioned a headache, and Elanna was all-around wretched. Lin and Glay rode at the back, with the pack-horses and the borrowed kitchen staff trailing behind them.

In front of him, Owen and Ettori were deep in conversation that Rane, mercifully, couldn't hear over the sound of the horses. He was trying not to think, because this whole excursion made him angry. Grief, which had at first been shock, was now raw and stinging, all the more because of the resentment he felt—directed at Kor—at being forced into this outing, with Kor either assuming or pretending that it was good for him and Owen not to be left alone. What Rane wanted was to be at home, with the witnesses gone, so that he and Owen could manage through this together. If Owen kept up his stoic pretense for too long, Rane worried that the sealed grief would fester, and the unseen damage it would do to Owen would hurt them both.

Of course it was entirely possible that even if they were home, Owen would be avoiding him. Quite likely he himself would be restless, and would by now have taken a fast horse—maybe even Owen's—for a reckless gallop to try to outrun his heartache. He would have gone to Dannpelier, where Tarken's even-tempered company would soothe him.

Instead, he was plodding north to gawp on command at Ettori's illegal dam and watch Owen fall over himself to stay in Kor's favor.

Tarken rode up beside him, leaving Manssorand, and Rane greeted him with a smile that he knew Tarken would see right through.

"I know, lad," Tarken said.

The sympathy in his voice almost broke Rane's control. He blinked a few times and looked at his hands until he was sure no tears would spill. Not yet. Not here.

Up ahead, Owen turned his head to say something to Ettori. "I don't know how he's doing it," Rane said. "Or why."

With a quick glance forward, Tarken dropped his voice and said, "Remember they can hear you better than you can hear them."

So Rane said nothing, and let his thoughts circle like vultures. Owen could have stopped this, could have told Kor it wasn't the right time to be away from home. Whatever advantage Owen saw from cooperating with Kor's every whim, it apparently was worth considerable sacrifice.

A mile or two later, the road started to climb and curve higher into the hills. They turned onto a rutted byroad that was so thick with mud that the horses had to unmire their hooves with every step. It was a scar through dense evergreen woods, and stumps lined both sides like guards at attention. At midday the woods were quiet except for the harsh call of a sentinel bird, and conversation stalled. Somewhere ahead and off to the left, he could hear rushing water. Rane felt watched and unwelcome, despite a contradictory sense of being utterly isolated as they rode.

The road bent sharply to the right and started to pull itself out of the mud. Soon they were riding along a track bearing northeast, gradually rising as it spooled around the base of a steep hill. A winterbourne, full after the recent rains, raced along beside them, collecting water that poured from the rocky hillside as it went. When they reached a wooden bridge that crossed this ephemeral stream, Kor reined in and pulled his horse about so that he was facing the rest of the group.

"The site is up there," he said, gesturing airily to the deep woods in front of them, where the road they'd been following tapered and started to cling to the steeper slope. Rane could see water coursing down a rut that had become a channel in the road, veering off the eroded edge before it reached them. "This little bridge was Dan Owen's suggestion," he said. "By crossing here and going around the hill, we can reach the lodge from the other side without having to go over the top. It's not as steep. And you can see, if we carried on this way we'd soon be wading upstream." He flicked a self-amused smile at them, then added, "We'll circle back onto Wyth land for a while, but we found it's worth the detour to spare the horses."

Rane glanced at Owen's face. Impassive. It was worse

than he thought if Owen wasn't just going along with Kor but was actively helping, and there was no sign from his brother that there were any scruples at all.

"So we can't see the worksite from the road?" Tarken asked, with casual interest.

It was Owen who answered. "No. From the lodge you can look up and see where the entrance to the tunnel is, but the work is all underground for now."

"What about the workers' camp?" Rane asked, trying to match Tarken's tone.

"There's not much to see for that, either—it's a cave further up."

"We'll have time to look at the worksite," Kor inserted, "if you like. For now, we'll go up to the lodge and relax a bit, and let the men know we're here."

The narrow road doubled back on itself a couple of times, ascending in stages. After circling nearly three quarters of the way, it broadened and straightened toward a clearing at the base of a cliff. The river, surprisingly far below them, crashed through its granite-walled channel.

Displaced earth and felled trees were heaped at the side, forming a rampart of sorts that spared Rane from vertigo. Gravel had been spread to cover the level area in front of a large, charmless, wooden building. From here, they were looking down at the tops of the tenacious evergreen trees that crawled up the slope from the river to the ridge. The rock face that rose above them was the only other interruption in the dense Caladen Forest around them. Its vertical shear looked like it had been slammed into the hillside, leaving the steep, forested slope untouched on either side.

A daunting footpath with rough-cut steps went up, stopping at a natural ledge that cut into the cliff. Starting there, Rane saw a series of vertiginous shelves that almost formed a switchback path up the cliff to another ledge. Anchored ropes hung down the cliff, and a length had been strung along the rock edge at the worst part of the pseudo-path as an insubstantial handrail. A tiny, dark figure on the upper ledge waved in salute.

Perpendicular to the main building, backed against the cliff, was a long row of open-front stalls sheltering only a handful of horses. A couple of small sheds seemed to have sprouted from weeds, and a battered cart tilted against the side of one, giving a strong suggestion of neglect. As the gravel crunched under the arriving horses's hooves, the rustic door of the main building opened, and a wiry man in House Ettori's dark uniform rushed out, wringing his hands. A second, more substantial man followed close behind.

"Lord Ettori! My lord, if we had known—"

Kor waved off the nervous greeting and dismounted. "Of course. We decided only yesterday to come." The second man took the reins from Kor, murmured that he would see to the horses, and that Carl would take them in and make them comfortable. Carl, in turn, gave his colleague a subtle but very black look behind Kor's back. In the few minutes it took for the group to dismount and ensure the horses weren't ready to bolt, Rane watched Carl keeping a chary distance from Kor.

"My lord," Carl said as he began to lead them toward the lodge. He was trying to bow from the waist as he walked. "We have had a bit of an unusual day today." There was a note of dread-filled apology in the way he said, "Another unexpected visitor arrived just a quarter hour ago."

The doorway was narrow, and low. Rane ducked as

he stepped over the threshold behind Kor and then Owen, into a large, open room that had more in common with a tavern than what he had pictured as a guesthouse. The windows that flanked the door provided only thin light, and the bare wood floor, walls, and rafters were unrelieved by any decoration. Four massive wooden pillars divided the space. Across the room from where he stood, a pair of closed doors huddled together in the middle of the long east wall. An abandoned game of chess was set near the large hearth at the south end, with a scattering of chairs nearby. At the other end of the room, a large slab table hulked in front of a smaller fireplace that looked as if it had not been used recently or often, and beyond that a ladder offered a way to the loft. As the House visitors entered and fanned out from the door, they set their weapons on the rack just inside. A trio of men hastily pushed away from the table, where a number of empty bottles and heavy mugs exposed their afternoon activity. They bowed to Kor and stammered greetings.

"Where is this visitor, then?" Kor asked.

An exchange of anxious looks, and then Carl glanced toward one of the shut doors and said tentatively, "Cleaning up, sir."

Kor laughed, and Carl and his mates produced cautious smiles, not yet trusting. "Well," Kor said, "we'll just wait then. Nothing too ominous if a bath is involved."

"No, sir." Carl took charge of making the visitors welcome, with a showy abundance of energy that Rane assumed everyone knew was just to cover his discomfort.

Ettori's men brought the two long benches from the table across the room and set them perpendicular to the larger hearth. They moved the game table away, and arranged a few chairs across the gap between the benches. Kor turned one of the large chairs facing the hearth into his throne, and seated Owen at his right. He kept Piers in his sight, and put Elanna to work with the kitchen staff.

Rane sat closest to the hearth, facing the interior of the room, with Tarken beside him and Manssorand across. He'd barely settled when someone handed him a mug of ale, which was even more welcome than the solid bench after hours of riding. The Ettori men filled in the remaining space on the benches, and hunched their shoulders and kept their eyes downcast unless their lord spoke directly to them. When one had to answer, Rane noticed that the man would look at the air over Kor's head, or at Kor's beard or his ear, but never at his eyes.

They had all gathered in the lodge, they said, because of the visitor. Two more Ettori men, whom Kor asked about by name, were in the tunnel with the workers, and the other three were at their stations. Kor asked how the work was going, and demanded a detailed report even though—or perhaps because—his guests were listening. The men were careful to keep it positive.

Heavy bread with honey was served, and the atmosphere eased. Elanna stayed away from the men, but Rane saw her watching, wary of Kor even from across the room. Rane started to perspire as the heat from the cooking fire spread into the room, and was grateful when one of the servants, mopping his own brow, opened the door and both windows. While Kor questioned Carl minutely, Tarken engaged the Ettori man beside him in a careful interrogation of his own. As usual, the target of Tarken's conversational trap had no idea when he'd stumbled into it.

"Oh, aye," the man said. "It's going well enough but slower than he'd like. Should pick up now the days are getting longer, since we can get one more shift from cave to tunnel before it gets dark."

"No work at night?" Tarken gave no indication that his trap had caught something unexpected.

The man shook his head. "No, they can work all right. It's always torchlight in the tunnel and the cave. Sometimes gives me a shiver thinking there's people inside that rock. Anyway, the tunnel and the cave don't connect, so we troop 'em up and down outside when they change shifts. You saw—it's about straight up and it's hard going even when you can see. It's too damn rough to make people try it at night. Actually had one fall to his death in the beginning, so we strung up ropes to hold onto, but none of us is keen to try it after dark, either."

Rane had to suppress a shudder. He was picturing the sheer drop from the overlook behind Dannpelier—the hills here weren't too different and this cliff was at least that high. It was terribly easy to imagine someone falling. If he'd seen it happen, he thought he would have simply refused to test his luck with another step.

He took a deep swig of his ale and tried to put the image out of his mind. He supposed it was more self-preservation than compassion that set the policy of not climbing the rock in the dark, but at least there was some mercy there for the poor Starborn. And for Piers.

A sharp creak announced that one of the interior doors had opened. Rane's view was blocked as Kor and the men who had been talking turned in unison. Then Owen leapt up from his chair with a sputtering sound as if someone had punched him in the gut.

Rane leaned to one side to see, and then shot to his feet. "Arissa!"

Even from halfway across the room, he could see her eyes widen as she registered on first Owen and then Rane. She froze, and he started toward her—only to hear a cautionary mutter from Tarken. It was enough. Rane held back as Owen crossed to her.

She stood with her weight on one foot, clutching her arms as if she were physically holding herself together. Of all things, she was wearing an Ettori man's dark tunic over her own clothes. It hung to her knees, and the volume of extra fabric enveloped her shoulders.

Owen took a few steps with purpose, and then stopped too soon, at an awkward distance. He should have gone right to her, Rane thought, and at least offered his hands. Betrothed as they were, it would have been perfectly proper for Owen even to embrace her, and right at the moment it seemed as if Arissa wouldn't have minded. Instead, Owen stood stiffly with his arms at his sides and looked her over. Her hair was loose and wild, and there were scratches on her face. Her leggings were stained and ripped, and mud had dried on her boots. As she waited for Owen—or someone—to say something, color crept into her face. It wasn't clear to Rane whether that meant embarrassment or temper, but she was most certainly uncomfortable with the scrutiny from Owen, Kor, and the whole group of men.

"Dane Arissa," Owen finally managed, at the same moment that Kor stood and crossed over to her. "I'm glad to find you safe."

Whatever she might have replied was swept aside as Kor approached and pretended not to notice how she hesitated before accepting his offered greeting and placing her hand on his. "Kor of Ettori. A pleasure to greet you, even under these circumstances. I had heard that my men had taken you to House Wyth—I wondered why I didn't see you. I can't imagine how you wound up here, dear girl," he said.

Her voice was small and quavering, but Rane heard her say, "Yes, they did. This was a mistake. I got lost, and my horse was stolen." At Kor's gesture, she took two limping steps and an Ettori man helped her into the chair Owen had just vacated. Kor sat at the end of the bench beside her. When the other men started to offer greetings to Arissa, Kor silenced them with an imperious gesture.

"Stolen?" Kor was humoring her, with a patient, paternal tone that was interwoven with doubt.

"Yes, I—"

"You shouldn't have left Wyth," Owen cut in. He hadn't moved from his spot and hadn't taken his eyes off her. He didn't demand to know what had happened, but spoke as if they were having a private conversation, with all his attention bearing down on her. That kind of intensity from Owen was paralyzing, Rane knew. He could imagine how Arissa felt, trapped between Kor's vaguely menacing politeness and Owen's hawkish focus. She looked over at his brother with dismay.

"No doubt she realizes that," Kor said, intending a reprimand that Owen didn't react to. "Sit down, Dan Owen," he said more sharply. "You're making the poor girl uncomfortable. All of you, sit down. Now, my dear, tell us what happened."

With a catch in her flute-like voice, she said, "I don't want to make anyone angry."

When Kor and Owen had both reassured her, absolving her, she raised her gaze. First she looked at Owen through her eyelashes, and then she tilted her head slightly and looked directly at Rane. It was a quick glance, and her blue eyes were pleading.

She said, "I was upset. Dan Rane...he said some things..."

"He told me you argued," Owen said.

"I...I have a temper. I needed to calm down, so I went for a ride. It's what I always did at home."

Rane was glad now for the miserable conversation he'd had with Owen that day. The others might think he'd been rude or worse, but since Owen already considered Rane at fault for her "escape" there was no outrage now. She went on, explaining that it was her first time riding alone at Wyth and she'd ridden out too far. She'd had to spend the night in the woods, and had gotten very lost. Somehow she'd ended up going down the hill, and then found her way to the road. She went back into the woods on foot for a moment, for privacy, and came back to find her horse gone. Her story was jumbled, and several times she corrected herself on the timeline, "No, I guess I twisted my ankle before I found the stream. I'm sorry…it's all muddled…" She went on describing how she wandered on foot for days with no sense of direction, staying near the stream, eating berries.

As she talked, Rane's remorse deepened. He'd thought she'd gone to the camp, to Davyn, and he'd been so angry that he'd let her go. Even if that had been her plan, it had gone so wrong that she had finally been overcome with everything that had happened to her. In the time they had spent together at Wyth, nothing had hinted at this side of her. She spoke haltingly, and looked mostly at her hands, clasped in her lap. If she would only look at him again, he could at least give her some sort of encouragement. But she huddled in her chair, and took deep breaths and long pauses, and the men were quiet as they listened for her next soft sentence.

Both Kor and Owen were leaning toward her, listening intently. On Owen's face, it was worry that drew his brows together. Kor's black eyes were more inscrutable, but like Owen he was full of solicitous sympathy for her. She talked about hearing terrible noises in the woods at night, and shivered. Then she batted her eyelashes.

Rane stared. Stars. She was pretending. She'd left Wyth five days ago, and as remote as House Wyth sometimes seemed, it would take uncommonly bad luck not to come across some hamlet or even a woodcutter's cottage in all that time. He heard her differently now, the meandering tale and the reticence: she was stalling. The shy voice and broken-wing lure held their attention and rallied their protective impulses. And not one of them looked even the slightest bit bored with the details of yet another night in the woods. Even Tarken was absorbed.

Her soft sniffling was interrupted from an anguished cry from outside, some distance above them—where the worksite must be.

A woman cried out, "My husband! I must see my husband!"

The spell broke. The Ettori men now sprang to the door, and the House visitors were on their feet and close behind. Arissa stood, and her knees gave out. The men closest to her wheeled as she gasped. Owen caught her, and Rane saw their eyes meet as she sagged against his strong support. Interestingly, Owen didn't flinch away, and even managed the start of a smile. She leaned against him and hobbled to the door behind the others.

Kor was at the doorway, saying, "Go! Up there!" On the lower of the two ledges, a slim, dark-haired woman was throwing stones at something.

In almost reverse order of their arrival, the visiting House lords took up their swords and filed out. Their footsteps on the gravel and the sound of buckles against leather sheaths made Rane feel like they were forming up for battle. The horses in the stalls shifted, ears swiveling, and the horses that were tethered in the open swayed and sidled as the men reformed past the edge of the building for a clear view of the cliff. There was still enough light for Rane to clearly see the black-clad Ettori men racing up the path to the first wide ledge. One stumbled and slid a few feet back down, recovered, and bounded goat-like up the rugged stairs.

Where the path ended, the cliff ledge was perhaps as wide as a small room, and the rock rose vertically behind it. It was as if a section of the cliff had been chipped off, leaving just this empty space like a stage. Where the ledge ended and slid back into the cliff, there were rock formations that looked like gargantuan shards. Facing that blocking wall of jagged rock, the woman shouted, "Let me see him!" She threw another rock as the men from below reached her. The first two pulled her back and held her arms. She struggled between them, but couldn't get free. "Let me go!"

Waving another of his men ahead, Kor himself started toward the path. As he did, Owen firmly pushed Arissa back toward Rane and followed. With Arissa now against his side, Rane murmured, "What the hell are you up to?"

She lifted her face and he was surprised to see that the scratches were fresh. Her eyes were deep, and there was real anxiety there. She just shook her head, and looked toward Kor and Owen as they climbed after the guards.

They turned the woman to face Kor, and Rane strained to hear his words. Then Owen's voice was clear and firm as he said, "No one will hurt you."

She shrieked, "My husband! Jeffrey!"

❧

At the signal, stones whizzed past. Even though she knew that was coming, Arissa cringed when one of the guards barked in pain and fell, with his hand clapped against his temple. The other staggered as a stone hit his shoulder.

Wild shouts erupted from the woods as two groups of men sprang out and rushed at the two ledges. There were only a dozen men, but concentrated in two small areas they seemed legion. Arissa saw Davyn with the lower group, and she shot forward with Rane close behind.

She scrambled the last few feet to the ledge, and then wished she hadn't. The ledge was narrow and crowded, and she would be in the way and probably distracting. Rane drew his sword, on the downhill side of the man Davyn was fighting. Owen stood between the fight and Lord Ettori, his own sword drawn to protect either Kor or Tienna—Arissa wasn't sure which.

As if she were seeing time slowed, she saw Tienna rise to her feet, with a dagger appearing in her hand. Kor reacted quickly. Tienna cried out as he grabbed her wrist, and the dagger flipped away and clattered over the edge. Davyn heard the cry and with a defiant shout, he leapt between them, sword raised in his left hand.

Kor's sneer vanished, replaced by a look of shocked recognition. "You!" It sounded like the word scorched Kor's lips, and he snarled. "No, Caladen is gone." His blade hissed through the air as he swung, and the clang and shearing slide of sword on sword raked Arissa's spine. She pressed against the rock, trying to be out of Davyn's way as he parried and dodged right in front of her. Sounds bounced and multiplied against the rock, adding to the disorientation.

Kor's blade was far more suited to this, a perfect weapon that seemed alive with its own instincts. When he thrust or swung, it was a smooth and lethal movement led by the sword. There was a grace to it, an awful grace, that drew her eyes to the flashing metal. The blades clashed again, but didn't immediately slide away this time. Davyn tried to press forward, to push Kor back, to move away from the rock wall, but Kor held his place. With a flip of his wrist, Kor let his sword twirl to the outside—Davyn rocked as the resistance gave way, and then danced backward.

His heel came down on loose stone and he lurched, throwing his bandaged right hand back to catch himself. Arissa saw Kor's brilliant blade starting to thrust toward Davyn's unprotected side. She shoved Davyn, as hard as she could, out of the path of the sword. She felt Kor's sword catch on her borrowed Ettori tunic as she tumbled over Davyn.

They hit the ground in a jumble of limbs. He landed on the back of his hip, half-twisted against the cliff wall, and she landed partly on him; her elbow jammed into his shoulder while her knee drove full force into the rocky ledge. She was trying to get her other knee under her when a merciless hand grabbed her arm and dragged her off, tossing her aside. Arissa caught herself on her hands and knees and flipped around to see Davyn, on his feet now but trapped against the wall. Kor's arm was in motion—she heard a hoarse sound from Davyn, and saw him sway.

Kor loomed over him in the thickening shadows and grinned. He lifted his sword high, poised with malice. "This ends, at last."

From beyond Kor, Owen shouted, "Kor!" There was command in his tone, which jerked Arissa's attention free from Kor's terrible face even before he wheeled to confront Owen. "Stop!"

Kor drew his arm back, preparing to swing. Arrisa saw Rane lunge toward Kor from the side, past Owen, his sword extended. Kor turned it aside easily, but Rane was already swinging again.

Owen's blade intervened. "Rane, no!"

There was shock on Rane's face as his brother's sword blocked his, and then anger. With a shout, Rane swung recklessly, trying to knock Owen's sword away. Owen countered, and Rane tried again.

"Stop, Rane!" Owen shouted, but Rane just swung again, fury lending him desperate strength. Owen parried, but didn't try to retaliate. He was just blocking Rane. Arissa wondered with dawning horror if Owen really were defending Kor.

With Rane occupied, Kor turned back toward Davyn. Davyn was backed against the rock, and his legs seemed to be buckling. His sword wavered in his left hand as he held it ready to parry, and Kor paused like a cat toying with his prey. Arissa cast around for some way to help and saw the sprawled figure of one of the Ettori guards. His sword was glinting on the ground near his hand, but it was too far. Closer, she spied a fist-sized rock and seized it. She hurled it with all her strength at Kor, not caring where she hit him as long as it kept him from raising his sword.

The rock sailed past him. It did catch his eye, and he whirled to her. The fathomless eyes were locked on Arissa's and he laughed. His lips were twisted in a malevolent sneer as he struck forward in two sudden steps, caught her by the arm, and flung her at the rock wall as if ridding himself of a cobweb. She slammed into it mere steps from Davyn, just as Davyn doubled over and his sword fell from his hand. Kor's sword was poised above her as she struggled to regain her balance. She heard another howl from Rane. Kor abruptly turned to face the threat behind him, but it was not Rane whose sword met his. Owen's face was set and grim as he engaged with Kor. Rane had stepped—or had been pushed—aside.

Dusk was beginning to blur details, and Arissa was still

dazed. Through the sweeping arcs of the swords and the kaleidoscope of shifting bodies, she didn't at first notice movement at the far end of the ledge. There was a large tooth of rock a foot or so away from the cliff that seemed to cast a shadow against the full wall. A man stepped out from behind it. Arissa thought one of the Ettori guards had been hiding there, but the man wasn't in uniform and a second man appeared. And then another, who was carrying a massive axe.

The distracted fighters paused momentarily as the Starborn workers crowded onto the ledge from the entrance to the diversion tunnel, which was concealed by rock and shadow. Tienna and Lord Dannpelier guided the stunned men and boys out from the tunnel and toward the woods. One of the boys recognized Kor and rushed at him with fists ready. Not a single blow landed before Kor's sword plunged into the boy's chest. Owen stared at the body that fell at his feet as Kor pulled his sword free, and then raised his eyes to Kor. Even from where she stood, Arissa could see Owen's rage ignite; she could almost feel it herself. He seemed to grow taller and broader, his presence expanding. It seemed to her that Kor stepped back before recovering and countering Owen's well-aimed stroke.

More Ettori guards arrived, maybe from inside the tunnel, and she saw Rane and Lord Dannpelier both start bouts with new opponents. A man she didn't recognize, who was wearing what seemed to be a House jacket, was fighting valiantly uphill on the path. She and Davyn were boxed in, with swords in motion all around them. Starborn continued to thread their way across the ledge and slip into the woods, and one or two hesitated with looks of compassion when they saw her, but the barrier of flashing weapons cut them off.

The fighters certainly paid them no heed. In the shifting patterns of the melee, maybe there would be a chance to run for it. "Can you move?" she asked Davyn. Davyn tried to stand straight, but groaned and clamped his right side as he doubled over again. He tried to catch his breath, and then—with a voice that hurt to hear—he told her to leave him.

She was ashamed that the temptation was so strong, even though it was brief: if it were the other way around, he wouldn't even consider leaving her. Not knowing what else to do, she picked up his sword. It was heavier than she expected, but she raised it as if to fend off an attack. All she could do was watch the strange choreography of the fights around them and try to hold herself together, in case she needed to defend him.

Her arms ached from holding the sword long before she realized that there were no more men coming from the tunnel. Looking past the four men fighting to her left, she could see the Starborn from the tunnel vanish into the woods. One Ettori man tried to follow, but a perfectly targeted arrow from an unseen archer sailed out from the woods and hit his thigh, toppling him. The last of the Starborn cleared the ledge, and only the fighters remained. Their swings were getting less controlled, their movements less fluent, as every one of them was tiring and becoming more desperate. She heard Rane shout a warning to someone. A man fell. Kor and three of his men still fought, and now only Rane, Dannpelier, the other House lord, and Owen were left to challenge them.

Kor slashed viciously at Owen, who twisted away even as his sword continued its sweep. Kor roared in pain and his yell was so harsh, so loud, that it flooded Arissa's mind. She saw darkness dripping on Owen's sword, and tried to see where he had wounded Kor. The dark fabric of Kor's shirt was soaked with sweat, and it was hard to tell if—

His arm. Something was terribly wrong with his left arm. It hung limp, and looked backward. Blood spurted from his shoulder, and Arissa felt her stomach roil. With a scream, Kor swung again as his legs gave out.

Owen crumpled, too. Arissa heard swords clattering to the rocky ground, Owen's and Kor's, and Rane's as he dropped his and ran to his brother. The Ettori men swooped like bloodhawks around their wounded leader and formed a protective ring around him. They hoisted him up, and Dannpelier and the other lord made no move to stop them as they fell back to the tunnel as a unit.

Near the center of the ledge, Owen lay supine with his brother kneeling at his side. Rane pressed his hand on Owen's chest and urgently repeated, "You're going to be all right. You're going to live."

Beside Arissa, Davyn sagged to the ground with his back still against the cliff. His right knee was bent, his left leg was stretched out. He still had his arm clenched to his side, and his head was bowed. With his dark hair falling forward to hide his face, he looked like he was resting, even dozing, and he made no sound. She crouched beside him.

"Davyn? Can you hear me?"

He turned his face toward her without lifting his head, and attempted to smile. His voice sounded strained, but his words were clear. "My ears are fine."

From the gloaming beside her came a deep voice. "We need to get away. Grit your teeth, lad."

27

INTRUSION

The Great Gorge

PIERS STOOD JUST outside the lodge, with Elanna beside him, and watched the flashing swarm of blades on the ledges above. He felt distanced from all of it, like none of it had any depth or substance. Actually, it was beautiful, in a way. The setting sun was at just the right angle to glint and glow on the metal, and the men seemed to be pirouetting around the blades.

Elanna pointed to the lower ledge. "That's Davyn!"

Piers could see Arissa; her fair hair gleamed almost like metal. It looked like Rane was defending her, and there was another man guarding her—Davyn, apparently. Elanna dashed toward the steep incline, abandoning Piers without hesitation. Anxiety slashed through Piers's detachment, a feeling like waking in the night with an ill-defined sense of dread and loss. He rubbed at the strange, bruised welts on his forearms. He was missing something, and his mind refused to identify it.

Halfway up the hillside, beyond the ledge, he saw Atto

burst out of the woods. Elanna intercepted him, and both of them looked down at Piers. Piers felt like a vent had just been cracked open, letting in a wisp of fresh air that was going to keep him alive. It was a gasping sort of relief. Atto saw him, shouted something, and beckoned to him to climb. He pointed toward the trees.

Piers started up the path. He wasn't far from the fighting when he felt his mind rip open. It was like being too close to a loud engine, or having a thunderstorm erupt in his head. The shockwave of pain staggered him, and then the storm was replaced by something more like a rushing river, dazzling, mesmerizing, terrifying. He saw Arthur's face again, felt his panic. The pain eased, but the dizziness didn't stop. His thoughts veered away from him.

"What is it?" Elanna was right beside him, holding onto him as if holding him up.

"Can't think," he said, and heard his own voice in the distance.

"Atto!" Elanna called. "Help me!"

Piers was buffeted by another wave. His legs seemed to be disintegrating; he couldn't walk. His mind was slithering. Both kids were with him then, one on either side, and they held him by the elbows like a doddering old man. They steered him, and he moved so slowly that a Starborn man tripped against him and swore.

When they were even with the lower ledge, he could see men crossing toward him, threading through the dance. There were bright slashes of steel everywhere, carving the air. An Ettori man saw them, shouted and pointed, and started to run at them. Two Starborn men overpowered the man as he got close, and one kicked the man's dropped sword away from him. Atto released Piers's arm and dove for the sword.

Piers and Elanna saw the second Ettori man just as he saw Atto. Elanna shouted to warn Atto, and the man looked their way. Blood ran from a gash on his face. His eyes met Piers's, and Piers felt a surge of frenzied, confused, and determined fury. The Ettori man took a bounding step toward Atto and raised his sword to strike.

Beside him, Elanna panicked. She flung a dagger—where had she gotten that?—with unaimed force. It struck the Ettori man in the throat.

Piers couldn't see, couldn't think, couldn't breathe. His mouth filled with copper. He swayed and then crashed to his knees.

Piers heaved. Atto and Elanna were pulling at him, urging him up. Reeling, he managed to get to his feet and blindly let them lead him on, past whatever hazards might have been between them and the woodline. As they passed into the dark woods, a two-note chime sounded in his left ear. He was aware that it meant something important but was not, just now, able to recall what he was supposed to do about it.

Someone was tugging at his hand at the same time something was ringing in his ear. Piers kept his eyes closed and tried to pull his hand away, but then his other hand was being pulled as well.

"Piers, you have to wake up," a voice said.

Another: "He is awake. He's pretending."

More pulling.

"Open your eyes, fielder." The second voice was familiar, and impatient.

The ringing was insistent. Why wouldn't they all just leave him alone? He felt like he'd been trampled. He didn't remember getting hurt. Was he sick? They must want him to go to the medic. If it was that serious, he ought to. He didn't want to get others sick.

He blinked. It was dark, but he could make out the outlines of the two people who were trying to haul him up. Bit by bit, the details came back: the woods, the Starborn, the fight, the pain. Before he moved, he took an inventory and found he wasn't badly injured. The pain, though, that had been real, and the effects still looped around him. Something had torn into his mind, ripping the fabric of his thoughts.

"What happened?" he asked. His throat was raw from retching.

The melodic chime came again. Annoyed, he tried to shove it out of his awareness. Not now! Then came another voice—this one seemingly in his imagination.

"Protocol override," the voice said. "Piers, reply."

"Jon!" It burst out, propelled by relief so intense he felt light-headed. For an instant, he was puzzled—voices in his head? With names, even?—and then it crashed into him. The ship. Somehow he'd forgotten about the ship. He shifted forward and let his friends pull him to his feet and steady him as he tottered. He thought he heard cheering in Jon's background.

"What?" Atto asked.

"The ship!" He switched to subvocals and said, "Jon, we got out. I'm all right." In fact he felt like he was going to fall over, and the disorienting mingling of his senses and his implant didn't help his nausea.

"You scared us half to death, kiddo. Your message came in hours ago and we haven't been able to reach you—you sounded desperate."

"Where've you been? Couldn't get through."

"It's been a disaster up here, we'll tell you later. But

Piers, we have *got* to land before everything fails. You're going to have to do it on your own."

"Do what?" Piers asked.

Atto was speaking, too, his words almost too fast to distinguish. "Come on, we gotta catch up with the rest of them. Rane's taking everybody to meet the ship."

The sudden recollection of *that* impending mess nearly did knock him down, despite the fact that Atto had tucked himself under Piers's arm and was half-holding him up. "What?" His brain couldn't process it.

"Just come on, fielder," Atto said, his voice rising. "I'll explain but you've got to get moving."

Piers apologized to Jon. "I need to focus—I'll link back in as soon as I can." He toggled out of communication mode with a few taps of his tongue at the back of his palate. He could imagine his synthesized voice playing through the speakers on the bridge, and Barston and Dad and the rest of the officers listening with miffed expressions.

Getting down the steep hillside through the trees in the dark was harrowing and took far longer than Piers expected. A supernova of a headache was coming, and with each passing minute it intensified. Atto promised him that once they found the Starborn, there'd be a healer who could help him. Or, he told himself, if he had to wait—and could make it long enough—the ship. He'd never had a headache like this, with so much pressure behind his eyes that he was half afraid and half hoping that he would black out.

They came to a moonlit clearing at the bottom of the hill. It was odd, Piers thought, that moonlight could be strong enough to cast shadows and yet not reveal color. There were perhaps a hundred people in the clearing, but he saw Arissa first, really just an impression of her. Then Rane came up to him and clasped his hand. Piers's every nerve was stinging, and it felt like a white-hot blade was being stropped on his skin.

"Davyn's hurt!" Elanna's shout yanked Piers into the present. He saw Davyn lying on the ground, and there was suddenly no air. He lurched sideways and collided with Atto, who buttressed him with help from Rane. Panic bubbled. Piers fought for breath and his legs suddenly dissolved.

28

HERITAGE

Caladen Forest

AVYN LAY ON his back, aware of the nighthoppers in the grass around him and glad for the bundle of threadbare fabric serving as his pillow. Both moons were up, and the clearing where the rescued Starborn had gathered was bright with their soft light and edged with sharp shadows. Tienna had checked on him, and then had apologized for leaving him in someone else's care while she attended to Lord Wyth.

If he turned his head a bit, he could see Arissa and Rane standing not far from him, watching Tienna tend to Owen and wincing with Owen's every moan. Once in a while, Arissa would look back at him, and he tried to give her some sign that he was bearing up. Rane only looked away from where his brother lay once, to glance down at Arissa as if to reassure himself that she was still beside him. Sometimes other people cut through Davyn's limited field of vision, and all of them looked like they were in various stages of unraveling, but so far everyone was holding on to a fragile composure.

His pain had new layers and angles. A biting torment had displaced the familiar discomfort of his healing shoulder, from Arissa's fall against him. Where Kor's sword had raked his side, the pain penetrated to his spine when he moved. He had stopped losing blood—Tienna said he likely still had telk in his blood from the doses she'd given him to help his shoulder heal—but he felt as if each beat of his heart jarred his wrist, as if the pain were flowing through his veins and rattling the fractured bones.

He had been healing well and feeling strong before they left the camp, but in answer to Tienna's most heartwrenching protests he had left the splint on, to avoid thoughtlessly switching his sword to his right hand. His left-handed drills had helped, and they had needed every fraction of a fighter they could muster, but he had suspected that when faced with threatening steel he would automatically grip his sword in his right hand if he could. Tienna had warned him that the impact of striking could do irreparable damage; if something went wrong, she'd said, he might never have use of that wrist again. So he had agreed to the precaution. And then he'd landed on his hand, and his wrist shattered inside the splint.

Lord Dannpelier, who had fought in the war, had enough experience with battle wounds that he'd been able to clean and bind the gash, though there was nothing he could do for the wrist. He'd been efficient and kind, but Davyn envied Owen for Tienna's gentleness.

Most of Davyn's previous interactions with House lords had been brief horse-related encounters at the inn. Now he was in the midst of a contingent from four of the Houses, and he had crossed swords with the lord of Prime House.

Rane had been upset to find that two other House lords had slipped away during the fight, but truthfully that was what Davyn would have expected from all of them. So many times, Van had told him that the Merran lords took self-preservation as their duty—because they couldn't trust their House Guards. Every man for himself. That was why the Queen's Guard swore such unyielding oaths. Because of their courage and skill, Van said, and her trust in those oaths, the Queen never needed to fear for her life. Van had been wrong; these men were risking their lives and more to stop Lord Ettori and free the Starborn.

Dannpelier sat near him, and talked quietly with Lord Manssorand. Davyn drifted. His own thoughts seemed to weave through their conversation, coming in and out of clarity. Dannpelier saw him looking across at Owen.

"Well, lad, they are doing everything they can," the man said. "As soon as she's got him steady, she'll be over here. Just hold on."

"I'm all right," he said.

"In the broad view, maybe," Dannpelier said, "but I think in the short term you'd be glad for a little help." He held up a flask, and then slid his arm behind Davyn's neck and lifted his head far enough that he could swallow.

Davyn felt a ripple of pain starting and braced himself. He fought off a cough, and got out, "True enough." Whatever was in the flask was searing. He wrestled with the pain and then said, "It would help if I knew Elanna and Atto were safe." He'd had a glimpse of them both at the cliff, and others told him they'd seen them—with Piers—make it to the woods, but they hadn't yet appeared here.

He saw movement at his periphery and tried to turn his head far enough to see. Lifting his head on his own was out of the question—he'd tried and it had felt like claws in his side. Tienna was walking over to Rane and Arissa, drying her hands on her tunic.

"He's resting. Just about asleep," she said. "We've done what we can. We had some basic supplies on hand, but he needs floodberries and of course we don't have those. For now we just have to let Owen fight."

"Will he live?" Davyn felt the dread in Rane's question.

Tienna's smile was weary but enough of an answer. Rane threw his arms around the healer. When he released her, she put a gentle hand on his arm. "He will live if we can keep him safe, but he has some hard months ahead of him."

She knelt at Davyn's left side. Her fingers were warm as she checked his pulse. The pain ebbed. Tienna seemed satisfied but her face was drawn and her hands trembled as she pushed his hair back from his forehead.

They'd traveled for three days to get here, keeping to the woods, and none of them had slept well since before they left the camp. When they'd arrived at the site this afternoon, Tienna and Arissa had gone unarmed into the unknown, counting on their wits—and men's assumptions—to get them through. The exhaustion and tension and stress had marked circles under Tienna's eyes. He reached for her left hand with his. "It worked better than it might have," he said.

"We were foolish not to plan for injuries."

"We brought a Starborn healer with us. That was a plan." The pain clawed at him again and he snatched a shuddering breath.

"I wish I could give you something for the pain. My kit wasn't fully stocked—and I don't have the things here to make paste." She looked down and turned his hand over in hers, and gently traced the lines of his palm. "Just when you were getting past the worst of it from before."

"I'm all right," he said, and heard a chuff from Dannpelier.

"He keeps saying that," the man said. "He's determined."

There were tears caught in her eyelashes, but she said lightly, "Sometimes we call it stubborn."

"It is bad," Davyn admitted, "but I can bear it. As soon as I can ride again, I need to get home to Trint with Elanna."

Now Tienna's tear dropped, landing on the inside of his uninjured wrist. She brushed it away with a broken-nailed finger and would not look at him. Then she took a long breath, met his eyes, and said, "Davyn, the Sweep took Elanna's mother. Tunny recovered."

Mira. The thought seemed to burrow into the center of his pain.

Tienna sat with him, wordless but soothing, while he lay still, cocooned in suffering, and listened to low murmuring voices. He felt as if the ground beneath him were swaying and dissolving.

Before the full reprieve of sleep came, Davyn heard a shout. He craned his neck and saw both Elanna and Atto running toward him. Elanna dropped to her knees beside him and tried to hug Davyn only on his uninjured side.

Davyn folded his good arm around Elanna. "It's all right, Elanna. I'm all right."

Atto glanced over his shoulder at the stranger they'd led into the clearing. Davyn had a momentary sense of familiarity, though he'd never seen this man. He looked like he was in agony, and Davyn was glad to see Tienna go to him. "Is that Piers?" he asked.

"Yes. He needs help—don't know what's wrong with him. He just kind of collapsed." Atto knelt beside Elanna. "Elanna saved my life," he told Davyn.

Elanna went pale. "I used your d-d-dagger," she said.

"I'm glad," Davyn said, and pulled the girl close again. "That's why I gave it to you."

In a thready whisper, Elanna said, "I killed him." She buried her face against Davyn's good shoulder.

Atto put his arm across her shoulders and explained, "She didn't mean to, but if she hadn't, I'd be dead instead."

There was so much more Davyn wanted to know, but he needed to collect himself before he could ask. The pain radiating from his wounds and injuries was brutal and commanding. He squeezed his eyes shut and focused on his breathing, and it made him think of lessons learned while sparring with Van. If you are fighting an honorable man, Carthen had taught them, don't get up until you are ready to re-engage. An honorable opponent won't strike you while you're down, but as soon as you stand, you are vulnerable. Don't get up until you can defend yourself.

On more than one occasion, Van had waited while Davyn lay flat on the ground, counting seconds and trying to gather his wits and catch his breath so he could spring to his feet and swing his blade. The question that came to mind now, with a grumbling, dark humor, was whether pain itself was an honorable opponent.

Elanna was still clinging to him, and even her light weight was becoming too much pressure. She was getting calmer by degrees and would surely stir on her own soon; Davyn didn't want to take this small comfort from her.

He took as deep a breath as he could through the pain, and opened his eyes. Atto was still on his knees beside Elanna, but looking over at the man from the stars, contemplating something. Finally, Davyn asked, "Do you still have the dagger?"

Atto nodded. "Elanna has it. I cleaned it as well as

I could." He wrinkled his nose, as if he were still in the middle of that gruesome chore.

"Thank you. I would hate to lose it."

A Starborn man approached, carrying a bucket of water and a ladle. He looked to be middle-aged, though it was only a guess; the left side of his face was smooth with scar tissue and his forearms were roped with it. "I'm Marlin. Tienna says you should drink." He crouched beside Davyn, ready to raise him up to drink, and put a hand on Elanna's back. "All right, there, lass. Need you to sit back there for a bit." Elanna pulled away, and Davyn saw that her face was wet with tears, though he hadn't heard or felt her crying.

The Starborn man noticed, too, and said, "What's this, now? The worst is over. You're all right."

Elanna sniffled. Her eyes were wide when she looked up, and Davyn thought she seemed puzzled by the man's comment, as if she couldn't quite work out why he thought everything was over. She tugged the sheathed dagger loose from her belt.

Hilt-first, she held it out to Davyn. The Starborn man's gaze started to move back to Davyn, and swept over the dagger. With a jerk, he looked again at the weapon, then looked up at Elanna's face with startled eyes. "Where..." He swallowed hard. "Where did you get that?"

Marlin's expression was impossible to read. Davyn's head swam. He said, "I've had it my whole life."

"Who gave it to you?" The man's voice shook.

"I don't know," Davyn said. "I was found on a doorstep in a basket, and that was one of the things that had been left with me."

With a strange catch in his voice, Marlin said, "I know that blade. May I...?"

Davyn handed it to him, and Marlin held the dagger

across both his palms like a mystic object, with intense reverence and a bit of caution. He closed his eyes, and a muscle near his temple started to tic.

He thought for a moment, then scrutinized Davyn and then Elanna. "My father was a master blacksmith," Marlin began. The summer before House Caladen fell, Marlin had been twenty and starting to earn his own reputation as a craftsman. The smithy was behind the row of cottages at the edge of House Caladen's park-like setting in the forest. He'd been in love with a woman named Sophia, whose sister and brother-in-law lived in one of the cottages.

He'd met Sophia that spring, the day after Lady Caladen had given birth to twins. Marlin held up a hand to forestall his listeners' questions. One of the twins was frail from the beginning, he said, and House Caladen announced only that an heir had been born. They didn't want to trumpet the good news of twins, only to have to publicly mourn if the likely end came. Sophia was hired into the House to help with the twins, and to help Lady Caladen and the nurse do everything possible to help both babies thrive.

In late summer, Lord Caladen hosted a party to mark his wife's twenty-fifth birthday. He invited everyone associated with the House—the House Guard, the servants, even down to the stable boys—to celebrate with them. He even made the traditional gesture and invited all the House lords, with no expectation that they would come.

But Sophia wasn't able to attend. The frail infant was in the nursery, tended day and night by a healer. His brother had developed a low fever the afternoon of the celebration and was banished from the nursery to keep his brother from contagion. So Sophia took the sick child to her sister's cottage. And where Sophia was, there Marlin was. He took his tools with him, to finish work on a dagger that he was honing and the leather sheath that he was still tooling, because they were to be delivered to the purchaser the following day.

That night, House Caladen burned. The conflagration was so abrupt and so fierce that no one escaped from inside. From the cottage, they'd first smelled and then heard the fire; they'd rushed out and seen the Great House blazing, its outlines flaring in orange and red. The scorched air thickened with screams.

"We saw—I know we saw—people being cut down by shadows." Marlin cringed at the memory. "We saw one of the shadows hesitate—seemed to look right at us." He pushed Sophia back into the cottage, and told her to flee with the baby. He'd given her the dagger, promised to meet her at the smithy in Ruatt. She'd slipped out the back of the cottage into the forest while he ran toward the burning House to save anyone he could.

Someone from a nearby Starborn camp had found him in the aftermath, with burns covering his arms and back. The Starborn saved his life, with months of care, but when he was well enough to ask about a woman and a baby at the blacksmith's in Ruatt, there was no trace of them.

"Davyn," Elanna said, without stammer or whisper, "does that mean...?" Her fascination was almost more compelling to Davyn than his own dizzying realization.

Davyn couldn't answer. His pulse pounded at his temples, and his breath rattled through his lungs. Though he was still lying on his back and could feel the cool damp of the ground under him, he felt abruptly unbound, like he could be swept into a current of air too powerful to resist.

❧

"His heart is racing." A woman's voice, and someone's hand around his wrist.

Piers was flat on his back, stretched out like Davyn, who was just a few paces away. He must have passed out. The healer woman was taking his pulse, and a man he hadn't seen before was hovering beside her. Atto was crowding them and shifting his weight from heel to toe and back, never taking his eyes off Piers's face. Piers couldn't speak, and his head surely was going to shatter any second now—which would be a mercy.

"Telk," the man said. "It's the best we can do for him. Is there any here?"

From somewhere outside Piers's view, Rane said, "I think Patrig has some."

"Double the syrup."

Some measureless time later, Atto helped Piers sit up. The woman offered him a metal cup that he could hardly hold. His hands were shaking too much to raise it to his lips, so she sat beside him and held it steady for him. It scalded his tongue and the top of his throat, but he drank anyway, and seemed to have no will of his own. He was racked with another surge of pain in his head and coughed against a swallow of telk. There was a circle of worried faces around him, and beyond them he could see Elanna and a Starborn man hovering over Davyn.

Arissa and Rane stood close together beside Davyn. There was almost an aura surrounding the three of them, an incandescent shimmer Piers wasn't sure he was seeing or feeling.

The woman urged him to drink more. Piers narrowed his focus, and tried to think only of the steaming syrup, the deep color of it, the rancid bite of it. The flavor was more intense than he remembered from the medicine Shea had given him. He concentrated on feeling the telk going down his throat, and imagined the warmth of it spreading into his veins. He inhaled deeply, and exhaled slowly, and willed himself calm.

"Good," said a newcomer, a short Starborn man with tufty red hair and oversized ears. He addressed Piers. "I'm Patrig, my friend. Telk is a wonder, isn't it?"

Piers had to agree. The pain seemed to partially drain away; he seemed to be skimming along the top of it now. It tried to pull him under, but there was a hum, more felt than heard, all around him, like remembered music. As long as he held on to that, he'd be all right.

"Can you give Davyn more?" Atto asked. "Will it help?" The earnest concern in Atto's question was touching. The hum swelled.

The man ruffled Atto's hair, which Piers—somehow—knew Atto didn't like, and said, "I think we may be able to give him something better than telk."

The woman said, "You have par-telk with you?" Piers didn't know the word, but whatever it was, she was excited about it.

"A few doses. Not much." He dug inside the satchel slung over his shoulder and pulled out a small vial containing something that looked like gold dust. He handed it to the woman.

"Thank the guiding stars," the healer said. "Owen needs this."

"And Davyn," Atto reminded. "Help him, too."

She set her hand on the boy's shoulder, but let her eyes rest on Davyn. Her lips parted and she shook her head, and Piers thought she winced, as if a sore spot were being prodded.

Patrig asked the woman something that sounded to Piers like, "Are you a sensor?"

"Untrained," she answered, "but I'm pretty sure he's got the gift."

"Then we can't risk it," he explained to Atto. "For some people—and Tienna thinks Davyn's one of them—par-telk causes madness. It's not safe for them to take it. I do have some herbs that will help ease his pain, though, and we can certainly give him more syrup."

Atto crossed his arms and fixed Patrig with a doubting glare. Davyn tried to reassure him, but Piers noticed the music was missing from Davyn's accent. Then Davyn's breath snagged mid-sentence and his body arched, like he was in the clutches of pain.

Piers felt as if someone kicked him, knocking all the air out of his lungs in one burst.

Both adults and Atto spun toward him. "Can he have some?" Atto asked.

Piers heard Patrig say no, they didn't know how it would affect him, and felt Atto's frustration push through the hum. "Lie still," Atto told him. "We'll get more telk for you."

The moons were gone, the sky was lavender and infinite and brightening, and the headache was starting to regain the upper hand. Piers lay still, trying to avoid even a twitch, while he had a fragmented debate with himself about whether to interrupt the conversation that was taking place around Davyn to ask for more telk. On one hand, if telk could help tame the pain, he wanted it. But he was drifting through a hallucination, or at least an imagining, that both terrified and fascinated him.

He felt he was at the center of an edgeless spiderweb, and he was able to feel the slightest touch to any silken thread. Atto and Elanna were in the web already, and he could swear he could feel their every breath, could almost feel their every thought. The healer—Tienna—was close, too, though she was still just beyond his reach. Beyond that, there were several strong presences that were eluding him. A series of detached emotions were taunting him, too; he'd feel a tug of some powerful impression that would dissipate as soon as he tried to home in on it. His head was splitting and he couldn't sort through the pain or the feelings to figure out what it meant.

While he tended his web, the others were satellites around Davyn. Piers himself felt wrapped in spidersilk, but it was shot through with a thread of loneliness. He didn't have the energy for hurt feelings, not with so much *hurt* and *feeling* to contend with, but there was no question that none of the others were thinking about him just then and he felt utterly alone. Then Tienna materialized beside him with another swallow of telk syrup. His web seemed to fade.

Davyn was still questioning, nearly resisting, the story he'd just heard. Piers hadn't heard all of it, but as Davyn was trying to make the pieces fit together, Piers had been able to get the idea. He knew he didn't understand all the nuances or implications, but he knew enough about the Great Houses that he suspected Davyn wasn't the only one feeling knocked out of orbit. A lost heir—sole survivor of a massacre—with a birthright to political power that everyone had thought was gone from the world. That had to have Rane and the other House lords wondering what came next, to say the least.

"It doesn't matter now," Davyn said. "There's no proof of it, and Caladen is gone."

"But Davyn," Atto said, "you're *Lord* Caladen."

"I don't think it works like that," Davyn said. He was

afraid of something, Piers thought, and the fear made his voice thin and strained.

From somewhere off to the right, there came a groan, and then, "Rane?"

Owen's rasp electrified the group that had been gathered around Davyn. Rane whirled and bolted out of Piers's view. Arissa tossed an apologetic look at Davyn while Tienna said something softly to him, and they both rushed after Rane, as did Patrig and then the two House lords. Atto and Elanna moved closer to Davyn, and now Piers felt abandoned.

It would take too much effort to sit up to see what was going on. Piers wanted the spiderweb back, so that he could at least know other people were there. He could imagine Rane's relief and joy, and the healers' gladness, and that was as good as seeing. The madness-inducing wonder drug had brought Lord Wyth back from the brink. He tried to imagine what Lord Wyth was feeling, and there was a moment of fear and confusion, and then he was slammed with a mix of pain, grief, and rage. As the emotions started to bind Piers, he felt like he'd just been snared in his own web. Except he was sure, with a soul-shaking certainty that made no sense, that the emotions weren't his.

His body objected. He felt himself go rigid, and nausea clamped down on his gut. He struggled against the fear. It took all his willpower, but he found a thread to follow up and out of the trap, and he dragged himself away from the powerful pull of those tangled emotions. As he fought free, he felt like he tore through the spiderweb, ripping it loose.

Piers tried to regulate his breathing, concentrating on his own heartbeat until he felt steadier. What the hell had just happened? One moment he was feeling abandoned by his friends, then relieved, almost happy that Lord Wyth wasn't beyond help. Then two successive waves of feelings that didn't match his perspective—and that didn't feel connected—and suddenly he was more enraged than he had ever been? That didn't add up. It was like he'd been taken over by someone else's emotions, which was taking empathy a little too far.

It clicked. Empath. The word was like a talisman he had fumbled for, and he started to remember.

He remembered Lord Ettori's black eyes, and the cold hands on his temples, and the feeling of having his psyche violated and exposed and then trapped. Ettori had walled him in, had caged his Empathic ability in barriers that Ettori constructed. And it had worked; Piers had forgotten the conversation and the blood and his own psi talent and even the nature of his mission. He'd been blocked from a core part of himself, until that curiosity and awareness of Lord Wyth's feelings had inadvertently freed him.

A few feet away, between Piers and Davyn, the two kids were whispering. Elanna slipped out of Piers's vision. Piers heard Atto tell Davyn, "We don't want you to be in pain."

Elanna returned, and handed a metal cup to Atto, who helped Davyn into position to drink and put the cup to his lips. Piers felt a jarring juxtaposition of guilt from Elanna and satisfaction from Atto. That combination was so familiar; he was blasted into a memory of how he'd felt prior to just about every misdeed of his teenage years. On reflex, he choked out, "Stop!"

※

There was no chance Davyn could drink without help; lifting his head pulled his side, which woke the wound. He wrapped his left hand around the mug to steady it. The telik Atto gave him was more pungent than what he was used to, but then, everything was more intense just now. He took a deep drink, grateful for whatever help it would bring, and was startled when Piers spoke.

"Stop!" Piers said, then groaned.

Atto said, over his shoulder, "It's all right, Piers. Elanna learned it from Patrig."

"Learned what?" Davyn asked. There was something important here. He needed to focus. He tried to shove the pain to the back of his awareness, then looked at Elanna, not Atto. Elanna wouldn't meet his gaze. "Elanna, what did you learn?"

"Patrig says if he isn't sure, he gives people just a little bit of par-telk dissolved in telik. He said it helps a little more than just the syrup but isn't enough to make people go mad." By the end of the sentence, Elanna was whispering. That was how she kept herself from stammering when she was anxious.

Davyn wanted to help Elanna keep her balance; whatever the par-telk would do, it wouldn't help any part of this situation for her to blame herself. She was already tearing herself apart over the death of the Ettori man. Throwing the dagger had been an impulsive act, and not like Elanna at all, but then again, she'd acted to save her friend and that was very much in her nature. Now she was struggling to absorb the truth that she had harmed someone to help someone else.

The comfort from the telik started to seep in. "It just feels like telik," Davyn reassured Elanna. "I'm sure it's fine." It was beyond the usual telik relaxation, though. His thoughts and his awareness seemed to be blurring, and the physical pain wavered, untethered.

The dagger was sheathed and lying within reach. It seemed strange to Davyn now that he'd never wondered why he'd been given a new weapon as a child, or that he'd never noticed that the familiar, scrolling vines on the leather were incomplete. As soon as he'd been old enough to be trusted with a sharp blade, his foster father had let Davyn carry it, and he'd worn it and used it almost every day. He'd never drawn the blade in anger; it had been more of a utility knife than a weapon. Now he could picture a young woman—Sophia—tucking it into the folds of his blanket as the only parting gift she could offer. She would have been thinking of Marlin, mourning him. Perhaps leaving her charge at Holden's door had been a relief, or perhaps it had just been one more loss for a girl who had lost all her friends and family at once. Davyn felt pity clutch his heart.

From a long distance away, he heard an agonized cry from Piers, but his imagination brushed his sensory awareness aside. Everything that Sophia must have endured pressed on him. She'd have had to get help, without revealing she'd fled from Caladen. She probably said the baby was hers while she waited in Ruatt for Marlin for days or weeks, afraid and alone, trying to care for a sick infant while keeping his existence—or at least his identity—secret. The unannounced twin would be safe as long as no one knew that an heir to House Caladen had survived.

A twin. The revelation of so many lost possibilities was acutely painful. He might have grown up side by side with a true sibling, in a brotherhood uncomplicated by issues of rank or differences in background or expectation. He had given up wondering about his birth parents years ago, but knowing, now, how they had died was a new ache. Lytaan and Jessa were the only parents he could remember, and Lord Holden had told him everything there was to be told. He'd been left on the doorstep, with the dagger, the wanderer's charm, and no explanation, so he'd been given to the farmer and his wife to raise.

The reasonable assumption had always been that whoever left him had been poor and desperate. Davyn had never felt the need to fabricate a more glamorous tale. He'd never imagined any version of his life that he would prefer to his childhood at Holden with Van. But Van was gone just as surely as his twin; what was and what might have been both vanished. Tragedy and cruelty had stolen dreams and possibility.

That cruelty had taken his birth parents, too—his first lost home. Then the tragic accident that had claimed Van had led to another exile, and he'd had to leave the only home he'd known, and the parents who had adopted him. And now, now Davyn had lost Mira, the mother he had chosen.

His pain had been floating, disassociated from any specific injury, just as his unstructured thoughts had drifted. As the compound loss took form in his imagination, it seemed to coalesce abruptly into a single, clenching grip around his throat. The pain was transmuted into grief and a sense of isolation so piercing it took his breath.

Davyn heard Piers make a sound as if his wind had been knocked out of him.

Davyn felt his body tense, and saw Elanna's anxious face, blurred by his own unexpected, burning tears. Atto rocked on his heels, arms wrapped around himself. Then Tienna was near, frantically asking him what was wrong. He couldn't answer. Could barely breathe. He focused on her eyes, so blue...so blue...and tried to find an anchor point in the world around him. He wanted to throw his arms around all of them and gather them close to him, and never, ever lose another parent or friend or brother. There was an aching, rending pull that now turned the grief into anguished yearning. Somehow he had to bring them into his heart, make them part of him in some way so elemental that they could never be taken from—

I'm here.

He thought he could make out words, as if someone whispered just at the edge of his hearing. There was a surge of comfort, and then warmth, like coming in from a long winter journey, and profound reassurance.

All the tension drained in an instant. The screaming pain from his shattered wrist still raged, and the wound in his side still felt hot and jagged, but now the pain had no hold on him. He knew he wouldn't have to bear it much longer, that some indefinite but certain relief was coming. The others looked at him in total confusion. "What happened?" Tienna asked. She brushed his hair away from his face again.

He wasn't sure he'd be able to speak, but his voice came out steady and strong as he said, "I don't know."

"I think I can explain," Piers said. Davyn looked over Tienna's shoulder and saw that the starman was sitting up and facing him. The man looked as if he'd been battling the wind—he seemed unharmed, but off-balance and exhausted—yet he was smiling, with a light in his eyes that belied the hollows under them.

⛬

Piers felt like weeping, but he grinned for Davyn's sake.

He'd been dead, he thought, or as close to death as a soul could get without taking the body with it. It had felt like a star exploded in his mind. It felt like being shredded and splintered, and every sliver of his psyche had become only pain. Time slipped sideways, and he had become a thousand sentient shards of a being who could never be whole again.

The Empathic onslaught of Lord Wyth had fractured something; the unfiltered feelings from Atto and Elanna had broken it wide open. Like a metaphysical reflex, he had tried to catch the pieces, and found himself in a hell of untrammeled emotion. Not just Atto, Elanna, and Owen, but other presences, other feelings, other minds that he couldn't distinguish. He couldn't find a coherent pattern, didn't know which pieces fit together. The boiling rage he'd felt earlier pulsed in the midst of the chaos in his mind, and this time he had recognized the familiar, tainted darkness of Kor's psyche in that, threatening to consume him.

Then he'd felt someone Reach to him. It was like seeing a beacon, finding a way out of a wilderness. It was something for his Empathy to tether to. As he Reached back, and Connected, it was like being pulled to safety.

The excruciating pain he'd felt when Atto and Elanna had been leading him into the woods made sense now, as he saw Davyn's bloodied bandages. He'd been feeling Davyn's indiscriminate Reaching, but Kor's intervention had kept him from recognizing it for what it was.

When he'd wondered about Owen's state of mind he had instinctively, inadvertently, Reached to Owen. In that Open moment, Kor had somehow found him and used that Open channel to reverse the signal. He'd tried to claim Piers's psyche, but through Piers he'd tapped Davyn. Davyn had resisted, and Reached—without direction—for help.

When Piers let himself Connect, the pressure in his head let up so suddenly and dramatically that it seemed like there should be an accompanying sound. The Connection shut out everything else, shunting Kor and all the other Empathic demands on him to the background, so that all his psi attention was on Davyn. If he tried to focus on a different presence, he could, but it would be like looking past a person who was standing nose to nose with him. It was such a relief—like a fresh dose of oxygen after nursing an empty tank—that he wanted to laugh.

Davyn's grey eyes were intense, filled with recognition that Davyn surely didn't understand. Piers sifted through Davyn's complex confusion, looking for the core emotion. When he found it, his relief doubled. It wasn't fear. Deep, deep down, Davyn was at peace. Of course, right now he was half-swamped with the confusion of an unfamiliar presence that seemed inserted between his own thoughts and his own feelings. Piers did what he could to dampen his own reactions. He even toggled off the implant, completely, just for a little while. The last thing he needed was to have to finesse his subvocalized thoughts and his subconscious feelings at the same time.

Atto, Elanna, and Tienna made room for him beside Davyn, all pulsing with their own emotions, all familiar as a favorite song. Piers sat down, legs criss-crossed, and smiled.

"I've been hearing about you for weeks," he said. "Especially from these two." The reference to Elanna and Atto caused a swell of gratitude and deep attachment. Piers saw them both as Davyn saw them, and he had to refrain from drawing them into the hug that Davyn wanted to give them. "I'm Piers Haldon."

"I don't understand," Davyn said softly. He didn't seem to notice the tears tracking at an angle across his turned face.

Piers Pushed as much acceptance toward Davyn as he could, and tried to stifle everything beyond the Connection. He couldn't tell if Davyn was getting psi input from the others directly, or only transitively through their Connection, but the fledgling Empath was close to panicking as he struggled against the emotions he couldn't place. Any shielding Piers could offer, he would. Davyn was fighting to preserve his sense of autonomy, and that was a losing proposition for any Empath—especially an unpracticed one.

Concern for Davyn radiated from Tienna, but she kept her face serene. She stood close beside Elanna, smiling when the girl looked up at her wonderingly. The smile was still on her lips when she looked at Piers, and in that moment he wasn't sure if he was in love with her or Davyn was. "You have the gift, don't you?" she asked. "And Davyn does, too."

He did his best to explain: the psi gene that the crew of the ship carried; the intensity of his own ability; the way Empaths could Connect with each other; and the awareness of others' feelings that infused his whole life until he'd arrived on the planet. "The crew on the foundation ship were all psi, too," Piers said. "We figured some of their descendants would be Empaths, and I think the Great Houses are the answer, or part of it. There are a few people I've been able to pick up, but only one other active Empath until now. I'd actually been wondering if after all this time there's now a different kind of psi here."

That was the part that still didn't make sense to him. He was picking up so much from the people around him, now. Atto and Elanna certainly had the concentrated, clear-edged emotions he associated with Empaths, and they were receptive to his Pushes—especially Elanna—and yet they seemed to have no inkling of it and therefore no control of it. Why hadn't the knowledge been passed down with the gene? Or had Kor somehow found a way to suppress awareness of it without contact? They didn't seem to be hiding it; Empathic ability hadn't been forced into the shadow by some sort of general, anti-psi sentiment. They just didn't know.

"On the ship," he said, "psi ability typically starts

flickering in adolescence. You start getting hints of it but it doesn't really take hold until you Connect the first time. That's what lights up Empathic ability—after that, you can start to learn how to focus." Piers shook his head. The words frustrated him, but metaphor was as close as anyone could get to explaining how it felt.

"People who think they might be psi try all sorts of dumb stuff to light up," he went on, "but I've never heard of anyone being able to initiate Connection before they were fully activated as an Empath. What happens is someone who's already activated Reaches out, to give you something to get hold of. It's kind of like someone has to pull you into your ability. Or maybe, someone shows you how to turn on the lights. It happened to me early, because both my parents are strong Empaths, but it took me years to be able to control it."

In a low voice, Davyn said, "You said I Reached out to you."

"Honestly, I don't know how it happened." Davyn shouldn't have been able to Reach if he hadn't already been active—before the first Connection, as far as Piers knew, a new Empath could only Push emotive energy in an unfocused broadcast. But if Davyn had ever experienced psi Connection before, he hadn't been aware of it; it was hard for Piers to imagine that someone could be an active Empath and not know it. Then again, language got in the way of understanding, sometimes. "I know how you feel" was something everyone said, when what they meant was, "I can draw from my own experience and imagine that you are feeling the way I would feel in your situation." Even using the word *empathy* for this psi talent was a bit off-center, because the meaning for a psi was so much more literal than the word's usual semantic purpose.

It'd be easy for people to decide that there were just a handful of individuals who were unusually imaginative and sensitive. Davyn might have figured that he was in that category. Those special people would have no way of knowing that what they experienced was more than just a different degree of emotional intelligence.

Piers said, "It seems like something else is the trigger here."

"The par-telk?" Tienna asked. "We know that people who have the gift—Empaths, I suppose—have a bad reaction to it. Some healers can tell if someone has the gift, but if we aren't sure, we don't give par-telk."

He asked what it was, and she explained that petals from telk blossoms were soaked and dried in some particular way, then ground up and mixed with the telk syrup. Piers started to ask one of the many questions that crowded into his mind, but stopped. They could investigate botanical pharmacology some other day, and in any case Kath should be the one to do it.

Kor had said something, hadn't he, about the plant having an effect on psis? If par-telk was a trigger that activated full Empathic ability, Piers thought, that would explain the madness they worried about: a newly triggered Empath—activated without Connection—who didn't know why he had so many inexplicable feelings might feel insane. Or, if par-telk removed psi barriers for an already active Empath, perhaps that would be even worse. Left Open to any psi signals, he'd be searching for something to cling to, but there'd be no one Reaching back. In the first scenario, he might feel isolation. In the second, it'd be closer to feeling rejected.

It made sense. If the drug only affected people with the psi gene, maybe it was something like the way hormones activated the gene. That would make par-telk a botanical trigger. It didn't explain the rest, though. The drug wasn't part of the equation for Elanna and Atto, but they also seemed to be gaining psi strength, or at least showing early symptoms of activation.

Symptoms. Ah. Kor had given him that answer, too. The virus. Only this mutation's affect on the gene wasn't blocking it—it was activating it.

"The Sweep," he said. "This Sweep is backwards!" He explained as well as he could, trying to convey the idea without mentioning DNA or genetics or cells or proteins.

As he talked, Rane started pacing, short distances that didn't take him out of earshot. Tienna and some of the other listeners were numb, trying to take it in. Atto said what they were thinking. "You're saying he made the Sweep? Every time? He did it on purpose?"

Piers confirmed, and both agitation and numbness kindled into burning rage. The immediacy of the reaction startled him, but that was outdone by the flare of Davyn's fear as he was thrust into the conflagration. Piers put a hand on Davyn's arm, using the contact to help Davyn feel the pull of the Connection; he drew Davyn out of psychic chaos, and shielded him as well as he could. He wished he could simultaneously Push calmness to the others, but he wasn't able to separate far enough from Davyn's panic to do it.

"It's over now," Piers said. "With the ship's arrival, the Sweep won't be able to take hold again." And somehow, he thought, we'll make sure Kor faces justice for this.

"I never caught the Sweep," Davyn said.

"Maybe you were already active."

"I think so," Tienna said. Her eyes shone as she looked at Davyn. "The way you understand animals could be part of it. And children."

Of course animals would be part of an Empath's development here. Piers should have thought of that. He'd had his own psi moment with the horse on the road, however that had happened. Maybe something like that would be enough to activate an Empath, the way it worked here.

"And if he's Caladen, it comes with the heritage." Piers hadn't noticed that the two other House men had come up behind him. The one who spoke was a youngish man wearing a vibrant jacket—a green that practically radiated. "There was always a legend that Caladen had the strongest gift."

Arissa, Owen and Rane were descendants of bridge officers, too, and they were psi even if they didn't know it. And Owen just took some par-telk.

That eruption of emotion from Owen earlier wasn't just a surge. That was another fledgling pushed out of the nest with no instinct to fly. And that trap Piers had resisted had been a Reach that he hadn't recognized. What a miserable beginning for the guy. And now what was Piers supposed to do? The Connection with Davyn was not a carefully calibrated sharing between experienced Empaths—Piers was going to have to manage it all from his end. He needed to get that under control, or he wouldn't have the capacity to handle multiple Connections just now, especially since Owen would be just as raw. Plus breaking from Davyn was going to be tricky. For now, he needed to focus on one thing at a time.

"I thought it was a myth," the other House lord said. "I don't think Ettori feels a damn thing."

Piers decided to save that news for later.

Green Jacket said, "I don't think House Manssorand does, either. My wife would tell you I'm emotionally blind." He walked to where Davyn could see him. The man was in his thirties, and his rugged features and weather-lined face made quite the contrast with Davyn's youth. Davyn was nervous under Manssorand's scrutiny; Piers was surprised by Davyn's insecurity and tried to shore him up with some confidence. The grey eyes flicked over to him with quickly suppressed surprise, and then a trace of a smile played at the corners of Davyn's mouth. So he'd felt it, and understood. Quick study.

"Dan Davyn," Manssorand said, "please know that House Manssorand stands ready to support House Caladen's recovery."

Davyn thanked him with as much dignity as he could, considering he was still flat on his back and still in pain. "I can hardly take this in," he said. "I was raised in Tyndaris...I'm hardly qualified to be a House lord, especially considering House Ettori's likely response. And one survivor doesn't really make a House."

"Ah. Rane proposed an answer for that," the older man, Lord Dannpelier, said, and Piers noted his psi presence now, too. He explained they'd wanted to rescue Piers so that he could guide the ship, and then to help the travelers settle. "And then, well, we thought that House Caladen might be a good home for the newcomers—but of course that has to be your decision now."

Davyn said to Piers, "Do you think your people would want that?"

That was beyond answering, since he didn't really know what the offer implied. He also knew Davyn had doubts, so he demurred. "We'll have to talk it through when they land." As he said it, the realization came that he'd forgotten—and, in his defense, been unable—to contact Jon as he'd promised.

Piers pinged the ship, and heard the two-note chime in reply. He turned away from the others, with some impulse for privacy that made him laugh at himself even as he started subvocalizing. "Sorry, Jon. You'll never believe what just happened!"

Jon was right there. "Dammit, Piers, don't ever turn it off like that! Especially after scaring everybody."

"I know, I know. But Jon, listen, you know I told you the Houses were founded by the crew? I was right! The descendants have the gene. And Davyn's active psi! Full-on, full-power Empath—and he didn't even know it. He's like a sunstorm, just blasting out in every direction with no control at all, and it was killing me until we Connected. I really need time to help him, because he's totally bewildered. Oh, and beyond that, turns out he's a lost heir to the fallen House I told you about. So he's kind of in over his head just at the moment and I'm in some kind of hyper-psi state."

"Or just hyper," Jon said. Piers was sure that was said with dry humor. "Not that I'm not interested, but can you by any chance fill us in on how you and these Empaths are going to get us down there?"

"I just need a little more time," Piers said. "They're all brand new, not even active yet, most of them, and I need to find the right way to pull them in. If there really is a beacon somewhere around here, maybe someone knows more. I can find the right person to talk to, I might be able to—"

Jon interrupted him, and that was not something Jon did. "We're probably down to countable hours, kiddo. A day or two. We're looking at the last of the stored food, and there's only one water system functioning now. Some people are pretty good at counting, and it's going to get really noisy up here if we don't announce definite and immediate plans to land *very* soon."

There was no way he could be reading Jon's emotions— not in any psi sense—through the implant, but Piers felt the anxious restraint just the same. Jon was on edge, but trying not to inflict that on Piers.

"I found the Empaths, Jon. I can pull this together and figure it out. Give me the chance," Piers pleaded. "I have the answer right here, we don't have to risk the crash."

"Not sure it matters, Piers. If we were a hundred percent sure of your welcoming committee, there'd be time to wait. But we aren't, and there isn't. Captain's set to try some theoretical engineering that they've come up. They think possibly we can cut the engines and let gravity do the rest if we come in at the right angle. Captain wants to land tomorrow, just in case, because if there's no help out there, we might need the time to cut our way out. We're headed for the open fields where you landed."

Dread rose in Piers's throat, with a metallic edge that lately had been the harbinger of heaving, though thankfully his stomach seemed content to stay in place. As far as they knew, the landing sequence might not even initiate if the right Empathic force weren't on this side. Cutting off the engines would put them on life support systems, and with the ship overburdened that wouldn't hold long. If some of the ship's Empaths could get out, perhaps through the maintenance airlocks, presumably they could open the hatch as intended. If for some reason that didn't work, would they have the time they needed to cut through a hull that had been built to withstand every force from the outside, or find or make some other way to evacuate everyone?

Piers had been worried about the shock of adjustment, on both sides. Given the timing, that concern moved to the bottom of the list. "I *am* a hundred percent certain, Jon. I can get the Empaths over there and I can channel all of it, pull them all together so we can do whatever we have to do. Give us time to get to the site."

After a moment, Jon said, "Sorry, scout. Captain says we're coming down, with or without."

Piers swallowed his arguments. Jon had as good as told him it was an official order—that telling *scout* when Jon's native impulse would have been a more sympathetic rejection. "I'll go as fast as I can, maybe we don't have to be right up close. What's the longest—the absolute longest—you can give me to get there?"

This time Piers heard the subtle click as Jon flipped off the encoder to talk to someone, probably his father. It seemed like he aged a decade waiting for Jon to come back. "Captain Haldon says day after tomorrow, shiptime. No more than forty-eight hours."

29

RECONCILIATION

Caladen Forest

A S HE LOOKED at the people scattered around the
glade, Rane had second thoughts about this plan.
There were ninety-odd Starborn here now, plus the
House group, and a few people were seriously wounded.
Including Owen. They weren't traveling quickly. And they
were farther from the fields of the valley than anyone was
admitting to Piers. Rane wondered what madness had over-
taken Piers, to tell the Starborn from the dam that the ship
was coming? Of course they wanted to witness that, and of
course that meant the welfare of a much larger group was
now at stake. They had few horses, and they had a long
walk through woods and down the hills ahead of them
before they got to the Truolt. And they had only two days.

It didn't help that Piers was prowling around the campsite when he wasn't sitting with Davyn. He talked to the
ship as he paced, and Rane had to keep reminding himself that Piers was not just muttering to himself. Heavy
concentration veiled Piers's eyes while he was "listening"

to the ship, and tiny muscles in his face rippled when he responded, and he seemed to cut himself off from his surroundings.

They'd started traveling mid-afternoon, with Owen in an improvised travois and everyone else limping along as well as they could. The healers were incensed, and they had pleaded for more rest before moving Owen and Davyn— and it was hard to argue against it. Both of them looked like they needed weeks. But they didn't have time, and Tienna said the par-telk would help them regain their strength more quickly than otherwise.

A couple of people had gone to fetch the others from Tienna's Starborn camp who were a little south of the lodge, waiting with the horses that the rescue party had ridden. Someone had proposed waiting for them, but Tienna and Davyn had supported Piers's assessment that the Starborn would easily be able to catch up with the slow progress of this group.

When they'd come to this clearing, just as the last of the sun was going, Rane had taken his stand. They wouldn't travel well through the night woods, this was a good place to bivouac, and rest now would help them tomorrow. Now he hoped his pity for the injured and struggling among them wasn't going to keep Piers from the rendezvous. That disaster might be more than Piers could handle.

The newcomers arrived as the daylight trickled away, leading a string of horses. There was a pair hitched to a wagon full of provisions, and some horses he didn't recognize, and then he saw his own Morning Star and Owen's Breeze, as well as the horses from the lodge at the dam— most still saddled with their House-embossed tack. That solved part of a problem, at least.

Rane watched Elanna and Piers help Davyn work his

way toward them with single-minded resolve. The horses all seemed to notice Davyn at the same moment. They lifted their heads in near unison, in the same attitude of alert interest, except for a magnificent black stallion who tossed his head and whickered. Piers laughed as Davyn greeted his horse with devoted affection, but Rane saw the starman's expression change to alarm when the stallion's attention fell on him. Then it was Davyn's turn to laugh. It seemed like an exchange of brotherly teasing, and Rane felt a twinge of loss.

Owen was in enough pain that the healers were keeping him still by sending him into a deep sleep. His face was taut even while he slept, a version of his stone expression that was worse for being entirely unguarded. Rane studied Tienna's face as she watched over Owen, and tried to trust her assessment that he was doing well and unlikely to come to harm from the par-telk. Now that they had an explanation for the reaction, and Piers at hand to guide them, they could work through the madness—if it came, and if that's what it even was.

It seemed like madness anyway. If Piers was telling the truth—and Rane couldn't doubt it, even though at one level he wanted to—then Owen was an Empath, and so was he. Piers promised to help them both as well as he could, and judging from Davyn's confusion and struggle, Rane was sure they would need it.

The small moon lit the clearing. Rane enlisted a Starborn man to help him build a comforting fire, and Piers and Atto constructed a couple of small lean-to shelters that no one wanted to use. Meanwhile Elanna was hardly a foot away from Davyn when given a choice, and Davyn stayed close to the horses. Blankets were distributed, food rationed out, and people started to stake claims on space around the fire.

Through all the preparation, Owen lay still. In the fire-light, he looked to Rane unbearably like their father on the night before he died. He sat beside his brother the way he wished he had sat with his father, to be there the moment he woke. Now the grief came.

When Owen at last shifted and moaned, Rane wiped his hand over his face, clearing away the traces of tears, and leaned over so Owen could see him. "I'm here," he said. He reached for Owen's hand.

"Some advice, little brother," Owen said, his words scratching through a parched throat. "Swords are dangerous."

The humor startled him. There was even something like a smile on Owen's lips. "Duly noted," Rane said, smiling back. "Glad you're here to share your wisdom."

Owen asked for water, and when Rane helped him drink from his flask, admitted that the pain was rising again. Before Rane even got to his feet to seek out a healer, Tienna approached, carrying a vial and a cup. "The par-telk is wear-ing off," she said. "There's some syrup here, which will help, but it'll make you drowsy again. I'll let you decide when you want to take it." She handed both to Rane and retreated.

"So many questions," Owen murmured.

"When you're stronger—"

Owen clutched at his arm. "Arissa?" he asked.

With all the things Rane needed to say to Owen, all the things Owen needed to know, this wasn't where he would have started. Yet there was urgency in Owen's eyes, and in the surprising strength of his grip. "She's here. She's safe."

His brother released his arm and subsided, closing his eyes. "Good." When he opened his eyes again, he looked more relaxed. "It's all right, Rane. I know you have feel-ings for her."

"I won't do that to you," Rane said, so softly he wasn't sure Owen heard him. "You need to marry her, for Wyth."

His brother gave him a tight-lipped smile. "You've got it wrong, brother. *She* needs to marry, for Aryn."

Rane stared. An owl whistled in the trees behind them. "You mean it's her idea?" That made no sense. Arissa hadn't even tried to hide that she wasn't happy about marrying Owen.

"No, it was mine. Someone has to save House Aryn before Ettori pounces on it. We can afford to do it. But it doesn't have to be me. You can help as much as I could—more, if she loves you." Owen was quiet for a moment, then added, "Though who knows what the politics will be, now."

It took Rane a few extra breaths to process that. He heard Piers and Atto laughing, as if from a separate reality. A silky breeze was starting up, trying to sneak through the trees without rustling any leaves. The larger moon, almost full, was visible through the lowest branches, bleaching the sky around it.

When he finally collected his thoughts and asked why Owen hadn't told him, the answer was equally disconcerting. At the crux of it, Owen had been playing a subtle game, keeping Ettori in view while he tried to learn how to be Lord Wyth. Saving House Aryn with a perfectly reasonable marriage would keep the situation among the Great Houses stable. "I didn't tell you because I didn't want to put you on the game board, not because I didn't trust you," Owen said. "I didn't want to risk you."

"Why did you stop me when I had a chance at him?" Rane asked. "I had a clear strike."

Owen seemed to be having trouble keeping his eyes open now, but Rane couldn't tell if he were resisting pain or sleep. "I couldn't let you do it," he said. "Couldn't let my little brother bear the consequences. You feel things too deeply."

"And you don't?"

"I know what I can handle. And I thought at first that I could still put off having him turn against us."

Then Kor had slain the Starborn boy and forced Owen to cast his lot. Rane knew a much, much longer conversation was called for, but Owen just gave him a fraction of a smile and reached for the vial of telk syrup.

30

HOMECOMING

Caladen Forest

PIERS USED EVERY technique he knew, and some he made up on the spot, to try to mask his impatience. For Davyn's sake, it really wasn't a feeling he wanted to broadcast. They had to go slow, and human decency alone would keep him from pushing to go faster. It's just that there was so little time to get to the landing site, and for sure the captain wasn't going to budge on that timeline. He couldn't.

The geography wasn't all against them; the others all insisted that once they got out of the Caladen Forest the rest of the journey would be fast. They said they could hire a boat and be swept down the Truolt River. Repeating the downstream experience Atto had given him wasn't very enticing, but at the pace they were going now they'd be lucky to get to the valley by next week unless there was some shortcut. Piers was tempted to break away, to race to the landing site and do what he could on his own if the others didn't catch up in time, but he didn't like the odds that he could stay on a running horse for hours. Better to be with the group and try not to spew his frustration. Piers wanted Davyn to be all right with Connection, and swamping him with conflicting personal priorities wouldn't help.

So Piers let his horse choose its own pace. They'd been on the move since just after dawn, and ought to be getting close to the Valon River. They were a sorry lot now, with dirty clothes and faces, and chafed and sore legs, but no one was complaining. Even Lord Wyth seemed to be in better spirits than he probably had any right to be, considering that he was jostling along in a wagon being pulled over ruts and roots. As for Piers: he was starting to think he might like to trade places with Owen.

The wagon trundled over the rough ground, and Piers thought the poor animals pulling it had probably had better days. Maybe he was just projecting his own misery—he ached all over. Davyn had no concerns about it, so Piers supposed it must not be an unreasonable thing to ask a horse to do.

Davyn rode beside Piers and was so assured and calm on that monster horse, despite his wounds and bandages, that Piers felt ridiculous for his own dread. His horse kept steady with the group, agreeably ranked in the middle of the small herd, and needed little guidance from him, which was a good thing. Piers was dependent on his horse's good will, since he was trying to keep in contact with the ship. Equine common sense and compliance were all that kept him from being left behind.

From time to time, he tried to Reach to the people he was sure of, trying to activate them or at least elicit *some* reaction. He held Davyn apart from that, which was exhausting but worth it. Protecting Davyn was a form of self-protection, because Davyn could do nothing to control his side of the Connection. Piers didn't want to experience the all-out assault of the rebound that would be the likely result of Davyn trying to assimilate multiple Empathic inputs.

He felt a little guilty for leaving Davyn to his own thoughts. Tienna occasionally fell in beside him to check on him, but when she had reassured herself that he was still all right she went back to the wagon to watch over Owen. No one else had much to say, and all Piers could hear were the birds in the woods and the tromp of the horses. He inhaled for a sigh, and the fragrance of damp evergreens and humus reminded him of the woods near the river where Arthur had died. He'd let his guard down, and the memory of Arthur's limp, battered body assailed him.

His horror-tinged grief flooded to Davyn before he could stop it, and he felt Davyn's recoil. Then there was a compounding effect, the kind of amplified reverberation of emotions that could happen if a Connection were too unconstrained. His own emotion came to him like backwash and carried the emotion it had provoked in Davyn along with it.

It brought him back to the moment with a shudder, and he focused on distinguishing his memories from Davyn's distress and bewilderment. "I'm sorry," he said. "I just thought of an accident." He couldn't face talking about it just now. It was strange to think that Atto was the only other person on the planet who knew about Arthur.

"You lost someone." Even as Davyn said it, he seemed to be taken aback by the emotional insight. Whatever his next thought was, it seemed to sting him. Piers thought it was probably the moment when the new Empath realized that the insight flowed both ways—it wasn't the easiest idea to process. "How does one get used to this?" Davyn asked, as if picking up a conversation.

Piers pulled in his lower lip while he thought, trying to find a non-alarming, truthful answer. Finally he said, "Time. And you can learn how to temper it a bit." He hesitated, and he knew Davyn felt his reluctance to go on. "I can try to break the Connection if you want, if this is too much. I don't know how that will feel to you, especially since the whole thing is involuntary on your part. For me, when a Connection ends I usually feel depressed for a few days, even if the relationship doesn't end."

"And you don't want to break it now."

"Honestly—selfishly—no. This feels normal to me, and I feel better than I have for a while. But maybe it's not fair to you."

Davyn stalled.

"Take your time," Piers said. He looked away to hide a smile at Davyn's effort to mask his relief, and the subsequent discomfort when he wondered if Piers felt that, too. "I'll try to give you some space while you work through it. And I promise we'll sit down and talk about it at some point, and I'll teach you the way I was taught how to handle it." He was surprised by the sudden echo of the words he'd said before he left *Redemption*, to a young friend who'd been struggling with activation. Maybe he was going to end up running seminars for new Empaths when his scouting days were over. Piers turned to his other side and started a conversation with Atto.

A couple of hours later, with the sun now over the tops of the trees and the woods washed with gauzy light, Piers saw that Davyn was holding his horse in place until Piers caught up. Davyn said, "Rane says we aren't far now. Another hour at most to the old road."

"That's good news," Piers said. "I'm ready to get off this horse." It was an understatement, but he didn't bother trying to disguise his complaint with humor. Davyn knew all too well how miserable he was. Unfortunately, any break would cost them time, and that added to his resentment of riding. It didn't help that as he looked around at the others, nearly everyone else seemed totally comfortable, except for Arissa and one of the Starborn men. The others, especially but not only Davyn, looked like they could spend all day in the saddle. Which, Piers thought, many of them probably often did.

"Hold!" Davyn called out, and the momentum of the horses ahead throttled to a stop. To Piers, he said, "I think you're not the only one." One corner of his lips twisted up, like he was suppressing a full smile. He rode ahead to catch up with Rane. Manssorand had already dismounted and was helping Arissa down.

Piers stayed where he was. Was he really going to have to ask someone to help him down? And how long would it take for all these people to have whatever stretch-break he'd just caused?

Atto fell in beside him, grinning. "Don't worry about it, fielder. No one's going to want to sit around here very long. We'll be there in time to see your ship come in."

"It's that obvious?"

"To me, anyway. Everyone understands, though. They don't want to miss the landing, either." He hummed a snatch of a tune and then said, "See that little ledge over there? That'd work for a mounting block, if you want down."

Not all bad to have people know exactly what you want, Piers thought. The ledge was twenty yards off to the side, almost concealed amid leafy bushes. As he turned the horse's head in that direction, he saw that Davyn was looking back at him, so he pointed toward the ledge and called, "Mounting block!" Davyn nodded and waved him toward it.

Atto hopped off his horse like he did it a hundred times a day, but was kind enough not to make too much of an issue of it when Piers, his left foot still in the stirrup, clung to the saddle and quested for the ledge with his right foot. Atto said something flip but stepped closer to steady him.

"Piers, look."

"What?" Piers asked, stepping down at last.

"*Look.*"

The knee-high ledge was the remnant of a stone wall, disguised by a jungle of ferns and weeds. On the other side of it, well-grown saplings and vines and a carpet of green filled a large clearing bordered by the forest on three sides. Farthest away from where they stood, the ruin of a building stood against the forest edge, so overgrown that it was camouflaged against the trees.

Atto looked at him, and glanced in the direction the others had gone. Then he grinned, clipped Piers on the arm, and stepped over the wall. "Come on, fielder. Let's go see House Caladen."

There wasn't much to see. The fire and the decades after it had erased any proof of human habitation. All that was left was part of the east wall. With the morning sun warming the crown of his head, Piers watched a pair of birds dart through a window-shaped hole in the second story of the isolated wall, and wondered what room would have been where he was standing. Generations had lived and died here, and the final tragedy had happened less than his lifetime ago, but there was a serenity about the place that sanctified it. He felt like there should be some ritual words to say or gesture to make, to acknowledge the memory and loss.

Atto suffered no such compunction, and monkeyed up the wall to stand in a hollow window. "Amazing!" he called down. "Can you believe they all just rode right past it? And we almost did!"

Squinting at Atto up there, framed against the green of the trees and the blue of the sky and leaning casually against the side of the gaping window, all Piers could think about was how easily he could fall. When had he turned into such a cautious old killjoy? Atto was as sure-footed a climber as any squirrel, but the wall itself might not be stable...

"Oh, damp it," Atto complained. "I'm fine, Piers."

Well, either Piers had let it show on his face, or Atto was getting pretty adept at picking up Empathic waves himself. Honestly, though, the strange link-that-wasn't-a-Link with Atto was baffling in its strength. Could Atto's psi ability be intensifying because of exposure to the Sweep through Elanna and Davyn, or to active Empaths? It was so much like Connection, but without the consuming intensity.

"If you get hurt I won't be able to get on the horse again," he said.

"Aw, you need me!" Atto said, as he started to climb down. When he was still a few feet off the ground, he pushed off and jumped the rest of the way. He landed on the balls of his feet, but there was a thud as if he had landed on something other than grass and soil. He knelt, brushed at something, and then called Piers over in a voice a notch higher than usual.

Atto was clearing weeds from a half-buried trapdoor a couple of feet from the wall. It took both of them to pry it open, with Piers pulling with all his strength on the steel ring until Atto jammed a thick branch in the gap to lever it the rest of the way. The top few rungs of a ladder were visible. Dank and ancient air swirled below, burnished with an amber glow.

"That's not natural," Atto said.

The two-note chime sounded in his left ear. "Hey, Jon," he said, distracted.

"Hey, yourself. We checked out the landing site—looks good. Baby Prethon joined the world last night. So far not too many people know, but word is getting out and it seems like it's pushing people across the line. They are taking it as a sign that we're out of time and they are demanding the captain land *now*."

"No, no, not yet!" He turned to Atto. "What's the soonest we could get to the site?"

Atto shrugged. "I still think tomorrow evening. As long as we get a boat before dark, and that should be easy."

To Jon, Piers said, "Look, I know—I *know*—how urgent it is. But it'll go better for everyone if we're there, for the psi reasons but also just the human ones. It's going to be a massive shock when you land, on both sides, and our people are going to need help even if no one gets hurt. At least give me the rest of the forty-eight, Jon."

There was a worrying silence from Jon that stretched on. "Jon?"

"We're thinking," came the answer. Another pause. Then it was Barston's encoding.

"We are out of time, Haldon," the commander said. The digital reinterpretation of his voice was hollow and lifeless.

"I know!" Piers tried pleading. "Commander, our arrival is myth, history, and religion all rolled into one for the people here. You've heard my reports—we really can't expect a universal welcome. The people with me are the ones who'll make the difference. They're the Empaths, our best chance of a safe landing. And some of them are the authorities, too. It's the welcome you sent me here to find. Please, please give me time to get them in place before you show up."

"Tomorrow, eighteen hundred hours." Barston said. "That's what the captain said." Typical of Barston, he abruptly disconnected, leaving Piers feeling like he had been robbed of the last word.

"I can't wait to see the ship," Atto said, bouncing from one foot to the other. "I can't even imagine it."

"Tomorrow. Late afternoon. We need to get moving in a few minutes."

"Then we don't have much time to explore!" Before Piers could stop him, he stepped into the hole and was standing on an unseen rung of the ladder.

"I mean it, Atto. Minutes!"

"Fine. I'm going down to see what that light is."

"Hold it, Atto! You're determined to get hurt, aren't you? That ladder could be completely rotted through."

"Nah," Atto said. "Feels solid." And he disappeared downward.

Piers hesitated, caught between caution and curiosity, then let curiosity win. He felt the wooden rungs sagging under his boots and clutched the side rails. He wasn't sure he was glad he couldn't see the bottom—the darkness spared him from dizziness, but left plenty of opportunity for imagination. So while he had less certainty that he *would* fall, he was fighting a stirring anxiety about what he'd find down there if he did.

He stepped onto a hard-packed dirt floor, and looked up at the square of daylight only a few feet above his head. It had felt like a longer climb than that. The strange glow was bright enough to cast Atto's shadow onto Piers as he followed Atto deeper into the subterranean space. The air was cool as it brushed his face.

They passed through a hallway just about as wide as Piers's arm-span, which led to a small room that contained nothing but what looked to be a waist-high stone block on a central dais. The light emanated from the top of the block, and Atto bounded onto the dais to see. With a guttural exclamation, he recoiled, and then more cautiously leaned forward over the block. "By the founders'..." He trailed off, abandoning whatever profanity he'd been about to utter.

Piers joined Atto on the platform. Sculpted in metal on the top surface of the block was a raised-relief map of the island, impressively detailed, set in a square border of thin striplights. The sculpture included different textures to represent forests and water and fields, and the hills and valleys were graded so precisely that Piers didn't doubt they were perfectly to scale. The carved lines of the rivers varied in width and depth. This wasn't an artist's interpretation. This was a scientific instrument.

The amber was reflected in Atto's eyes as he stared down at the map, then at the lights.

"Do you have lights like that?" he whispered.

Piers tried to answer, but had to clear his throat. It was probably just Atto's awe that was choking him up—but the lights were a vivid memento of home. "We do. All over the place."

"How do they keep burning?"

Piers wasn't going to try to explain electronics just now. The question that caught his attention was: how long have these been on? Striplights like this didn't use much power, but surely they hadn't been on for a thousand years. "I'll explain that some other time," he told Atto, "but this is definitely tech from the founders." He ran a finger over the cool plexi cover of the lights.

Atto set a tentative forefinger down and grinned up at Piers. "Not even warm!" He put his whole palm against the striplight. He looked at the map, and said, "This is really old. New Lake isn't even there." He pointed at the Wyth Valley, which was veined with rivers but didn't have any lakes or even sizable ponds. "Look, that's the wanderer's charm!" With his other hand, he touched a stylized compass rose in the corner. Where his finger tapped, Piers thought he saw an amber flicker. Atto jerked away, and then tapped the spot again, and once more, with a flicker each time.

Piers reached forward and touched the central valley, thinking it might even be the clearing where his shuttle had landed. There was a flicker under his finger, but the light was blue. Taps to other spots on the map resulted in faint flickers of blue—as long as one hand was touching the striplights. Both he and Atto started giggling like little kids and tapping random spots all over the island to see the blinking lights.

He pinged the ship. "Jon, you'll never believe what we found! It's incredible!"

"Sorry, kiddo. Can't talk. Crisis up here."

His excitement switched to concern. "What's happening?"

"Nav system just went haywire. Console flipped to ground visual and it's flashing and we can't get it to stop. The whole crew is beyond confusion—mayhem!"

Oh. Piers put a hand out to stop Atto from tapping. "Anything flashing now?"

"Uh, no."

Piers set his finger on the map, at the confluence of the rivers near Ruatt. "Is there a light now? Where two rivers join up?"

"A flash! All right, then, talk."

With a laugh, Piers said, "It's what I was going to tell

you. We found some ship tech—a map sculpture with striplights and haptic sensors. The beacon. But if you're seeing that, apparently it's a whole interactive nav guidance system."

There was a shout from the direction of the trapdoor. Rane's voice, calling their names. Atto yelled back, telling Rane to come down. They could hear Rane talking to someone above ground, and a man's voice responding.

"Whatever you're up to, it's giving Davyn problems," Rane said as he approached through the passageway.

Piers turned away from the map, and saw Rane stride into the chamber, with Lord Manssorand right behind him. He wanted to ask what was happening with Davyn, but when Rane saw the lights, he checked his progress and Manssorand almost collided with him. "What is that?" Rane said. He stepped up onto the dais beside Piers, and whistled through his teeth. "Something from your world, not ours?" The other man joined them, speechless and gaping.

"A bit of both. This has to be the beacon. Touch a spot on the map, and a display on the ship lights up in the same spot. The founders left us a way to guide the ship."

Manssorand watched the blue flicker under Atto's finger, then touched the map himself. There was no light. He tried a different point on the map, with the same disappointment. Atto coached him to have his other hand in contact with the striplight, but there was still no response. When Rane tried, the light flashed.

"Just me, then," Manssorand said. He forced a laugh. "Always knew Wyth had the magic touch."

Piers felt Rane's confusion and excitement clearly, and Atto's wonder was a force of its own. In contrast, Manssorand's humiliation was muted—a non-Empath's diffuse emotion. The Houses were supposed to be psi, and

Rane was and Manssorand wasn't. "You mentioned you don't think your family has the 'gift.' That's what triggers the lights."

His mother had worked for a while on developing a haptic-based machine-psi interface, without success, which had frustrated her to no end. *Redemption*'s nav system hummed along on psi energy, but didn't depend on physical contact. Since psi was in the DNA, and they used DNA-identification for all kinds of things, no one could ever understand why it didn't work.

As far as he knew, no one had solved it before the New Foundation Project ships launched, either. So the foundation crew, or someone after them, had designed this version of the beacon with next-generation tech that eighty years of science on the ship hadn't matched. He traced the striplight border with his index finger, marveling at the ingenuity. He told Jon, "The beacon is lit by the descendants of the bridge crew. I thought it was just going to be regular comms, but it's psi contact that makes it work."

Beside him, Rane was studying the map with his hands clasped behind his back. He said, "The Houses are marked." In fifteen spots around the island, Piers saw that there was a tiny symbol carved into the map: the ancient trident of the Greek letter psi. Rane directed his next comment to Manssorand. "Do you suppose it's like the Transference? Maybe we need a quorum."

Both House men were intent on the map, staring at the amber symbols. Atto was on the other side, palms on the striplights as he studied the map upside down. Rane held a tentative hand over House Wyth, as if expecting an electrical shock if he touched, and then tapped the symbol. It lit up, another amber light, and stayed on. More quickly, he tapped House Manssorand, and that light came on. Dannpelier, and the light came on. No others would illuminate.

The three amber-lit symbols glowed. Piers could feel his heart thumping. "Atto," he said, "can you go get the others? Tell them we need the Houses."

Piers was finding it hard to keep calm. Arissa was the last to set her hand on the striplights, and when she did, the amber lights on the map brightened so abruptly that the young woman flinched.

Piers hardly noticed; with five Empaths—the beacon counted Atto, so that settled that—in simultaneous contact with the beacon, it was like a portal had opened. He felt the psychic background of the Empaths on *Redemption* as if he were in the corridors of the ship—he could even pick out familiar presences. The doors had been thrown open and he'd been swept in, whether he willed it or not, and it was overpowering. All physical, sensory input stopped as he lost himself in tracing the Empathic connections. He was home. Perhaps Jon said something through the implant; Piers didn't register on words, but Pushed a feeling of welcome and encouragement that was brushed with his own elation.

From another direction, there was a wrenching psychic cry from Davyn, a desperate reaction to the inundation. It intruded on the homecoming and snapped Piers back into awareness. He found he was still by the map, both hands now on the striplights, swaying, his head thrown back and tears in his eyes. He shook off the trance and saw Atto standing across from him, looking disoriented. Beside him, Rane was shaking and braced against the block. Arissa and Tarken were both looking at the lights with pinned eyes; off to the side, Manssorand was staring at Piers in complete bewilderment. Remorse came hard on the heels of his joy as he felt the others' distress. He Pushed reassurance to all of them. Gently, he moved Rane's hands away from the striplights and steadied him with a hand on each shoulder. Atto saw, and lifted his own hands away, and nudged Arissa and then Tarken to do the same.

"Rane, it's all right, you're all right," Piers said.

"What in hell's name was that?" Rane's voice shook.

"That was an overwhelming dose of Empathic connection, even for me." Piers wiped his eyes with the back of his hand. "That was the full force of being Open to the emotions on the ship—and they are running high right now because of the landing—and you not having any way to process what you were feeling. You might have been getting it directly, or you might have been getting it through me, like Davyn did, but I'm sure it was a shock."

The young House lord shook his head, and ran his hands through his hair. Second by second he was getting calmer, but his eyes were still glassy and his breath was shallow.

"What's the point of that, just to put lights on a map?" Rane asked.

"I think..." Piers said, "I think this is set up so that both sides know where everyone stands. No surprises." He didn't point out that each of them would have been just as exposed to the ship's Empathic crew. It was clever, really. Multiple Empaths had to be here to activate the system, meaning a single House couldn't hoard secret knowledge of the ship's presence. And as a result of that forced Open state, neither side could successfully harbor a hidden agenda.

He heard an anxious female voice from above ground, and then a murmur of Davyn's musical accent. Atto sprang away from the beacon and shot to the entrance and out of sight, calling out to Davyn.

"You shouldn't be doing that, Davyn," Piers heard Atto say. There was no censure in his tone, only brimming excitement. "Can't you just hear Gran?"

"I may regret it," Davyn said.

"You won't! Two more steps. Wait till you see this!"

Elanna's higher voice cut through. "What's the light?"

Piers met them at the bottom of the ladder. Davyn was standing tall, and it didn't look like he needed the support that Atto and Elanna were providing. Tienna was at his side, radiating concern. With Davyn's injuries, the ladder must have been a trial, but when Piers traced the Connection to find Davyn's emotions, resolution and wonder were by far the strongest.

Face to face with Davyn, Piers felt another burst of responsibility for the younger man. Being Connected usually came with protective and possessive impulses, because in the tangle of the two psyches it was very difficult to separate their well-being from each other. This was even more than that, complicated by Davyn's neophytic need for reassurance.

"I had to come," Davyn said. "I don't understand." He pulled something out of a pocket and opened his palm to show Piers. It was a compass rose, burning with the same intense, amber light as the one on the map.

"And we saw things," Elanna inserted. "Lord Wyth, too—all three of us. Visions."

They struggled to find the words for things they had no way to recognize, but they knew as well as he did what it meant. Their visions had consisted of fragmentary images: the ground from above; trees flattened outward in a circle; a great shadow resolving into a gargantuan metal hull.

476

They'd been shaken by the emotions, too, excitement and anxiety, relief, joy, wonder, and fear.

From the chamber, Rane called, "Piers? There's something happening."

Piers stepped back up on the dais. The beacon was shining, the full border of striplights at max lumens now. House Caladen was lit up, though no one had touched the map. A diamond of white light pulsed a few inches above the map, moving diagonally across Merra from Portsay to Lin. It could have been a bird winging over the fields and forests, or a slow-moving shooting star burning its path over the hills.

"Jon, we see you." Piers spoke out loud, letting the others hear his side of the conversation. He was amazed that he sounded calm. "There's a light moving across— tracking your orbit." The light had reached the spot where his shuttle had landed.

"We see more lights," Jon answered, "but nothing moving. There's a new one, at your coordinates."

"That's House Caladen. Davyn's House."

Piers pulled Davyn up beside him, and asked Arissa, Rane, Tarken and Atto to put their hands back on the edge. The eastern part of the Wyth Valley started to fluoresce, as if the unmarked New Lake had been turned from water into blue light.

He took a deep breath and held it for three heartbeats, and then placed Davyn's hand on the strip.

The pulsing white light changed course and speed. It fled east across the map and merged with the blue light at New Lake. There was a spark, and the light turned amber, and then resolved into the very familiar shape of an NFP ark ship, hovering over the Wyth Valley.

"Holy stars of God," Jon said through the implant.

None of his usual flippancy was transmitted in the slow, soft utterance.

The shape spun at odd angles over the spot where New Lake should be, like a magnetic compass finding a bearing, and then stabilized, pointing toward the compass rose.

"Well, the landing instructions are clear," Piers said. It was much closer than the landing site they'd chosen from the ship. He grinned at the others around the map, who were each stunned in a different attitude of bafflement.

"Think you can climb the ladder?" he said. "Because the ship's coming and none of us wants to miss that."

They'd arrived in view of the landing site in the late afternoon, and the water of New Lake had been reflecting the brilliant red and tangerine sunset sky. Piers had a flash of doubt, since the beacon seemed to indicate that *Redemption* should try a water landing, but there were open fields just beyond the lake. He had entreated Jon and Barston to take the gamble. Since the combined power of his gathered Empaths had been enough to activate the beacon, Piers was sure it would be enough to guide the landing, to set the ship down just a little off the mark.

He convinced them to bring the ship down in the morning to give him time to do whatever he could to prepare the Empaths and the people who would witness it. Manssorand and one of the Starborn had ridden to the two closest hamlets with the news, and Piers had spent the evening trying to prioritize all the things new Empaths ought to know, and trying to learn their individual psi signals so that he could channel all of it into one coherent force.

Maybe Piers should have insisted that they all keep at it through the night, but they were overwhelmed and exhausted, and his confidence was high. So he ended the lesson and let them go off to think or sleep or worry or marvel as they liked. Except for Davyn. The man had borne the confusion on his own for long enough. They sat some distance away from the others, with the babble of the excited Starborn behind them and a clear view of the landing site and the night sky in front. Davyn had taken a little more diluted par-telk for the pain, and in the relaxed, psi-primed state, he was calm despite the refreshed awareness of the Connection.

"This closeness," Davyn said. "It's so strange. It's not reading your mind, but it's like I know what you're thinking. I wish I had words for it."

Piers fiddled with a twig and Pushed understanding and sympathy to Davyn, who laughed. "I want to learn how to do that," Davyn said.

"Oh, you do it already. You actually need to learn how to *not* do it."

"So you know everything I'm feeling?"

"I know you're really hoping I say no to that question," Piers offered.

Another laugh. "No privacy at all, then."

"No judgment, either," Piers said, and leaned back on his hands. It was a beautiful night, with a mild breeze making the leaves dance in the light of the first rising moon. For the first time, he was centered enough to really enjoy it, and the solace and pleasure that Davyn found as he looked at the stars carried through. It was true that there was no judgment; it would be like judging someone for the way his heart beat. Emotions flowed and morphed constantly, and it was what people did in response to them, what they chose to focus on, that mattered.

He was relieved that Davyn was accepting the intimacy of it without misinterpretation. There was a reason some people only Connected when there was a romantic attachment as well. For Piers, it had never been like that. It had just been an experience he wanted with people he cared about. Something in his Connection with Davyn had wiped away the physical price he'd struggled with. It was joy to rediscover the feeling of being fully himself because he was sharing his internal life with someone else. Davyn distinguished it easily and was unconcerned, which saved them from at least one awkward conversation.

"I've been thinking. Is it possible I had something similar with Van?" Davyn was unsure about saying more, but forged ahead. "Maybe because I had a twin, there'd been a Connection from the start, so I was already activated."

It seemed so obvious. He could imagine how that would have felt to the child Davyn, to be trying to find the other half of himself—without knowing that it was missing. "You might have been Reaching without knowing it. If Van was even a little sensitive, he'd have met you as close to halfway as he could." And then that Link had been severed, too.

"All this time," Davyn said, his voice low, "I felt like I was sleepwalking. I thought there was something wrong with me, that after losing him I was cut off from everyone." There were streaks of sorrow in his voice.

"You *were* cut off," Piers said.

"If I lose you..."

"No," Piers said firmly. "Someday we can choose to break the Connection—but we'll do it on purpose, when we're both ready. By then you'll know how to use your ability to enrich your other relationships." Piers grinned. "Tienna's pretty sensitive to Empathic signals, you know."

Davyn blushed, but grinned back. "It makes sense, now. I think I started falling in love with her just because she seemed to understand me so well." He grew serious again, with a pang that felt like bracing for loss. "I don't know if she'll leave the Starborn for me."

"She'll stay with you," Piers said. "She's pretty taken with you, too."

"And Elanna and Tunny. Their mother is gone, I don't want to leave them, too. If I'm supposed to restore House Caladen, can they come with me? Can their father?"

"Judging from what we saw of House Caladen—what's left of it—I think you probably have some time before that's a major issue. Lord Caladen pretty much has to live somewhere else for now, whether you rebuild that place or not."

Birdsong woke Piers the following morning, first a few simple trills that seeped into his dreams, and then a mingle of melodies and chirps that ruled out further sleep entirely. It wasn't a bad way to wake up, though it was hardly even light enough to count as morning. He had slept, but only for an hour or two after talking with Davyn through most of the night.

The ship was apparently out of range, maybe taking a victory lap around the planet. There were two recorded messages waiting for him. He listened first to the one from Kath. "*I can't get my head around the fact that this is finally happening,*" she said. "*It might be too soon for congratulations, but I'm thinking it anyway—it's going to be fine. I am really looking forward to seeing you, and hearing about everything, and seeing all of it and meeting everyone. Trees and horses and boats and clouds... Somehow I never really thought about the fact that the scouts would end up being tour guides. Anyway, just wanted to let you know I'm thinking about you. Good luck.*"

The second message was from Jon: "*You missed one hell of a party. See you soon.*"

Piers stood up and pushed the bedroll out of the way.

Last night, one of the Starborn women had diffidently handed him a bit of cloth, a bar of soap, and a razor. He wanted to shave, and try to look somewhat like he had his act together. Nothing he could do about his clothes, since his pack was somewhere in Ettori's possessions, but he ought to be able to manage cleaner hair.

Davyn and Owen had both slept in provisional tents, but most of the rest of them had just done the best they could to find a level, out-of-the-way spot where they could stretch out. Piers dropped his screens and tried to get a sense of the mood, and discovered that nearly all the others were still asleep.

As he made his way down to the river, Piers softly whistled a tune that Atto had taught him. He stared at the gently flowing water, and felt a deep ache. May the stars guide you home, Arthur.

He peeled off his rags and waded in, sucking in his breath as the cold water bit into him. Ducking his head under took care of any vestigial sleepiness; when he stood up, the icy drips from his wet hair coursed over his face. Unexpected bonus—he was glad for his dry clothes despite their pungency. He shaved with the borrowed razor, still astonished that he'd learned to do this by feel alone. Jon had said it: necessity forces skill.

Coming back into the camp, he saw that Davyn was up. He'd gotten one of the cook-fires going again and was heating a pot. Davyn laughed when Piers asked what he was cooking.

"Water," he answered. "Just heating up some water for telik. Want some?"

He did, actually. He was more than a little keyed up. In a few hours, *Redemption* would be home at last. The massive ship—and he knew just how massive it was because he'd looked over his shoulder as the shuttle dove for the planet—would appear in a bath of flames, then sink through the atmosphere, down through the sky, its shadow engulfing the clearing. The air would shudder and there'd be a rush of wind. The ground would shake, even if they managed the smoothest landing possible.

Inside the ship, people would be strapped in or holding tight, some of them probably regretting the party as they made history while battling their hangovers. The ship's automated systems would be making announcements none of them had ever heard. When the movement stopped, there'd be a stunned moment of silence, and then cheers. His father would say something succinct but stirring from the bridge, which only a few people would hear over the commotion.

Four generations on the ship had dreamed and planned for what would come after that, and lives had been built for this moment. When Kath's accident scratched her from the scouting mission, Barston had told her she'd be the first one off the ship. So she'd be in position beside the door that had never been opened. Piers could absolutely picture her, poised and beautiful and waiting for the signal.

Then they would be here. The door would slice open, folding down into a ramp, and his mission would officially be over. After that moment, he'd no longer be a scout. He'd just be one of three thousand people trying to figure out life after the stars. At least he had a head start on that.

EPILOGUE

The Great Gorge

THE TUNNEL WAS dark, until one of the guards found a discarded lantern. Kor closed his eyes against the burning light.

The Wyth boy had given him a serious wound, but he had returned the favor. And the other one, the boy with the face from his nightmares; that boy had fallen, too. So his wound was a fair trade. He would heal. Benino and his medicine would see to that. With luck, the boys would not.

Regardless, the world was changed now. Intense pain spiraled along his nerves, whether physical or psychological Kor didn't know. Everything he'd done in the long centuries since his father's death, everything he'd endured, was rendered needless by the ship's arrival. And descendants of his enemies had played their part.

The Great Quake, which Kor's great-grandfather had survived, had swallowed the technology that was supposed to guide the ark ship. The ancestor of House Wyth, the chief engineering officer of the foundation ship, had seen to it that a landing site was built in the valley. By then, Great-grandfather had decided the future would be better if the ark ship never landed. It had taken him a century and then some, but he had managed to flood the valley. Now only a lake remained to mark the second landing site, and in time the secret was lost.

For centuries, only a few people knew the other secret—the one that had kept Kor young. He'd been given several doses of Ettori's "elixir" as a young child, and he'd aged about one year for every five. He was now middle-aged at two hundred and thirty-four.

Priscilla Shen had tried to monopolize the telk plant and its mysteries, just for its known healing properties. She'd tried to eradicate the plant in the high plains, and there'd been a war about it—the three bridge-crew families in the fertile southern part of the island ended up breaking away, forming their own rebellious nation, which they named Tyndaris.

There was a year, barely a half-century after that, a year of strange weather and ruined crops, when the telk was blighted. It caused a virus, one that affected only the psis. Mainly it was the Tyndarans who suffered from it. Time and catastrophe had erased the memory of the secret of telk, too.

Except for what persisted with House Ettori.

So Kor alone knew these secrets, now, sharing only what he chose. He alone was leading the extended life; the longevity gave him power and time to sculpt the world according to his will. The children he'd fathered—and there were many—he ignored. Soon he would choose one to initiate into the secrets and become his heir, if his work was unfinished when his slow-approaching death finally drew near.

It had been a shock to feel the touch of the scout's mind. It had been a very long time since someone had tried. Most of the psis had no idea what they were or what had made them that way, so had no capacity to intentionally Reach. When he was physically near them, he could lock them inside their own psyches. It was a matter of reforming their barriers with his will, and it nullified their talent. Kor had managed, over a long time, to immure the Empaths of the Great Houses, but he was on guard for any signs of a reemergence. He'd been astonished by the scout's potency.

It had been a mistake, on Earth, when people gave in and accepted the psis. They'd let themselves be dominated by an accident of genetics, and that had ignited a thousand sparks of twisted innovation. A new accident gave this world a chance to try again.

The ark ship would bring more psis, maybe as powerful as the scout, and the damage was already done. The Caladen boy he'd fought today looked so like his father and had such overpowering psi energy that the truth of Kor's failure was obvious—all he'd done counted for nothing. He realized first that he hadn't eliminated Caladen.

Then he'd faced Owen and his brother and realized that they, too, were dazzling with Empathic talent. That was astonishing and humiliating. The younger boy he'd suspected but not bothered with, but somehow Owen's psi ability had resurfaced. The Aryn woman and others were active now as well, when their ability had been so deeply suppressed that Kor had disregarded it entirely. Something had woken the abilities of the House children—Wyth, Aryn, Dannpelier, *Caladen*—and with the addition of the scout, the Starborn, and the others, they'd triggered the buried beacon anyway. All those Reaching psyches had woven a net as blinding as the flashing swords. Was it the approach of the ship that had changed the balance? Or was it the scout's presence, spreading through them like contagion?

If the novice Empaths were drawing their psi stability

from Piers, then it was possible that if Kor shattered his mind it would spread to them all, like a psi version of the virus. His exchange with the scout had opened a channel to that mind, and as his men carried him away from the skirmish, Kor had flooded that channel. He had poured his centuries of control and power into the scout's psyche, to break the boy's will entirely. He'd enjoyed it, despite his wound, because it had been so long since he'd sought Connection at all, and this was not merely Connection but consumption. Piers had begun to weaken, and Kor had played with him, letting the onslaught ease just enough for Piers to start to let down his guard, without completely letting go, and then re-engaging.

That had been a costly miscalculation. In one of those interludes, another mind had Reached to Piers. The pull of that Connection had triggered Piers's natural psi response to disentangle his psyche from the other's, and that struggle had strengthened him. Kor had broken off from that Connection, rather than risk Piers somehow turning against him. He'd been surprised at the sharp bereavement he felt when he broke free. The boy was an extraordinary Empath, especially given his youth, and that Connection had been the first Kor had allowed himself in a lifetime. He felt, abruptly, a sense of isolation so total that he remembered every loss he'd ever suffered.

And so for now, he retreated. For now, Kor would shelter behind his own psi barriers, avoiding that touch, that awareness of other minds, and keeping his own presence safely caged.

The real nightmare was coming.

Kor howled, and the tunnel rang with his pain and rage.

Notes: The Great Houses

The original settlement on the planet (named *Valiana* to honor the foundation ship *Valiant Star)* was built at the landing site near at the northeastern edge of the island, close to what is now the Bay of Bangor. A series of earthquakes in the years 53-55 destroyed the site and that portion of the island is now submerged.

After the second major quake in the first year, most people moved to the interior region of the island, leaving only a small scientific community there. When the final quake sank the colony, the leaders decided to deliberately disperse around the Island. They established five regions, and founded three communities in each. Each community was centered around a large building that was originally communal but evolved to become the Great Houses.

Most of these Great Houses were named for members of the bridge crew of *Valiant.* Because the crew included four men named Daniel and a woman named Dana, it became the custom for members of the Houses to use "Dan" and "Dane" as honorifics attached to the given name when addressing one another, such as "Dan Owen." This convention is used by servants within the House as well. Formally, the senior member of each House is known as Lord or Lady of the House, such as "Lord Ettori," or just by the House name itself. Junior members of the House are addressed by non-House individuals by given name, sometimes with the House used in lieu of a family name, as in "Arissa of Aryn," or with Lord or Lady used unofficially, as "Lady Arissa."

When the Lord or Lady of the House is absent or indisposed, someone in the family (usually the heir) or a trusted third-party is named Head of House.

IN MERRA

The High East Houses

- Lin, Lord Chao
- Glay, Lord Terrance
- Estend (now part of Tyndardis, following the Estend War in 1042)

The Hill Houses

- Caladen (dissolved, 1036)
- Wyth, Lord Owen
- Dannpelier, Lord Tarken

The Northern Houses

- Ettori, Lord Kor
- Manssorand, Lord Gerrid
- Andali, Lady Lia

The Western Houses

- Chant
- Aryn, Lady Issanda
- Janoval, Lord Rick

IN TYNDARIS (since Border War)

- Uthen
- Pennington
- Shenterra

THANKS FOR READING!

Now that you've finished reading, I'd very much appreciate it if you would leave a review on Amazon—even a sentence or two is a big help.

Meanwhile...

Wondering just what was happening on *Redemption* while Piers was searching for a signal? That's the subject of *Safe Conduct*, which will be the next book published in the New Foundation Project series. Learn more about that on my website, where you can also keep up with my blog and my writing—and subscribe to my email list for updates right in your inbox.

(And if you're curious about what happens after the landing—yes, that will come, too.)

I'd love to hear from you. I don't spend much time on social media, but I keep a close eye on my email.

https://acmeehan.com | author@acmeehan.com

ONE MORE REQUEST

Will you help this book find its way to more readers?

I don't ask lightly, but if you feel you can recommend *A Signal for Redemption*, please let your friends and family know about it, through whatever channels you use.

Thank you!

About the Author

A.C. Meehan has lived in seven states and three countries, and is fascinated by the way interactions and environments shape personality. A self-described happy introvert with close friends in distant places, she enjoys reading, writing, taking courses, playing the piano and the harp, and taking long walks in the woods whenever possible. She currently lives in Northwest Ohio, where she works in strategic communications for a global manufacturing company. A Signal for Redemption, the start of the New Foundation Project series, is her first published novel.

Contact her at author@acmeehan.com.

Made in the USA
Middletown, DE
29 May 2022